THINK
OF ME
ONLY,

FABIO

"I'LL HAVE TO HAVE A KISS"

"Why, you reprobate!" Natalie exclaimed. "You have already helped yourself to several."

"But that was not the same. *I* kissed *you*—amid one devil of a skirmish on your part, I might add. Truth to tell, I shall never be able to convince my friends you spent the night with me unless you first kiss me—er, willingly."

"That is absurd!"

"Come on love. Put that satisfied gleam in my eyes."

"You, sir, should be condemned as a cad."

"Guilty as charged, my lady." He pulled her close and lowered his face to hers . . .

PRAISE FOR *PIRATE*

"I found myself unexpectedly enchanted. *PIRATE* is romantic fantasy at its best."
Chelley Kitzmiller, *L.A. Daily News*

ROGUE

by

in collaboration with
Eugenia Riley

AVON BOOKS ◆ NEW YORK

ROGUE is an original publication of Avon Books. This work has never before appeared in book form. This work is a novel. Any similarity to actual persons or events is purely coincidental.

AVON BOOKS
A division of
The Hearst Corporation
1350 Avenue of the Americas
New York, New York 10019

Copyright © 1994 by Fabio Lanzoni
Photograph courtesy of Fabio
Published by arrangement with the author
Library of Congress Catalog Card Number: 93-90814
ISBN: 0-380-77047-4

First Avon Books Printing: May 1994

AVON TRADEMARK REG. U.S. PAT. OFF. AND IN OTHER COUNTRIES, MARCA REGISTRADA, HECHO EN U.S.A.

Printed in the U.S.A.

RA   10   9   8   7   6   5   4   3   2   1

The author gratefully acknowledges
the contribution of Eugenia Riley,
without whom this book would not
have been possible.

One

Charleston, South Carolina
March 1821

Ryder Remington, Marquess of Newbury, stared across the sleazy tavern and saw what he most desired—a flame-haired wench.

The atmosphere of the Tradd Street Tavern was rowdy this cool spring night. A haze of smoke hung in the air, mingling with the odors of unwashed bodies, the stench of stale tobacco and soured beer, and the rank smell of the mutton stew that had simmered too long on the kitchen stove. Ryder could hear billiard balls smashing together in the next room, the strident sounds of a group of French sailors bickering loudly over their game of faro, and the intermittent roar of men cheering as darts thudded home on the board on the far wall.

But Ryder's attention was riveted on the comely wench. She was serving a trio of sea rats, pouring grog into the tankards of the bearded, unkempt sailors. Facing him as she did, he could see the dip in her nicely endowed bosom each time she leaned over to pour the brew from her pewter pitcher. Lust stirred within him. She was quite a shapely thing, dressed in a low-necked muslin gown with a dark, printed skirt and white bodice. Her heart-shaped face was graced by dimples, bright, laughing eyes, and an ample pink mouth. Her hair was shining red—albeit the color appeared a bit unnatural to him. The mass was pinned high on her head, with several tendrils trailing free.

As the wench finished her duties at the table, one of the

1

crusty sailors grabbed her and pulled her down on his lap. Unaccountably, Ryder almost surged to his feet to go rescue her. Then the woman's lusty laughter stopped him, and he observed her brazenly curling her arms around the old salt's neck and smacking his cheek. This female was in no need of salvation—she was obviously a seasoned whore.

"I say, Ryder, this place is an abysmal bore tonight," came a peevish voice next to him. "What say you we all go to Madame Chloe's?"

Ryder turned to regard his friend Harry Hampton. Hampton was forever the impatient one, he mused cynically. Along with his other three companions at the table—Richard Spencer, George Abbott, and John Randolph—Ryder had come to America from England four years past. All five men hailed from titled, aristocratic backgrounds; all five had been drifting through the Colonies aimlessly, living the lives of rogues and adventurers. They had arrived in "sinful" Charleston last fall, and intended to stay there and while away the fine spring days until the "sickly season" gripped the city with malaria and yellow fever.

Ryder mulled over Harry's suggestion that they all visit the bordello in nearby Simmons's Alley. He glanced at the others. "Is that what the rest of you gents want?"

"Aye," said an inebriated George as he lifted his tankard.

"I fancy a willing wench," added John.

"Perhaps Opal is free tonight," finished Richard. "She is woman enough to satisfy us all—eh, gents?"

"All five at the same time?" queried an eager George.

The men fell into bawdy laughter. Ryder again settled his gaze on the wench across the room. He watched her winnow her way out of the sailor's lap and continue on her rounds. He perused the nicely rounded curves of her backside, noting the subtle sway of her hips as she moved. Desire lanced him anew, with a vigor that brought a smile to his lips.

"Why don't the rest of you gents go on?" Ryder muttered, craning his neck to get a better view of the sumptuous maid. "I rather fancy staying here."

His companions at once picked up on Ryder's interest; all four turned to stare pointedly at the woman.

"Hers is a face I've not seen here before," murmured Harry.

"Hers is a face our Lord Newbury would like to lash to his lap," added George.

"Looks like the marquess is primed and aimed," taunted John.

"Aye—another unfortunate wench decommissioned on the morrow, after hours spent on *Ryder's* storm-tossed mast," put in a grinning Richard.

Ryder was rapidly tiring of the merciless gibes. "Ah, leave me be, the lot of you, and go harass Chloe," he grumbled.

"And miss all the frolic?" Harry said. Putting two fingers to his mouth, he whistled loudly. When the wench turned and stared at him, he motioned to her to come their way. George, Richard, and John joined in with catcalls of their own.

Natalie Desmond had been heading off to refill her pitcher when she heard the loud, rude whistle, accompanied by raucous huzzahs, from across the tavern. She glanced irritably at the five *gentlemen* who were gathered at a table in the far corner. All were ogling her, and three of them were waving and shouting like lunatics. She had not seen these particular reprobates before at the tavern—blessed good luck!—and she guessed they all were English. She knew their kind—rich, irresponsible dandies looking for sport. She resented their interruption, which kept her from her more important task this night.

Nevertheless, noting that Sybil, the girl who was supposed to attend their table, was busy mopping up a spill, Natalie sighed and started off. She consoled herself with the thought that maybe these five might provide a clue to aid her in her quest.

Arriving at their table, she quickly sized up each man. Her gaze was at once seized by the largest and most handsome one there. *Now, isn't he a fine one,* her woman's vanity forced her to concede. Even seated as he was, she could tell this man was a giant—the size of the sun-browned, beautifully shaped hand griping his tankard was proof enough of that. A glimpse of a gold-crested ring on one of his long fingers affirmed that her guess about his being English nobility was correct. With coal-black hair that hung wickedly around his shoulders, eyes as bright and blue as the ocean on a fine spring day, and a deeply tanned, aristocratic face with a long, straight nose, high cheekbones, a firm mouth, and a strong chin, his was a countenance that could have graced a general or even a king. His shoulders were broad and powerful, his flowing white shirt half open, giving her a provocative glimpse of a smooth, bronzed, splendidly muscled chest. Regarding her so steadily, he had about him the air of a man who easily conquered women and was well aware of his own mastery. Indeed, the very sight of this rogue shot a shiver through Natalie that she hastened to control, lest this libertine guess she sensed his raw virility. Nor could she let him see that she was a novice playing a dangerous game tonight, and totally out of her element.

Next to him was seated a blond, blue-eyed man with a rounded, youthful face; he, too, was handsome, though he lacked the riveting vitality of the titan. The other three men were ordinary—one brown-haired with a hawk nose, another thin and balding, a third with washed-out auburn hair and hazel eyes.

Reminding herself that these five might provide needed information, she forced a pleasant expression. "Good evening, gents," she began in a heavy Cockney accent. "I don't believe I've 'ad the pleasure of seeing the likes of you 'ere before. Be ye English lads?"

"Aye," replied the hawk-nosed one proudly. "We all hail from Mother England, where we distinguished ourselves in Wellington's cavalry by defeating the French tyrant to keep king and country safe."

Staring at the man, Natalie feigned fascination. "You mean you battled Napoleon 'imself?"

"Clever wench," he replied, raising a brow to his cronies. "Knows about Napoleon, she does."

"Why, everyone in the bloody Colonies 'as 'eard of bloody Napoleon," Natalie retorted with contempt.

"Certainly an East End lass such as yourself," put in the pretty blond one with a sly wink. "With that accent, you must have just gotten in off the boat."

As the others laughed uproariously, Natalie felt her hackles rising. "So, 'tis a bunch of gentlemen soldiers ye be—"

"Cavalry officers," corrected the balding one.

"Ah, cavalry officers," Natalie mocked. "And what 'ave you fine cavalry officers been doing of late?"

At this taunt, all five laughed heartily.

Chuckling, the auburn-haired man said, "My trusty comrades and I have been amusing ourselves terrorizing fair womanhood from one end of the American seaboard to the other."

Natalie feigned wide-eyed dismay. "Terrorizing fair womanhood? Why, I'm fair terrorized myself at the sight of you fearsome lads and your, er"—she paused to stare pointedly at the swords several of them wore strapped to their waists—"trusty rapiers."

That quip all but brought down the house.

Natalie winked at the pretty one. "So, gents—what would you ex-cavalry officers be fancying this night?"

Her question was met with more ribald laughter.

"Actually, miss," replied the blond man, "there is a gentleman present who fancies you."

Natalie rolled her eyes as more bawdy chuckles erupted. "And which of you gents might be fancying me?"

The hawk-nosed one spoke up, gesturing toward the black-haired giant, who, so far, had uttered not a single word. "Why, 'tis Lord Newbury here."

"Ryder Remington, Marquess of Mayhem," edified the balding gent in a slurred voice.

As the others guffawed, Natalie turned to regard the marquess, her lips twitching as he in turn sized her up with a wicked smile that revealed perfect white teeth, and a gleam of lechery in his blue eyes that again set her senses astir. Mayhem was what he was about, all right, she mused. Mayhem of the fairer sex, no doubt.

"Lord Ryder, is it?" she asked. She breathed an elaborate, disappointed sigh. "A pity 'tis no one special."

The other four doubled over with merriment at Natalie's slur, while the handsome rogue himself scowled magnificently at her.

"What, no rejoinder, m'lord?" she teased, figuring him to be somewhat dim-witted. "I reckoned you cavalry officer types were skilled at parry and riposte."

"Ryder here does his riposting in the dark," said the pretty one.

"Especially when a willing female is present," added the hawk-nosed one.

"A *willing* female?" Natalie repeated in mock astonishment. To Ryder, she clucked softly and said with sugary sympathy, "Poor lovey. Do you, then, favor a life of chastity, m'lord?"

That insult almost sent two of the giant's cronies sailing out of their chairs, but the raven-haired titan continued to glare formidably at Natalie.

Figuring she had successfully put the devil in his place, Natalie glanced dismissively around the table. "If you lads will excuse me, I must be refilling my pitcher."

The auburn-haired one spoke up. "Lord Newbury here would love to be filling your pitcher, wench—and refilling it."

As new, earthy chuckles erupted, Natalie glanced again at the quiet man, who still regarded her with a smoldering look. With a saucy smile, she shook her finger at the lot of them. "I might 'ave known you lads would be up to no good."

Yet even as she started off, the giant unexpectedly grabbed her around the waist and pulled her down onto his lap. Her pewter pitcher crashed to the floor as his large, strong hand gripped her chin and his splendid, scowling face descended toward hers. For a moment she was too caught off guard even to protest. She felt riveted to the spot as his strength, his scent, his heat tugged at her senses.

His vibrant, burning gaze held her pinned as, for the first time that night, the giant spoke up in an incredibly deep, sexy voice. "What I am up to, wench, you shall find very good."

A man of few words—but good ones at that, Natalie thought dazedly. She did not at first hear the coarse cheers erupting, for she was too mesmerized by the heat of Ryder Remington's mouth as his lips boldly engulfed hers— claiming, possessing, mastering her own. She reeled at his audacious assault, her mind galloping in fright, and she realized—too late—that she had clearly underestimated this man. In the days since she had started working at the tavern, several of the customers had brashly smacked her mouth, yet their sloppy pecks seemed nothing compared with this ravishment by fire.

The stranger's lips scorched her with the fervor of his passion. His hands tightly gripped her waist, branding her with his strength and heat, holding her to him with a power she knew could snap her spine. He radiated lust and vigor. Even as mortified and deeply shaken as she was, she had to admit his lips on hers did feel *very* good.

Then she felt his hot tongue teasing between her lips in a blatantly carnal manner. Panic and shock propelled her to her senses; she bucked to get free and beat against his chest. Yet her indignant behavior only seemed to encourage the scamp all the more. Her cries were easily smothered by his lips, her fists crushed against his massive chest—even as the other men hooted cheers.

Ryder was indeed having a grand time as he kissed the saucy wench. He had the woman squirming, writhing, twisting with lust at his touch—just as he wanted her. She surely deserved this for having goaded him so remorselessly, he told himself self-righteously. And the strangely unschooled nature of her response excited him. He loved feeling her tremble as he advanced and plundered. She smelled good, tasted even better, and her warm, supple body felt as if it were made for him . . .

Natalie was still floundering wildly, desperately trying to shake herself free of this impudent lecher. Then she felt something icy cold slip between her breasts, and sheer outrage produced the burst of energy needed to finally shove him away.

Freed from his smothering lips at last, Natalie was horrified to find herself breathing in ragged gasps. Meanwhile, the blockheaded miscreant only smirked back as he noted her rattled state. His triumphant gaze impaled her, and he raised a handsome black brow to mock her.

"So I am nothing special, eh, wench?" he taunted.

The merciless laughter of the other men lanced Natalie's ears. Somehow she heaved herself out of his lap, drew back her trembling hand, and slapped his arrogant face. He only laughed—the rogue!—while his friends were, by now, literally holding their sides. She again felt the cold object pinching against her bosom, and reached inside. She pulled out a five-dollar gold piece and stared at it in horror. As the insulting meaning sank in on her, she regarded the stranger with rage, the coin clutched in her trembling fingers.

He was totally unrepentant, glancing from her fuming visage to the coin in her hand. And then he even winked at her—the fiend!

"Is there a better place you would have me put it, wench?" he drawled.

Natalie flung the coin down on the table and faced the depraved Englishman with contempt. "You have not the price to attain me, sir—nor the countenance."

Hastily she grabbed her pitcher, turned, and with all the dignity she could muster, stormed off in the wake of the men's insufferable laughter.

As a glowering Natalie made a stop by the kitchen to refill her pitcher at the tap, Ned Hastings, the thin, sharp-featured owner of the tavern, sauntered up. "Natalie, are you all right?" he asked in a low, urgent tone.

Realizing she was still shaking like a leaf in a storm, Natalie managed to flash Ned a tremulous smile. He was the only other person at the tavern who knew her secret and whom she could trust. "I—I'm fine, Ned." Peering out the open kitchen door, she glared with contempt at the table she had just visited. "Just some rowdy English dandies out chasing skirt tonight."

"If those rogues have given you any grief, I'll cast the lot of them from the tavern," Ned insisted.

Natalie had to laugh. "Ned, every man here gives me grief—present company excluded." Watching him scowl, she touched his sleeve. "You fret about me too much. The fact is, I have no choice but to endure the pinching and the insults. There is simply no other way for me to get at the truth."

"I'm not sure, Natalie," Ned said worriedly as he mopped his brow with a kitchen towel. "I'm just not sure."

Before he could protest further, Natalie swept off with her filled pitcher. She returned to the main room and headed back to the table where she had previously been so successfully interrogating three Irish sailors.

"Ah, lassie, you are back," cried the dungaree-clad sailor who had pulled her onto his lap earlier.

Natalie forced herself to smile at the leathery-skinned, bearded man, who had a crooked nose and rotting teeth. "Aye, I am back, lads," she said brightly, refilling their tankards.

Setting down her pitcher, she plopped herself down on the lap of the youngest one, a sandy-haired youth who now gulped as he ogled her. Earlier, she had learned that the sailors had just arrived on a merchantman from London. The young man was an ordinary seaman, while the older two were first mate and sailing master on the square-rigger.

As the boy continued to gawk, Natalie grinned at the others. "Now you fine gents must tell me more about your recent voyage from England. Just what fancies did you bring for us to enjoy here in Charleston? Perhaps Bristol beer or Belfast linen?"

A guarded look flashed over the face of the bearded first mate. "You'd best take care with what you're asking, lass," he cautioned. "It could be that, at times, not everything found in the hold of our vessel is meant to be there."

"Why, at times," Natalie quipped back, dimpling prettily, "not everything found in the hold of *my* vessel is meant to be there."

The men roared with laughter, but afterward, the first mate still appeared skeptical, regarding Natalie narrowly as he scratched his jaw. "Just why are you asking us all these questions, lassie?"

She affected a shrug. "Why, 'tis a fussy lass I am. What if I was to decide to stow away on your vessel, lads, and keep you fine gents, er—entertained—during your voyages? I could never abide sharing your hold with fish-rot or livestock dung."

The three laughed heartily and appeared very intrigued by her suggestion. The bearded one leaned toward her and spoke behind his hand. " 'Tis cloth in the hold, lassie. But you must nary tell a soul that it be English."

"Ah, English cloth," Natalie murmured, batting her eyelashes at the salty dog hovering over her and fighting a wave of nausea at his odious breath. " 'Tis coarse woolens or fine cotton?"

" 'Tis the softest cotton made, lass," the man assured her.

"How very handy," she murmured back coyly. "I should not mind rolling about with a bolt or two"—she paused to look them over and lick her lips—"stowed by such handsome lads."

As the others guffawed, the bearded one grabbed Natalie and pulled her onto his lap. "You're welcome to share our hold, lassie—any time."

Across the room, Ryder watched with great resentment and

frustration as the saucy wench rocked in the lap of the scruffy seaman and brazenly flirted with him. How did she dare to impudently strut her wares to such scum and yet scoff at what he offered!

He had liked his taste of the wench—liked it far too much. Indeed, there had been an almost maidenly aspect to her response that would seem to belie her current occupation. Ryder longed to get the impertinent female beneath him in his bed, to take those ripe breasts in his mouth, to see if she would squirm and pant like a novice when he thrust himself into her.

More than anything, he longed to melt her ice, to replace her haughty sneer with a look of wide-eyed abandon. He was quite unused to having his desires thwarted by barmaids. Most came to him all too willingly. This wench, on the other hand, was begging to be set in her place—and he was just the man to do it.

"So the wench gave you your comeuppance, eh, Ryder?"

He turned irritably to the balding George. "I may well give her *hers* before the night is out."

"I'm betting you shall never bed her," chimed in Harry.

The hawk-nosed Richard nodded toward the bearded Irishman who held the female. "Aye, that wench must crave a bristle between her breasts."

This comment brought a dark scowl to Ryder's smooth-shaven face. For some reason, the very possibility made his blood boil.

"Face it, Newbury," taunted the auburn-haired John. "For once, you've met your match."

Ryder's hot temper was not cooling. "And I say I shall bed the wench by morning."

His claim was met with loud huzzahs and snorts of contempt.

"Care to back up your bravado with a wager?" challenged Richard.

"Why not?" Ryder retorted with a shrug.

Richard held up a hand sporting a dazzling ruby ring with a gold crest. "I am willing to bet my family ring, as well as the seal given to my father by George III, that you won't attain her by dawn."

"I'll bet my grandfather's dueling pistols that I shall," Ryder drawled back. He glanced coolly at the others. "What say the rest of you? Do you care to join in on the wagers?"

"Aye. I'm in for ten of the king's gold sovereigns," said George, "if you will throw in your jeweled rapier."

"Consider it tossed in."

"I shall bet my cavalry musket for your new Wellington boots," added John.

"Accepted," said Ryder.

Meanwhile, Harry was laughing at them all. Waving his hand in a deprecatory gesture, he declared, "You supposedly 'fearsome lads' wager with all the courage of ninnies at the knitting circle. Why not make the stakes a little more interesting?"

"What are you suggesting?" asked Ryder.

"I'll throw in my Baltimore clipper," said Harry, "if you'll plunk down your stipend for the next two years."

As the stakes escalated wildly, Ryder hesitated for no more than a heartbeat. "Done," he said.

Once all the details of the wager were decided, the five agreed they would meet the following morning to settle up the bets. Since Ryder did not want to take the wench home to the house he shared with the other four men on Queen Street, he asked his friends to meet him in the dining room of a sleazy hostelry in Roper's Alley, where he kept a cheap room for the convenience of just such assignations.

Anticipating an easy victory, Ryder glanced across the room. The presumptuous sailor was still pawning the wench he coveted. If he was to meet with success tonight—and he was determined to do so—then he had better cut out the competition posthaste.

As his four companions watched in fascination, Ryder got up, strode confidently across the room to the table, grabbed the startled wench by her arms, and yanked her away from the sailor.

Before the girl could react, the enraged Irishman shot to his feet to confront Ryder. "Wait a bleeding minute, mate—"

Ryder punched the man in the jaw, easily knocking him to the floor. By now he was well aware that almost everyone in the tavern had caught on to the small drama, and a tense silence ensued as the customers stared at the scene—the wench trembling in rage and mortification, and Ryder looming over the fallen sailor.

On the floor, the Irishman rubbed his stubbled jaw and glared up at the man who had punched him. "Why, you—"

But then Ryder totally amazed and momentarily disarmed the man when he grabbed his hand and pulled him to his feet. To the Irishman's utter stupefaction, Ryder stuffed two silver dollars into his hands.

"Trust me, my friend," he murmured to the Irishman, winking at the outraged whore. "You have neither the price *nor the countenance* to attain her."

The Irishman glanced from the grinning Ryder to the seething Natalie. "But—"

Ryder edged closer and whispered with murderous resolve, "And if you should linger here for another second, mate, I promise you will be holding something far more precious than two silver dollars in your hands."

For the Irishman, it took only one glance from Ryder's lethally purposeful face to the rapier strapped at his waist. He gulped, nodded curtly to his companions, and all three hastily retreated.

Ryder turned to the woman and spoke with consummate arrogance. "You, wench, may come with me."

For the second time that night, Natalie slapped the obnoxious devil, hard. "You, sir, may rot in hell."

Ryder was left to rub his stinging cheek while the maddening hussy stormed off, and every man in the tavern howled with laughter.

"Later, love," he murmured.

And meant it.

TWO

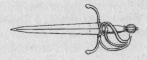

Two hours later, feeling exhausted and frustrated, Natalie Desmond emerged from the Tradd Street Tavern. Her feet hurt and her head throbbed from inhaling the smoky stench of the grog shop. Even the brisk, cool breeze blowing in off the bay failed to invigorate her. Wearily, she looked up and down the disreputable expanse of seamy tippling houses, sagging storefronts, and weatherbeaten cottages, only to note, to her chagrin, that her coachman was nowhere in sight. A fashionable carriage was parked at the corner to the north of her, the handsome conveyance awash in the wavering glow of a street lamp. A hatted coachman sat atop.

Still, there was no hint of Natalie's servant, Samuel, or the family barouche. Good heavens, had her loyal retainer gotten into the brandy again? And she could not have chosen a worse part of town in which to be stranded!

Natalie muttered a very unladylike curse. Samuel's failure to appear was the final straw capping off a very frustrating evening. Although necessity clearly dictated the course of her life of late, Natalie hated the nightly game she was compelled to play at the Tradd Street Tavern. Yet, on another level, she felt appalled that she was able to carry off her role with such bravado. It was almost as if some forbidden aspect of her nature were struggling to emerge . . .

As in her encounter with that maddening rogue! Fury had Natalie clenching her fists as she remembered his outrages. Not only had the scoundrel sorely tested her patience, his audacious kiss had sparked an appalling, illicit stir such as she had never felt before—a purely scandalous thrill that no woman of propriety could afford to experience. The entire incident left her feeling agitated and fearful of yet another danger lurking in the shadows of her nightly masquerade.

Now, to her further chagrin, she watched an obviously drunken vagrant emerge from a nearby punch house and stagger toward her. Bleary-eyed and unshaven, the man was clad in filthy dungarees and was guzzling liquor from a flask.

All too soon, the derelict loomed before Natalie and waved his flask in her face. His rank, rum-soaked breath almost made her retch.

"Hey, girlie," he slurred, "would ye be wantin' a bit of a nip?"

"Leave me be, you gutter tramp!" Natalie hissed back, resisting an urge to shrink from him. "My servant will be passing soon, and he can more than deal with the likes of you."

"A bit uppity for a tavern wench, ain't ye?" the man countered belligerently. He came closer, his leering features frightening her. "Give us a kiss, lovey, and perhaps I'll slip ye a coin or two."

He tried to make a grab for her. With a low cry of fright, Natalie dodged him. Yet even as she would have fled, his gnarled fingers caught her arm. She fought with all her might, screaming out for help, beating on his chest and arms. He grunted with pain, but still would not release her—

Until suddenly he was pulled from her! Natalie turned to see the very Englishman who had so galled her tonight holding her assailant by the collar and scowling magnificently at the man.

"Be gone, you filthy dog, and leave the lady be!" the giant roared, thrusting the drunkard away.

The man crashed to his knees, groaning loudly. He hurled her and the Englishman an angry glare, then grabbed his battered flask and stumbled off.

The Englishman turned to Natalie. "Are you all right, miss?"

For a moment, staring back at him, she found the sheer size of him staggering. She was not a short woman, but this titan loomed head and shoulders above her. Equally daunting were his devilishly handsome face and that long, rakish jet hair that gleamed in the mellow light. Unbidden, another memory of his brazen kiss streaked across her senses like the lick of a flame. She gave her wayward senses a quick, sharp tug on the moral reins.

Not about to reveal her trepidation—or her response to his riveting good looks—she replied primly, "Aye, I am fine, thank you."

He smiled. "May I see you safely to your lodgings?"

She shook her head. "My servant will be along any moment now to fetch me home in our rig."

This comment caused him to raise a brow. "A tavern wench with her own conveyance and coachman?" he murmured cynically. "How very odd."

She flashed him a nasty smile. "Sometimes tavern wenches can be full of surprises, sir."

"Aye, they can," he concurred ruefully, rubbing his jaw and coaxing another smile out of her. He glanced up and down the street. "Nevertheless, I must insist you not remain in this dangerous alley alone. There is no hint of this—er—servant you have mentioned, and obviously you are not safe here."

Watching two sailors emerge from the nearby tippling house and stagger toward them, Natalie could have screamed her exasperation. She felt caught between the devil and the deep blue sea.

"Miss?" the rogue urged her with a kindly, infuriating smile. "Don't you agree you are not safe here?"

"Obviously," she retorted sarcastically. Watching the drunkards weave closer, she heaved a great sigh. "Very well. I accept your offer."

He gallantly extended his arm, and while she did not for a moment trust the devilish gleam in his eyes, she had little choice but to endure his escort, before this new duo of rascals waylaid her.

At the corner, the Englishman assisted Natalie into his coach. She felt rather uneasy as he slipped in beside her on the leather seat, rather than taking his place across from her. She considered escape, but then he was shutting the door and calling up to his driver, and the conveyance rattled off.

"And now . . ." he murmured huskily.

"Now?" she repeated, perplexed.

He laid a hand on the bare skin of her forearm. A shiver streaked up her spine, and she heard him chuckle wickedly.

"You are trembling, wench. Let me warm you."

The next thing Natalie felt was his strong arms slipping around her, then his hot mouth descending on hers. Outraged, she struggled against him, trying to push away his massive body. She might as well have been beating against a brick wall. Oh, she should have known better! she thought in rising panic. This rake was clearly far more dangerous than the drunkard who had just accosted her.

And as his lips moved persuasively to coax hers apart, she found herself resisting the potent pull on her senses as much as she fought him! But battle him she would—for she would *not* allow this scoundrel to catch her emotions off guard again tonight!

Ryder felt the barmaid's resistance, but dismissed her struggles as part of her saucy game. He could not wait to get this feisty piece inside the hostelry and beneath him in bed. His manhood tightened to tortured readiness as he anticipated the dazed look in her eyes, the sobs of pleasure escaping her sweet mouth, when he filled her to the hilt and drove her to shattering pleasure . . .

Soon, and quite blessedly for Natalie, the carriage lurched to a halt. Ryder released her abruptly and hopped out. Still reeling from his presumptuous kiss, she saw him standing on the boardwalk, wearing a cocky grin and extending his hand. Furious and still fighting for breath, she glimpsed the door to the seedy hostelry beyond him, in an area she recognized as being filled with bawdy houses, and at last realized his full, insulting intent.

"Not long now, love," he murmured with a depraved grin.

Uttering a cry of rage, Natalie all but sprang from the carriage, her hand poised to slap the insolent smirk straight off his face.

Instead, she felt her hand being grabbed, her body being heaved over one of his broad shoulders. And the miscreant was laughing—actually laughing!—as he started off with her.

She screamed and beat on his back as he bore her inside the musty-smelling rooming house. He took no note whatsoever of her struggles. Images of tawdry furnishings, scandalous art, and sagging wallpaper swam past her eyes as he headed for the stairs. With her flailing body still dangling over a powerful shoulder, he navigated his way up the steps with a steadiness that amazed her, then turned down a narrow corridor. She heard the click of a key in a lock and the panel creaking open. After slamming it shut, he at last set her down.

Staggering on her feet, Natalie was dizzy, reeling. But the rogue did not miss a beat. Before she could even catch her breath, he pinned her against the door with his solid body, and his demanding lips tried to pry hers apart once more.

Abruptly, he jerked back and yelped in pain as she kicked him in the shin.

"God's teeth!" he bellowed.

Despite her state of extreme agitation, she glared at him in trembling triumph.

Her victory turned out to be short-lived, for she was grabbed, hauled against him, and swatted soundly on the bottom before he shoved her away. Then, as she watched in wide-eyed horror, the scoundrel began unbuttoning his shirt.

"I'll admit a token protest makes the game a bit more fun, wench," he informed her nastily. "But coming from your kind, too much coyness tempts a man to have you across his knees and thoroughly teach you your place. So off with your clothes, get your belligerent rump in that bed, and let's see you earn your coin."

Never in her entire lifetime had Natalie Desmond been so insulted as she now was by the infuriating devil who stood across from her. "You bastard!" she screamed, charging him with fists raised.

"Bloody hell!"

Scowling formidably, the rogue caught her wrists and pulled her roughly against him. She struggled not to cringe when she felt his male strength and saw the rage glittering in his eyes.

"You," he thundered, "had best watch who you call a bastard!"

"You," she shouted back, "had best release me right this minute, or I shall scream my lungs out!"

"I have ways to silence your protests, wench!"

"By raping me?" she taunted viciously. "Must you resort to force to get your ease from a woman?"

He propelled her away and cursed vividly, shaking a finger at her. "If you weren't a female, I would throttle you right

now! I have never had any wench give me so much grief—
certainly not a tavern slut!"

"Perhaps because I'm not a tavern slut!"

Even as Natalie made her rash declaration, she realized her
error. But caution came too late as she saw the Englishman's
gaze narrow on her, watched him advance on her menacingly.

"What do you mean by that comment?" he demanded.

"Never mind!" she cried in utter disgust, ducking him and
rushing for the door.

His steely fingers gripped her arm, yanking her around to
observe his fulminating expression. "Oh, no, you don't! You
are not leaving this room until you explain what you just
said. By Jove, if you have duped me—"

Seething, she thrust him away. "What do you mean, if I
have duped you? I have been doing everything in my power
to avoid your odious presence—and you are the one who
keeps assaulting me!"

Surprisingly, he fought a grin. Yet his voice held a steely
resolve. "I repeat, woman, that you are not going anywhere
until you tell me what you are really about tonight."

Defying him to her soul, she moved purposefully toward
the door. Thwarting her with ease, he sidestepped into her
path to block her.

"All right!" she cried. "By God, if you are not the most
exasperating devil I have ever met!"

With these words, Natalie succumbed to her temper,
yanked pins from her coiffure, pulled off her red wig, and
summarily tossed it down on a nearby chair.

Ryder's jaw dropped. "My God!" he exclaimed, staring incredulously at the rich chestnut-brown hair spilling down
around her shoulders. "Tell me who you really are—now."

She glared at him. "If I tell you the truth, it will put someone's life in danger—"

"Aye, 'twill put *your* life in danger if you don't start talking."

She gritted her teeth in continuing mutiny.

"*Now*, by God, or I'll—"

"My name is Natalie Desmond," she spat out.

"Proceed."

She hurled him another look of blazing contempt; he
reached for her with frightening purpose—

"Very well!" she all but screamed. "As you have already surmised, I am not actually a barmaid. Along with my aunt, Love Desmond, I have been running a textile factory here in Charleston."

Ryder stared at her uncomprehendingly for a moment, then snapped his fingers. "Why, I have heard of you! You are referring to the mill on Wentworth Street?"

"Aye."

"You are a gentlewoman?"

"Indeed."

"Then what in God's name have you been doing disguising yourself as a whore and working at the tavern?"

"It is a very long story," she snapped.

"We have all night."

"I sincerely hope not!"

He crossed his arms over his broad chest and leaned back to block the door. Natalie realized with supreme frustration that she would never get past him until she told him the truth.

Biting down a strangled sound, she glowered at him. "Six years ago, I came to America with my aunt. Aunt Love's son, my cousin Rodney, had been trying to get a fledgling textile factory off the ground here in Charleston. Only he was not meeting with success, given his—er—predilection toward dissipation."

"Ah," Ryder murmured meaningfully. "Go on."

"Aunt Love and I came here to assist Rodney, and we pretty much ended up running the factory for him. We had many obstacles to overcome—not the least of which was the fact that we were two women trying to succeed in a man's world."

"A formidable barrier," he concurred.

"We also faced stiff competition from cheaper English cloth—that is, until the American Congress passed a tariff five years ago imposing heavy import duties on English cotton. Better years followed for our factory—until lately."

"Lately?" Ryder grinned cynically. "Pray, do not keep me in suspense a moment longer."

Hurling him another nasty glance, she continued. "Aunt Love and I had been quite successful in selling our cloth to the merchants on King Street. We even established a few accounts in Boston and New York. All of that changed about

nine months ago, when the market here became glutted with
cheaper English cloth—obviously brought in by smugglers
who avoided the port and the tariff. As a consequence, most
of our accounts stopped buying from us."

Ryder scowled. "What does all of this have to do with your
posing as a barmaid at the tavern?"

"I was getting to that. You see, Aunt Love and I realized
our only hope would be to discover just who was actually
smuggling the cloth into Charleston. The local customs authorities were not of much help. Then, about ten days ago, I
arrived home to find a note from my aunt. She informed me
that drastic means were called for in order to save the factory,
and she had decided to go undercover to smoke out the smugglers."

He scowled. "Do you know what she meant by going
'undercover'?"

"No!" Natalie cried in exasperation. "All I know is she disappeared from the face of the earth that very day!"

"I see," Ryder said. "So you began working at the
tavern—"

"Because it is close to the harbor and is frequented by so
many sailors. I wanted to see if I could gather information
about the smuggling or Aunt Love's whereabouts." Drawing
herself up in outrage, she finished, "Indeed, tonight I was
having a very interesting conversation with some actual
smugglers when you stormed across the room and ruined everything!"

"You're speaking of the bearded Irishman in whose lap
you were sitting?" he asked tensely.

"I am!"

"He was a smuggler, I take it?"

"He most certainly was."

Ryder smiled. "A most amusing yarn."

" 'Tis true."

He regarded her skeptically for a long moment, then
sighed. "I suppose your tale is almost too outrageous *not* to
be true. Either that, or you've managed to lose your Cockney
accent with a dispatch that amazes me."

Natalie smiled sheepishly as she realized she had unwittingly slipped into her normal speech patterns with him. "I
told you, I am no tavern wench."

"So you are not." Now it was he who sported a rueful grin as he rubbed his jaw. "Then I must have botched things for you tonight, eh?"

"You surely did."

He slanted her a chiding glance. "Has it occurred to you that you might have bungled things for *me?*"

"For you?" Infuriated, she gestured wildly. "I did my best to avoid you! However could I have spoiled anything for you?"

"You posed as a barmaid."

"So what if I did?"

"Barmaids are not known to have the highest scruples."

"Agreed."

"You also taunted me quite mercilessly," he went on.

"You deserved it."

Fighting a grin, he drawled, "And thus I made a wager with my friends that I would attain you by morning."

"You did *what?*" she cried.

"Now you are responsible—"

"Why am *I* responsible?"

"Because if you had not posed as a barmaid, I never would have made my wager."

She rolled her eyes. "Oh, for heaven's sake! This is ludicrous! You cannot blame me for your own erroneous and disgraceful assumptions regarding my morals."

"But I do blame you." He pinned her with a meaningful look. "You see, I *never* lose wagers, Natalie."

She regarded him with scorn.

He moved closer, cupping her chin with his palm and tilting her mutinous face toward his. His eyes gleamed devilishly. "So what do you suggest we should do about it, love?"

She gave him a look that told him to go straight to the devil—

And *meant* it.

Three

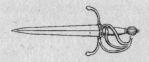

RYDER GRINNED DOWN AT THE APPEALING VIXEN WHO HAD turned out to be so full of surprises tonight. Never in his twenty-eight years had he encountered a woman who was such an intriguing enigma. He mused that he was having more fun with her now that he knew she was a lady posing as a whore than he'd had when he thought her to be a wench of loose morals acting the prig toward him.

"Well, Natalie, what do you suggest we should do?" he repeated.

"We are not doing anything!" she retorted with blistering sarcasm. "I am going home, and praying I shall never again have the ill fortune to set my eyes on you."

He gripped her arm. "Let's not be so hasty, love."

"I am not your love. And let go of my arm."

"I shall, but only if you will promise to hear me out."

"Oh, for heaven's sake!"

He released her arm, a thoughtful frown tugging at his brow. "Have you thought that I might be able to help you? Perhaps we can come up with an arrangement that will be to our mutual benefit."

"I have no need of your help—or of your *mutual benefit,"* she asserted.

"Don't you?" he countered. "That is not how it appeared to me outside the tavern an hour ago."

"The only reason I was in the slightest peril outside the tavern is because my manservant failed to appear."

"And what will you do the next time he neglects to meet your appointment? Has it occurred to you that it is both dan-

gerous and foolhardy for a gentlewoman such as you to fre-
quent taverns near the harbor?"

"Aye, 'tis dangerous," she retorted spitefully. "I could so
easily fall into the clutches of a rogue such as you."

He threw back his head and laughed. Still, his tone was sober as he remarked, "Perhaps I might be willing to help you
find your aunt."

"You?" she scoffed.

A dark scowl creased his face. "I am not without re-
sources, Natalie—nor without honor."

She glanced with scorn at his gold-crested ring. "Ah, yes—
Lord Newbury."

"I am called that back in England," he admitted guardedly.

"You seem more like the Lord of Debauchery to me."

"No doubt I've been called that as well," he agreed with a
grin.

She balled her hands on her hips and faced him down.
"Well, I do not want—or need—your help, Lord Newbury."

He lifted an eyebrow. "Are you sure you should be so
hasty, Natalie? Even though your aunt may even now be in
the clutches of these smugglers you seek? Even though her
safety—indeed her very life—could be in peril?"

Natalie ground her jaw in frustration and indecision. "And
you think you are the one to take on these scoundrels?"

He shrugged. "My friends will help."

"Those wastrels?"

A glint of anger sparked in his eyes. "Those wastrels, as
you call them, are all expert swordsmen who distinguished
themselves in the Napoleonic Wars. Besides, they will enjoy
such a caper."

She snorted with contempt. "A caper! It occurs to me that's
exactly how you view the entire proceeding."

His laughter was unrepentant. "Beginning the very moment
I laid eyes on you, m'lady."

"And what of you, Lord Rogue?" she continued in a
charged voice. "Are you, too, prepared to do battle on my behalf?"

Again he feigned that graceful shrug. "I was with Wellington at Waterloo. I would characterize my rapier as having
known vigorous combat."

"I'm sure you would," Natalie rejoined dryly.

Quelling a smile, Ryder asked, "Do you want my help or not?"

"You spoke of an arrangement that would benefit us both," she replied suspiciously.

"Aye."

"Exactly what would you want in return?"

Devilment sparkled in his eyes. "Your virtue?"

"Not a chance!"

He sighed. "Alas, I figured as much. Then I suppose I'll simply have to settle for second best—"

"Which is?"

He winked at her solemnly. "On the morrow, I want you to pretend to my friends that I have bedded you."

Natalie was aghast. *"What?* Why, the very idea! You want me not only to play the whore but to lie to your friends?"

"You needn't necessarily lie, only pretend to be—er—amorous toward me."

"But why?"

"Why?" He flashed her a dazzling smile. "So I may win the wagers, of course."

Her mouth fell open. "You are despicable!"

He chuckled. "I am indeed."

"You would deceive your friends just to win?"

"They would certainly stoop to equal chicanery toward me."

"But is it right to steal from your friends, to defraud them?"

"They needled me quite mercilessly tonight. Told me I would never be able to attain you."

"They were right," she snapped.

He stroked his jaw and fought mirth. "Well, I think they deserve to be taught a lesson."

Natalie stared in disbelief at the villainous scamp, then shook her head. "Oh, why am I even listening to this treachery? I could never trust you to help me. You have no scruples."

Something dangerous flared in his eyes. The cynicism fled, replaced by anger and steely determination. He reached out to grab her arm. "Natalie, I may be a libertine by your standards, but I am a man of my word. And I give you my promise that if you help me out in this, I will help you find your aunt."

Staring at him as he towered over her and frowned with such menace, she was tempted to believe him—for whatever reason. "You really would be willing to help me?"

"Aye." He laughed wryly. "And, Natalie, it seems to me that you are a young woman quite badly in need of assistance."

A valid point, she had to concede, though his smug attitude still rankled. "And will you agree not to divulge to your friends—or to anyone else—who I really am or why I am posing as a barmaid at the tavern?"

"My dear," he pointed out with forbearance, "how can I possibly hope to win the wagers if I tell my friends the truth?"

At that Natalie had to laugh. "I suppose you have a point." She bit her lip. "Then if you are indeed a man of your word, will you prove this by taking me home—now?"

"Will you come with me early on the morrow and help me convince my friends that we are lovers?"

She hesitated, then heaved a huge sigh. "Very well. I must be mad, but right now I'm too tired and frustrated to keep arguing with the likes of you."

"Splendid." He took a step toward her.

She held up a hand. "However, if you should betray me afterward and disappear before fulfilling your end of our bargain, I promise I'll make you rue the day you were born."

Undaunted, he smoothed down a bit of lace on her shoulder and drawled, "You may rue the day you met me, love, for whether you believe it or not, you are going to have a most difficult time getting rid of me."

She harrumphed.

He turned to pick up her wig from the nearby chair. "Don't forget your disguise, now. We'll have to sneak out the back door so we won't risk waking the landlady. My friends are meeting us here for breakfast shortly after dawn, and I don't want Mrs. Greentree to give us away by revealing to them that we didn't spend the entire night here together."

Natalie rolled her eyes and donned the wig.

He caught her hand as she moved toward the door. "Shall we seal our bargain with a kiss?"

"You may go kiss a water moccasin for all I care."

Moments later, sitting in the darkened coach with Ryder next to her, Natalie wondered just what kind of muddle she had gotten herself into. On one level, she appreciated the Englishman's coming to her rescue outside the tavern, but she felt more than a little uneasy regarding the devil's bargain the two of them had made.

Certainly, telling Ryder Remington the truth about who she really was and what she was about had seemed the only way to keep the amorous, arrogant rogue from ravishing her. And it was quite likely she would need a man's help in tracking down the dangerous smugglers and in locating a possibly kidnapped Aunt Love. But she still was not sure she should have trusted him with the details of her current mission. Indeed, she hardly trusted her own feelings for him. His first, brash kiss had fired in her yearnings she could not afford to unleash, let alone to acknowledge. And she feared all the more her own emotional response to his devilish ways—

For he was obviously a hopeless rakehell, a man so like the profligate males in Natalie's family—Cousin Rodney, even her own father. During her lifetime, Natalie had watched every woman in her family, including Aunt Love, endure endless humiliation and heartache due to the heavy vein of dissipation that ran in the Desmond men. Accordingly, Natalie had long ago resigned herself to the life of a maiden lady. Marriage was out of the question for her, since she was not about to join the ranks of the tragic Desmond women and trap herself in a loveless marriage that would only spell misery for her and her children. Equally forbidden, of course, was the lure of scandal, the tawdry love affair—and certainly *never* with a dissolute cad like Ryder Remington! Besides, at twenty-two, Natalie had come to cherish her independence, and enjoyed running the factory with Aunt Love. Now, if only she could find her aunt and get things back to normal before her own reckless, desperate charade drove her to ruin at the hands of some scoundrel—such as the rogue lounging so confidently next to her.

Sitting next to Natalie, Ryder, too, was mulling over the

fascinating time he had spent with her tonight. As the coach rattled past a street lamp that cast its radiance through the window, he regarded the profile of her lovely face. Why had he not noticed at once how her smooth brow, her nicely boned nose, her finely arched cheekbones, gave evidence of good blood and good breeding? Then he took particular note of the tiny worry lines around her mouth and eyes, the determined set to her lovely pointed chin.

He felt bewitched by this forthright, spirited Englishwoman who could play the gentlewoman or the whore with such ease. The gentleman in him wanted to help her, but more than anything else, the rogue in him was determined to have her! He had watched her play the coquette tonight—he longed to see her play the game with him in earnest. Indeed, it baffled him that she could flaunt herself so to others and then turn so prim and snooty when he demanded the same favors. How he would relish driving her to the ecstasy of her own defeat! Would it be such a sin to replace that haughty facade and anxious scowl with a smile of bawdy pleasure?

Natalie Desmond was clever, devious, and no doubt too headstrong for her own good. But most of all, she was damned irresistible. Her proper, holier-than-thou air only made her all the more challenging and appealing. Lust stormed his senses anew as he remembered the feel of her warm, soft lips on his, the gentle curve of her bosom against his chest, and her gasps of outrage and desire. There was surely much passion boiling beneath that prim exterior, which made him wonder how virtuous this intriguing spitfire truly was.

She would certainly profit from their arrangement and his protection. Left to her own devices, she would soon get herself into big trouble . . .

Left to his devices, her ruination would be equally assured, he mused.

The coachman halted before a charming double house on upper Church Street. In the Charleston style, the two-story, red brick structure faced sideways to the street. Ryder glanced appreciatively at the rows of shuttered windows gracing both floors, then at the high-pitched, gabled roof stretching above. The house was flanked on the left by a double gallery running its length perpendicular to the street. The pillared veranda was sealed at the street end by a porticoed entry door flanked by colonnettes and topped by an elegant entablature. He glimpsed hanging baskets on the upper, open gallery, as well as honeysuckle curling around the wrought-iron carriage gates and fence that sealed off the yard.

An alien emotion filled him at the sight of this cozy home. The elegant house represented a world of society and respectability he had long ago turned his back on.

"This is where you live?" he asked.

"Aye, along with my cousin Rodney and my manservant, Samuel." Her sigh was heavy with frustration. "Until just over a week ago, my aunt lived here, too."

"We shall find her, love."

Natalie struggled with a desire to tell him again that she was not his love, then quashed the rash instinct by reminding herself that she might well need this rogue's help. He hopped out and offered his hand, and she allowed him to escort her up to the portico. The darkness of their brief journey was relieved only by the dim, distant glow of a street lamp. The Charleston night, with its intrinsic blend of starry skies, heady moist air, scents of jasmine, and sounds of crickets, swirled around them.

Once they arrived at the street entrance, he tarried in the darkness. "Tomorrow I shall call for you before dawn. We shall breakfast with my friends and collect on my bets."

"Very well," she replied guardedly.

He looked her over. "I'd advise you not to dress too elegantly. Indeed, the more disheveled you can manage to appear, the better. After all, we want to give the impression that—"

"You needn't elucidate further!" she cut in primly. "And am I to assume that after this meeting with your cronies, you will help me search for my aunt?"

"You assume correctly."

"Good night, then."

Moving squarely between her and the door, he obviously had other plans.

"Is there something else?" she asked irritably.

"As a matter of fact, there is." He edged closer and teased huskily, "I'll have to have a kiss, you know."

"What?" she cried, shoving him back against the panel.

"Why, you reprobate! You have already helped yourself to several."

"But that was not the same."

"Pray tell, why not?"

"Because *I* kissed *you*—amid one devil of a skirmish on your part, I might add. Truth to tell, I shall never be able to convince my friends you spent the night with me unless you first kiss me—er, willingly."

"That is absurd!"

"I shall never be able to affect the proper smug grin," he insisted with a maddening smirk.

"You have been doing a splendid job of affecting it all night long."

"Come on, love," he urged. "Put that satisfied gleam in my eyes."

"Now it's a gleam in your eyes you wish to find?"

"And is it your aunt *you* wish to find?"

Natalie made a sound of frustrated rage. "You, sir, should be condemned as a cad."

"Guilty as charged, my lady." He pulled her close and lowered his face to hers.

She glowered at him. He waited and smiled.

She smiled back, then abruptly slammed her foot down on his instep.

"Hellfire and damnation, woman!" He jerked away and glared at her. "You are lethal!"

"Oh, spare me your protestations of injury!" she snapped back. "I didn't step on your foot that vigorously. Besides, you asked for it."

"Madam, I am about to give you what *you* are asking for!"

Natalie, in front of her own house and in her own element, was not about to be outmaneuvered again. With a saucy tilt of her head, she retorted, "Not if you want me present during your little experiment in larceny tomorrow morning."

His reaction was actually comical, going from a blustery, disbelieving scowl to a grimace of uncertainty and finally to a more calculating, cajoling grin. "But what of the gleam in my eyes?"

Natalie accompanied her next gibe with a sneer. "Go find it the way your kind always does—with whatever sleazy creature happens to strike your fancy."

Yet his riposte was impeccable. "But *you* are the sleazy creature who has struck my fancy."

In the next moment, her hand almost struck his face.

He grabbed her wrist. "Vicious vixen! I'll do it, then!"

"And I shall weep into my pillow all night long!"

"Ah, the devil with you!" he swore.

As Ryder turned and stormed back down the path, he heard Natalie's low chuckle, just before she creaked open the door. Damn the confounding woman, anyway! He felt perplexed, intensely frustrated—but, through it all, maddeningly intrigued.

Four

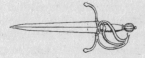

STROLLING DOWN THE PILLARED PIAZZA, NATALIE APPROACHED the inner entrance to the house. She creaked open the door and stepped inside, shutting it behind her. Inside the central hallway, all appeared normal. The wall sconces on either side illuminated the soft rose Persian runner, the carved mahogany Empire tables, and the caned Duncan Phyfe settee. Moving further inside, she sighed as she caught her reflection in the gilt-and-ebony Federal mirror with its gold eagle menacing above her. The fierce gilded bird seemed to disapprove of her current disheveled state, and Natalie couldn't agree more. Mercy, she did look a sight in her tawdry attire, with her image so bedraggled from her struggles with the Englishman.

Still, hadn't she gotten in a nice parry or two before he'd left? The memory brought a smile.

Shoving aside for now a reexamination of the entire scandalous encounter, she proceeded down the hallway and, according to habit, removed and hid her wig in the drawer of a bird's-eye stand which held a trailing fern. Smoothing down her hair, she noted a ragged brown edge on the lovely plant and frowned. Tomorrow she must remember to water all of Aunt Love's plants and hanging baskets. She had kept putting off the task, as if taking up her aunt's duties would be an absolute admission that Love Desmond was indeed lost to her.

She must also air out her aunt's room so it would be ready upon Love's return, Natalie added to herself firmly. She and her aunt owned no slaves; both women highly disapproved of the institution so deeply ingrained in the American South. Their servants consisted of a German widow lady, whom they

31

paid to come in twice weekly to do the laundry and heavy cleaning, and Samuel, a free man of color who was their combination coachman, gardener, and handyman.

Where on earth *was* he?

Wearing a perplexed frown, Natalie wandered into the drawing room. Her gaze became riveted on the portrait of Aunt Love that hung on the far wall, above her aunt's inlaid satinwood rolltop desk. Done by Samuel Morse when he had come through Charleston two seasons past, the vibrant painting revealed a bright-eyed widow with a pleasing, angular face, silver-streaked brown hair upswept in a bun, and a happy smile curving her generous lips. Natalie's expression grew wistful. Aunt Love might be an eccentric, flighty soul, but she had also been a second mother to her. Natalie had been only fourteen when she had lost her own French mother; in 1813, the headstrong matron had deserted her family and returned to Paris, even as England and most of Europe were rising up against the tyrant Napoleon. As far as Natalie knew, Desiree Desmond remained in Paris to this day.

If only she could know where her aunt was!

Natalie left the room and continued her search for Samuel. She did not have to hunt for long. At the archway to the dining room, she groaned at the sight that greeted her and sniffed at the unpleasant odors of cigar smoke and brandy.

Samuel and Rodney were passed out at opposite ends of the Queen Anne table. Both men were snoring, their heads propped on crossed forearms. Natalie mused that Samuel's hair was as crinkled and gray as Rodney's was blond and curly. Samuel's dungarees were dirt-streaked, Rodney's velvet tailcoat stained with food and liquor. The table was littered with cards, grimy glasses, and an overturned, obviously empty brandy bottle, which had oozed a sticky dark puddle onto the fine wood. Natalie gritted her teeth as she noted several cigar butts crushed out in Aunt Love's best Wedgwood bowl, and a new burn mark on the mahogany.

Damn Rodney! It was bad enough that he spent his days drinking and gambling, but did he have to lure Samuel into his debauchery? The servant was responsible and right as rain, except for the periodic times when Rodney corrupted him with drink. She wondered how on earth her cousin had gotten money for the brandy—she knew his monthly stipend was not due to arrive for weeks yet.

With suspicion needling her, Natalie hurried over to the breakfront, opened the drawers, then sighed in relief after quickly determining that none of the silver was missing. Perplexed, she turned back toward the table and again eyed her pitiful cousin. She supposed she should not think of him so harshly; perhaps it wasn't entirely his fault, but rather a cruel quirk of nature, that he was the way he was, the very image of every other wastrel in the Desmond family. And, truth to tell, he had not totally thrown away his life.

It had been Rodney's inheritance that had bought this house and the Charleston factory in the first place, albeit both had been in a deplorable state when Natalie and Love first arrived in America. Nonetheless, it was Rodney's home in which they lived, Rodney's factory at which they worked. Her cousin had always seemed a rather sweet, lost soul, and while he drank or gambled away every penny of the small stipend remaining from his inheritance, he had on only two occasions grown so desperate that he had actually resorted to selling the silver.

The question remained—where had he gotten the brandy?

Natalie walked over to her cousin and nudged him gently. "Rodney—please wake up."

After a moment or two of being prodded, he stirred, and blinked up at her through bloodshot blue eyes. Although he was only twenty-seven, his skin was blotchy and traced by spider veins, and heavy jowls framed his button mouth. In his present state, Rodney seemed to take no note of Natalie's rather risqué costume. She reflected ironically that it might be a blessing that her dazed cousin seemed incapable of fathoming the details of her present, daring mission.

"Ah, Natalie, dear," he slurred. "Good to see you."

Natalie gritted her teeth as his liquored breath wafted over her. "I can see you have gotten into the drink again."

"I'm sorry, m'dear," he muttered with a vague wave of his hand. He rubbed his forehead and hiccuped. "I've one demon of a headache."

She harrumphed. "Not surprising to me."

"Have you—er—heard anything from Mother?"

"Not at all. I was hoping you had."

He shook his head miserably. "We must notify . . ." He struggled for a moment, then stared at her helplessly. "Who must we notify?"

"The constable. It is already done, and the City Guard have been ordered to keep an eye out for her as well."

"Ah, very good," he mumbled, yawning. "Wish I knew where she went off to. Most unlike her, you know." His head slid back down on his forearms.

Natalie shook him again. "Rodney!"

"Yes, dear?" he muttered.

"Did you have to get Samuel drunk again? He was supposed to fetch me home tonight, but he did not appear."

Rodney lifted his head and struggled to focus on her. "What was that?"

"I said, did you have to get Samuel drunk?"

Rodney's watery gaze remained befuddled. "But, Cousin, Samuel was the one who brought home the brandy."

As Rodney laid down his head and began to snore again, a perplexed Natalie hurried to the opposite end of the table and nudged her servant. "Samuel."

He looked up, his dark-eyed gaze equally bleary. "Yes'm?" he muttered, scratching his grizzled scalp.

"Where were you tonight? Why did you not meet me at the appointed time?"

"You not there, missus," he mumbled.

"I certainly was!"

He shook his head. "I come, but you not there."

"Then you must have come at the wrong time, because you did not appear when I left the tavern."

Stifling a yawn, he lowered his head and drifted back to sleep. "Sorry, missus. You not there."

With thinning patience, she cried, "Samuel!"

"Yes'm?" The groggy man did not even look up.

"Where did you get the brandy?"

He was silent for a moment, then mumbled, "Dice."

"You mean you won the brandy in a dice game?"

Loud snoring was her only answer.

Expelling an exasperated breath, Natalie went about snuffing out the downstairs lamps, lit herself a taper, and trudged upstairs. Her headache flared again with blistering force. Both Samuel and Rodney were lost causes—at least for tonight. Now she desperately needed to catch a few hours of rest before that infuriating rogue showed up again and took her off to deceive his friends. Oh, what had she done? Had she truly cast her lot in with the devil?

She had definitely thrust herself into the path of danger, associating herself with a man who had few, if any, scruples. And damn his eyes for being so appealing and charming in spite of it all! Mercy, how could she have responded to him so scandalously, if only for one brief, unguarded moment?

As a morally devout woman, a woman committed to spinsterhood, she was clearly flirting with disaster. Would she find Aunt Love only to lose her own soul in the process? Indeed, she feared that same traitorous part of her nature—no doubt the reckless French in her—took perverse delight in her nightly masquerade at the tavern, a game made so much more risky by the rogue's appearance tonight.

All of this turmoil made Natalie's temples throb even more, but she inwardly vowed to stiffen her spine, to better control every wayward instinct to ensure that the sober, righteous side of her prevailed.

Passing her aunt's empty room on the upper story, she ground her jaw and bucked up her courage. Did she really have a choice other than to continue her disguise—and to enlist the rogue's help? She feared the unknown enemy who might have harmed her aunt, she feared Ryder Remington, and—most of all—she feared herself.

Over at the hostelry in Roper's Alley, Ryder sat naked in bed in the darkness, a sheet draped across his middle. He would have to stay here for the night, else go home and give away the game to his cronies.

Wan moonlight spilled in from the window behind him. A breeze, smelling of fish and refuse, wafted in, billowing the moth-eaten curtains and sending shadows dancing over the room's shabby furnishings, the scarred dresser and sagging bed. Across from him, a large cockroach slowly climbed up the door panel, while a mouse nibbled on some unknown tidbit in the corner.

Ryder sipped wine and half listened to the bawdy sounds of a sailor and a prostitute bickering loudly on the street below. The two were quarreling drunkenly over the price of a night of sport. At last the argument ended with a lusty shriek from the whore; Ryder heard the pair's laughter, their footsteps trailing off into the night.

Not that the night would ever be silent in this disreputable district so close to the docks. Even the wee hours inevitably teemed with noise—watchmen making their rounds and rousing drunkards asleep in doorways; sailors brawling as they left grog shops. Toward dawn, water wagons would clank past, lamplighters would bang around snuffing out the street lamps, and the scavenger would clatter past on his rounds, carting up the slops and rubbish.

None of the sounds could ease the unexpected emptiness inside Ryder right now, or the sharp, nagging feeling of sexual frustration—a torment so skillfully inflicted by the little tease he had met earlier at the tavern.

Ryder was accustomed to constant distraction and lusty entertainment from the opposite sex; moments like this, when he was actually alone and impelled to reflect on the shabby state of his life, were rare. He mused that the tawdry room in which he now reposed was really no more tidy than the cluttered abode he shared with his four compatriots over on Queen Street. He wondered idly what had become of his finer days back in London, when he had slept in a mahogany four-poster laid with the finest embroidered linens and silk hangings; when he had drunk the most expensive wines and eaten the best foods; when he had gambled at his club on St. James's Street and cantered his thoroughbred down Rotten Row in Hyde Park, tipping his hat at giddy young debutantes and filling them with equal measures of fascination and fear.

Of course, he was far from eager to return to England and the bitter memories he had left behind there. He relished his life of freedom and sensuality abroad—although, at solitary moments like this, he had to concede that his hedonistic existence felt somewhat empty.

He wondered why he had chosen to spend these long, dark hours alone, when a brief trip to the nearby, notorious Bear bordello would no doubt have secured him a willing wench with whom he could have rolled around on the lumpy tick for the rest of the night. He had vowed to Natalie Desmond that he would do just that—then he had gone to his room minus female solace.

Why? His fingers clenched on the stem of his wineglass. Because no doxy could really ease the taut aching that consumed him now. Because ever since he had laid eyes on fair and lovely Natalie Desmond, he had become obsessed with the thought of possessing *her* alone. The maddening minx had thrown down the gauntlet—nay, flung it in his face!—and now he had to conquer *her* before he moved on to the next conquest.

Abruptly, he grinned. What an enigma she was—a proper gentlewoman who was unorthodox enough to run a textile factory, a haughty lady who was audacious enough to pose as a tavern wench in order to find her missing aunt.

Would she be equally inventive and unorthodox in bed? He smiled in anticipation at the very thought. He longed to rip away her facade and find out what she was really about—whether she was saint or sinner underneath. Although she had offered him compelling excuses for her scandalous masquerade, the circumstances of their meeting spurred increasing doubts about her scruples. She might defend herself like a lady when the occasion demanded, but she had strutted about the tavern like a whore. Even now, memories of her titillating little charade sent a new thrill of potent arousal pulsing through him and generated hope for eventual, great heights of passion between them.

Yet Ryder also realized that taking on this woman's cause held danger—and in this he was not fearing the smugglers they would likely pursue together. While he longed to sweep staid Natalie into his world of unfettered sensuality, her proper side might well pull him in quite an opposite direction. He remembered dropping her off at the neat, prosperous house on Church Street. Eccentric though she might be, Natalie Desmond represented a proper, polite society Ryder had long ago abandoned, when he had forsaken a life of luxury and nobility for one of exile and profligacy abroad.

Was there still some remnant of the soul of that Englishman left to be saved? he wondered cynically. Or had the rogue supplanted him entirely?

As much as Natalie Desmond captivated him, some instinct

warned him that she might try to lure him back into a world that had once strangled his spirit and shattered his peace—a world that had crumbled on a cold night in London four years ago, when he had lost his beloved mother.

Five

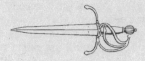

As DAWN WAS BREAKING THE FOLLOWING MORNING, NATALIE and Ryder sat at a small table in the dining room of the notorious hostelry known as the Greentree House. The innkeeper, Gerta Greentree, a large, lumbering woman in a stained gown and ratty shawl, was pouring coffee for them from a battered tin kettle. Watching the woman trudge over to serve a ragtag seaman and his prostitute companion—a loathsome creature who was actually smoking a cigar!—Natalie felt a stab of sympathy for this world-weary innkeeper who had to deal with such disreputable clientele in order to earn a livelihood. She watched the first rays of dawn creep through the grimy windows and illuminate the chipped and stained pottery cup sitting before her. She noticed with repugnance the slick of grease floating on top of the brew, and the odor rising from the steaming cup was fetid. As tired as she was, she decided she could do without the fortification of coffee this morning.

"The others should be along any moment now, love."

She glanced up at Ryder. Looking no worse for wear, her partner in crime sat across from her in a shaft of pale light, the golden rays glinting off his mass of shiny black hair. So shocking, that hair, she mused, noting again the way it hung around his shoulders without even a queue to restrain the decadent raven strands. More scandalous still seemed the grin sculpting his handsome mouth, the mischievous gleam in his bright blue eyes. The rogue was obviously anticipating their chicanery with great relish! She took in the slant of his noble nose, the aristocratic arch of his dark brows, the height of his cheekbones. The dark shadow of whiskers along his jaw only emphasized his dark handsomeness—and his debauchery. Mercy, if he wasn't sinfully handsome—and a devil to his very soul!

The cigar-smoking whore at the next table had also noticed Ryder and was ogling him with a greedy leer, Natalie observed with nagging irritation. Had he sought out the favors of just such a wanton hussy last night, as he had vowed he would? She seethed. She would not put it past the lecherous wastrel at all!

With distaste, she watched him lift his coffee cup. "Eeek!" she cried as he took a gulp. "How can you drink that foul brew?"

He set the cup down with a shrug. "I've tasted worse."

No doubt he had, she thought ruefully.

Ryder in turn was assessing the beautiful woman who sat across from him. Natalie wore the same gown as she had last night, with its white bodice and full printed skirt. The low neckline again afforded him an exciting glimpse of the cleft in her nicely rounded bosom. He longed to plant his hands on her tiny waist and pull her over to him for a proper good-morning kiss—even willing to risk the thorough dressing-down she was bound to deliver if he so dared! Such skin she had—pale as ivory, yet tinted with the blush of the rose. Again she wore the red wig, but the bright tresses appeared tawdry this morning compared with the remembered splendor of her rich, fiery chestnut-brown curls; their scattering of gold strands near perfectly matched the mellow gleam of her light brown eyes. Roving his gaze over her finely boned nose and wide mouth, he hungered all the more to taste her again. He would soon enough, he promised himself.

"You were wise to wear the same gown and wig," he murmured. "Still"—he paused to stare at her elaborate coiffure, the curls tightly mounded on top of her head—"you look a bit too well put together for a woman who ostensibly spent the night in my bed."

"You, sir, are a depraved, contemptible heathen!" she retorted.

"Doubtless." He chuckled and stroked his jaw. "Nevertheless, what do you suggest we should do to remedy your lack of the proper—er—morning-after air?"

Her mouth was pursed to spew out a rejoinder when he abruptly reached over and caught her hand. With a strength that surprised her, he pulled her to her feet and tugged her around the table.

"Just what do you think you're doing?" she demanded, trying—without success—to yank her fingers from his firm grip.

He hauled her down onto his lap and grinned devilishly. "Giving you that just-kissed look?" he suggested.

Further attempts at speech were squashed by Ryder's insistent mouth. His lips captured hers as his fingers slid into her tightly arranged wig and began almost roughly to pull tendrils free.

Shaken and mortified, Natalie struggled against him, fought the seduction of his lips, and at last managed to shove him away. "Stop this at once!" she cried, batting at his determined hands, feeling even more embarrassed and rattled as she noted several bleary-eyed diners staring at them.

"But I cannot, love, else I may lose the wager," he countered smoothly. "You see, had we spent the night together, your lips would, I presume, be quite bruised. You would have a suitably dazed look in your eyes—and I suppose you might creak a bit."

"Creak?" she repeated, outraged.

"I'm not known to be a gentle lover," he murmured with a depraved, husky chuckle.

"You, sir, could be Attila the Hun," Natalie retorted. "But I'll have you know that English gentlewomen *never* creak!"

"You don't say?" he countered glibly.

"And if you seek to shock me with your sordid gibes, I am afraid you are going to be sorely disappointed. I'm made of far stronger stuff than that."

"Are you?" He looked her over with a cocky grin. "Of course, we have not even addressed the matter of how—er—shopworn I might appear after a night of being thoroughly plundered by you."

"If I thoroughly boxed your ears, sir, would you be satisfied then?"

He stroked her cheek in a trailing caress that left her gasping. "No, but I am getting there, Natalie," he rejoined, leaning toward her for another kiss. "Indeed, love, I am getting there."

As his face continued to descend toward hers, Natalie was appalled to find herself mesmerized by the gleam of laughter in his wicked eyes. Oh, he was beyond redemption! She braced herself to resist him again, but he startled her when he ducked his head lower, latched his lips onto her neck, and began to suck and bite.

Aghast, Natalie realized this rogue intended to leave a blatant memento of his passion on her throat! She squirmed mightily, but could not shake the leech free.

"Stop it!" she hissed. "What do you think you are—a bloody vampire?"

He chuckled against her throat, his hot breath sending shivers of gooseflesh down her body. "Like a vampire, I've been known to leave my mark."

He was about to fasten his mouth on her neck again when they heard the loud sounds of male laughter and catcalls coming from across the room. Both of them stiffened. Ryder's head snapped up as, scowling, he observed his four friends advancing toward them. Natalie tried to bolt out of his lap, but he held her fast.

"Let me go!" she cried, still trying to twist free.

A menacing and equally mortifying pinch on her behind effectively quashed her struggles. "Ah, my cronies have arrived," he murmured evenly. "Look lively, love."

While Natalie glared murder at him, Ryder's four friends stepped up to the table. Harry was the first to speak as he glanced from Ryder to the hot-faced, voluptuous wench on his lap. He stared pointedly at the love mark on Natalie's neck, and his lips twisted into a grimace.

"What have we here, Lord Newbury?"

With his arms still tightly clamped about Natalie, Ryder grinned up at the others. "What we have here, gentlemen, is a lost wager." At the ensuing groans, Ryder winked at Natalie. "Natalie, my dear, may I introduce my friends— Harry Hampton, George Abbott, John Randolph, and Richard Spencer."

As Ryder nodded toward each man in turn, Natalie quickly realized that Harry Hampton was the blond, blue-eyed one, George Abbott was thin and balding, John Randolph was auburn-haired and hazel-eyed, and Richard Spencer was the man with the hawk nose. All four were dressed in cavalier style, in flowing white shirts and dark breeches. All wore sabers or rapiers strapped to their waists.

Remembering—albeit unwillingly!—her promise to Ryder, Natalie changed to her tavern-wench persona and flashed the group a saucy grin. "How do you do, gents?"

The men mumbled greetings.

"Won't you join us for breakfast?" Ryder asked them. "I've already ordered coffee, gruel, and sausage for us all."

The men sullenly took their places around the table. Richard Spencer eyed Natalie's mussed coiffure and raised an eyebrow to Ryder. "So you had your wicked way with the wench, eh, Newbury?"

Ryder kissed Natalie's cheek, his fingers lazily caressing the side of her breast. "What does it look like to you?"

While Richard and George exchanged a meaningful glance, Harry said, "I'd like to hear it from the wench herself."

Ryder stared Natalie in the eye. "Well, wench?"

She would have liked nothing more than to throttle the maddening devil—especially since his depraved fingertips were now straying dangerously close to her nipple, which had traitorously begun to tingle and tighten, as if in anticipation of his scandalous touch! Mercy, what was happening to her? She would have loved to strangle Ryder Remington in front of his cronies—but she remembered in the nick of time that she needed his help to find Aunt Love.

Still, perhaps this rake was playing a game in which two could participate. He had made her squirm aplenty; maybe it was *his* turn to wiggle on the hook a bit!

She smiled at Harry and drawled, " 'Is lordship and I 'ad a rousing good time last night. Fair make me creak, 'e did."

As the other men howled with ribald laughter, a gleeful Natalie watched Ryder's face darken. Relishing her small triumph, she underscored her brazen remark by mussing his hair, to the wild hoots of his cronies.

"Hey, Ryder, would the wench be interested in *rousing* any of us tonight?" George put in with a mischievous grin.

"She can make me creak any time," added John.

A flustered Ryder all but shoved away the suddenly attentive Natalie. "The wench is not interested," came his prompt and surprisingly cold reply.

George whistled. "Taken a fancy to you, hasn't he, woman?"

"Aye, I reckon 'e 'as," Natalie replied, tweaking Ryder's ears, to the intense amusement of the other men. "Put that dazed look in my eyes, 'e did."

More chuckles followed, while Natalie continued to savor Ryder's sudden discomfiture. Perverse delight filled her; *he* could be gotten to, after all. She noted that he appeared very agitated—especially when she teased the stubbly curve of his jaw with seductive, trailing flicks of her fingers.

At last Ryder took charge. Heaving a grunt and grabbing Natalie's wrists, he turned decisively to his friends. "All right, then, gents. Time to pay up."

They grumbled among themselves. Then Richard tossed down a stunning ruby ring and a gold seal, while George threw in a heavy purse.

Ryder regarded the two holdouts. "Well, gents?"

"My cavalry musket is back at the house," John said resentfully.

Ryder looked at Harry. "Hampton?"

Harry sighed explosively. "The *Wind* is tied up at Middle Dock. But you can gather your own damned crew."

"Why, Harry," Ryder chided with a grin, "how stingy of you."

Meanwhile, Natalie turned in alarm to Ryder. "What is the *Wind?*"

"A Baltimore clipper."

Natalie's eyes grew huge. "You mean you are taking your friend's ship?" she cried, so appalled that she momentarily forgot to feign her accent.

"What's this?" cried Richard. "A whore with a conscience?"

Ryder's head at once swung around to Richard. "You," he snapped, "will watch who you call a whore!"

"But, Ryder, if she spent the night with you, then she is—"

"Curb your tongue, Spencer, or I will call you out!" Ryder roared.

This comment caused the other men to glance at one another in perplexity. The awkwardness ended as the innkeeper's daughter sauntered by with a tray and deposited bowls of gruel before each person. Ryder's cohorts ate with relish while discussing their agenda—they planned to hunt quail that morning, attend a horse race at the York Course that afternoon, and visit the gaming tables in the evening. Their profligacy and lack of purpose disgusted Natalie.

But what agitated her most of all was having to remain on Ryder's lap as they all lingered an eternity over their breakfasts. He had once again seized the advantage and was making *her* squirm—he pawed her, nibbled at her face with his lips, and even spoon-fed her the lumpy, unpalatable gruel. The fact that her hands were tied, figuratively speaking, and that she was duty-bound not to rebuff him in front of his friends, nearly drove her mad. When he missed slightly with the spoon, spilling gruel at the corner of her mouth, he dabbed it up with his forefinger, then placed the morsel in her mouth. The lecherous gleam in his eyes, combined with the blatant sensuality of his gesture, left her thoroughly rattled. She narrowly quelled an instinct to bite his finger—whether with exasperation or with a far more shocking emotion, she was not quite sure. This recklessness he spurred in her, she did not like one bit!

Just as the men were finishing up the meal, the very drunk who had accosted Natalie last night staggered by the table. As she cringed from his nauseating breath, the whiskered man spoke to Ryder.

"Good morning, your lordship. Glad to see it worked out so well."

Ryder appeared most ill at ease. "Yes ... well, thanks again."

"What worked out so well?" Natalie demanded, at once suspicious.

The shabby man winked at her. "Why, his lordship here slipped me a coin to accost you last night, miss. Paid me quite handsomely, he did." He grinned at Ryder. "Anytime you want me pawing the wench again so you can play the hero, just say the word."

"Believe me, I will," Ryder rejoined dryly. His friends fell into new torrents of mirth.

"So you left nothing to chance last night, eh, Ryder?" Harry taunted.

"Newbury is a crafty one, isn't he, love?" George said to Natalie.

Natalie was already staring daggers at Ryder. "You bribed that horrible man to accost me?" she demanded furiously.

"Aren't you glad I did?" he countered with taut, underlying menace.

Undaunted, she persisted. "Did you also give my servant the bottle of brandy?"

"This wench has a servant?" queried an amazed Harry.

Ryder pinched Natalie's bottom hard, eliciting a horrified squeak from her. "This wench is having delusions." He grinned at his cohorts. "Too much sin and pleasure last night."

Fuming, Natalie shot to her feet.

Ryder caught her hand. "Now, Natalie," he warned in a tense whisper. "Don't go off in a huff, love. My friends may assume you are no longer kindly disposed toward me."

"Heaven forbid."

Feeling both reckless and enraged, Natalie leaned over until her lips hovered just above Ryder's, and her eyes blazed down into his. Spotting the look of lusty anticipation in his eyes, and hearing the other men hoot encouragements, Natalie jerked her foot beneath the table and kicked Ryder's shin with all the force she could muster. His sudden groan of agony gave her fierce pleasure.

When she straightened, he was white-faced. She was grinning as she grabbed her cloak and tossed it around her shoulders. And she grinned the entire time it took her to turn and walk out of the room.

Six

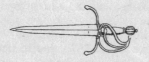

"Natalie, wait! Wait!"

Outside, Natalie heard Ryder's near-frantic voice as she rushed down the fetid alleyway, heading away from the harbor district. She glanced back, noting to her satisfaction that he was chasing her with a decided limp. Whirling to continue her breakneck journey, she stifled a scream as a buzzard, feeding on the offal of the garbage-strewn lane, shrieked and flapped its wings before her, then soared off in the blue skies overhead. Clutching her heart, she rushed forward, emerging on the corner of upper Meeting Street. She glanced from the dome of St. Philip's to her right, to the merchants opening up their shops to the south of her, and to the conveyances already clogging the street. Realizing she might well be spotted now that she was in Charleston proper, she ducked into the shadows of a doorway, removed her wig, and stuffed it into the large pocket of her cloak.

She was back on the corner, waiting for a dray to pass, when Ryder caught up with her.

"Natalie, wait," he said, grabbing her arm. "You must at least allow me to drive you home."

"My house is only two blocks from here," came her prim reply. She shook loose of his grip. "I can walk the rest of the way, thank you."

Leaning over to rub his shin, he grimaced. "That doubtless would be safer for me, yet I fail to understand why you are tearing off this way."

She was mystified. "You fail to understand?"

47

"Don't you want my help?" came his equally perplexed response.

Starting off, she laughed humorlessly. "Actually, I don't."

He hobbled after her. "But why?"

"Why?" She glanced at him in astonishment. "Tell me, Lord Newbury, is there anything or anyone on this earth you take seriously?"

"Why, I take you seriously, love," he replied ruefully.

She lowered her voice. "Aye, you're sincere about getting me into your bed."

A guilty grin pulled at his lips. "Natalie, we have an agreement. That I do take to heart. You fulfilled your end of our bargain—now it is my turn."

"Your gallantry is commendable, m'lord," she sneered, "but I will not hold you to your vow. Rather, I shall count myself fortunate to be rid of you."

"What's sticking in your craw now?" he demanded with an exasperated wave of his hand. "After all, I am the one who just got cudgeled—for the third time—by your vicious foot! Why are you all of a sudden playing holier-than-thou?"

She looked at him in amazement. "You can ask that after your disgraceful demonstration back at the hostelry?"

He feigned disappointment. "You didn't enjoy my kisses?"

She felt outraged enough to throttle him. "Don't delude yourself that I was the least bit moved!"

"Aha—then you must be referring to the bets?"

"Aye, you scoundrel!" She emphasized her remarks with angry gestures. "How could you deceive your friends in such a wholesale manner? I assumed you had made only token wagers. But family jewelry, purses filled with gold, a Baltimore clipper for heaven's sake!"

He grinned sheepishly. "I told you my friends deserved to be taught a lesson. I always planned to return all the bounty later on."

She rolled her eyes. "So even that you did not take seriously. Tell me, is everything in life a mere lark to you?"

"Pretty much," he conceded.

"Then, thank you very much, Lord Rogue, but I have no need of a man with such a cavalier attitude, a man who has proved himself neither trustworthy nor honorable."

Now she had angered him, and his strong hands caught her

arms, pulling her toward him. "Now wait just a minute. I
may be a rogue, but I do have honor, and I can be trusted. I
am seeing our bargain through, whether you like it or not.
And if you'll just allow yourself a bit of time to cool off, I
think you'll see it's high time you quit putting your own ruffled pride above the safety of your aunt."

"I am not being proud!"

"Oh, yes, you are. I have not known you long, Natalie, but
I have managed to ascertain that you are a headstrong, determined woman. But there's a big difference between being
spirited and resourceful and being foolhardy. The waters you
are braving are clearly dangerous, and whether you want to
admit it or not, you need my help."

She scowled at him murderously.

"Well, Natalie?"

She expelled a frustrated sigh. "Are you promising you
will return your friends' property?"

"In due course."

"What does that mean?" she asked suspiciously.

He shrugged. "Within a fortnight."

"And what if my aunt cannot be found *within a fortnight?*"
she returned sarcastically. "Are you saying that after you return your friends' possessions, you will still be willing to help
me?"

"But of course. A bargain is a bargain. And don't we have
one?"

"Nay." In a huff, she started off again.

"Damn it, woman, what's ailing you now?" he demanded
in supreme frustration while limping after her.

"You have to ask?" she flung back at him. "May I point
out that you did your best to mortify and humiliate me in
front of your friends?"

"And you did not make *me* squirm in the least?"

Her face heated with guilt and embarrassment. "That is
only what you deserved, you lecher, and is totally beside the
point—"

"Which is?"

She stopped and glowered at him. "I cannot possibly accept your assistance, Lord Newbury, unless you promise to
stop trying to force yourself on me."

The infuriating devil only grinned. "Force myself on you?"

Still fighting laughter, he clipped into a mocking bow. "Then of course you have my word that I won't, m'lady."

She eyed him dubiously. "You are sincere?"

He raised an eyebrow. "As sincere as your foot is lethal. Now—where shall we begin our search for your aunt?"

She groaned. "I must be demented."

"That makes two of us. Suggestions, Natalie?"

She shook her head as they turned onto Church Street and headed toward her house. "I wish I knew where to begin. I really felt I was on the verge of a breakthrough last night, until you intervened."

"You are referring again to the Irishman I knocked to the floor?"

"Yes."

"Why don't I make a few discreet inquiries around the harbor and see what I can find out?"

She glanced at him in bemusement as she realized he truly was serious about helping her. "That might be of benefit. I would join in the search, except that I really do need to get to the factory."

"So you actually run that enterprise all by yourself?"

"Until recently, I had Aunt Love."

They were now paused before her house. Spotting the anxiety in her eyes, he said, "Don't worry, love. We shall recover her."

Staring at him, for reasons she could not quite fathom, she found herself believing him.

"In the meantime, I should like to see this factory," he went on.

She nodded. "We do have a couple of samples of the smuggled English cloth, and I suppose seeing them might be useful to you."

"Of course." He scratched his jaw. "Let me see . . . The facility is over on Wentworth Street, is it not?"

"Yes."

He slanted her a chiding glance. "Not the best part of town for a gentlewoman."

"True. But the exalted Low-Country planters here have ensured that such enterprises are confined to the town's perimeter."

He nodded. "I shall call on you there this afternoon."

After Natalie went inside, Ryder backtracked to the hostelry. His shin was throbbing—damn, but the wench had a nasty aim!—as he stumbled into the dining room. He was pleased to note that his friends were still there, tarrying over more coffee.

"Well, gents," he said, taking his seat and grinning at them, "isn't she a beauty?"

"You needn't gloat," Richard remarked.

"Actually, I did not come back to gloat. I have a proposition for all of you. How would you like to earn back the possessions you just lost in the bet?"

The four men exchanged glances of astonishment, followed by smiles of lively interest.

"We are all ears." Harry spoke for the group.

"Good," Ryder said. "You see, my lady friend has an aunt who worked as a weaver over at the textile factory on Wentworth. About a week ago, the woman disappeared, and there are rumors that cotton smugglers may be involved."

Ryder's cohorts appeared baffled; Richard scratched his head, while John and George scowled and mumbled to each other.

"So what do you expect us to do?" asked Richard.

"I want all of you to scour the harbor district and try to find out anything you can about cloth smuggling along the coastline—suspicious nocturnal movements of ships, cargo being unloaded at clandestine locations, anything like that."

"Why don't you just ask us to put a camel through the eye of a needle?" demanded Harry. "What are we supposed to do? Walk up to some midshipman on leave and declare, 'Say, old man, do you know any smugglers?' "

"No, of course not," said Ryder. "You must at all times be discreet. But you can visit the tippling houses and eateries near the harbor, strike up conversations with various people, and see what you can learn. You can start by trying to locate the Irishman I punched to the floor last night."

"Why him?" asked John.

"Because, according to my lady friend, he and his cronies may be smugglers."

"What about the missing aunt?" queried George.

"The lady and I shall see to her," Ryder replied smoothly.

"I want the four of you to concentrate on finding out every-thing you can about activities in the harbor district or along the coast."

"And you are saying if we help, you will return our be-longings?" asked Richard.

Ryder nodded magnanimously. "Each man who brings back a clue leading to the capture of actual smugglers re-ceives the prize he forfeited today. Is that fair, I ask you?"

The others exchanged questioning looks, then nodded in unison.

After George, John, and Richard left, Harry lingered be-hind with Ryder. He rapped a spoon on the tabletop and re-garded his friend through narrowed eyes.

"There's something troubling me, Newbury," he murmured ominously.

"And what might that be, old man?"

"Is this woman—"

"Natalie."

"Ah, yes, Natalie." Harry stared Ryder in the eye and drawled, "Is she truly a tavern wench?"

While a skitter of apprehension streaked up Ryder's spine, he kept his composure intact and his tone impassive. "What makes you ask?"

Harry laughed derisively. "One minute the wench has an accent, the next minute she doesn't. She also spoke of having a servant—another marvel for a woman of her supposedly humble circumstances. And something tells me that red hair of hers isn't quite real, either."

"Just what are you implying, old man?"

Harry leaned toward Ryder and snarled, "I'm saying that if you have deceived us all, Newbury, there's going to be the devil to pay."

Ryder shrugged. "Is that all?"

"Well—is the woman a tavern wench or not?"

Anger flared in Ryder's eyes. "She *is* my mistress, and that is all that should concern you, and only as it applies to our wager. Otherwise, why don't you mind your own damned business?"

Harry's smile was cynical as he watched his friend rise and limp out of the room.

Seven

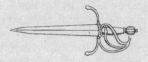

THAT DAY, RYDER WENT BY THE UNITED STATES CUSTOMS House and inquired about smuggling activities in the Charleston region. A clearly distracted clerk informed him that smuggling was rampant in the vicinity, and that the overworked agents could not possibly apprehend every vessel determined to evade the customs and tonnage duties levied at the port by Congress. He could offer Ryder no specifics on cloth smuggling locally.

Wanting to make certain his cronies were about their assigned tasks, Ryder made a stop at the house on Queen Street. There he roused George and John from bed and dispatched the two shirkers to investigate with Harry and Richard in the harbor district.

That afternoon at four, Ryder called at Natalie's factory on Wentworth. In the corridor, he collared a thin, harried-looking clerk and convinced the young man to lead him to Natalie's office on the second floor.

As the two men stepped through the open doorway, Natalie, at the desk, did not at first look up. Ryder was amazed by the dramatic change in her. Had he not known better, he could have sworn the near-mousy woman scribbling away before him bore no relation at all to the ravishing, earthy, flame-haired wench who had so captivated him last night. No wonder she had not worried about being recognized at the tavern! In the scant hours they had been apart, she had become utterly transformed. Gone was the risqué gown that had so well displayed her voluptuous body. Now she was swathed in an ultramodest, high-necked, dark broadcloth

frock; her hair was pulled up into a severe bun, and she wore
the most unbecoming steel-rimmed spectacles he had ever
seen in his life.

Yet through it all, she could not hide her beauty from him.
Her rich chestnut hair, with its lovely gold strands catching
the light, enthralled him far more than the gaudy wig. Her
skin possessed the same youthful glow, and he well knew that
behind those atrocious spectacles, her eyes held the same
tawny, seductive gleam. Also well remembered were all the
delightful curves hidden beneath that shroud of somber brown
cloth. He found that her modesty now excited him as much
as her brash earthiness. The contradiction of this lady/wench
intrigued him thoroughly. He longed once again to unravel
the mystery of her—to pull all the pins from that tight coiffure, unbutton all the tiny buttons on that high bodice, undo
her . . .

The clerk addressed Natalie. "Miss Desmond, you have a
guest, Ryder Remington, Marquess of Newbury. His lordship
says he has business with you."

Behind her desk, Natalie glanced up, staring from her
openly curious young clerk, Gibbons, to the tall, masterfully
handsome Englishman who stood there grinning at her—as if
he knew all her secrets.

Did he? The thought set her pulse to racing.

Nevertheless, Natalie's facade was properly demure as she
stood and nodded to Gibbons. "Yes, his lordship does have
business with me. That will be all, thank you."

Wearing a disappointed expression, the young man left.
Natalie looked Ryder over with amusement. "Well, this is
quite a change—Lord Newbury."

Indeed, she added to herself. Gone was the rogue; in his
place stood a fashionably attired, clean-shaven English gentleman, garbed in a long coat of black wool, matching trousers, a waistcoat of brown velvet, a white shirt, and a
matching Byron cravat. His black silk top hat was held in one
hand, a gilt-tipped walking stick in the other. His hair was as
jet-black and scandalous as ever, yet restrained now by a
queue to lend him an air of respectability. All in all, he
looked very much the proper dandy about town, although
Natalie felt far from complacent in the presence of this dash-

ing scamp who had already done so much to threaten her well-ordered life and her emotional equilibrium.

"I must say you appear quite transformed yourself, Natalie," he said. "As for me, I did not wish to embarrass you when I called here at the factory, so I dressed appropriately." He smiled wryly. "The trappings of a gentleman are not unknown to me."

"I'm pleased to hear that." She stepped toward him. "Would you like to see our facility?"

"Of course. I caught only a cursory glimpse as I came in."

As they started toward the door, he took her by the arm, restraining her. A puzzled smile tugged at his lips. "Tell me something."

"Yes?"

He touched the steel rim of her spectacles. "These eyeglasses—do you need them, or do you use them to hide from the world?"

Removing the spectacles and laying them on her desk, she met his gaze evenly. "I don't see well at close range."

"Can you see me?"

"Oh, yes."

He chuckled.

"At any rate, the spectacles help me when I am working on the account books." She cleared her throat. "Shall we go?"

Yet he tarried, smiling wickedly as he reached out to run his index finger across her soft lower lip. Her sudden low gasp as she jerked away and glowered at Ryder told him that beneath that prudish exterior, she was far from being *all* straitlaced and priggish.

"Unless I can persuade you to take a moment to greet me more properly?" he teased. "Actually, I was thinking it might be fun to discover who you really are, Natalie—prim maiden or shameless wench."

To his amusement, it was all proper lady who now shoved past him and marched for the door. "Save your persuasions for those tawdry creatures who may be moved by them," she snapped over her shoulder.

Shaking his head, Ryder followed her out of the office, down a stairway, and onto the main floor of the factory. A riot of sights and sounds greeted him. The expanse was filled with carding machines and spinning mules. Workers—both black and white, male and female—manned the noisy equipment. Cylinders carded ginned cotton, stretching all the fibers in the same direction, while on the mules, spindles clicked and rollers hummed, spewing out vast yards of mule yarn. Overhead, drums rotated on rumbling shafts, turning the huge belts that drove the machines.

"We buy our cotton from the gin at Goose Creek," Natalie began, shouting to be heard. "All our equipment is steam-powered." She pointed to the drums and belts overhead.

"Aye, I noticed the steam engines outside when I arrived," Ryder replied. "Very up-to-date."

She led him out of the building and across to the weaving shed, where they looked in at the neat rows of whizzing power looms manned by a mostly female work force. This shed, too, was bursting with cacophony—shuttles flying, healds slamming up and down, merging warp and weft into the raw product on the cloth beam. The clamor was played out to the loud reverberations of belts and shafts.

"There is another small building at the back of the property, with vats for bleaching and dyeing," Natalie explained. "Of course, we have excellent dyes available due to all the indigo planting in the Low Country, and we have some wonderful French Huguenot dyers trained in Paris. We also have a cylinder press for imprinting calicoes. I'd take you back there, but the odors tend to be quite vile, despite the good ventilation. I have to change the workers frequently in the dyeing shed."

"So—a totally self-contained operation," Ryder remarked as they left. "You do your carding and spinning on the main floor of the factory, your weaving and dyeing in the sheds. I'm impressed."

"Aunt Love and I have tried our best."

"Where do you get your workers—besides your French dyers?"

"Some are free blacks, others are new immigrants." She smiled rather guiltily. "Also, once it got around town that Aunt Love and I pay fair wages, we also attracted a few— shall I say—soiled doves."

"Aha! Tell me, did you consult any of them regarding your role last night?" he inquired with a wink.

"I'm sure I do not know what you mean," came the predictably straitlaced response.

"Oh, yes, you do," Ryder retorted, wagging a finger at her. "For instance, however did you acquire that wretched accent you used at the tavern?"

She smiled sheepishly. "Was my accent that bad?"

"Pitiful," he assured her. "Not to mention the fact that every time you became angry, you promptly shed it. Hampton has already noticed."

"Oh, dear." She fought a smile. "Actually, several of our female loom pickers are from the East End of London, and I have tried my best to pick up the dialect."

"You need further instruction—or, better still, to give up the game entirely."

Her tawny eyes flashed with defiance. "I can't do that, and you know it."

He decided not to press the issue. "At any rate, it is good of you to supply suitable employment for so many who might otherwise be destitute here."

She nodded, but her expression was troubled. "Truth to tell, I shall be thrilled if I can continue to meet the payroll for the next few weeks. That is why I had my spectacles on when you arrived. Until this past year, things had gone so well for the factory—given the dip in world cotton prices two years ago, we were even thinking of expanding. But due to all the accounts we have now lost to the smugglers, I'm afraid the figures for the factory are no longer adding up."

A frown drifted over his countenance. "Is it truly that grim, love?"

She nodded. "Before long, I shall have to think about releasing workers—a prospect I dread."

"And what of the owner of the factory—can't he help you?"

Her gaze beseeched the heavens. "You mean Cousin Rodney?"

"Yes. Where is he while all these disasters are amassing?"

She harrumphed. "I would imagine he is where he usually is—at home in bed, recovering from another hangover."

He touched her hand. "I'm sorry. And is there no one else in your family—"

She shrugged off his touch and spoke bitterly. "The other men in my family are, unfortunately, just like Rodney."

He pulled her to a halt just outside the main building and regarded her with a curious smile. "That is why you hide your beauty from the world, isn't it?"

She raised her chin and stared back at him with cool indifference. "I am sure I do not know what you mean."

"Oh, but you do. Have I missed the mark, or are you determined never to marry?"

"Matrimony is certainly not in my foreseeable future."

"A true bluestocking," he murmured. "But underneath, perhaps a scared little girl who is afraid to trust men?"

Her jaw tightened. "I will not have you presuming my thoughts, Lord Newbury."

"But that is why you are afraid of me, isn't it?"

"I am not the least bit afraid of you!"

"Whatever you say." But his knowing grin belied his statement as he opened the door for her.

They headed back to her office, where she showed him samples of the factory's product—the finest muslins and brightest calicoes, the softest Sea Island cottons.

"An outstanding array," Ryder murmured, setting down a swatch of blue muslin. "And yet you cannot effectively market your product?"

She nodded in extreme agitation. "We've hundreds of bolts rotting in the warehouses even now—because of this." Reaching into her desk drawer, Natalie pulled out a square of gray cloth and tossed it at Ryder.

He held the cloth up to the light and examined it for a long moment, an intent frown on his face. "A very distinctive warp," he murmured at last.

"Are you so familiar with the terms of the industry?" she asked.

He shrugged and tossed the sample aside. "As a gentleman, I've been schooled to appreciate the finer things—British cloth being among them. Has it occurred to you that the answers you seek may be in England?"

She waved a hand in frustration. "Yes, but I cannot even consider such a prospect until I thoroughly investigate here. What if Aunt Love is still somewhere in the vicinity? Besides, I would not even know where to begin in England."

He picked up the sample again. "I would think at the largest and finest factory in the land."

She snatched up the piece of gray fabric, balling it in her fist. "It is good English cloth, isn't it?"

"Aye."

Growing more agitated, Natalie tossed down the cloth and began to pace. "But ours is of the same quality—or better."

"I can't argue with that."

"Only we cannot compete with the price!" she cried. "When we first got here, the factory was in a most antiquated condition. All the spinning and weaving were done by hand. Aunt Love and I invested everything we had in new equipment, ordering power looms and spinning mules all the way from Birmingham. We increased the output tenfold. Things were going so well, especially after Congress passed the tariff which made domestic cloth more affordable. Now this—these cursed smugglers ruining everything for us—and they may even have harmed Aunt Love!"

He crossed the room and touched her arm. "We'll find her, and put a stop to the smuggling."

She braved a smile at his obvious sincerity. "I suppose it is good of you to help."

"My pleasure, m'lady."

Her expression tightened with suspicion. "Why are you taking on my cause, anyway?"

"Our bargain, remember?"

"Not the real reason," she commented shrewdly.

He wiggled his eyebrows lecherously. "I can think of a few others."

"I suspected as much," came her tart reply. She moved away from him, her expression turning serious again. "Did you have any luck today, trying to locate those Irishmen?"

With regret, he shook his head. "Not yet, love, but I'll keep trying. I've drafted my cohorts into the search."

She eyed him with sudden trepidation. "You didn't tell your friends who I really am, did you?"

"Of course not, love," he assured her. "I only have them seeking general information on smuggling in the region. They are unaware of your masquerade at the tavern."

Satisfied with his explanation, she laid a finger alongside

her jaw. "I must go back to the tavern tonight, see what clues I can ferret out—"

That drew a scowl from him. "Do you really think that is wise? You could—"

"End up the object of another nefarious wager between *gentlemen?*" she inquired snidely.

He chuckled. "Natalie, I do wish you would let me do all the investigating."

"I'm sorry, but that is out of the question. Especially with my aunt's life quite possibly in danger."

Reluctantly, he nodded. "Very well. But if you insist on this madness of posing as a tavern wench, then I must insist on being there to watch over you."

She feigned an amazed smile. "How fortunate I am—to have my very own guardian angel. Or should I say guardian *rogue?*"

Eight

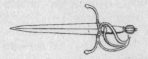

"WELL, GENTS, WHAT SHALL I BE GETTING YOU TONIGHT?"

That night at the tavern, Natalie, once again attired in her revealing frock and garish wig, stood before a table occupied by six crusty English seamen. Her expression was one of lively impertinence, even though she was half choking on the smell of their unwashed bodies and the stench of their cigar and pipe smoke. The sailors, mostly bearded and dressed in motley attire, were definitely not off a respectable merchantman or a Navy cruiser. From their battle-scarred appearances, they might well be involved in smuggling or outright piracy.

The largest of the six, who sported an eye patch, malarial coloring, and a jagged red scar running from his left ear to his stubby chin, spoke up lecherously. "What would you be offering us, wench?"

As the others howled raucously, Natalie took the taunting in stride. "Well, sir," she responded with a gamin grin, "we 'ave grog, rum punch, beer, or Madeira to whet your whistle. Or, if you gents is 'ungry, we 'ave roast pigeon or shepherd's pie."

"And what if our appetite ain't for food 'n' drink?" asked a cocky, pockmarked sailor with crooked teeth.

"Then we 'ave billiards and faro in the back room, and I 'ear a cockfight is starting up over at Wragg's Alley."

At this rejoinder, the half-dozen sailors roared with laughter. "She is a saucy one, ain't she?" remarked one to another.

"Aye, and 'ers is a sauce I'm lustin' to sample," came the lascivious reply.

"When did you lads get into port?" Natalie inquired casually.

"This evening, wench," answered the youngest and most handsome of the six. He looked her over slowly and insultingly. "You must know how 'tis for a man, after spending such a long time at sea. A mate gets an itch for feminine solace, if you know what I mean."

"An itch, sir?" Leaning toward him, wide-eyed, Natalie murmured soberly, "Would you be needing a female to pick the lice off ye, then?"

The boy colored miserably while his cronies rocked with mirth. "That ain't the kind of itch I was meaning, wench," the lad snapped.

Natalie continued to feign innocence. "Well, I ain't rightly certain what kind of itch that might be, sir. But whatever the torment, I'm sure 'tis a pity for your wife."

The young man blushed even more vividly as Natalie's barb scored; the other sailors jabbed him and added taunts of their own.

"You are a clever one, wench," the scarred one remarked. "How did ye know Billie here is wed?"

Natalie winked at the blond, blue-eyed lad. "Lovely ones like him ain't left standing at the altar." As the men grinned appreciatively, she went on matter-of-factly. "What brings you lads to Charleston?"

Immediately a suspicious pall fell over the group. "Why would you be asking, wench?" inquired their leader.

She shrugged. "Well, a lad 'ere earlier said he thought you gents brought in kegs of fine rum from Jamaica." Lowering her voice, she added conspiratorially, "If you lads be running rum, then Ned, the tavern master, 'e might be eager to do some trade with ye."

"We brought in no rum, lass," the man retorted.

"Now don't get a gale in your rigging, lovey," Natalie teased him with a wink. "Just making conversation to pass the time."

"Well, there are some things a wench 'ad best not ask," came the ominous response.

"Aye," put in the pockmarked one. "The captain here just ran through a nervy bastard who asked 'im too many questions down in Savannah."

While the scarred man hurled a glare at the talkative sailor, Natalie clapped her hands and grinned at one and all. "Ah, so 'tis danger you speak of? And tall tales to tell? Now, I'm a lady who purely loves danger—and stirring stories." She crossed her heart and grinned winsomely. "I promise you, lads, my lips are sealed."

At this, even the captain chuckled, and the previous tension dissolved.

"Bring us a pitcher of beer, wench," said the young, pretty one, "and let us talk some more."

Across the room, Ryder sat watching Natalie, his bright gaze smoldering and his fingers tightly clenched around a tankard of rum. Had the woman no regard for her own safety? How did she dare to criticize his reckless streak when here she was, brazenly flirting with the most disreputable crew of harbor rats he had ever seen in his life! All his self-control had to be summoned to keep him from charging over and prying her loose from the clutches of those odious knaves. Even though he knew such a move would only infuriate her, he was sorely pressed not to smash in a few faces and carry her off for a thorough scolding, and—God help them both—for more than a few thorough kisses!

He grinned ruefully as he thought of how the woman had gotten beneath his skin, into his blood, in a brief twenty-four hours. She maddened and inflamed him, this exciting mix of angel and whore. Why did she keep shoving him away, playing the snooty virgin, when she never hesitated to brazenly tantalize other men? Her behavior made him feel outraged, perplexed, but, through it all, more determined than ever to possess her.

He wondered which persona she would truly take to bed with him. Would the proper lady blush and shy away? Would the tavern wench quake with desire and eagerly toss her knees over his shoulders?

Both prospects excited him unbearably. And, watching her at work now, he was again left wondering how truly innocent she was. For a lady who claimed to have little amorous training, she played the coquette with considerable ease.

He drew a sigh of relief as she moved away from the table of sea dogs. But all too soon she returned with a tray bearing a large pitcher of beer and half a dozen tankards. After she had poured each man a brew, the largest of the six pulled her onto his lap—and the shameless wench rocked with laughter. Ryder's blood boiled.

He was half out of his seat when, all at once, the door to the establishment banged open, and he watched his four cronies march in. Led by Harry and grinning to a man, the troupe made a beeline for Ryder's table.

"We've news," Harry began as the crew noisily took their seats.

"Pray, don't keep me in suspense," Ryder drawled, still observing Natalie from the corner of his eye.

"We did manage to ferret out some information on the Irishman you set down last night," Richard said. "It seems he and his compatriots sailed out of port today on a merchantman bearing rice to Liverpool."

"Very helpful," came Ryder's sarcastic response.

"There's more," chimed in John. "By questioning some Dutch sailors over at the Bowling Green House, we learned that sometimes smugglers have been spotted unloading cargo west of Charleston along the Ashley River."

His curiosity piqued, Ryder sat up straight in his chair. "The Ashley?"

"Aye," said Harry. "It seems most smugglers sneaking into Charleston do so through the back door, proceeding up the Stono River and through its estuaries into the Ashley."

"Ah, I suppose that makes sense," Ryder said with a thoughtful frown. "Smugglers would naturally want to avoid any customs inspections at the harbor on the Cooper River. Did you learn of any specific location on the Ashley used for such activities?"

George said, "No, but one bloke mentioned a general area north of the Broad Street Canal where, in the past, there have been some customs seizures—mostly of Africans brought in illegally."

Ryder nodded decisively. "I want all of you to start watching the area at night."

There followed a litany of groans.

"But, Ryder," protested Richard, "you said if we brought you clues, you would give us back our possessions."

"I said clues leading to the *capture* of smugglers," Ryder

countered. "So far, all the four of you have brought me is rumor and innuendo. When we actually get our hands on these brigands, then all of you will be repaid. In the meantime, it won't do any of you a bit of harm to spend your nocturnal hours in more productive pursuits."

Richard muttered a curse and glanced at Natalie across the room; she was leading the sailors in a bawdy sea chantey. "All of this for a tavern wench and her lost aunt?"

"Never underestimate the power of a tavern wench," Ryder murmured cynically.

The others grumbled to one another, then got up and strode off to the back room to shoot billiards.

Late that night, when Natalie left the tavern, Ryder was waiting for her, his tall form outlined in the wavery light of a street lamp. Beyond him was parked his coach.

"May I give you a ride home, m'lady?" he called out sardonically.

Spotting him striding toward her, Natalie was in no mood to be toyed with. "Thank you, no," came her crisp reply. "Samuel should be along at any moment in our barouche."

"Aye, he has already made his rounds, and I took the liberty of sending him along," Ryder responded adroitly.

"Like you did last night?" she demanded, suddenly furious.

"Last night?" he repeated innocently.

She balled her hands on her hips and glared at him. "When I spoke with Samuel, he claimed I had given him the wrong time to meet me here last night."

"Perhaps you did," Ryder drawled.

"But someone else gave him a bottle of brandy."

"Perhaps someone did."

He was being slick as a street magician, and she was tempted to stamp her foot. "Oh, you are insufferable!"

He merely took her arm and firmly towed her away. "And you, my lady, are at my mercy, at least for the moment, so you may as well enjoy our little jaunt. Besides, we have some matters to discuss," he finished ominously.

"Oh, grand," she sneered.

He propelled her toward the coach and ushered her inside. "Did you enjoy yourself tonight?" he asked with deceptive mildness as they rattled off.

"Enjoy myself?" she repeated. She yanked at pins, pulled off her wig, tossed it aside, and drew her fingers through her flattened hair. "Do you actually think I could enjoy being pinched, pawed, and smacked by every stinking, repulsive sailor there?"

"You seemed to be suffering little from my perspective," came his equally nasty reply. "And have you even considered what you were risking, tempting such disreputable men in such a brazen fashion? Why, one of them could have tossed you over a shoulder and carried you off upstairs—"

"That would never happen!" she cut in vehemently. "Ned would never allow it."

"Ned?" Ryder queried.

"Ned Hastings owns the Tradd Street Tavern. His wife is a weaver at our factory. Both of them are fond of my aunt, who has shown their family numerous kindnesses in the past. That is how I got the position as serving wench in the first place. Ned knows who I really am, and he promised he would keep my secret and ensure my safety while I investigated Aunt Love's disappearance. Besides, he runs a clean establishment."

"A clean establishment?" Ryder mocked. "So only the hands pawing you are filthy?"

With considerable restraint, she managed not to slap his arrogant face. "I do not appreciate that comment in the least!"

"Then perhaps your *appreciation* can only be acquired in a more direct manner," he shot back. "Come over here and give me a little of what you so generously bestowed on the others."

"Rot in hell!"

In the next instant, Ryder hauled Natalie across the carriage into his lap, and captured her lips in a punishing, possessive kiss. Indignation and traitorous arousal hit her with simultaneous, blinding force. She drew back her hand and slapped him. He bellowed a curse, and a split second later, she managed to shove him away and clamber back to the relative safety of her own seat.

Ryder had to struggle hard to keep from strangling her. "Isn't this pretense of innocence a bit late, love?" he sneered, rubbing his cheek. His features appeared harsh in the wavering glow of a passing street lamp. "You bounced around on half a dozen male laps tonight, and now you dare to spurn me?"

"I bounced around on half a dozen male laps tonight in order to find my aunt!" she railed. "Do you have any idea of the indignities I suffered having those men try to touch my breasts, pinch my bottom, and plant their nauseating, rank kisses on my face? Now I find that you are no better than they are—*and* after you promised to behave yourself!"

That comment brought stony silence.

"Well, what do you have to say for yourself, sir?" she half shouted at him.

He was quiet for a long, charged moment. "All right, maybe I . . ."

"Maybe you what?"

"Overreacted."

"You don't say?" she snapped.

"Well, I was jealous!" came his fierce reply.

"You—you were what?"

He stared at her straight in the eye. "Jealous."

For once, Natalie was totally at a loss, disarmed by his honesty, the blinding intensity in his eyes. Her heart pounded in the charged silence. She was quite unused to inspiring such passion in men—especially a dashing and handsome man like Ryder Remington. She realized she was recklessly, irrationally tempted to cross the distance between them and somehow soothe his wounded vanity.

Was she mad? Instead, she smoothed down her skirts with fingers that trembled. "Oh," she murmured primly. "I see."

He surprised her by roaring with laughter. As she observed him in bemusement, he pinned her with a rakish glance.

"Natalie," he warned softly, "one more coy remark like that will doubtless see you undone by me."

She stared back, at first too unnerved to speak. At last she dared to ask, "What did I do wrong?"

He leaned back in the seat and regarded her lazily. "It's what you did *right,* darling—playing a teasing little game that women have been using to drive men to lunacy since the dawning of time."

She started to say, "Oh," again, then clamped a hand over her mouth. She was sorely tempted to ask him more about this "game" she was ostensibly playing, then swiftly decided she would likely not benefit from a full explanation—or a demonstration. She clenched her fists in her lap and tried to calm her flustered senses.

They were now turning onto her street. He glanced out the window and spoke with some lingering tension. "Did you meet with success tonight?"

She was still floundering in the wake of the sexual repartee. "Success—in what?"

"In finding the smugglers," he supplied patiently.

"Oh, that." She shook her head. "As things turned out, all my efforts were for naught."

"Indeed?"

"The men I spoke with tonight were smugglers," she went on with disgust. "I realized that much as soon as we struck up a conversation. I even tried to draw them out by suggesting they might be bringing in rum. But it seems their schooner, based in Cuba, smuggles slaves from Africa into Charleston."

He chuckled. "Ah, yes, I must presume that Africans are a most coveted illegal commodity here, ever since the Congress outlawed the trade in 1808."

"But my point is, I'm no closer to finding Aunt Love!" she declared in exasperation.

"Poor heart," he sympathized. "And after all that pinching and pawing."

"Including at your hands as well," she pointed out ungraciously.

He rubbed his forehead. "You really aren't going to give me any peace about this, are you?"

"No!"

"Are you going to insist on an apology?"

"Yes!"

He reached out to pat her hand. "Very well, love, I am sorry. Clearly I misjudged you."

"And *clearly*, I am overwhelmed by your sincerity."

"Take heart, fair Natalie," he went on teasingly. "All is not lost. My friends were able to uncover a clue or two today."

"They were?" she asked, both shocked and pleased.

"It seems your Irish seamen sailed out today with the tide."

"Oh, damn," she muttered.

"Now, Natalie," he chided. "You are beginning to sound much more like a tavern wench than a proper lady."

He was right, and Natalie was glad the darkness hid her guilty blush. "Did your friends discover anything else?"

"Yes. Evidently most smuggled goods come into Charleston via the Stono River, and from there into the Ashley."

"I suppose that makes sense."

"And I have even convinced some of my cronies to watch the area at night."

"Have you?" All at once she felt remorseful; he was trying to help, in his way. "Then perhaps I owe you an apology, too."

He grinned.

"I am sorry I snapped at you so," she said stiffly. "It was simply a very frustrating evening for me."

"For me as well, I assure you. And mayhap I can suggest a way to ease our mutual agitation?"

She shot him a chiding glance. "Now, none of that. If this association is to succeed, Lord Newbury, we must keep things on a strictly amicable basis."

"Amicable?" he mocked. "Not exactly what I have in mind, Miss Desmond, but I do suppose we must begin somewhere. Only you must tell me something."

"Yes?"

He stared at her fervently. "Do my kisses disgust you, Natalie?"

Taken aback, she stammered, "Why—why would you ask?"

"Because a moment ago, you said I was no better than the others, pinching and pawing you, planting disgusting kisses on your face."

Natalie fought the potent pull of his wounded, yet still very seductive, expression. "You really cannot expect me to address such crude subject matter."

"Crude?" he exclaimed.

"I will not stroke your vanity, sir!"

Pleasure and mischief danced in his eyes. "Ah, Natalie, there is much of me I would love you to stroke." Watching her puff up to spew out a new rejoinder, he held up a hand. "Very well, we will try to keep things—er—amicable. But I think I would like a friendly little kiss to seal our congenial bargain."

She glowered.

"I'm waiting, Natalie."

Feeling flippant, she brushed her fingers across her lips, then blew him a kiss. *"That* is all you will ever get from me, Lord Rogue."

Ryder threw back his head and laughed. "But, Natalie, you are forgetting the challenge you are issuing."

"What challenge?"

His tone was sensually teasing. "That kiss was like the slap of a glove across the cheek, an invitation to duel."

"A duel begins with an insult!" she flared.

"Ah, so it does. But you are missing my point."

"Which is?"

In the darkness, he winked at her. "When you blew me the kiss, you dared me to take more. Ten kisses full of seething passion couldn't have done it better."

Natalie turned away to hide her smarting face. She was very much afraid the rogue had just spoken the truth.

Nine

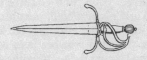

AFTER DROPPING NATALIE OFF, RYDER FELT RESTLESS. HE HAD
his driver take him to a tavern on Queen Street not far from
the house where he lived with his cronies. He dismissed his
coachman and sat in the smoky, raucous grog shop alone,
scowling at the noisy revelry surrounding him and trying to
drown his sexual frustration in a tankard of rum. At one
point, when two brawling Scots crashed onto his table, over-
turning his drink, he was compelled to get up and heave both
scoundrels halfway across the room. He decided Natalie was
making him demented, between her reckless disregard for her
own safety and her maddening determination to tease other
men before his very eyes—while still thwarting him
soundly!—and drive him to new heights of crazed lust.

Ryder realized his torment could not really be eased until
Natalie was his. Although the minx continued both to tempt
and to frustrate him, he knew now that winning her over
would require a more subtle strategy—because the direct approach had clearly failed, and because of the pledge he had
made not to force himself on her, a pledge she was obviously
enforcing to the letter!

Damn her eyes anyway for exacting the promise in the first
place, then for reminding him of it tonight—and of the fact
that he had broken it. She had an amazing ability to appeal
to the hidden English gentleman in him, and to stoke up his
guilt while still stoking *other* parts of his anatomy—without
even touching him!

Overwhelming her, then, was out, but couldn't he still persuade, cajole, or somehow seduce her? He chuckled at the

very thought. Technically, he could. How long had it been since he had played the suitor, the flatterer of women? During the past four years, the wanton types he had pursued had been easy prey. A slap on the rump, a kiss, a lusty comment or two, were usually all it had taken for a woman to fall at his feet.

This woman clearly *never* would, not unless he first refined his approach and coaxed, teased, beguiled, tricked—whatever it took to outsmart her and win her favors.

As guilt assailed him at the thought of his nefarious scheme, he reminded himself that Natalie Desmond was a repressed bluestocking who very much needed to learn to let go and enjoy life's pleasures—not only the ones he could bring her in bed, but also all the delights of the world surrounding them. Would it be such a crime to awaken her to the sensual when she was already missing out on so much of life's richness? He well knew that her passionate side lay smothered just beneath that prim surface, all her delightful secrets merely waiting for him to unlock and savor—if only he could persuade her to drop her ironclad guard!

When Ryder left the punch house an hour later, he found his hunger for the maddening wench had only increased. Whistling a favorite tune, "The Rogue's March," under his breath, he headed home along the darkened street. As he approached the final corner, four dark figures suddenly jumped out at him. Every nerve and fiber in Ryder's body jerked to awareness as he faced down the menacing group. Unfortunately, footpads and thieves were not at all unusual in this seamy part of town.

"Well, what 'ave we here, lads?" called a surly voice.

"A pampered dandy with a fat purse," snarled another.

"Leave me be or meet your death," Ryder warned.

" 'E's a cocky bastard, ain't 'e?" came a nasty response.

With that, the four charged him. Ryder was prepared, not about to become easy prey. Even as the scoundrels swung at him, landing painful punches to his ribs and arms, he retaliated swiftly, striking one man in the jaw, hitting another squarely in the gut. The night echoed with the sounds of blows, grunts, and curses as the men battered him from all directions at once. Ryder managed to slam one of his assailants across the shoulders, knocking him to the ground. Like savage animals, the other three roared with fury and stormed Ryder, hitting, kicking, flailing viciously, trying to grab him even as he swung back with powerful punches that somehow kept the trio at bay.

"Damn it, Will, get off your bleedin' arse and give us a hand with this demon!" one of the attackers yelled to the fallen man.

Catching a glimpse of the prone man struggling to his knees, Ryder realized he might soon be overwhelmed. He tried to grab his rapier. But the other three villains managed to seize his arms, restraining him while the fourth assailant staggered toward him. Struggling against his captors, Ryder glimpsed a look of rabid rage gripping the fourth man's grotesque, filthy face just before the scoundrel's doubled fists whacked him violently in the midsection, then across the jaw. The brutal pounding continued until stars swam before his eyes.

At last Ryder crashed to the ground, his body burning with pain as he gasped on the putrid stench of garbage. One of the brigands kicked him viciously, and he grunted in misery. Another dug his bootheel into Ryder's back, while a third reached down and ripped away his purse—and his pocket.

"Nervy bastard!" he heard one of them jeer. "Well, 'ere's a message for you and your dandy friends. Stay away from the 'arbor. A nosy scoundrel like you is apt to get 'is nose cut off—that, and a lot more."

The next morning, Ryder awakened feeling the effects of his battering. At first he felt so stiff and sore that even getting out of bed was a trial. A glance in the mirror confirmed his worst suspicions. His face looked as if it had been at the receiving end of a game of ninepins. His jaw ached and his stomach and ribs were bruised.

Ruefully he recalled how a loose, grazing pig had roused him last night in the filth of the slop-strewn street. Stiff with agony, he had staggered home, stripped himself naked behind the garden wall, drawn several buckets of water from the well, and poured the cool ablutions over himself until he felt reasonably clean. Finally, exhausted and shivering, he had gone inside and tumbled into bed.

Awkwardly pulling on a pair of trousers and a shirt, and

grabbing his boots, Ryder made his miserable way down the upstairs hallway of the house he shared with his friends. Inside one of the unkempt rooms, Harry lay snoring, still fully clothed, his body half on and half off the sagging mattress. Ryder tossed one of his boots, hitting his friend squarely on the backside.

"Bloody hell!" Bleary-eyed, Harry jerked awake and turned toward the doorway. Spotting Ryder, he threw the boot back at him.

Ryder caught it neatly. "Get up and roust the others," he ordered. "Time to be about our business."

Harry rubbed his backside and his eyes, then squinted at Ryder. "My kingdom, Newbury, what has happened to you? Your face looks as if it had been used to wipe up the streets."

"It was," Ryder drawled. "Four scoundrels accosted me last night. They beat me, robbed me, and left me in the street to be collected by the scavenger."

Harry's features snapped to alertness. "You don't say, old man! By Jove, do you suppose the incident has to do with the smuggling?"

"From the warning I was given, yes," came Ryder's grim reply. "And you had best advise the others that this mission could become considerably more dangerous than we had first assumed."

His features aglow over the adventuresome possibilities, Harry surged to his feet. "I'll gather the troops at once."

Rolling his eyes, Ryder went downstairs to the parlor, where he shoved a sleeping Richard off the settee. The wastrel only groaned—then resumed snoring as he landed facedown on the rug! Ryder shook his head as he sat down and pulled on his boots. Despite the cool, fresh breeze blowing in off the piazza, the room emitted a stale stench. The dusty expanse was littered with discarded clothing, empty liquor bottles, dirty dishes, cigar butts, scattered cards and dominoes. Ryder knew their cleaning lady, Mrs. Smead, was due shortly to make her weekly rounds, and Lord only knew why the kindly matron put up with the five of them and their debauchery. Even their coachman, Joseph, who cared for their animals and slept in a small room at the side of their stable, lived in regal splendor compared with the squalor of this pigsty.

Again, at this solitary moment, Ryder was left reflecting on the tawdriness and purposelessness of his existence. Strange, but he had not devoted a thought to his sloth and lack of ambition until a winsome beauty had first given him his comeuppance two nights ago—

Not that he was in any hurry to abandon his life of decadent pursuits, he added firmly to himself. Indeed, the idea of reformation definitely took a backseat to his determination to win Natalie.

And now it appeared they could both be in grave danger. He scowled as he considered the ominous warning the scoundrels had issued last night. Word had certainly gotten around town quickly that he and his friends were investigating the smuggling. However, he had no way of knowing if the attack was directly linked to cloth smugglers. He and his friends might have unwittingly stirred up an entirely different hornet's nest. From what he had learned so far, all types of commodities were being secreted into Charleston via the back door. His attackers last night could have been slavers, illegal traffickers in rum or whiskey—the possibilities were endless.

Nevertheless, now that he was aware of the dangers, he remained more convinced than ever that Natalie should not continue her daring masquerade at the tavern. Yet he knew that, without resorting to physical force, convincing her to desist would be difficult at best. Even telling her about the assault on him would likely backfire and send her charging further into danger.

In the back of Ryder's mind was the nagging fear that his coming to care for Natalie and her problems could threaten his entire audacious scheme to conquer her and then move on to the next challenge. Still, he felt too intrigued and fascinated—and too consumed with lust for her—to bow out now.

Ten

OVER THE NEXT FEW DAYS, RYDER AND HIS CRONIES CONTIN-
ued trying to ferret out clues regarding the smuggling. While
Natalie ran the factory by day, the men circulated through
seamy sections of Charleston, drinking grog with sailors, asking discreet questions, and keeping their eyes peeled.

Despite their attempts to be circumspect, it became more
and more apparent to Ryder that all of them were indeed
playing a very dangerous game. Harry exchanged fisticuffs
with a couple of less-than-cooperative Welsh sailors he questioned at the Old Market; and one night as Richard was heading home, he was pelted in the back of the head with a rock.
Increasingly, Ryder suspected there was an organized cloth-
smuggling ring in Charleston and that he and the others had
incited its wrath.

At night, both Ryder and Natalie continued their probes at
the tavern. When Natalie first noticed Ryder's battered face
and questioned him about his injuries, he told her the truth
about having been robbed, but withheld the warning the brigands had issued. Each night he kept an eagle eye trained on
her; his cohorts were out patrolling a long expanse of shore-
line along the Ashley River, looking for any shallow draft
vessels trying to sneak commodities into Charleston under
cover of night.

On Saturday, Ryder finally got a chance to begin imple-
menting his new approach to win over Natalie. After spending so many nights with her at the tavern, he was eminently
weary and frustrated from watching the scum of the earth
paw and pinch her—while he could only watch, tormented

and powerless, from afar! He realized they needed some time alone, away from their troubles. Thus he decided to invite her to a concert at White Point Gardens that afternoon.

Well groomed and whistling a jaunty tune, he arrived at her door long before noon with a bouquet of flowers and a tin of bonbons in hand. When she answered his knock, wearing a modest day dress and appearing bemused, he extended both flowers and candy with a grin.

"For you, my lady."

"What are you doing here?" came her predictable, exasperated response.

"Why, my dear Miss Desmond, I have come to pay you court."

She rolled her eyes. "You can jolly well go play your games elsewhere!"

"Now, Natalie," he cajoled. "I have decided we both need a respite from our taxing—and so frustrating—nightly endeavors. A few hours of leisure might even clear our heads and give us new insight into our investigation, don't you think? To this end, I'm inviting you to join me at a concert at White Point Gardens this afternoon at two."

Though Natalie was secretly amused and even enticed by Ryder's eloquent persuasions, she had been exposed to that lethal charm of his all too often lately, and she didn't need another dose today. With cool courtesy, she replied, "Thank you so much for your kind invitation, Lord Newbury, but I'm afraid I'm far too busy today to attend the concert with you."

He feigned a wounded air. "Even though 'twill break my heart to be denied your lovely presence?"

Now her patience was wearing thin. "Spare me the hearts-and-flowers rhetoric. I am well aware of what your true purpose is."

He chuckled. "And what might that be?"

"Corruption and debauchery. Of my person, I might add."

"Indeed? What a stimulating consideration. May I call for you at one-thirty, then?"

"You may go call the cows for all I care."

Sighing elaborately, he again extended the gifts. "If you won't at least accept my presents, Miss Desmond, I vow I shall tarry here at your door and howl my anguish until the cows you mentioned come home."

"Oh, for heaven's sake!" Natalie grabbed the items, swung around, and slammed the door in his face.

Ryder walked away grinning.

Ten minutes later, Natalie heard a new, earsplitting clamor out at her street entrance. Figuring the exasperating devil had returned, she stormed out of the house, down the piazza, and flung open the door to the street, only to view four burly, disgruntled-looking Irishmen standing there with buckets of water, the first one wearing some sort of badge.

"May I help you?" she asked, totally perplexed.

"All right, little lady," said the husky and ill-humored leader, "where is the fire?"

"The *what?*"

"The fire. You sent your boy to the barbershop to give us the alarm—"

"My boy? But I do not have a boy! And who are you?"

"We're the bucket brigade, ma'am," explained another.

"The bucket brigade!" she cried.

Wearing a massive scowl, the man with the badge glanced around at the house and the roof. "Aye, and by the looks of it, little lady, you've just given us a false report—"

"What do you mean, a false report? I tell you, I have no boy and I gave no report!"

As the men stood grumbling to one other, Natalie noticed Ryder sauntering up to join them, wearing an innocent grin. Her eyes grew huge as realization dawned on her. The villainous scamp was doubtless behind this treason!

"May I be of some assistance here, gentlemen?" he asked the firemen mildly.

The head fireman turned to Ryder while jerking his thumb toward Natalie. "The lady made a false fire report. Sent her boy—"

"You blockheaded idiot! I have no boy!" Natalie burst out, even as she saw Ryder stifle a chuckle. She could have killed him on the spot.

Meanwhile, the insulted fireman leveled a glare at Natalie. "So I'm an idiot, now, am I, miss? I've a mind to turn you in to the constable, I do!"

"Oh!" she seethed.

Ryder stepped closer and stroked his jaw. "When was this false alarm given, gentlemen?"

"Less than ten minutes ago, sir."

Ryder winked at Natalie. "Then the lady could not possibly have raised the alarm. You see, I've been here all morning trying to woo Miss Desmond."

While Natalie gasped her outrage, the firemen, to a man, began to snicker. "Are you certain about this, sir?" their leader asked Ryder.

"Oh, yes," he returned solemnly. "I've been courting Miss Desmond for an eternity now, it seems. I'm sure you gents are aware of how stubborn these lilies of the South can be."

"Aye," they concurred.

"At any rate, I was plying Miss Desmond with candy and flowers, and just before you men arrived, she finally agreed to join me at the concert this afternoon." Dramatically, Ryder finished by saying, "You're not going to whisk her off to the jail house now and spoil all my well-laid plans, are you?"

The head fireman hesitated. "Well, sir—"

"In fact, I was only just now leaving Miss Desmond's scintillating presence when the ruckus you gents created drew me back. So you see, the lady could not possibly have dispatched a boy to fetch you here."

The men frowned and consulted one another. "Well, if you say so, sir," their leader conceded.

Ryder grinned at the fuming Natalie. "If you have any doubts at all, why don't you stop by White Point Gardens this afternoon at two? I promise you will see the lady there with me."

"Very well, then," the man mumbled, and the four trooped off, sloshing water.

As soon as the firemen were out of earshot, Natalie charged on Ryder furiously. "Oh, you despicable cad! Raising a false fire alarm!"

"Me?" He pressed a hand to his heart in feigned bewilderment. "Who said I raised a false fire alarm? I merely happened along in your hour of need and most generously saved you from almost certain disgrace and incarceration—for which I think you should be most grateful—"

"Oh, you exasperating devil! Of all the gall! And telling those men you were wooing me!"

He grinned maddeningly. "But I *am* wooing you, Natalie."

Growing more rattled by the moment, she stammered. "And—and after you promised to behave yourself!"

"Now wait a moment," he chided. "I promised not to 'force' myself on you. Have you been ravished, Miss Desmond?"

"No, only thoroughly mortified! You are going to ruin my reputation in this community!"

Undaunted, he quipped, "Indeed, I may find a way to do just that if you won't promise to come out with me this afternoon."

Natalie was too agitated to mouth a retort, although the sound rising in her throat spoke volumes.

He bowed elegantly. "Miss Desmond, will you kindly do me the honor of—"

"Very well!" she exploded. "But for now, I'd advise you to leave my presence before I strangle you and save you the trouble of appearing here again this afternoon!"

He left, chuckling, and she stormed back inside, a secret smile curving her lips.   .

The concert was held in a treed park at the tip of the Battery, which fronted the wide, gleaming Ashley River. Standing with Natalie in the midst of an audience composed of Charleston citizens, Ryder grinned as he listened to the concluding strains of "The Rogue's March"—which was surely being played in his honor, he mused. He had enjoyed the band's repertory of patriotic tunes, just as he relished the sunny spring day and the tangy scent of the sea breeze wafting through the gardens and sweeping up the heady scents of blooming jasmine, dogwood, and magnolia.

Most of all, he savored being with the elegant lady standing beside him—and what a struggle it had been getting the feisty wench here! This afternoon, for the first time, he saw Natalie decked out as a vision of lovely womanhood. Her form dappled by bright sunshine, she looked as delectable as a spring flower in her rose silk organza dress, with its empire bodice and long, puffed sleeves. She wore a matching bonnet crowned with silk roses and tied in a taffeta bow beneath her chin. She carried a lacy silk parasol. With her wide gaze fixed on the bandstand and her toe tapping a rhythm, the average citizen would never guess that each night this proper lady donned a crimson wig and a low-cut gown and bounced about on sailors' laps at a squalid punch house.

Nor would the casual observer ever know that he spent his nights in equal notoriety, Ryder reflected ruefully. Out of respect to Natalie, he had donned a chocolate-brown, single-breasted tailcoat and buff-colored pantaloons over Wellington boots. His long hair was again drawn back in a queue, but in deference to his own nonconformity, he carried his top hat in his hand. How he hated the stuffy confinement of hats!

Ryder and Natalie clapped with the others as the band finished its last tune, "Hail Columbia." As the gathering began to disperse, he turned to her. "Well, Natalie? Has it been torture?"

She smiled grudgingly. "Very well—I did enjoy the music immensely. Indeed, I had almost forgotten how nice a Saturday excursion could be. Thank you for asking me."

Ryder whistled. "Do my ears deceive me?"

"Stop gloating or I shall box your ears."

Ryder was grinning, about to offer Natalie his arm, when two frail, elegantly attired elderly ladies stepped up, a Negro manservant following them.

"Why, Natalie," declared the taller of the two as she peered through her quizzing glass, "how good to see you out and about today—and with such a handsome gentleman."

At the pointed reference, Natalie said, "Miss Rose, Miss Grace, may I present a friend of mine, Ryder Remington, Lord Newbury, from England." To Ryder, she added, "I would like you to meet two of Charleston's finest ladies, Miss Rose Peavy and her sister, Miss Grace, who attend my church."

"Ladies, I am enchanted," Ryder replied, taking and kissing the gloved hand of each spinster and prompting both to beam with delight.

"Sister and I are so pleased that you have brought Natalie to the concert, Lord Newbury," Rose informed Ryder. "This young lady spends far too much time slaving away at that factory."

"I agree," murmured Ryder.

"As does her aunt," added Grace, who glanced around in perplexity. "By the way, where is Love today?"

Natalie forced a pleasant expression to hide her discomfiture. "Actually, my aunt is at Summerville visiting some friends."

"How nice. Do give Love our best," said Rose.

"I certainly will."

"We shall look forward to seeing you at church tomorrow, Natalie," added Grace. She glanced hopefully at Ryder. "And perhaps Lord Newbury as well?"

Ryder bowed to the two spinsters. "Ladies, do take care."

The two women were still smiling as they strolled off.

Natalie shook her head and regarded Ryder ironically. "So, Lord Newbury, you can be a gentleman when you want to be."

"I was hardly reared in a rookery, Natalie."

She eyed the gold-crested ring on his hand. "No—I do suppose you were raised in high style."

Offering her his arm, he did not comment. " 'Tis a truly lovely day. Go with me for a walk, Miss Desmond?"

It *was* a lovely day, Natalie thought. She found that she, too, didn't want the excursion to end—just as she had to admit she felt secretly charmed by the gentleman in Ryder. "Yes. That would be nice."

They crossed the grassy expanse of the park, pausing by Ryder's coach so that he could inform Joseph that he was taking Natalie for a stroll. Then they navigated their way across Battery Street, with its row of gleaming, shuttered, and verandaed houses positioned to catch the breezes off the Ashley. They continued down Meeting Street, which today was clogged with both carriages and people.

Ryder glanced around at the throng of fashionably dressed families, slaves, vendors, and even a few Indians in white men's clothing. "What is this press of humanity I've noted in town of late?"

" 'Tis the height of the season," Natalie explained. "From January until May, all the planters from the Low Country bring their families in to shop on King Street, to enjoy the social and cultural activities."

"Do you run in such circles, Natalie?" he inquired.

"Not at all," came her forthright reply. "Oh, my pedigree is likely as good as anyone else's here, and when Aunt Love and I first arrived in Charleston, there were definitely overtures made to us by some of the city's grand dames." She laughed. "Actually, at first I do believe there were suspicions the two of us might be abolitionists, given the fact that we were English and owned no slaves. I presume we passed that test, but as soon as it was discovered that my aunt and I spent our days running a factory instead of doing needlework and making social calls, we quickly slipped into disrepute. Alas, you shall never see either of us receiving invitations to the Jockey Club Ball, or to join the Academy of Fine Arts."

He chuckled. "You hardly seem brokenhearted over the ostracism."

She shrugged. "My passion is not for soirees, masquerades, the theater, or sewing circles. I've much more important things to do."

"Ah, yes, you are a young woman of consummate industry."

"And you are a gentleman of consummate indolence."

"Touché," he murmured. "And what of the two charming old ladies to whom you just introduced me? Haven't they heard that you and your aunt are social pariahs?"

Natalie had to smile. "Miss Rose and Miss Grace are two of the kindliest and most gracious ladies I've ever known. They spend most of their time in charitable pursuits, volunteering to nurse the ill at the pesthouse and the orphanage. But both are also fiercely independent, and I am sure they are unconcerned regarding their standing in the social register. Like me, they attend the Anglican St. Philip's, even though attending the Episcopal St. Michael's is now considered much more the vogue." Feeling the tug of her Christian duty, she went on politely. "And, as the ladies just mentioned, you would be welcome to join us at services."

"I don't attend church, Natalie," he practically snapped back.

"No, I suppose you would not," she rejoined coolly.

Ryder ground his jaw. The instant he had uttered the harsh retort, he had regretted his words. Yet how could he make Natalie understand why he had turned his back on formal religion, when the pain of his alienation still seemed so fresh? Worse yet, by speaking so precipitously, he had lost the opportunity not only to be with her again, but also to demonstrate to her in a small way that he was more than just a hopeless profligate.

They fell into silence as they arrived at the intersection of Meeting and Broad streets. Here, near the center of town, the noise and activity only intensified. Shoppers with slaves bearing packages shouldered past one another on the crowded walkways. Brightly dressed City Guardsmen drilled across the yard of the Guard House. A group of ladies in fringed carriage dresses and silk bonnets traipsed into St. Michael's Church. A half-dozen elderly men lounged on the steps of the Court House, reading newspapers or playing dominoes. In the distance, at the base of crowded Broad Street, Ryder could spot the looming Palladian facade of the Exchange, and a slave auction being conducted on its steps.

Natalie, too, was taking in the bright chaos. "Should we not head back?"

He nodded. "Let's go back via King Street and stop off for tea."

They chose a hostelry at the corner of Broad and King, where the innkeeper's wife served them a sumptuous repast of tea, crumpets, and fresh fruit.

Handing Natalie a crumpet spread with strawberry jam, Ryder thought of how much he relished being alone with her and sharing this elegant little jaunt. It was strange, he mused, that even wearing formal clothes—a prospect he normally found confining—could be fun when she was along. Then he thought of the night to come, and felt frustration—and no small amount of jealousy—surge anew within him.

"I do hope you are not planning to return to the tavern tonight," he remarked.

She accepted the roll and took a delicate bite. "I shall work there for a few hours, but I have already informed Ned that I must leave early."

He groaned. "Must you go there at all?"

"I must."

"At least you will be leaving early." Suddenly suspicious, he asked, "And why is that?"

"You really have no idea, do you?" she returned resentfully.

"Not a clue." Rather testily, he added, "But you sure as blazes better not be planning to steal off to some midnight lovers' rendezvous—with a man other than myself."

Fighting the smile his roguish remark prompted, she set

down the crumpet and straightened her cuffs primly. "You are forgetting that tomorrow is the Sabbath. While I am certain that such matters hold no interest whatsoever for you, I do teach a Bible study class and have much preparation to do."

At this revelation, Ryder almost choked on his tea. Setting down the cup, he shook with mirth. "What an enchanting mixture you are—Sunday school teacher and tavern maid."

Caught up in the mood despite herself, Natalie taunted, "And which do you prefer, Lord Newbury?"

His devilish gaze raked over her, and he spoke huskily. "I think I would like to take the Sunday school teacher upstairs with me—and then take the tavern wench to bed."

"Oh!" she exclaimed, her face flaming. "And I thought you were going to be a gentleman this afternoon!"

He raised a black brow. "Whatever gave you that idea, Natalie?"

She tossed her napkin at him, and he caught it with a smirk.

Watching her lower her gaze demurely, Ryder was not about to drop this delicious subject matter. "You mean you don't want me to arrange for a room for us here?" he teased. "After all, we're both so respectably attired that I'm sure I could convince the owners we're a proper married couple."

"Indulging in an afternoon of *improper* frolic?" she shot back, while fighting a smile. "You really are determined to ruin me, aren't you?"

"Are you so certain 'twould be ruin?" he whispered, leaning toward her. "It might well be heaven instead."

"Your modesty astounds me, sir."

Amused by her retort, he continued to look her over in a smoldering way, but his words no longer came so glibly. "Actually, darling, you look so lovely and refined today that it makes me realize anew how much I detest your working at that sleazy tippling house."

She lifted her teacup with fingers that trembled—especially since he had called her "darling." "I realize you disapprove of my strategies—just as you must realize you have no say in the matter."

"I am far from convinced that you are accomplishing anything at all there, other than subjecting yourself to needless danger and harassment. I think that if any answers were to be found at the establishment, you would have found them by now."

"I disagree," Natalie said stoutly. "There is a constant change of clientele at the tavern. Every time a ship docks, a new group comes in. Sooner or later I'll find someone who has information on Aunt Love."

"I think you are whistling in the dark. I still say we might be better off going to England and trying to uncover this smuggling ring at its source."

"Talk about whistling in the dark!" she mocked. "However can we hope to track the smugglers all the way to England? And shall we then visit every factory in London, Manchester, and Lancashire?"

He was broodingly silent.

Later, after they had left the hostelry and were walking down King Street, Natalie caught Ryder's sleeve, pulling him to a halt in front of a dry-goods shop. Wearing an expression of intense frustration, she pointed to a length of fabric in the window. "See that bolt of blue muslin? It's smuggled from England, but you will never get the shopkeeper to admit it. I should know—I have asked him."

"Then why don't you acquire a post as a shopgirl here on King Street and investigate things from this end?" he suggested. "That would be far safer for you."

"You are forgetting that I must run the factory by day. And besides, all the shopkeepers know me. Until recently, most of them bought cloth from us. Then, when cheaper British fabric became readily available, they demonstrated no scruples at all about canceling their accounts. But they are all too wily to admit that they have broken the law."

He frowned, making a mental note to investigate some of these shops on his own. "I should think the local merchants would demonstrate more support toward a Charleston enterprise."

"Many of them are Tory loyalists," she replied.

He was silent, his expression abstracted as they continued. They were crossing Tradd Street when suddenly the roar of an approaching carriage had Ryder jerking his head to the right. He yanked Natalie back just in time to avoid the out-of-control conveyance. The coach crashed by, careening mere inches from their noses in a clamor of thudding hooves, jangling harnesses, and shrieking springs.

On the safety of the walkway, both of them stood half in shock, catching their breath. "Are you all right?" Ryder asked solicitously.

"Aye—but where on earth did that carriage come from?" she cried, her hand on her heart. "It seemed to materialize out of thin air."

"I know," came Ryder's tense reply. "That was a really close call. We must be more careful in the future."

With both of them still feeling shaken, they headed back to the Battery. Ryder felt far more disturbed by the incident than he was willing to admit. When he had escorted Natalie into the street, he had seen the carriage down the block, but had judged they had plenty of time to cross. Then he had heard the snap of the driver's whip, and the carriage had borne down on them like a demon from hell. It was as if the driver were deliberately trying to run them down—

This possibility, coupled with the assaults on him and his friends over the past week, chilled Ryder's blood.

That night at the tavern, Ryder was as nervous as a tomcat on the prowl as he watched Natalie make her rounds among rowdy patrons who swung their mugs, hooted catcalls, and tried to grab her derriere as she passed. After having had her all to himself that afternoon, he felt more jealous, frustrated, and bemused than ever, forced to watch so many scoundrels try to fondle her. She was *his,* by damn—or so he sorely hoped!

Memories of their brush with danger today, combined with the reality that Natalie could well be in equal peril now, only further fueled his temper and grated on his patience. When he saw a bald sailor with a mustache reach out and pinch her behind, outrage surged in him. Observing Natalie turning to slap the scoundrel, and the seaman rising to confront her, Ryder quickly decided enough was enough. He bolted to his feet, charged across the tavern, and slammed his fist into the jaw of the cad who had dared to touch her. The man tumbled to the floor, and before his companions could react, Ryder grabbed Natalie's arm, sending her pitcher spinning from her grasp as he yanked her toward the door.

"What in God's name do you think you are doing?" she cried, struggling to get loose.

"Getting you the hell out of here."

Outside, she was still trying to pull herself free of his steely grip as he tugged her toward his carriage. "Why are you all of a sudden acting like a madman?"

"I'm mad?" he mocked furiously. "Has it never occurred to you that a woman who blatantly invites rape every night may have more than a few bats loose in her belfry?"

"You are well aware that I am only trying to find my aunt. What is wrong with you tonight?"

He released her arm and drew a heavy breath. "Natalie, I think we may both be in danger."

"What do you mean?"

"I didn't want to worry you about this before, but last week when I was attacked, the thieves warned me we should stay away from the harbor. Since then, some of my cronies have had run-ins with ruffians as well. And I suspect the incident today with the carriage was not an accident either, but another warning."

To his mystification, she appeared intrigued. "Ryder, you know how sorry I am that you were harmed by those brigands. But doesn't this prove we are getting closer?"

"Closer to what?" he raged. "Certain death for you?"

She thrust her chin high. "No one has harmed me yet."

At that moment, Ryder's hands were itching to throttle her. "For a supposedly straitlaced spinster," he snapped, "you have one hell of a foolhardy and mulish streak!"

Anger sparkled in her eyes. "Well, Lord Newbury, who asked for your opinion—or your help—anyway? If you consider our activities too dangerous, then by all means bow out. As for me, I am willing to do whatever it takes to uncover the truth and find Aunt Love."

She pivoted and started back toward the tavern, and Ryder, with a blistering curse, fell into step beside her and seized her arm. "If you are not the most stubborn woman I have ever met! Before this is over, you may well have me resorting to brute force just to save you from your own recklessness! Furthermore, I am taking you home."

"No, you are not!"

In answer, Ryder spewed out a blasphemy, grabbed Natalie

around the waist, and heaved her up over a broad shoulder, then swung around and stalked off with her. "I said I am taking you home," he repeated with deadly determination.

Natalie was seething. When she struggled to get free, his warning pinch on her bottom only exacerbated her fury. But as he strode along so briskly, the inevitable rub of her breasts against his warm, hard back ignited her senses in a far different and more shocking way. Her face was burning by the time he set her down.

In the coach going home, the anger and tension still flaring between them was hot enough to make the very air sizzle.

Eleven

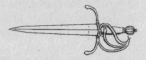

THE NEXT AFTERNOON FOLLOWING CHURCH, NATALIE WAS SUR-prised when Ryder again appeared at her home. Still dressed in her Sunday best, she opened the door at the end of the veranda to spot him standing on the steps, this time casually attired in a flowing white shirt and dark breeches. His long black hair was unrestrained, and he carried no hat. Beyond him in the street was parked his coach, with his driver sitting atop.

At the sight of him, Natalie felt her heart trip with excitement, and, unbidden, a memory of last night, when her breasts had bounced so provocatively against his hard back, rose to haunt her. She grappled with her errant senses.

"Lord Newbury." She greeted him with some perplexity. "You seem to be making a habit of appearing here."

He flashed his most engaging grin. "I've come with a peace offering."

She raise a delicate brow. "I wasn't aware we were at war."

"We hardly parted on the best of terms last night."

"I am surprised you even remembered."

"Miss Desmond, you never fail to make an indelible impression on me," he teased.

"And the reason for your call today?"

"I thought you might enjoy coming with me to take out Harry's schooner. We could sail her over to James Island."

She crossed her arms over her bosom. "I thought you were planning to return the vessel to Harry."

Devilment danced in his eyes. "You cannot expect me to

relinquish the schooner before I experience the joys of sailing her."

There was a hidden sexual innuendo in his statement that left Natalie secretly stirred and fighting a smile in spite of herself. "Now you propose to make me your partner in crime?"

"And aren't you already, darling?"

She harrumphed.

Deftly, he continued. "Besides, I have already hired a crew for the day, and I also stopped by that charming hostelry where we had tea yesterday, and implored the innkeeper's wife to pack us a most scrumptious picnic dinner."

"My, you are one for the grand gesture," she murmured. "But I do have so much to do today—"

"On the Lord's day?" he mocked. "You are not being a very good Christian, Natalie."

"And what you have in mind will doubtless not make me a better one."

He chuckled. "Doubtless."

Natalie struggled for a moment, then made a decision. Firmly, she said, "Lord Newbury, I again appreciate your kind invitation, but I did go out with you yesterday, and enough is enough. I have so much to catch up on today—"

"Very well, Miss Desmond," he said with a dramatic sigh. "Break my besotted heart."

Watching him turn and stride away, Natalie scowled, musing that he had given up far too easily. Then she remembered the glint of mischief in his eyes as he had turned away.

Her brow knitted in suspicion, she watched him continue toward his carriage, then pause to speak with a passing constable. A moment later, both men turned to stare pointedly at her.

Mercy! What disgrace was Ryder planning to heap upon her now?

Wild-eyed, Natalie rushed over to join the men. She smiled frozenly at the constable while muttering under her breath to Ryder, "I'll go."

At her words, the rather bemused constable smiled, tipped his cap, and strode on.

Ryder raised an eyebrow to Natalie, grinning his delight.

"Why, my dear Miss Desmond! What prompted this sudden—and so endearing—change of heart?"

She shot him a fuming look. "How dare you even ask, you villainous scamp!" As he shook with mirth, she demanded, "What chicanery were you planning to engineer *this* time to force my hand?"

He pressed a hand to his heart. "Why, Miss Desmond, I swear you misjudge me—"

"Spare me the protestations of innocence and 'fess up!"

He was literally bursting with repressed merriment as he reached out to toy with a ruffle on the cuff of her dress. "Why, I thought I might suggest to the constable that you are running a house of ill repute—"

"Oh, of all the nerve! You wouldn't!"

"Wouldn't I indeed?"

"You devil!"

Totally unrepentant, he continued. "Now, before the lure of such trickery becomes irresistible, why don't you be a good girl and go change into a more casual frock?" He eyed her high-necked blue silk gown with its myriad mother-of-pearl buttons traveling up the bodice. "You definitely do not look properly attired to walk the beaches with me."

Natalie glowered at him and protested a bit more, but ultimately, Ryder's charm and good humor prevailed—along with the certain knowledge that the rogue would wreak unholy havoc in her life if she failed to cooperate. She escorted him inside to wait for her in the drawing room, then went upstairs. Changing into a white muslin chemise gown with a low neckline and an Empire waist tied with a blue satin ribbon, she couldn't repress a smile as she recalled his brazen shenanigans. She realized she was treacherously excited at the prospect of going out with him again. Scamp though he was, Ryder did have a way of turning even the mundane into an adventure.

Natalie let her rich chestnut hair fall down around her shoulders, and completed her outfit with leather slippers and a wide-brimmed straw hat decorated with small silk flowers. She entered the drawing room to find Ryder sipping brandy and playing cards with Rodney. Both men set down their cards and drinks and stood, and Natalie noted Ryder's gaze lingering on her appreciatively. She also observed with amazement that Rodney actually appeared halfway genteel and sober today. Although his coloring was wan and he swayed slightly on his feet, he was dressed in his best tailcoat and trousers, his shirt linen was starched, his face clean-shaven, and his hair slicked down with pomade. Natalie hadn't even been aware that Rodney had gotten out of bed as yet!

Puzzled, she glanced from Rodney to Ryder. "I see you have met my cousin."

"Indeed, we were just discussing our mutual admiration for you," Ryder said.

Rodney coughed. "Lord Newbury has informed me the two of you are going on a picnic."

Natalie's gaze swung back to Rodney. "That is right. Do you—er—have plans yourself, Cousin?"

"Yes, I do," he replied. "I am attending a harpsichord recital with Miss Prudence Pitney and her family at the Queen Street Theater."

Natalie struggled not to gape at her cousin. "Why, that sounds delightful, but I don't seem to recall your mentioning this young lady before."

Rodney colored miserably and shifted from one foot to the other. "I only met Prudence two days ago. You see, I—I spent a night at the workhouse." As Natalie and Ryder exchanged amazed glances, he quickly added, "Strictly by accident. Prudence was among the ladies from the Beneficent Society who came calling with baskets of food the next morning, and she—er—intervened with the warden on my behalf and helped me straighten out the—er—misunderstanding."

"How generous of her," Natalie murmured.

Ryder stepped toward her. "We should be going."

"Of course."

He nodded to Rodney. "It was a pleasure meeting you, Mr. Desmond."

"And you, too, Lord Newbury."

Taking Natalie's arm, Ryder added wryly, "Good luck with Prudence."

Once they were driving away in his conveyance, both of them burst out laughing.

"So that was Cousin Rodney," Ryder said. "He is your aunt's son?"

"Aye."

"Where is his father, if I may ask?"

She sighed. "Uncle Malcolm died in London years ago. He was killed in a duel over a woman of ill repute—for which my father always blamed Aunt Love."

Ryder touched her hand. "I'm sorry. So Rodney has not been reared around admirable examples of the male species?"

"To put it mildly."

"If he is such a hopeless cause, how did he manage to get the factory off the ground?"

"Rodney hasn't always been such a reprobate. In fact, he was very wise to use his inheritance money to buy the factory and house here in Charleston."

"And then what happened to him?"

She slanted Ryder a chiding glance. "You of all people should not have to ask that. Charleston is a very sinful place."

"So it is, love," he said with laughter in his eyes.

"I can't conjure what Rodney might have done to end up in the workhouse," Natalie went on. "But I'll never forget how, on one occasion, the constable fetched him home after finding him asleep in a cow lot."

"Ah, but it appears there may be hope for your dissolute cousin after all," Ryder remarked. "It is a giant leap from cow lots to harpsichord recitals."

Her expression grew wistful. "You really think this young woman he met could reform him?"

He took her hand, pressing her soft fingers to his cheek. "Darling, I am eminently aware of the redeeming effect the right lady can have on even the most seasoned rakehell."

Though she did not believe him for an instant, his silky eloquence had her again fighting a smile as she pulled her fingers away.

They continued to Bay Street, where the coachman halted the carriage at the end of Middle Wharf on the Cooper River. As Ryder helped Natalie out of the conveyance, she glanced up and down a vast street fronted by long, jutting wharves that moored a huge flotilla of vessels—everything from mighty square-rigger cargo ships to Navy frigates to the new steam packets to smaller sloops and fishing boats. Although

the nearby street market and the shops were closed for the
Sabbath, the docks themselves teemed with industry. Barrels,
boxes, and bags were stacked everywhere, and muscled roustabouts were unloading sacks, huge cuttings of bananas, casks
of rum, and crates of china. Gulls swooped around the ships,
squawking loudly, and the air reeked of rotting fish.

Carrying the hamper with their picnic meal, Ryder led
Natalie down a wharf to the gangplank of a two-masted
schooner.

"Welcome to the *Wind*," he said.

Natalie followed him up the gangplank. On board, she took
in the well-scrubbed teak decks, the handsome ship's wheel,
and the tall, straight masts. "Poor Harry," she murmured.

"Harry will recover his property in due coarse," Ryder assured her.

The half-dozen sailors he had hired for the excursion were
already at their posts, weighing anchor and unfurling sail. Ryder strode off to speak with the helmsman, and Natalie
moved toward the bow of the ship as the tide pulled them out
into the bay. The day was bright and cheery, and the crisp sea
breeze caressed her skin and filled her senses with its invig-
orating essence. She studied the profusion of vessels beyond
in the bay: sailing sloops and rowboats, heavy-sitting mer-
chantmen and passenger ships making for the docks. In the
distance, she could spot the palmetto logs of Fort Moultrie at
the tip of Sullivan's Island. A frigate flying the Union Jack
was tied up nearby at the pesthouse—there, she assumed, to
drop off ill passengers for quarantine before entering the harbor. Across from Fort Moultrie, Fort Johnson on James Island
stood sentinel at the southern entrance to the harbor.

Glancing behind her, Natalie observed Ryder trying his
hand at the wheel, while the helmsman gestured nervously
and issued rapid instructions. It struck her that he was like a
big child with a new toy. Shaking her head, she turned to
gaze ahead. With amusement, she again recalled how he had
tricked her into coming along. Ryder might represent danger
and all the forbidden temptations to which she was determined not to succumb, but she had to admit his sense of mischief and joie de vivre could be infectious. As during their
outing yesterday, she could feel her spirits lifting. Indeed, out
here in the gleaming bay, she found it difficult to believe her

troubles even existed, with the wind singing in the rigging and the spray bathing her face as they glided over the smooth waves.

Then, all at once, the schooner veered so hard to starboard that Natalie was forced to grab the railing to keep from losing her balance on the tilting deck. She heard violent cursing behind her, and the screaming of the masts as the yards crashed crazily above them. Clinging to the bulwark, she watched two crewmen scurry aloft to tie down severed lines and restore the proper trim to the canvas. Within less than a minute, the craft achieved stability and tacked to the south.

Ryder came over to join Natalie at the railing. "Are you all right?"

"Aside from almost losing my breakfast, I'm doing quite splendidly," she retorted. "What happened?"

He smiled sheepishly. "I wanted to try my hand at steering, but evidently I have a rather heavy hand at the wheel. I find myself summarily dismissed as apprentice helmsman." He reached out to tweak her chin. "And I was hoping to make you proud of me."

Her gaze beseeched the heavens. "Everything in life is just one grand adventure to you, isn't it?"

Staring out at the rolling waves and taking a deep breath of the sea breeze, he began whistling a jaunty tune they had heard at the concert yesterday—"The Rogue's March." Natalie chuckled, realizing she had her answer.

They fell into a companionable silence as the schooner slipped into the wide Ashley River, taking them past the verdant gardens and stately homes of the Battery. To the south stretched the marshes, palmettos, and glistening white beaches of James Island.

They dropped anchor close to the island, and two crewmen lowered the longboat. Ryder clambered down into it with the picnic basket, then helped Natalie descend the rope-and-cleat ladder.

Close to shore, Ryder hopped out and pushed the small craft to the beach so Natalie's skirts would not get wet. As she stepped out, he grabbed the basket, and they climbed to the top of a small dune, where he spread out a tablecloth for them to sit on.

"What of your crewmen?" she asked as she smoothed her skirts around her.

"They will wait for our return."

She glanced out at the anchored ship. "It would have been nice to let them come ashore as well."

"And give up being alone with you?" he replied irately. "That is not the plan, Natalie."

"What is the plan?"

His response was a devilish chuckle as he looked her over. "You look so adorable today, my dear Miss Desmond, that I am supremely grateful I was able to whisk you off."

Natalie could only shake her head. "You really are shameless, you know."

"Shameless?" He feigned innocence. "Now what have I done?"

She slanted him a chiding glance. "Were you actually going to tell the constable that I was running a bawdy house?"

He regarded her lazily. "Actually, darling, I was thinking of donning a mask and charging in with my sword to kidnap you."

His dashing repartee secretly charmed her. "You wanted me to come along that much?"

"More than you will ever know." Eyeing her covetously again, he turned to reach inside the hamper. "Hungry?"

"Starving."

Ryder took out a veritable feast: sweetbreads, wafer-thin slices of ham and corned beef, sections of oranges, whole strawberries, clumps of grapes, an apple pie, and a bottle of Madeira to wash it all down. He served up Natalie's repast on a gold-trimmed Bristol tea plate and handed it to her along with a filled crystal goblet of wine.

"You are spoiling me with all these pleasure outings," she remarked as she took a sip of the rich wine.

"I would say you are in need of being spoiled," he replied. "Time to get you away from all your troubles and put a bloom in your cheeks."

"It is difficult to allow the world to press in too heavily here," she agreed, glancing behind them at a huge, moss-draped oak tree, where a bevy of warblers was singing sweetly, and then beyond them to the beach, where small waves lapped at the shore. "It is such a lovely spot."

He watched the wind tug at her thick, shiny hair. "And even lovelier with you gracing this dune."

Again Natalie felt charmed, though she was careful to steer their conversation into more neutral territory. "I haven't been on a picnic like this in—oh, I guess eight or nine years."

He whistled. "That long? You need to learn to play, woman. Why, you must have been a child when you last went on pleasure outings."

She nodded and spoke wistfully. "When I was small and my parents were still together, we used to summer at Brighton, and go to the beach to bathe and picnic. I miss those times."

"You were an only child?"

"Yes."

"And what happened to split your family apart? That is, if it is not too painful to discuss."

She sighed. "My mother hailed from a prosperous, middle-class French family. My grandfather hovered on the fringes of the French aristocracy until the Revolution, when he became a member of the Directory and, later, a minister to Bonaparte. My mother came of age just as Napoleon was rising to glory as commander of the French armies."

"How did your parents meet?"

"My mother and father met in 1797, when she was eighteen. My grandfather brought his family to London on a business trip. You see, Grandfather owned a huge furniture factory in the Faubourg Saint-Antoine in Paris, and my father was just starting his own career as a factor at the London Exchange. Those were the days before Bonaparte's Continental System escalated the hostilities between England and France and crippled trade for Great Britain. Anyway, the two men conducted business together, my mother and father met . . ."

"And the bargain ultimately included a contract for matrimony?"

She smiled. "Although I am convinced my mother and father were deeply in love at the time, theirs was always a turbulent marriage. The fighting between them intensified after Napoleon was crowned emperor of France, especially when my father's business suffered as a result of the Berlin Decrees. Nevertheless, my mother remained a republican with a great passion for Bonaparte."

Ryder raised an eyebrow.

"Political, not carnal, passion," Natalie clarified primly.

He chuckled. "I am relieved to hear it."

Her gaze grew turbulent and bitter. "Long before Bonaparte was exiled to Elba, my parents had a dreadful argument over the emperor's aggression, and my hot-blooded mother packed up and returned to Paris."

"I'm sorry." Thoughtfully, he added, "And I had not realized we share so many elements in common."

"Do we?"

He nodded. "First of all, we are both motherless, so to speak. We are both only children. And we are both the products of dual cultures. You are half French, half English. I am half Italian, half English."

"You are?" she inquired with keen interest.

"As a young man, my father met my mother while he was on his grand tour of the Continent." Ryder's countenance became stony. "After the two were married in Florence, he brought my mother and grandmother back to live with him in London. My parents' union was what I would call an empty shell—effected mainly for status and to secure my father an heir—although my mother was a wonderful parent to me. Tragically, she was killed in an accident four years ago."

Her expression crestfallen, Natalie touched his hand. "Oh, Ryder, I'm so sorry. And your father? How is he faring?"

"He still lives in London today."

She regarded his abstracted expression with sympathy. "I take it the two of you are not on good terms?"

"No, we are not."

They fell silent, concentrating on their food. Ryder ate heartily and finished his meal before Natalie. He reclined on one elbow and watched her avidly as she more daintily sampled bits of fruit and meat.

While the tension that had terminated their discussion seemed to have eased, Natalie was well aware that an entirely different—and potentially more dangerous—tension was taking its place. The ardent gleam in Ryder's eyes unnerved her mightily. Occasionally, even as she protested, he reached out to stuff a strawberry or a crust of bread in her mouth, his fingers brushing her lips and stirring those traitorous longings

within her. He repeatedly refilled her wineglass and kept
shamelessly urging her to drink up.

Feeding her a grape, he chuckled. "You know, I am really
glad we have had this discussion today regarding our families. Now I know how you acquired your headstrong, passionate streak."

· Setting down her wineglass, she at once became defensive.
"What reckless, passionate streak?"

He raised a dark brow. "Natalie, don't tell me you are arguing that a woman who dresses up like a doxy and endlessly
charges into jeopardy is altogether sober and prudent?"

She wiped her mouth delicately with a snowy napkin. "I
fail to see what bearing my heritage has on any of this."

He threw back his head and laughed. "Darling, you are
half French. That explains precisely why you are left constantly struggling between the prim little spinster in spectacles who runs a respectable factory and the hot-blooded
wench in a low-cut gown who flirts with the seediest elements of society at the tavern each night."

She raised her chin and spoke forthrightly. "I do not see a
conflict at all. Furthermore, I do not flirt. I merely do what
is necessary to find my aunt."

He slanted her an admonishing glance. "Are you honesty
trying to convince me that you don't enjoy your nightly masquerades at the Tradd Street Tavern?"

"Not in the least."

"There is no part of you that savors flirting with the unknown and teasing potentially dangerous men?"

"Correct."

He took her dishes, set them aside, then leaned toward her
intimately. "You don't enjoy this?"

Fighting her own fierce yearnings as he ducked his head to
kiss her, she braced her hands on his shoulders. "Shall we go
for a walk?"

"A walk?" he repeated. "My, but you are an industrious
Englishwoman, to have us marching about with our stomachs
so full." He stroked her cheek with his fingertip, wrenching
a gasp from her, and raked his gaze up and down her body
with a thoroughness that curled her toes. "I think I'd first prefer a little nap with my favorite, tempestuous Frenchwoman."

Natalie was hovering somewhere between panic and passion when he abruptly turned back to the picnic basket. "Oh, I almost forgot."

"Forgot what?"

She heard a low chuckle, and in the next instant, one of his strong hands gently pushed her shoulders back until she was reclining beside him.

"Ryder!"

Anticipating some nefarious stunt, she was about to pop back up when he disarmed her by laying a pale pink rose across her breast.

"A rose for my lady," he whispered, smiling tenderly into her eyes.

Another little gasp escaped her. His gesture was just too sweet! Moved despite herself, she fingered the velvety, dew-drenched blossom. "How lovely. A single rose."

In reply, Ryder ducked his head down to her bosom and deeply inhaled the essence of the bloom—and of *her,* she was sure! "Ah, yes. Heaven."

"You devil!" Although flustered, Natalie dimpled all the more, secretly thrilled by his teasing. She touched the blossom again. "The petals are so soft . . ."

"Aye, if one is ever mindful of the thorns."

Natalie stared up at him. His expression was now very intense, almost as if she were some sugary confection he hungered to devour. A strange heat curled treacherously in her belly, leaving her feeling vulnerable and uncertain. Ryder's fingertip moved to caress her jaw, sending shivers streaking over her.

"Have you ever watched a rose bloom, Natalie?" he asked huskily.

Wide-eyed, she shook her head.

Seductively, he whispered, "First, the bud is closed up like a tight little fist. Then it gradually opens itself to the heat of the sun, drinking in the warmth, trusting, then at last blossoming fully, in a burst of joy . . ."

His words trailed off provocatively, leaving Natalie awash in agitation, her cheeks hot. She knew he was brazenly trying to entice her, but worse yet, she was not entirely immune to his skilled persuasions. And she could not admit how well she grasped his hidden, sensual meaning—not without giving herself away!

Even as his gaze continued to hold her captive, his titillating finger began sliding down her throat, prompting a new riot of gooseflesh, making her squirm with a great deal more than discomfort. "Ryder, please don't—"

"Don't what?" he baited. "You can't claim I'm forcing you now, can you, Miss Desmond?"

No, but you're ravishing me with words—and your eyes! she was tempted to retort.

"You need to start watching roses bloom, Natalie," he whispered soulfully. "Indeed, there's an entire world I would love to awaken you to. A world of purely sensual delights. You'd enjoy it so much if you'd let yourself go a bit, darling."

No doubt she would, she mused in mingled fascination and horror. "I can't," she denied breathlessly.

"Why? Because you fear you'd end up trapped in a miserable marriage, like your parents were?"

She laughed without humor. "Aye. More likely I'd end up ruined—at your hands."

"Oh, Natalie." Now the errant finger was dipping even lower, caressing the rose, then brushing the tender flesh of her upper bosom like the lick of a flame. "Why grapple with all those dire consequences, and the rest of our lives, today? Why not just enjoy the moment?"

"The *seduction* of the moment?" she inquired in a cracking voice.

"If you so desire, darling."

At his skilled rejoinder, Natalie braced herself for an direct assault that still did not come. Instead of claiming her lips as she would have expected, Ryder continued the slow, debilitating caress of his finger, toying with the lace of her décolletage, straying dangerously close to the cleft in her bosom, making her demented, while further arousing her with ardent looks and the heat of his breath on her cheek.

"Just relax, darling. Smell the sea breeze. Watch the birds fly above."

Watch *him*—smell *him*. Ryder's sheer masculinity was so riveting, how could she be conscious of anything else? He was too near, and far too tempting! She was jolted by the longing in his bright blue eyes, and enchanted by the fierce beauty of his face, the jet gleam of his raven hair whipping around his noble visage. Even as his words had titillated her, his scent now further inflamed her floundering senses. She felt increasingly rattled, out of breath, out of control, unable to remember all the reasons she should fight him.

Ryder sensed her building excitement and continued to woo her slowly. Removing the rose—and its perilous thorns—for safety's sake, he began planting tiny kisses all over her sweet face. She shuddered, and the skin of her cheeks felt hot, yet incredibly soft, against his mouth. He continued unhurriedly, moving aside her fragrant hair to nibble at her earlobe—a most sensitive spot, he discovered— waiting to hear a small, incoherent moan rise up in her. When at last he heard that tiny, helpless cry, he eased his lips over hers.

The tenderness of his kiss was devastating to Natalie. Something burst in her then, as if Ryder's warm, firm lips were claiming hers for the first time. Inexorably, she felt herself beginning to uncoil to him, just like the tiny bud he had planted in her imagination. The hot mastery of his mouth on hers thrilled her deeply, and the pressure of his hard chest felt crushingly sensual against her soft breasts. When his tongue teased between her lips, the combined torture and delight were like nothing she had ever felt before—potent, shocking pleasure. Heat and languor suffused her, and her heart thrummed at a frenzied pace. The wine was in her blood, and he was storming her senses. Somehow, her arms found themselves tightly wrapped about his strong neck, and her lips moved tentatively against his . . .

The heat of desire rushed through Ryder as well as he tasted Natalie's lips and felt the incredibly sweet, first stirrings of her response. How he had waited for this moment, to feel her quivering with pleasure against him. He nudged her lips further apart, gloried at her aching gasp, then thrust with his tongue slowly, deeply, possessing her utterly, telling her sensually that she was *his*. She moaned again, a little sob of both pleasure and torment, and the poignancy of it tightened his chest with emotion as he crushed her closer. Ah, she was heaven, tasting of fruit, heady wine, and sensuous woman.

Growing bolder, he trailed kisses across her throat. He felt the wild, hot throbbing of her pulse against his lips, and his own heart responded thunderously. He moved lower, trailing his tongue over her soft skin, pausing at the warm, quivering flesh of her upper bosom and inhaling the sweet, musky scent of her. But as his fingers moved to ease along her bodice, he felt her stiffen and could sense panic rising in her.

"Ryder, no, please stop," she gasped.

At once he pulled back and stared at her. Her cheeks were bright, her eyes dark with yearning, frustration, and uncertainty. Her breath was coming unevenly and her lips were slightly parted, as if, through it all, she were still begging for more of his kisses. Delight surged in him that he had awakened her to his passion, even if not with the full abandon he would have preferred. In truth, he burned to stoke her desires to the boiling point, to drive her to dizzying heights of ecstasy. That sweet victory would come in time, he vowed.

For now, though, it was best not to press, else he could spoil that eventual triumph for them both. Better to tease her again.

"You were saying, Natalie?" he murmured innocently.

She again mouthed the word.

"No?" he repeated, stroking her wet, luscious mouth. "I could barely hear you, darling. Are you quite certain it's 'no' you said?"

"No—that is, y-yes," she stammered.

Chuckling, he nuzzled his lips against her cheek. "Which is it, darling? Didn't you enjoy my kiss?"

"That—that is beside the point."

"And what is the point?"

Catching a ragged breath, Natalie managed to push Ryder away and sit up. He noted with tender amusement how deliciously flustered she appeared as she smoothed her rumpled clothing and her mussed coiffure with fingers that trembled. Already she was struggling to play the prim virgin again, but she had been moved by his kiss . . . ah, yes, and much more than she would ever admit!

He savored the delightful little victory. "Well, Natalie? Are you quite certain you want to stop?"

Turning to him, she spoke with extreme agitation as the proper lady at last seized control. "How can you even ask such a question when we are both well aware that you are a man determined never to stand at the nuptial altar and I am a woman committed to spinsterhood?"

Ryder roared with laughter. "Committed to spinsterhood? What an unconscionable-sounding fate for you, darling."

Her expression was utterly sober. "It is the choice I have made for my life."

"But to call yourself a spinster! How unromantic a term!"

"I am sorry if the unvarnished truth fails to charm you, Lord Rogue. You doubtless would prefer a more tawdry term such as 'mistress.' "

" 'Mistress,' " he repeated thoughtfully. "Now, that has a nice ring to it. Tell me, are you volunteering?"

"No."

Stifling a groan, Ryder stood and offered his hand. "I suppose we may as well go for our walk now."

"If you wish."

The tension between them abated as they strolled along the edge of the water, although Natalie remained confused and appalled at herself for having allowed Ryder to take the liberties that had stirred her so. He led her down to a salt marsh, where he pointed out the antics of various birds—a sandpiper skipping along the marsh, a Louisiana heron comically flapping its wings as it strutted through the waves, a long-billed curlew digging in the marsh for sand crabs. Everything about the setting seemed to fascinate him: he showed Natalie an unusual conch shell, pointed out a large turtle snapping up a small fish, and plucked several small wildflowers and stuck them in the brim of her hat. Again she found his sense of joy endearing, although it saddened her that they were too different for her ever to share fully his zest for life, other than at fleeting moments such as this.

They studied the bright skies, trying to discern faces in the wisps of clouds, attempting to identify the birds flying overhead. At one point, when they watched a small, bright bird fall from the sky into the edge of the surf, Ryder dashed out into the water and retrieved a gorgeous, though listless, painted bunting. Natalie stared in wonder at the scarlet, violet, and green bird in his hand; it lay perfectly still, though its breast was pulsating rapidly.

"What happened to it?" she cried.

"I suspect the bird has just migrated here from South America," he replied. "It is likely exhausted after flying over the ocean for many days."

"Oh, the poor thing. Will it live?"

Ryder petted the bird gently with his fingers. "Perhaps if we give it a little help."

At Ryder's instruction, Natalie fetched a napkin from the picnic hamper. She watched in fascination as he dried the bird and stroked it back to life. Moments later, it flapped its wings and took off out of his hand. The look of delight on Ryder's face as he watched the brilliant bird soar into the blue sky was something she would never forget. He and the bird were much the same, she mused—untamed and carefree.

As they headed back, he picked up a piece of driftwood and studied its gargoyle lines and twisted angles with a quizzical expression. "An interesting bit of flotsam," he murmured, casting it aside. "Rather reminds me of my father's face."

She turned to him with a puzzled frown. "What an odd comment."

He touched her arm. "Natalie, about yesterday. I didn't mean to snap your head off when you invited me to church. One day I'll explain a little more about my family history and why my feelings regarding the church are so bitter."

"You needn't explain."

He appeared startled. "Indeed?"

She picked up the piece of driftwood he had dropped and examined it with resignation. "Nothing holds you, Ryder. You have no aspirations in life, no goals. You're as free as a bird, as fanciful and wayward as this piece of driftwood." She tossed the chunk of wood into the surf, watched the frivolous waves toss it about, then nodded toward the moored schooner beyond them in the river. "And I am as steady and unchanging as an anchor."

"A rather grim characterization of us both."

"I'm only trying to be truthful. You have no roots." She stared at him with regret. "No allegiances, no ties."

"And that is why I am fully committed to your quest?" he asked in a charged voice.

She shrugged. "I am sure you are helping me because it amuses you. And I am also convinced you will give up the game as soon as you grow bored—or realize you cannot seduce me."

He caught her hand and spoke vehemently. "Natalie, what happened between us just now—it meant something to me."

"Aye, I am sure it did—for the moment," she conceded. "But you have also made it clear that you do not ever want a wife."

Frowning, he asked, "Did I say that?"

"Did you have to?"

He ground his jaw and glanced away.

Though his consternation was obvious, Natalie could no longer avoid the sobering realities of their situation. "I can see that I must be an irresistible challenge to your male vanity. But the truth is, the two of us are just too different. You are the rogue, I am the lady—"

"I thought you said you were the spinster," he reminded her.

She ignored that and pressed on. "You are not ready to settle down. You would never want me as more than a mistress. I am not looking for a lover, nor could I ever settle for a husband who is no more than a will-o'-the-wisp. Nothing can ever come of—of what we've shared."

Ryder was silent, bemused, as they went to retrieve the picnic basket.

Twelve

THE NEXT EVENING RYDER WAS SITTING AT THE TAVERN, scowling fiercely, trying his best to keep a watchful gaze on Natalie as jaundiced eyes ogled her and greedy fingers harassed her path. He had called on her late that afternoon, again prevailing on her to see reason and not continue her reckless masquerade. But as always, the maddening minx had turned a deaf ear, much to the distress of his male vanity and his thinning patience. Once he had bedded her, would he be able to lay down the law and stop this nightly mischief of hers? But then, why was he even considering such long-term complications if his goal was only to become her lover?

Well, they still had her aunt to find, hadn't they? That would take some doing—if he didn't strangle the wayward wench first!

Following their outing at the beach yesterday, Ryder felt more intrigued by Natalie than ever—and even more frustrated. Yes, she had responded to him, but only to successfully marshal her own forces afterward and lecture him soundly until his ears were blue.

He grinned at the memory. Dash the woman anyway for appealing to the gentleman in him! All this pious rhetoric about anchors and spinsterhood—and about what an irresponsible cad he was! To his chagrin, he found he was not entirely immune to her assaults on his sense of honor, her stirring up some proper Anglican guilt in him. If only the prim lady in her would drop her guard long enough for the rogue in him to have her—before the gentleman in him became caught up in far more complications than he desired.

All at once, Ryder's thoughts scattered as his four cronies came charging in. Hampton, Abbott, Randolph, and Spencer appeared almost comical, all heavily armed with pistols and sabers and wearing flowing white skirts, dark breeches, and outdated, cavalier-style hats.

"Well, aren't the four of you modestly attired to reconnoiter for smugglers," Ryder drawled. "I am amazed you did not bring along a brass band and a few fireworks."

"Ryder, this is no time for your usual sarcasm," Harry said impatiently. "You must ride with us at once. We have just spotted a smugglers' vessel coming up the Ashley, not far from Charles Town Landing."

"They are likely planning to unload their cargo on the peninsula somewhere north of town along the Neck," added Richard.

Ryder's entire body tensed. "You are sure the vessel belongs to smugglers?" he asked Harry.

"Why else would she be slipping from the Stono into the Ashley under cover of night?" came Harry's impatient reply. "If she were a legitimate merchant craft, she would simply wait for daylight and make for the harbor on the Cooper River."

Nodding soberly, Ryder turned to observe Natalie. He groaned when he saw a leering sailor reach out to make a grab for her bottom, then chuckled as she whirled and thoroughly boxed the scoundrel's ears. For a moment he felt torn between his desire to protect her and his determination to nab the smugglers. He quickly realized it fell to him to assume a role of leadership.

He turned to John. "Randolph, I'll need your pistol and your horse. But keep your saber. I want you to stay here and guard the wench."

"But, Ryder!" John protested, crestfallen. "Why must I miss all the fun?"

Ryder stood with his hand at the hilt of his rapier. "Perhaps because I'm a better swordsman than you are."

Harry punched Ryder's arm. "That depends on what type of swordplay you are engaging in, eh, Newbury?"

"I can outparry the lot of you with any blade you choose," Ryder drawled. As the others exchanged droll glances, he extended his hand toward John. "Your pistol, Randolph. And don't forget to keep a good eye on the wench, or you'll have me to reckon with."

Muttering a protest, John handed over his pistol, and the other four men left to mount their waiting horses.

Across the room, a scowling Natalie watched Ryder depart with three of his cronies and wondered what knavery he was up to now. Was he already bored with spending his nights at the tavern? Were the men headed out to seek their sport elsewhere, at a bordello, a poker game, or a cockfight?

She muttered a curse and went off to refill her pitcher. What a fool she had been to give any credence to his passionate pleas at the beach yesterday. She might have known she could not count on him, that he was too much of an irresponsible rogue to honor his part of their bargain!

Moments later, Ryder and his friends were on horseback, galloping along the peninsula in the moonlight. To the west of them, beyond palmettos, marsh grass, and bald cypress, flowed the wide, silvery Ashley River. To the east loomed deep forest. The night was cold, damp, and foggy. The hooting of owls, the crying of swamp birds, and the rustling of leaves mingled with the rushing of the river, the pounding of the horses' hooves on the sandy loam, and the animals' labored snorting and huffing.

As the four rounded a bend, Ryder held up his hand, signaling to the others to rein in their horses beneath the shelter of an oak tree. Ahead, through the shifting banks of fog, Ryder spotted the shadowy outlines of two parked wagons. Across from the drays were beached a couple of heavily loaded canal boats; blurry, darkly clad figures skulked about, unloading crates from the boats and carrying them to the drays.

"Do you suppose those are the smugglers?" George whispered tensely at Ryder's side.

"Is that the same craft you men spotted earlier?"

"It's roughly the same size," replied Harry, "although I didn't expect to see two of them here now."

"A larger ship could not have made it up the Stono, even with the spring tide," explained Richard. "I'm betting the smugglers put their illicit cargo on lighters somewhere farther down the coast."

Watching the men heave the crates, Ryder nodded grimly.
"And those boxes could well hold English cloth."

"What do you propose we do?" asked George.

"I propose that we apprehend the lot of them," Ryder said.

Harry snorted in contempt. "Can't you see we are greatly
outnumbered? There must be at least eight of them. That's a
lot to risk for the sake of a tavern wench, if you ask me."

Ryder raised an eyebrow at his friend. "This is the same
brilliant swordsman who dispatched six Thomières infantry-
men at Salamanca?"

"That was for king and country, not for smuggled cotton
and the favors of a red-haired wench," Harry rejoined.

"Enough trifling—let us ride," said Ryder.

After a bit more grumbling, the other three men spurred
their horses and followed Ryder's lead toward the wagons.
The fog was rapidly thickening, which masked their approach
but also made navigating difficult. Hearing a curse behind
him, Ryder turned his head to see Richard tumbling off his
horse into the Ashley. He groaned at the sight, but realized
there was no time for a rescue now. Indeed, at Richard's loud
calamity, the smugglers had noted their advance; the burly
men ceased their labors, drawing out pistols and swords as
they menacingly faced the riders.

Then Harry imprudently called out, "I say—what goes on
there?"

A second later, his hat flew off with the force of a pistol
blast.

"Great Scot!" he cried.

"Let's get them!" urged George.

Near the wagons, the three reined in their horses and leapt
to the ground. Instantly, the angry smugglers converged on
them from all directions. Fists flew, pistols fired, and razor-
sharp swords sliced through the fog.

At first, the three men fought in a tight group, surrounded
by the smugglers. Ryder punched out one brawny fellow with
ease. Then, spotting a bearded blackguard about to fire at
Harry, he unsheathed his rapier and slammed the pistol out of
the man's hand, nicking the scoundrel in the process. The
smuggler charged at Ryder with a bellow of rage. Sidestepping his bulk, Ryder kicked him in the belly and, as his as-

sailant doubled up in pain, hit him across the shoulders, knocking him to the ground.

The next thing Ryder saw was a shorter man lunging at him with saber drawn. He feinted as the man would have gutted him, then charged with his own rapier, locking swords with his opponent, then parrying aggressively, leaping forward with each explosive stroke, beating the man back. Visibility was almost nonexistent now, and while Ryder had lost sight of Harry and George, he could still hear curses, swords shrieking, men groaning, all around him. The acrid smell of smoke from discharging pistols grew heavy in the air.

Once again Ryder feinted as his opponent lunged at him, still intent on impaling him with his deadly saber. Missing his aim, the man careened away crazily into the fog. Ryder tore after him until he spotted a new flash of metal engaging him. He swung aggressively, but now his opponent seemed to have acquired considerable skill, and was blocking each blow like a master. The two battled for long, desperate moments, their weapons screeching and banging, the fog threatening to make their slightest miscalculation a lethal error.

Then he heard a decidedly English remark: "Bloody hell!"

"Richard!" Ryder cried.

"Damn right it's me! Is that you, Newbury, who just nearly cut off my bloody balls?"

Ryder stepped closer and was just able to make out the features of a dripping, ashen-faced Richard. Glancing lower, he spotted a thin slash across the front of his friend's trousers. "Sorry, old boy. I see you managed to crawl out of the river after you fell in."

"My bloody horse stumbled!" Richard burst out.

Harry's voice joined in. "Newbury, is that you and Spencer over there? By Jove, Abbott and I have been hacking away at each other like a couple of gladiators in the arena."

"Where are the smugglers?" asked a perplexed George.

"Quiet a minute!" cried Ryder.

The four fell silent. Listening intently, Ryder heard wagons creaking off in the distance.

"Damn this miserable fog!" he exploded. "We've all been swinging at each other, and now the smugglers have escaped!"

Thirteen

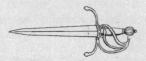

THE NEXT MORNING NATALIE WAS AT HER DESK, PORING OVER A production schedule, when Ryder barged into her office at the factory.

"Natalie, I must speak with you at once," he said urgently.

"You!" She whipped off her spectacles and glared at the exasperating devil who had already done far too much to disturb her life—and her peace of mind. She surged to her feet. "How dare you even make an appearance here this morning!"

"What do you mean?" he cried, looking genuinely perplexed.

She rounded the desk and punched his broad chest with two fingers. "We had a bargain, you scoundrel! And you abandoned your end of it and deserted me last night!"

"Deserted you?" he repeated. "But I left Randolph to guard you!"

"Your friend John Randolph departed with a prostitute shortly after you did—"

"I'll throttle him!" Ryder cut in angrily.

"Well, then throttle yourself while you're at it—since I'm sure you were similarly occupied!"

Ryder stared at the irate Natalie—at her heaving bosom, blazing eyes, and clenched fists. Abruptly, he broke into a delighted grin. "You're jealous!"

"I am not!" she retorted.

"Oh, yes, you are, and I had no idea I had so managed to endear myself to you," he teased.

"You are about as endearing as a horde of mosquitoes!"

"And equally determined to devour your lovely flesh?" he suggested with a lecherous wiggle of his eyebrows.

Not at all liking the turn of the conversation, she snapped, "Where were you last night?"

He whistled. "My, but you are in a raging temper this morning."

"And if you are not prepared to 'fess up, you may as well leave."

"But I've been trying to explain," he pressed on with forbearance. "George, Richard, Harry, and I had a run-in with some actual smugglers."

Her eyes widened. "You did? Where? How?"

He held up a hand. "One question at a time, please. As you know, I've had my cronies watching an area along the Ashley where smugglers have been spotted previously. Last night the others informed me they had observed a canal boat coming up the Neck. Four of us rode out and confronted the scoundrels as they were unloading their cargo north of town."

"Did you capture them?" Natalie asked eagerly.

"Unfortunately, we lost the villains in the fog."

She heaved a disappointed sigh. "All of them escaped?"

He nodded grimly. "After we lost visibility, the smugglers slipped off in their drays and boats, leaving us to slash away at one another in the darkness. My rapier came within inches of castrating poor Richard, who had the earlier misfortune of falling into the Ashley."

At this, Natalie had to giggle. "At least you did try. I thought you had—"

"I'm fully aware of your distrustful thoughts regarding me, love." He winked at her. "How could I even look at another female after you have bewitched me so?"

She dismissed his flirtation with a wave of her hand. "Oh, spare me your roguish charm." Her features tightened in a scowl. "As for finding the smugglers or Aunt Love, we appear to be no better off than when we started."

"I disagree," Ryder said. "I think we are definitely moving closer to nabbing the smuggling ring."

"But how can you even know it was cloth these men were unloading?"

His eyes danced with triumph. "I haven't told you the best part yet. You see, we stumbled over a smashed crate on the beach." He pulled a piece of cloth from his pocket and proudly handed it to her.

Natalie grabbed her spectacles and perused the material intently. She spoke through gritted teeth. "It's the same distinctive warp—the very British cloth that has become our ruination!" In disgust, she tossed the scrap down and yanked off her spectacles. "Now what shall we do?"

"We can continue to monitor the area at night, and I suppose we should also keep watch over the merchants on King Street, to see if the smugglers make contact with any of them." He shook his head. "Otherwise, I must admit it could be weeks before we make a second breakthrough or spot another vessel coming up the passage. I still say we are better off investigating in England."

"Not until we find Aunt Love!"

"Hasn't it occurred to you that she might have returned home by now to track the cloth down to its source—or that the smugglers might even have taken her to England by force?"

"Yes," she replied in frustration. "But I still feel we must do everything we can here first." She flashed him a conciliatory smile. "Still, I do owe you a debt of gratitude. Thanks to your efforts, at least we are moving closer."

"Are we, love?" Catching her off guard, he grinned and pulled her close. "You know, I would simply love to collect on that debt."

"Oh, you are impossible!" she cried, but with a guilty smile.

"Impossibly smitten," he concurred solemnly. "Now, to get back to your jealousy—"

"I am not jealous!"

"We both know you have no plans to marry," he continued smoothly, running a bold, tormenting finger across her throat. "But if your more carnal appetites should ever get the better of you, love, let me assure you that I am both a consummate lover and a discreet one!"

Trying to squirm out of his embrace, she retorted, "You are brazen! And when will you get it through your thick head, Lord Rogue, that I am not the least bit interested in you?"

"Oh, but you are, darling," he told her. "You gave yourself away at the beach on Sunday."

"I did not!"

His cocky grin clearly bespoke otherwise. "Oh, yes, you did. The little gasps, the eloquent sighs . . ."

Her face was smarting. "Oh! Only a cad would speak of such matters!"

"Not to mention your high-minded, moral discourse about being devoted to spinsterhood."

"And what of it?"

Unholy mischief gleamed in his eyes. "Natalie, you must realize that *every* rogue lives to abolish spinsterhood."

At last she managed to wiggle out of his embrace, though she struggled against a smirk and spoke with a telltale quiver. "You forgot to add 'humility' to your vast list of accomplishments. And as I have already informed you, a torrid love affair between us is *not* part of the bargain."

His smile was all rogue as he dipped into a gentlemanly bow. "But, my dear Natalie, I always try to give a lady much more than she has bargained for."

After he had left, Natalie found she still trembled. For Ryder had spoken the truth. She had been jealous when she assumed he had gone off with a prostitute last night. Ryder was chipping away at her normally ironclad control of her life, her emotions, and she did not like it in the least! He had awakened something in her at the beach—with tender words, gentle touches, and one incredible kiss that still made her burn every time she remembered it.

Since then, she felt more flustered, more frustrated, more at war with herself whenever she was around him—and even when she wasn't! She remembered the night in the carriage, when he had told her she could incite his passions without even touching him. Now she found the same was true for her. When he lifted an eyebrow, grinned at her, or just looked at her with such devastating lechery, she erupted into shivers.

What agitated her the most was how much he seemed to enjoy rattling her composure and stirring up her senses. He was clearly wrong for her, he maddened her—but oh, he tempted her, too!

That night at the tavern, Natalie sat talking with a young cabin boy, Simon Miller, who had shown up earlier, politely begging for a cup of water. Natalie's heart had gone out to the near-emaciated child wearing a filthy, ragtag jacket and trousers, and a cap that appeared to have been dragged through the mud. She had at once brought the boy mutton, sweetbreads, and milk from the kitchen. Squashing his protests about accepting her charity, she had insisted that he eat, and finally he had devoured the repast with an urgency and relish that had twisted her heart.

Over the last hour, she had learned Simon's tragic story. Hailing from Liverpool, the lad was only fourteen; he had run away from home to join the merchant marine, only to be discharged from his ship at Charleston because he could not carry a man's load. He had been loitering around the harbor for weeks now, scavenging for food, doing odd jobs, trying to sign on to another ship.

"Was this your first voyage at sea?" she asked him.

A grin split the boy's thin features. "Aye, miss. It's kindly of you to ask."

"It appears as if your superiors starved you," she added with concern as she noted the way his clothing hung on his frail frame.

He shrugged a bony shoulder. "When we was out to sea, I took the chills and ague somethin' awful, miss. That's why the captain discharged me, I reckon."

Natalie touched his forearm, which bore a yellowed, fading mark. "And was it the ague that gave you these bruises?"

He avoided her eye. "We hit a gale in the mid-Atlantic, and all of us was tossed about like twigs. 'Tis a wonder I was not swept overboard."

"You are far too young for such a grueling life," Natalie said in outrage. "You need to return home to your family."

The boy's pale eyes grew moist with melancholy. "Me mum is in heaven, and me dad will only beat me worse than the quartermaster did, once the drink is in 'im."

"I'm sorry." Natalie frowned, trying to think of what to do for the boy. "It's clear you don't belong in an establishment like this."

"And what of you, miss?" he inquired with an endearing grin.

Natalie had to laugh. She glanced up to observe Ryder, who had been watching them from across the room, amble over to join them.

Folding his large form into a chair, he glanced from the boy to Natalie, then winked. "Do I sense competition here?"

Natalie smiled. "Ryder, this is my new friend, Simon Miller." To Simon, she added, "This is my friend Lord Newbury."

Simon was staring up at Ryder in awe and recognition. "Your lordship, it is good to see you again."

Ryder squinted at the boy. "Again?"

"Again?" repeated Natalie.

"Aye, miss," Simon informed her happily. "A few days back, 'is lordship 'ere gave me a silver dollar to go give warning of a fire."

As the connection dawned on her, Natalie glared at Ryder, who grinned sheepishly when recognition evidently struck him as well. "You're saying Lord Newbury paid you to summon the bucket brigade?" she asked Simon.

"Aye, miss."

While hurling another seething glance at Ryder, she asked, "Tell me, was this a fire at a lady's house?"

"Aye, 'twas," replied Simon. He snapped his fingers. "Was you the lady, then, miss? 'Is lordship told me you was getting mighty 'ot to be saved—"

"Oh!" cried Natalie.

"So she was, Simon," Ryder interjected, laughing.

"Then you managed to save 'er, your Grace?" Simon inquired earnestly.

"In a manner of speaking, yes," he replied.

"You cad!" Natalie almost shrieked.

Simon appeared bewildered. "Didn't the lady want to be saved, your Grace?"

Ryder slanted Natalie a wink. "Oh, don't mind Miss Desmond, Simon. She only became a bit peeved when her *bluestockings* got singed." Before the fuming Natalie could spew out another rejoinder, he rushed on. "And please, young man, I am nobody's Grace here. Such deference is truly head-spinning."

"As you wish, your lordship."

Ryder glanced curiously from one to the other. "What are you two conspiring about, anyway?" he asked Natalie.

Still indignant, she retorted, "You're a fine one to talk about conspiracy!"

He stroked his jaw. "It seems my sins always do come back to haunt me."

His remark gave Natalie at least some measure of righteous vindication. And soon, her concern for Simon took precedence over her irritation. As the boy continued eating, she leaned toward Ryder and whispered, "I'm trying to think of a way to help him. He signed on to a merchantman in Liverpool—then they mistreated him during the voyage and dismissed him here in Charleston."

Thoughtfully, Ryder eyed the lad. "You know, young man, I share a house with some friends over on Queen Street. Our coachman, Joseph, could use a stableboy."

Simon's features tightened with pride. "I don't want your charity, your lordship."

"You'll not be saying that after you've mucked out the stables for a few days."

Simon drew himself up in his chair and thrust out his chin. "Very well, sir. If you'll pay me fair wages. Five shillings a week is what I demand. I shall do a man's labor for you, but I don't come cheap."

"Certainly." Ryder leaned forward to shake the boy's thin hand. "And you may also be able to help the lady and me with some inquiries we are making."

Simon turned to Natalie. "What might that be, miss?"

"My aunt disappeared a few weeks ago," she confided. "It is a long story, but we have a feeling she may be trying to track down cloth smugglers."

"Cloth smugglers?" the lad repeated in a tense whisper, his eyes widening. "Why, now that you mention it, miss, I seen a gentlewoman in the 'arbor a fortnight past, and askin' about cloth, she was."

Natalie paled. "You aren't telling tall tales, are you, Simon? This matter is of the utmost gravity."

"Oh, no, ma'am. Cross me 'eart." He paused to do so. "I reckon I even know where the lady be."

"You do?" Natalie cried.

"Aye, miss. Like I say, she was 'round the 'arbor during the day, askin' questions near the wharves and such. Then that night, I seen 'er stealin' onto a packet. I was sleepin' behind some crates, you see. Anyway, miss, from the talk of the sailors loading up the frigate, she was bound for London. That's where your aunt must be."

Natalie and Ryder stared at each other in a moment of joy

and astonishment. "You are sure?" Natalie asked Simon intently.

"Oh, yes, miss." He scowled at her. "Looked a bit like ye, the lady did. But older, of course."

"Do you know the name of the vessel this woman sailed out on?" Ryder asked.

The lad shook his head. "Sorry, your lordship. 'Twas night, you see."

"Never mind, Simon." Ryder reached out to hand him a coin. "You have just earned your first bonus."

Simon's eyes went wild with joy. "A crown, sir! But this is too dear!"

Ryder grinned. "You deserve it, lad. You have helped the lady and me more than you can know."

Moments later, Ryder and Natalie sat across from each other in his coach. Simon lay asleep with his head in Natalie's lap. Ryder's thoughts were tender as he watched Natalie stroke the boy's hair and stare at the youth with such concern. She truly was a very fine human being, he mused with pride—and one hell of a desirable lady.

"Poor child," she murmured. "It is good of you to take him under your wing, Ryder—although I cannot believe you actually paid him to give a false fire report."

"It was an entirely innocent ploy, love."

"Really?" She lifted an eyebrow at him.

"Well, Simon's role was innocent, at any rate," he admitted sheepishly. "For the rest, I take full responsibility."

"I'm relieved to hear you taking responsibility for something."

Chuckling, he glanced at the boy. "My first task will be to have our cleaning lady give him a thorough scrubbing. I suspect that dingy brown hair of his will turn bright blond after a good shampoo. I do hope he is not infested with vermin that are now crawling all over you."

Natalie did not even flinch. "The poor lad has been through hell, and he gave us our first major breakthrough on Aunt Love. We owe him."

"Aye, we do. Now we know your aunt has almost certainly sailed for London."

Frowning, Natalie glanced up. "But why do you suppose she stowed away on the ship?"

"Perhaps she uncovered a smuggler vessel sailing out of the harbor with legitimate cargo, and she decided to track the ring down to its original source."

Natalie nodded. "Were Harry and the others able to find out anything more about the smugglers you tried to detain last night?"

"Nay. And the vessels and the drays have evidently vanished as well. No doubt we thoroughly spooked the villains. But we are back on the track now."

"So we are."

He leaned toward her. "You realize, of course, that we must sail at once for England."

"You mean *I* must sail at once for England," she replied firmly. "You've done enough for me, Ryder."

Anger assailed him that she was dismissing him so summarily. And after all the effort he had put in to win her, he was not about to allow her to traipse off to England alone. "So you are that eager to be rid of me?" he asked darkly.

"And why would I want to do that?" she inquired with some measure of flippancy.

"Perhaps because I make you feel things you would rather not feel."

"That is ridiculous!"

To his distinct pleasure, he saw color creep up her face as they passed the winking lights of a tavern. "Is it?"

"Yes. I've imposed on your generosity long enough. And I can handle things from here on."

His laughter was cynical. "You cannot even handle getting yourself home from the tavern unmolested!"

At his harsh retort, Simon stirred, and Natalie raised a finger to her lips. "Please, you are waking the boy," she admonished.

"Natalie," he continued in a low, resolute voice, "I simply cannot allow you to travel to England alone. 'Tis too dangerous, a gentlewoman unescorted."

"Have you considered that it might be far more dangerous for me to travel with you, my guardian rogue?" she retorted.

Though a low laugh escaped him, his tone was firm. "I am coming with you to England, and that is final." With unaccus-

tomed tentativeness, he added, "Besides, it is high time that
I visit my grandmother."

"Your grandmother?"

He nodded. "As I believe I've mentioned, my mother was
killed in an accident four years ago. But her mother—my
grandmother, Francesca Valenza—still lives in London."

"Does she live with your father?"

"Hardly. The two are not on speaking terms."

"And what of you and your father?" Natalie asked gently.

"If anything, our relationship is worse."

She stared with compassion at his drawn, tense face. "Oh,
Ryder, I cannot ask you to confront what surely must be a
painful situation—"

"Natalie, I am coming with you," he interjected vehemently. "Furthermore, I will check on my grandmother."

She expelled a sigh. "You are absolutely determined to do
this?"

"Just try to stop me."

She stifled a groan. Clearly, he was immovable. "Very
well. Tomorrow I will look into booking us passage—"

"We shall sail on Harry's clipper," Ryder said decisively.

"What? But I thought you planned to return it—"

"I do. Actually, Hampton seems bored with the Colonies at
present, and I'm sure he would not be averse to sailing home
with us."

She shook her head. "This is still one big caper to you,
isn't it?"

He stared at her. "In truth, Natalie, it has become quite serious."

The gleam in his eyes told her just what he took most
seriously—her own seduction. "Then we will have to hire a
crew—"

"I'll talk Hampton into financing the voyage. He is far better funded than I at the present time." Abruptly, he flashed
her a grin. "Actually, love, my stipend is rather exhausted at
the moment, and I do not know how else we shall get to England, save on Harry's ship."

Staring at the charmingly stubborn rogue sitting across
from her, Natalie silently questioned her own sanity and said
a prayer for them all.

Fourteen

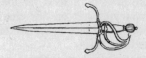

AFTER HE DROPPED NATALIE OFF AND MADE A PALLET FOR SImon in the stable, Ryder felt restless and saddled up his horse. With the cool night air whipping around him, he galloped the large bay stallion north on King Street, passing the crowded tenements where the town's poor huddled together just south of Boundary Street. At the town's gate, he turned his horse and headed back home at a canter.

In a day or two, he would sail for England with a woman who intrigued, aroused, and fascinated him. The possibilities were wonderful—if he didn't die of unassuaged lust before they reached London! He would get to see his beloved Nonna again, a prospect that also warmed his heart. But knowledge of the myriad complications and bitter memories awaiting him in London filled him with conflict and turmoil.

With irony, he recalled Natalie's words: *I cannot ask you to confront what surely must be a painful situation.* The woman had a penchant for understatement. Painful wasn't the half of it, as far as he was concerned.

He knew now that he would have to meet with his father in England—an event he thoroughly dreaded. Nevertheless, the interview would be necessary, for reasons Natalie so far had not fathomed. It was truly ironic how their lives were linked. How much longer would he be granted this reprieve? Would it all begin to unravel when they reached London and Natalie learned the truth?

Meeting with his father would also mean dealing anew with his pain over his mother's death, and this possibility further unsettled Ryder's emotions. He smiled wistfully as he remembered Carlotta Remington—a tall, stately woman, blue-eyed, raven-haired, and graceful. His mother had been a rare and lovely jewel. She had been blessed with a noble, beneficent spirit and a devotion to those less fortunate; there, she and Natalie were much alike. As a child, he remembered helping her prepare baskets of food for the poor, and sometimes even accompanying her on her charity rounds to the most squalid rookeries of London, where the masses huddled in dark, rat-infested hellholes.

He remembered tender, happy times as well, when his mother used to read or speak to him in Italian. His father, catching them, would often scold; although the duke took much pride in having married the daughter of a Florentine count—and especially in winning a bride with such a sizable dowry—he considered Italian to be an inferior, vulgar tongue. Still, even when Ryder was grown, sometimes he and his mother would sneak off together; she would converse in her native language, and he would answer her in his own stilted English-Italian. He recalled her endearing platitudes, which in time he learned to translate from Italian: "The secret of life is a generous heart," and "Be happy, my son," she would always say.

Indeed, those were the last words she ever spoke to him.

He missed those days, loved and missed his mother even more. And being blamed by his father for Carlotta's death had only added to his burden of pain and guilt. With anguish, he recalled his father's scathing condemnation four years ago . . .

The terrible words echoed through his brain. "You worthless reprobate, how dare you carouse at White's tonight while your mother was being waylaid by thieves and murderers! I told you never to allow her to visit those deplorable slums alone."

Ryder had tried to defend himself. "Your Grace, I was not aware that Mother had plans. And where were you?"

"I was at Parliament, where I properly should have been—while my dissolute son was drinking and gambling away his mother's very life. And may you burn in hell for it, you miserable wastrel!"

Even today, as much as his pride had struggled to bury the deep wounds, his father's denunciation still hurt. At times his guilt over his mother's death ate at him like an acid. Perhaps it was simply easier to hide from his pain here, to lose himself in a life of debauchery.

Four years ago, only Nonna's complete refusal to blame him for his mother's death had saved him from utter despair. Now, his return to England raised the very real possibility that he would have to battle not just Natalie's demons but his own as well.

The next morning, Natalie awakened filled with restless tension. She had little time to reflect on the foolhardiness of her decision to sail for England with two rogues—one of whom attracted her mightily while still shamelessly plotting her ruin. At least she would be traveling with a male escort, and the sooner she packed and they all set sail, the sooner she could find Aunt Love.

She turned her mind to the tasks and problems at hand. Samuel was responsible enough to care for the house, she quickly decided. But what about the factory? She groaned at the thought of turning the business over to her dissolute, irresponsible cousin, knowing he would doubtless bring the enterprise to the brink of ruin once more.

Nonetheless, realizing that she had no other choice, she dressed and went downstairs to find Rodney. Outside the drawing room, she paused at the unexpected sound of an angry female voice.

"Rodney, you have been drinking again!" she heard the woman exclaim. "There is simply no way I can take you to the meeting of the St. Cecilia Society in your current, disgraceful state! Mother will swoon, and Father will have apoplexy!"

"Now, Prudence, I swear I only had a small nip before retiring," Rodney whined. "Perhaps if I have just a little more coffee—"

"You promised me you would never again touch a drop of spirits!"

"I truly am sorry, dear. Won't you forgive me?"

Natalie ventured inside the room. Her cousin, pale and bleary-eyed, and looking eminently downtrodden, was seated in a wing chair and raising a china cup to his lips with trembling fingers. Hovering over him was a dainty young woman in a mauve silk dress and matching bonnet.

"Good morning," Natalie called.

Both of them glanced at her, and Natalie was pleased to note that Prudence had a delicate, china-doll face and shiny, wispy brown curls sprouting from beneath her bonnet.

Rodney set down his cup and struggled to his feet. "Er, Natalie," he began unsteadily, "may I present Miss Prudence Pitney. Prudence, my dear, this is my cousin, Natalie Desmond."

Prudence swept forward eagerly and offered Natalie her hand. "How do you do, Miss Desmond? Rodney has spoken so highly of you."

Natalie shook the girl's hand, already liking this forthright young woman. "I'm pleased to meet you as well, and do call me Natalie." She smiled at Rodney. "Are you two on your way out? If so, I mustn't detain you."

Coloring, Rodney fell back into his chair. He waved a hand vaguely. "I—I think I must have at least one more cup of coffee before we venture forth."

"By all means," murmured Natalie. She turned to Prudence and lowered her voice. "While Rodney fortifies himself, may we have a word in the hallway?"

Although Prudence's expression was bemused, she responded in the affirmative and followed Natalie from the room.

"I don't mean to thrust all my troubles on you so soon after we have met," Natalie began urgently, "but the truth is, I'm really in a spot, Miss Pitney."

"Please, you must call me Prudence—and I should be delighted to be of any assistance."

Natalie was liking Prudence more with each passing moment. "Splendid. Has Rodney told you his mother is missing?"

"Why, yes. A most tragic turn of events."

"As it happens, I have just learned news of my aunt's whereabouts. It seems she has returned to England—"

Prudence clapped her hands with glee. "Oh, how wonderful! Rodney will be thrilled to learn she is safe."

"Well, we do hope she is unharmed, at any rate. And I need to sail for London at once."

"I understand." Prudence frowned quizzically. "Do you suppose Rodney will want to sail with you?"

"I doubt it," said Natalie. Leaning toward the girl, she confided, "The problem is, I need Rodney to oversee the factory while I'm away. It is his factory, you see."

"Ah, it is?" Prudence murmured, her eyes gleaming with keen interest.

"Yes. And currently, Rodney is . . ." Natalie's voice trailed off and she shook her head.

Prudence's expression was equally perceptive. "I do grasp your point."

"I couldn't help but overhear the two of you arguing," Natalie continued, "and I do hope you haven't given up on Rodney entirely. Perhaps you could . . . check on him from time to time while I'm away?"

Prudence laughed. "Oh, Natalie, you needn't worry at all on that account."

"I needn't?"

"Of course I must be stern with your cousin at times," Prudence explained, "but I assure you I am far from abandoning him. Why, I am convinced his complete redemption is close at hand. Mother agrees."

"She does?" Taken aback, Natalie flashed a quick smile. "Then you are willing to help?"

"Certainly. Just tell me what needs to be done."

"Oh, bless you!" Eagerly, Natalie proceeded with instructions. "If you could just try to keep Rodney away from the brandy and the grog shops, and see he goes to the factory as often as possible. He is at least passably qualified to run the enterprise. Otherwise, if you should need anything, you can always consult my assistant, Mr. Gibbons."

"Mr. Gibbons. I shall certainly remember that name. And do not worry, Natalie. I shall see that Rodney is at his desk daily." Dreamily, she continued. "I believe your cousin only needs some meaningful endeavor to utilize his talents. Father agrees."

"Oh, he does?"

Patting Natalie's hand, Prudence smiled brilliantly. "Now, Natalie, you must go on to London, and do not fret about a thing. Your cousin is in very good hands here. Shall we go tell Rodney the wonderful news about his mother?"

Following the determined young woman back inside the drawing room, Natalie shook her head at meeting this well-intentioned young crusader who was so confident in her own ability to reform a wastrel.

Fifteen

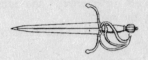

THEY SET SAIL FOR LONDON TWO DAYS LATER, ON A COOL, balmy spring morning. Standing on the main deck of the *Wind*, Ryder watched Natalie stroll up the gangplank, followed by her manservant, Samuel. She was dressed in a braided traveling frock with a matching, feather-bedecked hat, and she looked very much the proper lady. Nevertheless, excitement stormed his senses at the thought of the glorious, decadent weeks stretching before them. He had some surprises in store for this captivating woman that might well prove her undoing—and his own delight.

He hurried over to escort her on board, and took the small satchel she carried. "Good morning, love. All set to sail for the mother country?"

Natalie harrumphed. "You have no idea how unnerving it is to have to go off and leave my dissolute cousin Rodney in charge of the factory."

Ryder chuckled. "Believe it or not, love, not all men are hopelessly incompetent."

"This man is. At least his new friend, Prudence Pitney, has promised to keep an eye on him."

"Ah, good for Prudence. What would we libertines do without you noble ladies to save us?"

They crossed the deck, Samuel following with Natalie's trunk. She glanced at the dozen or so crewmen who were busy tying down lines or stowing gear. The dungaree-clad men were definitely a motley crew, swarthy, bearded, and battle-scarred, several of them malarial in appearance and one of them even sporting a peg leg. All stared pointedly at

Natalie as she passed. She also spotted Simon, up high on the mainmast, tying down a line. The boy looked so much better with his clean clothing and neat haircut; she noted that, just as Ryder had predicted, he was a towheaded lad. She waved to him, and he waved back.

"So Harry hired on a crew," she muttered to Ryder. "Where is he, by the way?"

"He's down in the hold with the quartermaster, inspecting the hull for leaks."

Natalie rolled her eyes.

"Do not worry, love. The *Wind* is as seaworthy as they come," Ryder replied with a grin.

"How did Harry manage to acquire the schooner, anyway?"

"Oh, he saved her from being scuttled at Liverpool," Ryder rejoined dryly. At Natalie's horrified look, he chuckled and quickly added, "Actually, Hampton's father owns a shipping line. He rewarded Hampton with the *Wind* following his valor in the Napoleonic Wars."

"And no doubt Harry's put the vessel to no good purpose," she muttered.

At the companionway, Ryder inclined his head toward Samuel. "Is your man coming with us to London?"

"No." She turned to the manservant, laying her hand on his sleeve and flashing him a gentle smile. "Samuel, thank you very much for your help this morning. You may set down my trunk and return to the house now. Remember, the money I gave you must last until my aunt and I return. Don't forget to water all of Mrs. Desmond's plants—and for heaven's sake, stay out of the brandy, and try to see to it that Mr. Rodney does the same."

"Yes, miss." Samuel set down the trunk and tipped his hat. "You just find Mrs. Desmond and bring her home safe and sound."

"I shall certainly try my best."

As Samuel left, Ryder motioned to a seaman to come get Natalie's trunk, and the muscled sailor hurried forward to hoist the steamer over his shoulder. They proceeded down a companionway and belowdecks. Ryder led Natalie into a small cabin that was furnished with a narrow bunk, a dresser, a desk, and a chair. Grinning, the man deposited Natalie's trunk and left.

Putting her satchel on the desk, Natalie turned to Ryder; he looked altogether too rakish, lounging against the dresser, attired in tightly fitting breeches that displayed the hard muscles of his thighs, and a partially unbuttoned, flowing white shirt that showcased the tanned muscles of his chest.

She scowled at him. "Just what did that sailor find so amusing?"

He stroked his jaw thoughtfully. "Perhaps the fact that the two of us are sharing the same cabin."

Natalie was horrified. "Why, you cad! We shall do no such thing!"

"Shhh!" Appearing alarmed, Ryder stepped forward and pressed a finger to Natalie's lips. "We mustn't forget Harry!"

"What about Harry?"

"I have possession of this schooner, love, only because Harry thinks we are lovers."

She glowered at him.

"And if he should learn that we have duped him . . ." Ryder made a clucking sound. "I shouldn't doubt Hampton would become incensed enough to dump us both in the mid-Atlantic."

"Oh, for heaven's sake!" she cried in exasperation. "It *is* his ship, anyway. Why don't you just give it back?"

"I will—the instant we dock in London. In the meantime, can we risk this entire venture, not to mention your aunt's safety, on whatever whim may strike Harry if—and when—he learns the truth?"

Natalie made a strangled sound. "Just how did you explain me—and this trip—to him?"

He shrugged. "I said you are my mistress now, and are accompanying us back to London."

She balled her hands on her hips. "Oh, of all the gall!"

"Natalie, think for a moment. It was the only way to secure his cooperation."

She eyed him narrowly. "Whether 'twas the only way is certainly debatable—but it is an inspired bit of chicanery, I'll grant you that!"

"The die is cast as far as Hampton is concerned," he

pointed out with forbearance. "Do you want to sail for London today or not?"

She almost mouthed a very unladylike curse. "Are we going to tell Harry what our real purpose is?"

"We may, in time. As I've mentioned before, Hampton is already aware that we are trying to find your lost aunt—and he is also suspicious that you may be something more than a barmaid." He hooked an arm around about her waist, pulled her close, and grinned lecherously. "Nevertheless, for the sake of our mission, we must continue to play the amorous lovers. That won't be so difficult, will it, darling?"

She shoved him away. "You just want to share the same cabin with me."

He crossed his arms over his chest. "The prospect hardly devastates me."

"Well, I shall see to it that your little intrigue does not work."

"Will you indeed? How?"

She thought fiercely for a moment, then said through gritted teeth, "You, Lord Rogue, are going to sleep on the floor!"

He threw back his head and laughed. "Whatever you say, Miss Desmond."

"Furthermore, I must have your promise that you will not molest me."

"Molest you?" Mischief danced in his eyes. "I take it this is another promise like the one you exacted from me recently—that I would not 'force' you?"

"It is indeed."

His tone was one of consummate eloquence. "Let me assure you that I am not a molester of women." He looked her over and finished in a deliberately sensual tone, "As it happens, there has never been such a necessity in my life."

"I must have your promise nonetheless," she insisted, a tremor of nervousness cracking her forthright tone.

"You have it," he replied. "But aren't you forgetting something?"

"And what is that?"

Leaning toward her intimately, he murmured, "It is a very long voyage to England, Natalie."

She was already eminently aware of that. And despite his promise, she did not for a moment trust him. After all, he had made her a similar promise in Charleston, and they were both well aware of how seriously he had taken *that*.

When Ryder escorted Natalie back on deck, he spotted Harry next to the helmsman at the wheel. The rest of the crew were busy stowing gear and preparing to launch the craft.

"Natalie, love!" Harry greeted her brightly. "Glad to see you made it on board. Has Ryder settled you into his quarters?"

As a couple of nearby crewmen laughed ribaldly, Ryder watched Natalie's face flame. She glowered at Harry and demanded in an undertone, "Why don't you take out an advertisement in the *City Gazette*, telling all of Charleston that I am accompanying you two libertines on your voyage?"

Appearing appropriately chastened, Harry muttered, "Sorry." He regarded Natalie with a bemused frown. "By Jove, how did you manage to dispense with your red hair—and your accent?"

Ryder decided to intervene, grabbing Natalie's arm and towing her off, while drawling over his shoulder to Harry, "Barmaids can be full of surprises."

Leaving behind a puzzled Harry, Natalie and Ryder went to stand at the railing as the clipper, tugged by the tide, slipped out of its berth and into the bay. Simon joined them, his hair wind-tousled, his eyes glowing with exuberance.

"Isn't she a beauty, miss?" he asked Natalie proudly.

Natalie glanced about at the *Wind*'s rippling sails and handsome masts, then turned to smooth down Simon's mussed hair. "She is indeed."

"Lord Newbury says when we arrive in London, 'e will take me to meet 'is grandmother."

Natalie glanced over the boy's head at Ryder, who grinned at her. She had to admit that, rogue though he was, he had done an excellent job of seeing that Simon's needs had been met. "I am certain we shall all have a splendid time," she told the boy.

The *Wind* was now tipping her sails toward the harbor entrance, passing between the twin forts on James and Sullivan islands. Natalie enjoyed the rhythmic rocking of the ship, and the breeze and spray on her face. She laughed with Simon over the antics of some sea gulls swooping around a fishing boat and harassing the fishermen.

After a few moments, the boy went off to continue with his duties, and Natalie turned to Ryder. "So you are truly looking forward to seeing your grandmother?"

"Aye."

"Tell me about her."

His expression bespoke pride. "Nonna is a unique person, very wise, very self-possessed. In fact, she is something of a seer."

"You don't say! I would love to meet her."

"And you will. I think she had a very happy life with my grandfather, a Florentine count. When my parents met, she had been a widow for several years, and decided to come with them to London, where she could live close to her daughter and son-in-law."

"Then you have had her with you all your life?"

"Aye." He smiled wistfully. "I remember once when I was a child, she took me to the circus and taught me all the names of the animals in Italian."

"Do you speak the language?"

"*Ben poco,*" he replied with a grin.

"No doubt you're about as proficient at Italian as I am at French. Where does your grandmother live now?"

"She has a town house in the West End, off Grosvenor Square. I'll likely stay with her while we're in the city."

"Then you won't stay with your father?"

"No." His lips hardened into a bitter line. "My father is quite content with his prayers—and his hatred."

She laid her hand on his. "I'm sorry." Tentatively, she added, "If it is not too difficult, I really would like to know what prompted the estrangement between the two of you."

He was silent, his fingers clutching hers.

"Please, Ryder."

He sighed, his features tight as he gazed ahead at the blue, rolling waves. "On a bitterly cold night four years ago, my mother set out alone, with her coachman, to take baskets to the poor in the slums of Southwark. On their way back to the city, some ruffians waylaid the carriage on London Bridge and tried to rob my mother. The horses spooked, and the carriage careened off the bridge into the icy Thames—with my mother inside."

"Oh, Ryder, how horrible!"

"Her death was a massive shock for my entire family," he went on. "And the tragedy was worsened by the fact that my father blamed me for her death."

"But how could he?" Natalie cried, outraged. "Your mother's death was an accident that obviously had nothing to do with you."

"My father and I were well aware that my mother used to indulge in such reckless, albeit noble, pursuits. She was far too devout and kindhearted for her own good. She used to spend her days—even her nights—ministering to the less fortunate in such dangerous rookeries as Stepney and Jacob's Island. My father's argument was that I should have been with her that night. I really had no excuse, since I was gambling at my club on St. James's."

"And where was your father?"

"At a meeting of the Privy Council. At the time, the country was immersed in labor riots, and there was some parliamentary crisis over the Seditious Meetings Act and the suspension of habeas corpus."

"The Privy Council," Natalie repeated, bemused. "So your father is an advisor to the king?"

"My father is the Duke of Mansfield," he murmured.

"The Duke of Mansfield?" She was stunned. "I knew you were of titled stock—but a duke's son!"

"My father was once in good stead with George III—until the king succumbed to permanent madness. After my mother died, my father acquired his peculiar bent toward religious fanaticism. At least he had a reasonable excuse for not being there on the night my mother was killed—while his profligate son had none."

She squeezed his hand and regarded him with keen compassion. "I'm so sorry. But you can't blame yourself."

He regarded her fatalistically. "Can't I?"

"Of course you can't!"

His words poured forth with bitterness and turbulent emotion. "How much worse can it be than for a son to be condemned for his mother's death—and doomed to hell?"

"But that is so unfair!" she cried.

"Tell that to my father."

"You left because of his denunciation?"

"Aye. At least, thanks to the trust set up by my grand-mother at my birth, I have not had to depend on him for material support."

"Will you call on him at all?"

He hesitated, then muttered, "Probably. As a matter of fact . . ."

"Yes?"

He shook his head. "Never mind."

Noting his troubled expression, she sensed she should not probe further into his thoughts right now, although his disclosures had made her feel much empathy for him. Touching his arm, she said, "Ryder, it troubles and touches me that you are willing to confront your painful past for my sake."

Abruptly, as with the shifting of a sail, he changed moods, smiling and pulling her into his arms. "I could use some comfort, love. I would savor all the soothing you might give me."

Before she could protest, he leaned over and quickly kissed her lips.

Just as hastily, both sprang apart at the sound of Harry's loud whistle. "Hey, Newbury, stop pestering that young woman and put yourself to good use."

Ryder turned, scowling, to see his friend stride up with a sword in each hand. "Why don't you go keelhaul yourself, Hampton, and leave the lady and me alone?"

Undaunted, Harry laughed. "Now that we're out to sea, I do find I'm feeling bored." He handed Ryder a saber by its hilt. "Time to practice our fencing, old man. We mustn't let all our good training at the Haymarket Academy go to waste." He winked at Natalie. "Besides, who knows what challenges we may face in seamy London?"

Watching Ryder lift his blade and examine it as the bright sunlight glinted off sharp steel, Natalie was horrified. "You can't mean to practice swordplay with him—on a moving ship?"

Ryder shrugged. "Why not? Hampton and I have certainly fenced on the deck of a moving vessel before. If you'll excuse us, love, Harry seems to be in a mood to see his blood spilled."

It was on the tip of Natalie's tongue to protest further, but the two men were already moving toward the center of the main deck. Standing about five feet apart, both assumed stances of readiness, with feet spread and sabers extended.

Natalie could not believe her eyes—the pair of them belonged in an asylum!

At Harry's energetic *"En garde!"* the melee began. Natalie's teeth went on edge at the awful sounds of shrieking steel. The two men danced back and forth, charging and striking, Ryder parrying Harry's blow, Harry lunging into Ryder's riposte. How the two managed to keep from slicing each other to ribbons was totally beyond her. For an agonizing eternity, she watched the razor-sharp sabers flash and dip and bang and thrust, while the two deranged rogues laughed, danced around with precision, and yelled out blasphemies. In the midst of the frenzied lunacy, the two swordsmen deftly sidestepped the mainmast, vaulted over skylights, dodged smoke heads and pump handles.

Natalie was terrified and amazed. She would have looked away, yet her gaze was riveted on the scene with perverse fascination as she feared that at any second now, she would watch Ryder's head go sailing off—a possibility she found horrifying.

When had she come to care for this rogue so much that the prospect of his being harmed—or even nicked—was devastating to her? Whenever it had happened, she realized now that Ryder Remington had charmed himself under her skin and into her blood.

Yet, on another level, she was even more appalled to find herself feeling excited, even aroused, as she observed the beautiful rhythms of his arms and legs as he leapt and swung and feinted, his strong muscles rippling, his clothing pulling against splendid sinews, his raven hair gleaming in the full sunlight. Never in her life had she felt quite so panicked, or so exhilarated, or so inundated by lust. How she feared this reckless side to her nature that he inevitably roused!

At last, following a howl from Ryder, the two men sprang apart.

Harry, grinning, held up his sword as Ryder scowled at the slice in his shirt.

"Ready to beg for quarter, old boy?" Harry asked with a grin.

Ryder's response was to shout a battle yell and charge into a new, explosive *flèche* which Harry barely managed to repel. Natalie watched in awe and deepening horror as Ryder sprang forward, whacking powerfully at Harry, driving him onto the hatch cover, while Hampton blocked and retreated.

At last, with a scream of steel hitting steel, Ryder knocked the sword from Harry's hand and pressed the tip of his saber to Hampton's gullet.

"Well," Harry said with a grin, showing remarkable aplomb for a man with a sword at his throat. "I'm famished. Why don't we all go get something to eat?"

Natalie was subdued during the meal, which was served at a small table belowdeck, outside the galley. The fencing practice had evidently put Ryder and Harry in jovial humor. The two ate heartily, dipping biscuits in their stew and exchanging war stories from their days in the cavalry. They also made a wager regarding whether or not all of them would arrive back in London in time to see the coronation of George IV, the former Prince Regent, who a year earlier had succeeded to the throne on the death of his blind, insane father.

When Natalie watched Ryder reach across the table for the salt cellar, and saw the cloth of his shirt pull against his torso and reveal a spreading blotch of red, she suddenly felt half nauseous. She got up and abruptly fled the table.

Harry glanced up to spot the flash of Natalie's retreating skirts. "What ails the wench, Newbury?" he asked Ryder.

"I'm not sure."

Frowning in perplexity, Ryder followed Natalie into their cabin. "Natalie? What is it, love?"

She turned to him with hot tears welling in her eyes. "Are you a complete imbecile?"

"What do you mean?"

"The fencing!" She pointed to his shirt. "You are hurt!"

He glanced down. "Oh, that. 'Tis only a nick, love." He eyed her quizzically and reached out to brush a tear from her cheek. "No reason for you to weep."

"No reason! It could have been your head that was lopped off."

A devilish grin spread across his face, and his teeth were

white against his deep tan. "Why, Natalie, I do believe you care about me after all."

Her face flamed. "I—I care because I need your help when we arrive in England—and because it infuriates me to watch anyone flirt so recklessly with death."

"And you were not reckless yourself back in Charleston?" he chided.

"That was entirely different. I had a legitimate mission—to search for my aunt. It is not as if I were enjoying myself—"

"Ah, so it is perfectly acceptable to behave with careless disregard for one's own safety, as long as one is not enjoying oneself?" he countered skillfully.

She stamped her foot. "Oh, you are infuriating! My point is, the fencing is both dangerous and unnecessary."

"But, darling, don't you want me to be prepared when next we encounter the smugglers? Besides, ever since we served together in Wellington's cavalry, Hampton and I have regularly practiced our swordsmanship. We've never hurt each other—aside from a few harmless nicks. And what is life without a few risks?"

"I guess that is the difference between us," she informed him in a voice hoarse with outrage and fatalism. "You're willing to gamble your life away. I'm not."

He gestured in entreaty. "Natalie, for the love of heaven, you are making too much of this—"

"And your shirt has a nasty bloodstain on it, and you haven't even cleaned the cut."

Abruptly, he whipped off his shirt. "Then cleanse it, love."

He caught her totally unaware. Natalie's mouth went dry as she stared at the muscles of his magnificent bare chest—the bronzed sinews and satiny skin glowing with male sweat. She gazed at the small cut that still oozed. She smelled the musky scent of him, and felt the warmth of his body, his vitality. Suddenly he seemed so powerful, so rivetingly sensual, in the small cabin.

Heavens, this man was making her demented!

She could not help herself. Like one mesmerized, she walked toward him, rationalizing to herself that she *must* examine the cut, and knowing all the while that the wound was hardly at the root of her sudden fascination. She placed her trembling fingers on his chest—

With a groan, he hauled her close, until her lips were touching the gleaming flesh as well.

She shuddered against him, then tasted him, tasted salt and man. Her trembling arms encircled his massive torso.

"You are so beautiful," she whispered achingly. "You have the body of a god. How can you be so careless with it?"

Feeling overjoyed, even slightly humbled, by this touching evidence of her caring, Ryder kissed Natalie's hair, then tilted her face up to his.

Natalie wanted to scold him more, but the burning look in his eyes pinned her to the spot, breathless with anticipation. He leaned over, gently kissing away her tears. She sobbed and gave him her lips—this time eagerly.

He crushed her to him and devoured her mouth with demanding lips and ravishing tongue. She clung to him dizzily as the room seemed to whirl around them and lightning bolts of arousal repeatedly staggered her. Everything about the moment was so intense—the fierceness of her yearnings, the heat of his body, the taste of his sweat.

"I promise I'll take better care, love, so I may savor you, too," he whispered into her ear. "You have the mouth of a goddess, the eyes of an angel, the body of a courtesan. In time, I promise you I will explore, and delight in, every delectable inch of you."

Fearing she might demand such a demonstration at once, Natalie managed to break free. Appalled at her own lack of restraint, and breathing in gasps, she muttered, "I—I must wash that cut now."

"Aye." He watched her go to the basin and dampen a cloth. "But now another part of me smarts with a torment that will not be so readily eased, I reckon."

In mingled fascination and horror, Natalie stole a glance at the bulging front of his trousers. She hastily flicked her gaze away and wrung out the cloth. As she returned to him and began to dab unsteadily at the wound, her hot face told him that she now shared that same potent aching, and that it would indeed take a great deal more than a cool compress to soothe her.

When they returned to the table, Ryder noted Harry grinning as the latter spotted a small blotch of blood on the bodice of Natalie's dress.

Sixteen

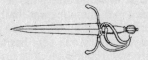

BY EVENING THEY WERE WELL OUT TO SEA. THE *WIND* WAS A spectacular sight, with the brisk sea breeze catching her full suit of sails and the golden light of sunset emblazoning her decks. She glided over the huge, gold-crowned, rolling blue waves of the Atlantic.

After supper, a lazier atmosphere prevailed. Except for the helmsman manning the wheel and a couple of sailors working the rigging, the crew and passengers savored their leisure. One old salt lounged against the mainmast, playing the haunting strains of "Barbara Allen" on his harmonica. On the forecastle hatch, four other seamen were involved in an animated game of dice.

On the main deck, Ryder, Simon, and Harry played ninepins, while Natalie looked on with an indulgent smile. She mused that the two men were every bit as callow and carefree as Simon, rolling the ball and cheering over each small triumph.

She remained embroiled in turmoil regarding her passionate and emotional encounter with Ryder earlier that day. After witnessing his reckless swordplay with Harry, she had felt every bit as tempted to murder him as she had been to rip the clothes off his glorious body and devour him alive.

Never had Natalie been so conscious of the riveting power Ryder held over her. The knowledge that this man could bring her to tears, to terror, to raging anger or unbridled lust, was hardly comforting. She was a woman accustomed to controlling her own life and her own feelings, a woman determined not to succumb to any rakehell. Yet Ryder Remington

141

and her own traitorous desires had other ideas in mind. The fact that they were sharing the same cabin presented the very real anxiety that she might allow the rake to ruin her—and eagerly so—before they reached London.

Dash him for being such a winsome charmer!

While Harry was resetting the pins, Ryder strode up to Natalie and handed her the ninepins ball. "Give it a try, love."

She rolled her eyes. "Someone here has to show some maturity."

"Oh, quit being such a wet blanket," he scolded, tugging her toward the center of the deck.

"Knock 'em all over like I did, Miss Natalie!" Simon encouraged her, jumping up and down.

Fighting a smile, she leaned over and rolled the ball. Her face flamed as the ball veered off to the side, missing the pins entirely. The men laughed heartily at her failed attempt.

She balled her hands at her waist and glowered at them. "The deck tilted."

"If it did, why didn't the pins fall over?" teased Simon.

"It appears the ninepins ball is possessed," added Ryder.

"Care to make a wager, Natalie, to sweeten the pot?" taunted Harry.

Ryder retrieved the ball and handed it to her. "Here, love, we shall let you have another chance," he said with a solemn wink. "It appears you need all the practice you can get."

From the devilish glint in his eye, she could tell just what kind of "practice" he had in mind. Gritting her teeth, she leaned over and rolled the ball. Straightening, she flashed Ryder a triumphant smirk as all nine pins went crashing over.

"So much for practice," she told him, tossing her head and striding off.

When Ryder returned to the cabin at nightfall, he found Natalie in the bunk, her spectacles on as she scowled at a book. She looked like such a studious bluestocking that he perversely hungered to undo her, to expose again the passionate wench who had kissed him so ardently earlier. His pulse quickened at the delectable memory, and especially at the thought of creating quite a few more.

He went over, snatched the book out of her hands, and

chuckled. *"Dictionary of Trade and Commerce,"* he read. "My, aren't we ambitious."

She grabbed the book back. "I try to improve my mind whenever possible."

Quelling an amused smile at her remark, he sat down on the chair facing the bunk and crossed his booted feet on the edge of the mattress. "Meaning you do not indulge in frivolous pastimes such as games of ninepins?"

"I've never had the luxury of such frolic," she replied.

"You issued from your mother's womb a grown woman?" he inquired mildly.

She ignored that. "How do you think Aunt Love and I kept the factory running and learned about all the latest equipment and inventions? It required constant research, reading, letter writing, even travel."

"Those were choices you made, Natalie."

"Choices?" She snapped the book shut. "Has it never occurred to you that the Charleston factory would have failed had not Aunt Love and I—"

"Has it never occurred to you that your cousin might have fared better had you simply left matters well enough alone? Not every man in the world is totally irresponsible and incompetent."

"No—only those men like you who have the luxury of living on a stipend and whiling away their days in indolence and debauchery."

He whistled. "Whatever did I do to deserve such a denunciation? Simply by indulging in a game of ninepins?"

"Everything is a game to you. And have you thought of the example you're setting for Simon?"

"Now I'm corrupting a child?" he asked incredulously.

"You're hardly creating the best environment for him. For instance, what plans do you have for his future?"

He shrugged. "I see him as, perhaps, a suitable valet for me once he is grown."

"But if he is to become a gentleman's servant, he must have training, education," she argued in exasperation. "Indeed, I have brought along some primers, and shall begin his schooling tomorrow."

He rolled his eyes. "Before you know it, you'll have us all in monks' clothing, and on bread-and-water rations."

"You needn't make me out to be a villainess," she replied. "I just feel that we should create an atmosphere of industry and dignity."

He was shaking his head. "What on earth is stuck in your craw now, woman?"

"I'm sure I have no idea what you mean."

"Oh, yes, you do. Are you still angry about this afternoon?"

"Foolishness always makes me angry."

He leaned closer. "Which foolishness, love?" Watching her face grow hot, he added wisely, "Ah, I see. *That* foolishness."

She threw the book at him. He caught it with a wicked grin. She glowered at him through her spectacles until he handed her back the volume.

"What of fun, Natalie?" he teased.

"Fun?" she scoffed. "That is all you think of."

"While all you think of is sober industry." He regarded her with a pensive frown. "What are your parents like?"

"I've told you before that my father is altogether too much like you."

"And your mother? You told me she is French—and may I presume she is not like you?"

"You presume correctly," Natalie related bitterly. "She is exactly the opposite—flighty, passionate, cavalier."

"Ah . . . so I see."

She whipped off her spectacles. "What do you see, Lord Rogue?"

"The way you are is a reaction to the way your parents were."

"Now I do not follow you at all."

"It must frighten you, Natalie, to think you could become like one of them—that you might succumb to the profligacy and self-indulgence of your father, or to the impulsiveness and hotheadedness of your mother. So you hide what you really are beneath that prim and proper facade."

"This is ridiculous!" she flared. "I have no facade—I am exactly what I am!"

"A minx who teases sailors at a sleazy tavern?"

"That was a necessary deception. And as I have told you before, I will not have you presuming my thoughts or motives."

"But someone needs to, because you desperately must acknowledge the woman you really are."

"And who is that, pray tell?"

He reached out to stroke her cheek and gazed into her eyes. Pleasure stormed him at her sudden, low gasp, and at the way her tawny eyes flared with hot emotion, giving her away.

"You are hiding, love, hiding beneath a world that is too weighted down by problems and responsibilities. You are denying yourself all the pleasure, all the richness, life has to offer. I sense that you will not be happy until you find a man who can unleash the passionate Frenchwoman in your soul."

"And you intend to be that man?" she scoffed, if in a quivering voice.

"Aye. That is why you are so angry, isn't it, Natalie? That is why you are burying yourself behind steel spectacles and in dreary tomes."

She was silent, staring at him.

Seductively, he went on. "You are frightened that ultimately, you will give in to me—and even more scared that you will love every minute."

"That is not true!" she blazed. "I will not have you telling me what my own feelings are. Furthermore, please get out of here and leave me alone!"

"But I cannot, love," he replied patiently. "We are sharing the cabin—remember?"

"How much longer until we arrive in England?" she demanded.

His grin bespoke that he was thoroughly enjoying her agitation. "With good fortune—and good winds—perhaps three weeks."

While Ryder watched with amusement, Natalie disgustedly got up and flung open her trunk. "You, sir, will kindly leave my presence while I—er—prepare my person for slumber."

"Prepare your person for slumber?" he mocked. "That sounds like such a daunting task. Are you certain you don't need my assistance?"

A second later, a shoe came sailing out of Natalie's trunk and sent Ryder scooting for the door.

Natalie grabbed her nightgown and wrapper and disappeared behind the dressing screen—in case the rogue, whom

she trusted not at all, should dare stick his head back inside
again. The accuracy of his accusations haunted her as she undressed. She *was* angry at him because of what he made her
feel. And how would she bear three more weeks of this type
of torture?

Later, trying to fall sleep was sheer torment for Natalie.
Though the cabin was immersed in darkness, she was pain-
fully aware that Ryder lay only a few feet away from her, on
his pallet beneath her bunk. She could hear his regular breathing and smell his male scent. Even the gentle buffeting of the
ship, which she had found to be soothing six years ago when
she had sailed to America with Aunt Love, seemed distracting tonight.

On the floor, Ryder smiled as he listened to Natalie flip-
ping about. He longed to be in that soft bunk with her, next
to her warm, voluptuous body. He promised himself that before this voyage was over, he would know that pleasure.

It was strange, he mused, but the more snooty, aloof, and
judgmental she acted, the more determined he was to unravel
her secrets. It had become his mission, almost his obsession,
to make her stop denying the woman she really was, to make
her admit that part of her really had enjoyed playing her provocative game at the tavern—especially with him. That hidden, passionate woman was an intoxicating creature he was
determined to have in his arms, to arouse not only to passion
but also to joy in life. In time, he would level her pride and
decimate her inhibitions, and then she would know what true
ecstasy, what true glory, were.

He considered this delicious prospect as he drifted off to
sleep . . .

It seemed only a moment later that Ryder jerked awake as
he heard Natalie screaming and flailing about frantically
above him.

"What is it, love?"

In answer, she came sailing off the bunk to land on top of
him. He uttered a grunt of mingled surprise, pain, and arousal
as her shapely body covered him.

"Natalie?"

She was trembling violently. "Th-there was something
c-crawling on me!"

He stroked her spine. "There, love, calm down. As you can see, it wasn't I who assaulted you. Probably just some spider or cockroach skulking about in the darkness."

She shuddered violently. "I—I hate insects!"

He laughed. "So the paragon of virtue has a weakness after all?"

"This is not the least bit amusing!" she railed, and he felt a tear slide onto his face.

"Natalie?" he murmured tenderly, clutching her closer. "I hadn't realized you were so genuinely frightened. I'm sorry, love."

"Please," she murmured breathlessly as she fully realized the scandalous positioning of their bodies. "You must let me up at once."

"To allow you to be assaulted again by the nefarious creature in your bunk?"

"Is it better that I be assaulted by you?"

He chuckled. "Me or a cockroach? Now, that is a contest I shall win hands down. Do tell me whose touch you prefer, love."

And before she could protest further, he hooked an arm around her neck and drew her lips down to his. Natalie tried to squirm away, but the treachery of his nearness, and her own reckless desires, tugged potently at her inhibitions. Shock waves of delight jolted her as his lips moved with tender seduction over hers. His tongue eased between her lips, and when she moaned, he plunged roughly, deeply, engulfing her with new waves of frenzied excitement. She was all at once losing her mind. When his hands swept downward, pulling her nightgown up over her naked hips, she wiggled violently, a protest smothered in her throat as he continued to kiss her so masterfully. Soon even her writhing ceased as the feel of his strong, bold fingers on her bare bottom seemed to mesmerize her, the audacious stroking sending darts of arousal between her thighs.

When his lips moved away to her cheek, both of them were breathing raggedly. "You have the sweetest lips I've ever tasted," he murmured huskily. "Your hair is so silky, and smells of honeysuckle. As for your bottom, I've never felt anything so soft. I may have to sink my teeth into you before this night is out."

"Ryder!"

Reeling, Natalie tried to protest, even though she coul
hardly hear her own frantic plea over the hammering of he
heart. Then, abruptly, Ryder yanked away the sheet that sep
arated their bodies, and she was electrified—

"You are naked!" she gasped, her words near frantic wit
panic and lust as she felt the hard, hot shaft of his desir
pressing into her.

"A delightful state, love, and one I would have you share,
he murmured wickedly, tugging further upward on her nigh
gown.

She struggled to restrain his determined fingers. "Ryder—
please, don't—"

She heard him heave an exasperated sigh. "Natalie, if yo
are going to say no, you had best mean no," he warne
"Otherwise, this situation will soon be beyond my control—
and yours."

"I—I mean it," she managed.

Again he stroked her bare bottom. "Are you so sure?" h
asked hoarsely. "Is that why your posterior is covered wit
gooseflesh and I can feel the tightness of your nipples eve
through your gown?"

"You—you did this to me!"

"Wrong. You started it, you maddening wench!"

He kissed her again, nipping with his teeth and strokin
with his tongue as his fingers relentlessly tugged her nigh
gown toward her waist. She shoved his hands away while sh
could still gather the strength to do so.

"Very well, you excite me!" she admitted with equal mea
sures of passion and frustration. "But not every desire i
meant to be indulged."

"And that is precisely what is wrong with you, Natali
Desmond. Desires *are* meant to be indulged—"

"And that is precisely what is wrong with *you*, Ryde
Remington!"

Muttering a curse, he nudged her off him and got to hi
feet. She heard a second blistering expletive escape him as h
stumbled around in the darkness. A moment later, the roo
was flooded with light—

At first Natalie was afraid to look. Then a banging soun
compelled her to glance up at him.

"Your cockroach, madam," Ryder said.

He was extending his boot toward her, and on its sole was the smashed insect. But Natalie noticed the icky mess for only a split second. Her heartbeat pounded in her ears as her gaze became riveted on Ryder's glorious body—

He was starkly, magnificently naked—all beautiful sinew, muscled chest and arms, and hard thighs and long legs covered by sexy black hair. His jaw was rigid, his eyes filled with passion's dark fire as he stared back at her. Shamelessly, her gaze slid down his gorgeous body and settled on his aroused shaft, which rose so high and full against his belly. At the thought of that beautiful instrument claiming her, probing her most intimate parts, she felt heat streak up her face, set her nipples tingling, and burn between her thighs like relentless flames licking—

"For heaven's sake!" she cried. "Have the decency to cover yourself!"

His grin was depraved, with a full flash of white teeth. "May I suggest that you have the decency not to stare?"

"Oh!"

"But then, I'm forgetting your determination to improve your mind, aren't I, Miss Desmond?" he baited sardonically. "Tell me, is it male anatomy that has aroused your intellectual passions now? Shall I fetch you your spectacles so you may have a better look?"

For once, she spoke entirely without thought. "Who could miss *that?*"

While Natalie trembled in mortification, Ryder threw back his head and laughed. "Natalie, I'll have you know that I am not decent and, unlike a certain stuffy Englishwoman I know, do not wear clothing to bed. Yours is a ridiculous, prudish habit that I intend to divest you of before we reach England."

"You will do no such thing! Furthermore, will you kindly—"

"*Furthermore,* I cannot cover myself, since you are sitting on my sheet."

"Oh." Natalie all but sprang to her feet and clambered back into the bunk.

Ryder tossed down the boot, snuffed out the lamp, and plopped down onto his pallet. "Your bed has been secured, madam, and I assure you that you are safe from all molestation."

As Natalie took refuge, trembling and achy, beneath the
covers, she could only muse that she was not at all safe from
her debilitating desire for Ryder Remington.

Seventeen

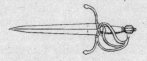

O VER THE NEXT SEVERAL DAYS, THEY SETTLED INTO A ROU-
tine. Natalie spent much time tutoring Simon on his reading
and sums, while Ryder and Harry busied themselves with the
workings of the ship, or playing dice or cards with the crewmen. To Natalie's chagrin, the two rogues continued to practice their fencing daily. She had long since given up trying to
dissuade them from engaging in the reckless swordplay. At
times, watching them leap around on deck and wield their lethally sharp sabers, she did wonder how they managed to remain alive. Yet, aside from a few nicks and cuts, both men
miraculously concluded each session with their heads still at-
tached.

Natalie often mused that living in such close quarters with
Ryder was as much an emotional peril for her as the fencing
lessons were a physical hazard for him. These days she
seemed in a constant state of agitation—and, yes, lust. She
was haunted by the memory of the night when she had hur-
tled off the bed and landed squarely on top of Ryder's hard,
aroused body, when he had roved his hands so intimately
over her backside and kissed her with such devastating mastery. She found herself treacherously wanting him more with
each day that passed. Sharing the cramped cabin with him
only heightened both her desire and her sense of frustration.
His body was a splendid, living sculpture of bronze and
sinew and vibrant energy, and he displayed no sense of modesty as he dressed and undressed daily. When she protested
his audacity, he would only laugh and tell her she could always choose not to look.

Could she? As she found her gaze straying, again and
again, to magnificent arms, powerful thighs, and muscular
chest, she had to wonder if she truly had a choice at all. One
time when she had entered the cabin, he had been sitting lan-
guidly in the tub. Natalie had felt both horror and amazement.
When she scolded him that he should have warned her he
was bathing, the rogue had merely grinned and said, "And
miss your delicious reaction? Never!"

Ryder, too, took note of Natalie's unsettled state due to the
enforced intimacy of their living quarters—and her undoing
was his delight. Each time he watched her guilty yet captivated gaze stray toward him as he dressed, he knew it was
only a matter of time before she was his. Of course, if the
priggish wench needed to so much as retie a hair ribbon, she
banned him from the cabin and scurried behind the dressing
screen like a scared little rabbit. He was delighted when he
strode into the cabin one gusty morning and the screen tipped
over, revealing glorious Natalie wearing only her
undergarments—and a very hot blush! He winked at her solemnly, and when the mortified girl struggled to right the
screen, and succeeded only in toppling it again, he howled
with laughter—until her hairbrush hit him squarely in the
midsection.

Harry constantly taunted Ryder about his relationship with
Natalie. But as Hampton continued to note Natalie's changed
demeanor and dress, and watched her working with Simon, it
became clear to Ryder that his crony was also growing increasingly suspicious about her background.

One day the three were gathered outside the galley, eating
oyster stew and biscuits for the midday meal. Harry decided
to confront the issue. Winking at Natalie, he said, "My dear,
you are truly a delightful creature who has put a new gleam
in my old friend's eye. But I must say you have some peculiar habits for a tavern wench. Aside from tutoring Simon—
hardly typical behavior for a barmaid, you must admit—you
tend to leave some of your texts lying about on deck." He
picked up a book and dumped it in front of her.

Staring at the volume, she smiled guiltily.

"I would have expected Fielding's *Tom Jones* or perhaps
Clelands's *Memoirs Of A Woman of Pleasure*," Harry went
on with an cynical grin. "But Adam Smith's *Wealth Of Na-*

tions? I would have thought your passion would be for unfettered sensuality, my dear—not free trade."

Ryder chuckled. "Natalie likes to improve her mind whenever possible." He turned to her with a sheepish grin. "I guess our secret is out, love. We simply cannot escape Hampton's brilliant deductions any longer."

"Then Natalie is not truly a tavern wench," Harry stated reprovingly. "Something I have suspected all along."

"Ah, yes, you have us, Harry," Ryder conceded wryly. "Natalie is not truly a tavern wench."

"Then who is she?" Harry demanded. "And why was she posing as a barmaid?"

"Why don't we let the lady answer for herself?" Ryder suggested.

"Well, Natalie?" prodded Harry.

She smiled ruefully. "Actually, I did work at the tavern under disguise. My full name is Natalie Desmond. Along with my aunt, I ran the textile factory on Wentworth in Charleston."

Harry regarded Natalie with astonishment. "Why, I've heard of the two of you! You are a gentlewoman, then?"

"Yes."

"Then how on earth did you end up working at the Tradd Street Tavern?"

Natalie told Harry the story of how she and her aunt had come to the Colonies to run the factory, and how her aunt's recent disappearance had compelled her to resort to extreme measures.

"By Jove, this is fascinating," said Harry afterward. "A gentlewoman posing as a barmaid. So what made you and Ryder decide to sail for England?"

"A tip from Simon," Ryder replied. "He saw Natalie's aunt stealing on board a merchantman bound for London."

"I see." Harry scratched his jaw. "So you feel the smugglers are headquartered there?"

"Yes," said Natalie.

"Funny the ring wouldn't be based in Lancashire or Manchester, with all the textile factories there," Harry murmured. "Although God knows London has its share of such facilities." He snapped his fingers and turned to Ryder. "By Jove, doesn't your father own a textile factory in Stepney?"

Natalie turned at once to Ryder. "Does he?"

Ryder shrugged. "My father has holdings in a number of different industries, and as you are both well aware, he has not discussed his affairs with me for many years."

An awkward silence descended, but Harry quickly filled the gap, grinning at Natalie. "So, Miss Desmond, have you family to see in London?"

"Well, I certainly hope to find my aunt. And I've also a father there, Charles Desmond. He is the younger son of the Earl of Worcester, and a factor at the Exchange."

"Ah—marvelous. So we'll all be returning to the cozy bosom of home and hearth." Inclining his head toward Ryder he continued. "But tell me, just how are you planning to explain dear Newbury to your family—not to mention the rather compromising circumstances of your passage together across the Atlantic?"

While Natalie paled, Ryder spoke with an edge of steel in his voice. "There really is no need to divulge the actual circumstances of Natalie's arrival in England to anyone—is there, old man?"

"Perhaps not," Harry conceded tightly.

"Indeed, I was going to suggest that Natalie tell her family she and I crossed the Atlantic together on a legitimate passenger packet. Do you see any reason we can't *all* of us say that?"

"No reason at all, I suppose," Harry muttered, but with an edge of vexation and suspicion in his voice.

Later in the day, the wind began to gust, and the skies grew ominous. Higher than normal waves began to pitch the vessel. Nonetheless, Ryder and Harry met for their daily fencing practice, while Natalie looked on in horror. The brooding skies opened, but only to make way for a sun shower of brilliant proportions.

The two men stood in readiness across from each other with feet spread and sabers extended. The wind whipped at their clothing and hair, and fat raindrops pelted them.

Harry shot Ryder a contemptuous glance. "I've a bone to pick with you, old man."

"And what might that be?"

Harry lunged with his saber, and Ryder parried and riposted.

"You deceived me about Natalie," Harry accused, advancing with quick, vigorous strokes. "She was never truly a tavern wench."

Ryder feinted, then burst forward with a thrust that Harry deftly dodged. "Our wager had nothing to do with her being a tavern wench."

"Balderdash." Harry charged with slicing blows, skidding on the slippery deck. "The fact that she is a lady, not a whore, is what I'd call a material omission. I suspect you never even bedded her on the night the two of you met."

Ryder laughed, blocking blows with skillful circular parries. He, too, was fighting to keep his balance as the rain splattered them, and the feeling of danger was exhilarating. "Then why do you suppose she and I are sharing the same cabin?"

Harry vaulted onto the scuttle hatch, beating back Ryder's charge. "No doubt because you contrived some devil's bargain—perhaps that you would help her find her aunt if she would pose as your mistress."

Ryder launched into a powerful *flèche* that sent Harry sailing backward off the hatch. Ryder bounded after him, springing into a reprise. "Would I engineer such a Machiavellian scheme?"

Harry retreated and blocked. "Oh, yes. You would resort to any chicanery in order to steal my ship and best your friends."

As the vessel buffeted, Harry barely managed to dodge Ryder's thrust. Furious, he whirled about and wielded his blade.

Ryder lunged. "A pity there is no way you can prove your suspicions."

Harry feinted, then charged with fierce, hacking strokes. "Aye. If there were, I would call you out in earnest, or perhaps have the crew dump you and the lady overboard to the sharks."

"My! So bloodthirsty, old friend. Isn't it enough that I plan to give you your ship back once we all dock in London?"

"Nay. It is the principle of the thing. It is a matter of honor."

"You possess honor?"

Harry roared into Ryder's shrieking blade.

As the two continued to dance to and fro and cross swords, Natalie watched in deepening terror from across the ship. The wind was now screaming through the masts, the deck was tilting crazily against the rising waves, and the two lunatics across from her continued to hack at each other like demons, leaping frenziedly around the lethally slick deck.

Natalie was convinced she was going to watch Ryder die before her very eyes, and equally certain she would never recover from it. It no longer mattered why she felt this way, her entire world and all her emotions turned topsy-turvy by this rakehell. She simply felt it. It was surely the curse of all the Desmond women, she mused bitterly, being consumed with fascination for a hopeless profligate.

Then she saw Harry make an aggressive stroke, heard Ryder howl an expletive, and watched him spring back and clutch his chin.

Natalie raced across the deck, trembling so badly that her voice came out an enraged whisper. "Are both of you totally mad? How dare you chop away at each other while the deck is spinning! You should both be confined to Bedlam!"

Ryder dropped his hand, revealing a thin cut along his jaw. "But, Natalie, it is only a nick—"

"You may rot in hell," she told him, then swung her fulminating gaze to Harry. "And that goes double for you!"

Before either man could comment, Natalie raced off for the companionway. Ryder pursued her, and he entered their cabin to the heart-wrenching sounds of her sobs.

"Natalie, darling, I didn't mean to—"

She turned, beating her fists on his wet chest as she screamed at him, "Go away and leave me alone!"

"Darling, it was only fencing practice—"

"In the midst of a gale?" she shrieked. "You could have lost your bloody head—"

"But I didn't—"

"That is not the point! Only a lunatic would risk his neck for the sake of sport—"

"I assure you, my neck was never—"

"It was! The wind was howling, the rain pelting, the deck whirling, and yet you two imbeciles were just slicing away at

each other! You're like a big, spoiled baby who must forever
be amused and distracted—"

Abruptly, Ryder grabbed her wrists and hauled her hard
against his hot, solid body. She gazed up, defiant yet captivated.

His words were low and hoarse as his burning gaze impaled her. "Then amuse me, love. Distract me. You do it so
well."

She should have been furious. She should have throttled
him. Yet, pressed against him so intimately, with his incredibly blue eyes blazing down into hers, she could think only of
how wet he was, how wet she was, and how she ached to
ease the hurt and need inside her. As on that magical day
back at the beach, a dam burst in her, but this time a flood
tide of raw emotion was unleashed. Moaning incoherently,
she stretched on tiptoe to kiss him passionately. He responded
with a groan of desire, crushing her closer and plundering her
mouth with his tongue.

"Don't you know we can avoid this no longer?" he whispered roughly, his lips against her cheek. "You were meant
for me, love."

"Meant for heartache and ruin at the hands of a rogue, you
mean." But even as she said the words, she pressed her lips
lovingly to the exposed flesh of his upper chest.

"Why heartache, darling?" he teased, his hand cupping her
breast and tearing a moan from her. "I'll be gentle with you.
You can trust me."

"Trust you and trust Bonaparte not to escape from St. Helena," came her rueful, tremulous response.

With a low, husky chuckle, Ryder swept Natalie up in his
arms and carried her to the bunk. She quivered as he pressed
her down beneath him and kissed her feverishly. She tangled
her fingers in his long, wet hair and whimpered softly.

"You know I'm not going to stop this time, don't you?" he
asked raggedly.

He pulled back then, and began purposefully unbuttoning
the bodice of her frock. Floundering in her own raging heartbeat, she stared up at him. Spotting the smoldering intensity
in his eyes, she panicked and almost did beg him to stop. But
then he was kissing her again, so passionately, and raising her
skirts. And then it was too late.

Eighteen

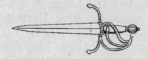

Beneath Ryder, Natalie trembled with both passion and fear. Somewhere in a far recess of her mind, she knew she was being reckless, but for once she did not care. Being in Ryder's strong arms, being totally consumed by desire for him, simply felt too good. For the first time in her life, the prim lady was thrust aside as the passionate woman emerged. Natalie felt powerless to contain the potent longings streaming through her as Ryder's wonderful lips seduced hers and his massive, hard body crushed her soft flesh.

Ryder, too, was reeling with desire and exultation. He gloried in Natalie's surrender, in making her his at last. In the back of his mind, his conscience nagged that he was a cad to proceed with this, but for now, he was too caught up in the glory of loving her, awakening her, to care. He wanted her so desperately, had waited so long for her. She was like a fire burning in his heart, his spirit, his blood. Emotion shook him as he anticipated all the ecstasies they would share.

He ran his lips over the incredible softness of her face. At her low cry, he claimed her mouth, sucking her tongue, her very breath, deeply into him. Her moan stirred even wilder longings; the sweet taste of her left him ravenous for more. He stroked and probed with his tongue while pulling the pins from her hair and sinking his fingers into the thick, velvety mass. He held her to his demanding mouth and ravished her with his tongue until she sobbed in delight. His senses swam with the delicious womanly scent of her.

His lips roved down her throat, and his heart gloried to her sharp gasp. He finished unbuttoning the bodice of her dress,

pulled down her chemise, and bared her lovely breasts, taking
avid delight in the way the mounds rose and fell so rapidly
with her tortured breathing. He pressed his ear into the hollow between her breasts and listened to the wild thrumming
of her heart. That was where he wanted to be—inside her,
making them one heart, one body.

He cupped one of the soft, round globes in his hand, then
glanced upward, desire storming him anew as he glimpsed
the languid, passionately dazed look in her gorgeous tawny
eyes. The thought of how those lovely eyes would darken,
glow, dilate, as he drove into her, ignited his loins to unbearable arousal.

"You're so beautiful," he whispered, smiling at her.

"As are you," she whispered back.

He leaned over to take her breast with his mouth . . .

The instant Ryder's lips brushed the tight, aching pink bud,
Natalie went insane. The hot pleasure of his tongue flicking
across the sensitive peak was like nothing she had ever felt
before—jolting, raw pleasure. She cried out his name, slipped
her hands beneath his shirt, and caressed his strong shoulders
while breathing in delirious gasps.

Her ardent response further fueled his own desires; slowly,
he sucked her turgid nipple inside his mouth. She made a
sound of strangled delight and dug her fingers into his shoulders.

He glanced again at her exquisite face, at the cheeks so hot
with passion and maidenly wonder. Lord help him, she was
so adorable, so incredibly lovely! He wondered what color
that bright face would burn when he introduced her to realms
of ecstasy she had never known.

He leaned over, running his lips over the soft, firm contour
of her breast. Tenderness filled his heart as he felt her fingers
slide into his hair, holding him tightly to her breast, as if she
truly did crave him.

"You do know what to expect, darling?" he murmured as
he licked her smooth flesh.

"I—I'm a mature woman," came her breathless response.

"Are you?" With a husky chuckle, he caught her hand and
pulled it downward, pinning her fingers to his rock-hard erection.

Her mouth fell open on a gasp. "Well, perhaps not *that* mature."

Nonetheless, she did not shy away. Ryder's mirth soon faded to burning need as Natalie explored the swollen shaft with an untrained eagerness that left him heaving huge breaths of tormented arousal.

He raised himself to find her staring at him with fascination and ardor. She smiled, hooked her arms around his neck, and drew his face down to hers. This time, she possessed *his* mouth—at first tentatively, running her tongue over his lips, his teeth; then boldly, thrusting inside his mouth, eliciting a torrid response from him that left both of them totally engulfed in delight and made Ryder's chest tighten with poignant emotion.

He moved with feverish haste, pulling her clothing down her body, following with his burning lips, kissing the concave plane of her stomach, undoing the ties of her drawers, caressing her soft, womanly curls. All the while she twisted and panted, stroked his rough face, his satiny hair, and encouraged him with low, wanton cries. He was on fire, barely able to contain the urge to join their bodies.

She was sobbing with pleasure by the time he moved upward again to kiss her, gently parting her thighs and exploring with his fingers. His merest touch on her sensitive, aching bud had her writhing against him. By now he craved her so fiercely, he felt close to drowning in his own raging heartbeat. But he continued slowly, arousing her passions until she was slick, ready for him. His fingers trembled as they finally moved to the buttons of his breeches, freeing his stiff, agonized erection. He pressed his mouth deeply into hers as he teased and parted her further. He pressed at the portal of her femininity. So delicious. So tight. He probed harder, heard her muffled cry, and drew back to look at her face.

"I—I'm not entirely sure this will work," she murmured raggedly.

He couldn't contain a chuckle. She appeared so earnest. "Oh, Natalie," he whispered. "Poor love. It's too late to back out now. I'm going to fill you until you beg for mercy."

Kissing her again, he pushed harder, and she squirmed. He slid his hands beneath her, sinking his fingers into her soft bottom, holding her to his possession. She whimpered as he just invaded her small slit. She enveloped him like a hot, wet noose, making him burn to bury himself in her. He gritted his teeth and bore down, breaching her maidenhead.

She cried out, and he comforted her with his lips while inexorably pressing into her, unable to stop now, groaning with tortured pleasure as the velvety wet vise of her clenched around him. By the time he sheathed himself fully, she was trembling, gasping, digging her fingers into his arms—

"Darling, I'm sorry," he whispered, kissing her mouth, her cheek. "I won't hurt you again, I promise."

Natalie stared up at him. In truth, she felt torn apart, bursting with him, yet never had she known such powerful intimacy as she did with him so deeply inside her, with his warm, solid body crushing her nakedness. He made her feel wild, wanton, but most of all, he made her feel *his*—as alive with pleasure as she was throbbing with pain. She stretched upward and passionately kissed his mouth.

Her sweet surrender shook him to the core. He kissed her back tenderly and moved within her gently, unhurriedly, not wanting to hurt her again, holding in the reins of his passion as tightly as he could. During the next few moments she gasped and clung to him as the slow, deep friction of his stroking drove her to new heights of demented arousal. At last she wiggled against him tentatively, and he responded with a flurry of driving strokes that had her tossing her head and crying out, rubbing her breasts against him.

A grunt shook him, and then he was lifting her hips, plunging vigorously, until she whimpered with the exquisite torment of it and arched to meet him. A soft sob escaped her as he pressed her higher, and a cataclysm of rapture shook her in riveting waves that lifted her eagerly into his driving heat. A groan was ripped from his throat, a ragged whimper from her, as he pressed home with the force of his climax.

He fell on her, breathing frantically, devouring her mouth with ardent kisses. She clutched him tightly to her heart.

Nineteen

NATALIE DOZED, AND RYDER STARED AT HER WITH GREAT TEN-
derness. What ecstasy she had given him! She had definitely
come to him a virgin—the streaks of blood on the sheets confirmed this—which made him feel all the more hellishly
guilty for having taken her. She was a lady, and under the circumstances, an honorable gentleman should offer marriage.
He wasn't entirely ready for that, but neither was he ready to
let her go.

It was so odd. He had always assumed that once he bedded
Natalie, the challenge would be gone and she would be out of
his system. Now he found quite the opposite was true. Instead
of feeling sated by victory and ready for the next challenge,
he felt more intrigued, more fascinated, and—aye!—more
hungry for her than ever. This enchanting mix of wench and
lady would be in his blood for a long, long time, he mused.
Today a purely passionate creature had supplanted the prim
spinster, and he longed to get to know that hot minx better,
even as he continued to tease and tantalize the proper lady in
her. It was her own damn fault, anyway, for being so gorgeous, so desirable, so alluringly feisty.

To that end . . . He stroked the curve of her hip and nibbled
on her jaw. She stirred, and smiled up at him. Joy filled him
anew . . .

Then he felt her tensing, watched her eyes fill with realization and panic. It was almost as if he could see the proper
lady rise up and take charge again.

"What have I done?" she gasped.

He smiled tenderly and caressed her cheek. "Easy, darling. It's not quite that dire."

"B-but I can't do this!"

"Not to contradict a lady, but it seems to me you already have."

"Oh, heavens!"

Uttering a wince, Natalie squirmed out of Ryder's embrace, grabbed the sheet, and stood, wrapping herself in it. She began to pace, appearing confused, disheveled—and more irresistibly sexy than ever.

Wearing a bemused frown, Ryder sat up at the side of the bunk and watched her. Hoping to soothe her, he said, "I can understand your agitation, darling, since you were a virgin—"

She turned on him in trembling outrage. "So you wondered about that? I suppose you would have, you cad!"

He ground his jaw. "Many women have lived through this before, Natalie. It's not the end of the world—"

"Speak for yourself, sir!"

He grinned. "You will survive it and be better for it, I predict."

His arrogance infuriated Natalie, particularly since she felt so close to an emotional collapse. "Oh, will I? What if there is a child?"

He scowled and gazed at her for a moment. "Then I suppose I would have to do the honorable thing, wouldn't I, love?"

Natalie's eyes began to sting. His obvious reluctance hurt more than any refusal to take responsibility ever could. "Overwhelm me with your enthusiasm, why don't you?"

With a groan, he stood. "Darling . . ."

She stared wide-eyed at his nakedness, reeling with both horror and new waves of lust. "Will you kindly put on some clothing?"

Now the rogue spoke up. "I think not, love."

Making a sound of frustrated rage, she turned her back on him.

Ryder felt at a loss. "Darling, why fret so about such dire consequences right now—"

She whirled, her eyes blazing. "You don't have to worry about such consequences at all, do you? As a man, you can simply ruin me, then go about your merry business!"

Her words lanced his conscience and brought a new frown to his face as she reminded him of his original, more dastardly intentions toward her. He no longer felt quite that way—though he couldn't really define the change in his feelings. He did know he felt an obligation and a deep affection toward Natalie—she was not merely some doxy to be bedded and abandoned. He also knew it was killing him that she was denying the magic between them, that she was holding herself apart from him when he wanted so badly to hold her again—and when he felt convinced in his heart that she wanted him, too.

"So I've ruined you, now, have I, love?" he asked gently.

Her lower lip quivered and she turned away. Ryder watched one lovely shoulder sag and couldn't bear it. Neither could his manhood, which had traitorously grown more aroused throughout their titillating conversation.

He walked over to her, moved aside her disheveled hair, and stroked the creamy curve of her shoulder. She shuddered and he smiled.

"Was it torture, love?"

She shook her head, and he heard her sniff.

He curled an arm around her waist and pulled her close against him. Another squeak of misery escaped her. He splayed his fingers downward toward her belly. "Did I hurt you?"

Natalie fought tears at his devastating nearness. "You . . . at first. Not very much."

He nibbled at her cheek while reaching upward to gently pry her fingers loose from the sheet. "I'm sorry you're so distraught, darling. I suppose I'll just have to comfort you, won't I?"

She spun around, her eyes enormous, especially since she had spotted how enormous *he* now was! "You can't mean like that!"

"No, I mean with just a little kiss"—he paused to demonstrate—"a tiny caress . . . a few tender words."

Natalie was reeling, gasping, but still clinging tenaciously to the sheet. Ryder's nearness was so electrifying that she knew she was within a hairbreadth of falling apart—and falling into his arms again.

Her words came out in desperation. "Please, will you go—or at least have the decency to put on some clothing!"

He appeared genuinely concerned. "And leave you here so overwrought?"

She turned away and squeaked again. His hand reached around her, his fingertip trailing down her neck to stroke the tight fist clutching the sheet to her breast. She shivered.

"Why don't you drop the sheet and come back to bed with me, darling?" he whispered huskily. "I promise I'll make you feel so much better."

Trembling, she fought the assault on her emotions, and as his seductive finger continued to stroke her fist, she remembered what he had once said about a rosebud unfurling. She almost lost all control, then gasped and clutched the sheet even tighter.

Then he turned her in his arms and kissed her, so tenderly, and whispered against her mouth, *"Let it go, love."*

With a cry of torment and desire, Natalie dropped the sheet, and then she was in his arms, her aroused breasts crushed against his hard, warm chest.

Ryder carried her back to the bunk, pressed her beneath him, and kissed her achingly. "Please don't cry, darling. I can't bear it when you do."

"Aye, even as you prime me for new tears," she replied tremulously.

He pulled back. "Didn't I pleasure you when I loved you?" he demanded hoarsely. "Tell me, please."

"You did," she gasped.

"And don't you want me again now? I want you so badly I'm about to die of it—"

In response, Natalie hauled him close and kissed him. After all, enough was enough, and her emotions were certainly at the breaking point.

Her ardent response drove him wild. He caressed her breasts, ran his fingers over her silky thighs, and kissed her. Unable to contain his feverish desire, he drew her thighs apart, and he heard her whimper slightly as he began pushing himself inside her again. Though the hot feel of her all but made him demented, he again managed to move slowly, stoking her passions to unbearable intensity, waiting patiently for her cries and sighs of surrender, then thrusting more deeply, burying himself in her, creating a delicious friction that had him groaning and her sobbing in delight. His mouth smothered hers as they climaxed together. He was left half dazed, breathing raggedly.

When at last he withdrew, he felt bemused that she turned to the wall, curling up in the blanket and sniffing.

He stroked her spine. "Natalie? What's wrong now, love?"

"Could you *please* leave me alone for a while?"

"Darling, can't we talk about this?"

"Talk about it?" she repeated with hoarse fatalism. "You use your words to trap me."

He felt hurt and angered. "So now I've trapped you? You were not a willing participant at all?"

"You've gotten your way!" she burst out. "You should be quite proud of yourself. Please, just go."

Hearing the hurt and confusion in her voice, Ryder felt consumed by turmoil. He desperately wanted to reach out to her, to truly comfort her somehow, but realized his words could not really reach her unless he could give her what she most needed.

At war with himself, he got up and dressed. With a last look of longing at the huddled figure on the bunk, he left the cabin . . .

Natalie continued to sob quietly. She couldn't believe what she had done—lost her head, lost all control, given herself to a rakehell. Yes, it had been glorious, and she half feared she was in love with him. Yet Ryder Remington was the last man on earth whom she could ever trust with her heart.

What scared her even more was that her own traitorous desires now seemed even less trustworthy than he was!

Twenty

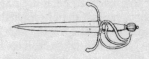

Two and a half weeks later, as the *Wind* glided up the wide estuary of the Medway toward London and the Thames, Natalie stood at the rail, gazing out at the marshes and farmlands, watching ducks and geese feed among the waving grasses. Harry was behind her at the helm. Ryder had climbed up into the mains to help Simon brace the yards. Natalie had long ago all but given up on trying to curb his suicidal tendencies.

Not that she was a paragon of caution herself. She remained both appalled and traitorously fascinated by her own conduct in allowing Ryder to bed her. In his arms, she had discovered a wanton, reckless side of herself that she was not pleased to see emerge, yet was still, at times, powerless to deny. For this reason, she felt thankful they were finally approaching London—and a respite from the excruciating tension of living in such close quarters with Ryder. Perhaps now she could come fully to her senses, dubious though the prospect sometimes seemed.

Twice during the voyage she had again succumbed to the shocking, potent pull of her passion for him. The first instance had been an even more tormenting reenactment of the night the cockroach had assaulted her, but this time the culprit had been a gust of wind that had rocked the ship in the middle of the night and sent Natalie tumbling off the bunk to land on top of Ryder. Hearing his pained grunt, she had felt immediate concern for his person. *Have I hurt you?* she had asked. *I'll show you what hurts,* he had answered, drawing her fingers boldly lower. She had squirmed only for an instant. The next thing she remembered, her lips had been on his, her arms tightly wrapped around his neck, her nightgown raised . . .

The second time, he had burst in on her unexpectedly while she was dressing. She had been wearing only her drawers and camisole and had been digging in her trunk for stockings. That time, he had merely looked at her. Heavens, that look! The fire, the need, even the endearing uncertainty in his eyes. 'Twas all it had taken to melt her—to her great shame! Totally rattled, she had dropped her stocking. He had picked it up and handed it to her, their hands had brushed, and then . . .

Both times afterward, Natalie had withdrawn into herself, refusing to talk or to be cajoled. Ryder had glowered and grown grumpy.

Yes, 'twas best they would soon live separately, though the possibility still depressed Natalie's spirits, since she cared for this rogue far more than she wanted to admit. Indeed, ever since the ship had slipped from the Channel into the Medway, she had felt weighted down by the problems she would have to address—finding Aunt Love and dealing with her father, who was likely to be in a far worse state than he'd been in when Natalie had left him.

She turned to watch Ryder shimmy down the mainmast, hop onto the deck, and stride over to join her. He looked very handsome this mild morning, with the wind whipping his hair around his patrician face, and his loose-fitting white shirt billowing around his tanned, muscular torso, although she was pleased to note that his visage appeared abstracted, too. She hoped he was suffering as much as she was, but she doubted she could hope for that much!

Arriving at her side, he rubbed his jaw, which was stubbled with black whiskers. "I guess I'd best get below, shave, tie back my hair, and put on a proper suit of clothing—so I will not give poor Nonna too much of a shock."

She braved a smile. "You are excited about seeing your grandmother, aren't you?"

"Aye. As I mentioned before, I'll likely stay with her." He frowned quizzically. "And you will reside with your father, I presume?"

She nodded. "His house is on Devonshire Terrace, near Regent's Park."

Drawing a heavy breath, he reached out to stroke her cheek, his expression suddenly wistful. "I'm going to miss you, you know."

Though his words were laced with charm and tenderness, Natalie fought against the powerful pull. "Why, Lord Newbury, I would have thought that by now you'd be eager to go on to the next conquest."

Her words did not please him in the least, judging from his dark scowl. "Actually, I find myself not eager in the least. And what of you, Miss Desmond? Are you so impatient to be rid of me? I could have sworn that over the past weeks, you've discovered in me a redeeming feature or two."

She blushed vividly. "Just because during the voyage I succumbed to a momentary lapse or two—"

"Or three or four," he reminded her.

"—doesn't mean I'm prepared to offer myself as your mistress!" she finished in a mortified whisper.

He chuckled. "Why, Natalie, are you tossing down a new gauntlet now?" As she heaved herself up with indignation, he held up his hand. "Contain yourself, darling. I won't try to trap you into the life of a demimondaine before we dock. It's just that . . ." He paused to look her over covetously, and sighed. "You've been such a charming cabin mate— especially when you fall out of your bunk."

Fighting the titillating effect of his words, she snapped back, "And 'tis entirely for the best that we are cabin mates no longer, sir!"

He lounged against the bulwark. "Why is that?"

"How dare you even ask! You know you have no interest whatsoever in matrimony, and neither do I. You know we're far too different—"

"In some ways, we're very much alike," he cut in devilishly.

She turned away moodily and crossed her arms over her bosom.

Groaning, Ryder reached out to touch the tip of her nose. "But we *shall* continue to see each other, love. After all, in a number of ways, our investigation has only begun."

She glanced at him tentatively. "Ryder, I—I'll not continue

to hold you to our bargain, if you would prefer to be released."

He frowned. "I think you have things backward, love."

"Do I?"

"Aye. 'Tis you I am not ready to release—and thus I'm seeing our bargain through, wherever it may lead us."

She glanced away, feeling secretly charmed and relieved that he would not merely desert her now that he had had his wicked way with her, although she was cynical enough to realize that his "devotion" to her stemmed not from true gallantry, but from the fact that he had not entirely satisfied his lust for her.

Mercy, did *she* ever think of anything else? She resolved to steer the conversation toward more neutral territory.

"Do you suppose we'll have any luck finding Aunt Love here?" she asked.

"We shall try our best. You said she no longer has quarters in London?"

Natalie nodded. "She gave them up when we sailed for America. Although her relationship with my father is wretched, I presume it is always possible that I may arrive home to find her sitting there, doing her knitting or some other such nonsense. If so, I shall surely wring her neck."

"Not likely, as overjoyed as I know you will be to see her. You really are very concerned about her safety, aren't you?"

"It's a nagging fear, forever at the back of my mind. Of course, my aunt is a flighty sort, not inclined to seek my counsel before she launches on her various exploits. Still, this particular stunt of hers goes way beyond the pale."

Ryder nodded. "Try to keep your spirits up, love."

He strode off to the companionway, and Natalie turned her attention back to the passing sights. They had now moved into the main pool of the Thames, and already the air had become tinged with the soot of London factories and chimneys. The river was rapidly growing crowded with vessels of every variety, from huge three-masted merchant ships to smaller schooners, sloops, and barges, and even some of the new steamers they had spotted in the Channel. To the north loomed the forbidding façade of the Tower of London, ravens swirling about its turrets; across from it on the south bank spilled the appalling tenements of Jacob's Island. Ahead, near

London Bridge, stretched the somber gray outline of the Customs House, and beyond soared the Monument to the Great Fire. In the distance rose the dome and baroque towers of St. Paul's.

Harry was turning the ship to starboard, veering off into one of the many docking areas where murky, foul water slapped against ships, barges, and wharves. Natalie drew a deep breath. They were home—and in her heart, she was gripped by the demoralizing fear that things would never again be the same between her and Ryder.

Aye, it might well be for the best that their days of sharing the same cabin had ended. Still, her heart ached as she anticipated the inevitable anguish of losing him.

When they docked, Ryder made a small ceremony of turning the *Wind* back over to Harry, along with an expensive bottle of brandy. After everyone had disembarked, Ryder, Natalie, and Simon parted company with Hampton, who was bound for his family's lodgings in Mayfair. Ryder hailed a hansom cab; he and Natalie squeezed inside, while the driver crammed himself, Simon, and all of their luggage on top of the rattletrap conveyance. They clattered away from the cluttered, filthy docks, moving through the gray, yawning slums of the East End and eventually onto Ludgate Hill. Natalie gazed out the window at the grandeur of St. Paul's. Sir Christopher Wren's masterpiece stood tall and splendid, a shining jewel sitting solitary amid the harsh encroachment of Newgate Prison to the north and the ramshackle intrusion of Doctor's Commons, with its menage of courts, to the south.

They headed through the center of town, past the soaring Georgian and Palladian buildings of the Strand. The streets were crammed with conveyances. Drays lumbered by, laden with wool or cotton, iron or produce. Gleaming custom coaches squeezed their way past wagons, while carts pulled by mastiffs competed with stanhope gigs and even a few of the newfangled, two-wheeler hobbyhorses. The walkways were clogged with humanity, from businessmen trooping briskly past, to vendors calling out raucously and waving their wares, to raggedy street urchins darting about, looking for pockets to pick.

Catching a glimpse of Bow Street as it curved off toward

the theater and market districts, Natalie remembered happier days when she had attended the Royal Opera House with her parents and had shopped at Covent Garden with her mother. What state would she find her father in now?

"Has the city changed much since you've been gone?" Ryder asked.

She twisted about to stare at him sitting next to her. Clean-shaven, with his hair drawn back, he now appeared the consummate gentleman in his black cutaway coat, crisp shirt linen, and top hat. "The city seems more congested—and filthier."

"Ah, yes, due to the thousands still thronging to our cities to man the new factories—and, no doubt, not improving their lot as they thought they would, as evidenced by the Spa Fields riots and the Peterloo Massacre."

Natalie was compelled to raise an eyebrow at him. "Why, Lord Newbury," she taunted, "could it be that you have an awareness of the plight of your fellow man after all? I thought your entire passion in life was for amusement and debauchery."

He shot her a forbearing glance as they continued past St. Martin-in-the-Fields, with its stately Corinthian columns and a breathtaking spire dotted with pigeons. To the south, Natalie could spot the familiar outlines of Whitehall, the Palace of Westminster, and the Abbey. As they passed verdant St. James's Park, she spotted ducks paddling in the pond.

Edging along the back side of Buckingham Palace, they turned north and followed the contour of Hyde Park, passing grand Georgian town houses designed by Kent and Adam and Nash. From there they proceeded through Mayfair to Devonshire Terrace.

Natalie felt herself tensing as the driver pulled the conveyance to a halt outside a brown brick, three-story Georgian town house framed by chestnut trees and fringed by ivy, ferns, and blooming roses.

As Natalie ground her jaw and gripped the edge of her seat, Ryder reached out to pat her hand. "It can't be that bad, love."

She laughed. "You haven't met my father."

Further conversation was curtailed as the driver opened the door. Ryder hopped out, instructed the man to haul down

Natalie's trunk, and offered her his arm. He called up to Simon that he would return momentarily, then led Natalie up the path.

They climbed the steps to a porticoed entrance flanked by beautifully carved Grecian urns. Ryder knocked, and a robust, gray-haired man with bushy eyebrows and wearing a butler's garb opened the door.

The man stared at the newcomers in consternation, then cried, "Miss Natalie! Praise the saints, child, is it you?"

"Fitzhugh!" Natalie gave her old family retainer an affectionate hug. "How good it is to see you again."

The butler beamed, and then his gaze narrowed on Ryder. "And who is this with you, miss?"

"My guest is Ryder Remington, Marquess of Newbury," Natalie answered smoothly. "Lord Newbury and I met in Charleston, and we crossed the Atlantic together on the same passenger ship. When we docked an hour ago, he offered to escort me home."

"Ah." Although the butler was frowning, he acknowledged Ryder with a bow.

"Fitzhugh, is my father in?" Natalie continued worriedly.

"Bless my soul, I'm forgetting myself," Fitzhugh muttered. "Come in, please, and let me take your things."

They moved inside to the center of the rotunda, followed by the cabdriver, a bedraggled, crusty character who muttered and grumbled as he dragged in Natalie's trunk. Ryder asked him to wait at his conveyance, and Fitzhugh summoned a footman to carry Natalie's trunk upstairs.

As Fitzhugh gathered up their gloves and hats, Natalie glanced around at the familiar surroundings. Ferns and Grecian couches languished beneath a soaring dome embellished by gilt-edged plaster medallions and scrollwork. Ahead, a carved, oaken staircase curved up three dazzling stories. Intricate plaster panels, classical statuary, and magnificent oil paintings graced the walls and stairwells.

Natalie leveled her anxious gaze on the butler and repeated, "My father, Fitzhugh?"

"Indeed, miss, he is in," Fitzhugh informed her ruefully. "I am afraid Mr. Desmond has sequestered himself in the study for days now, and hasn't even made an appearance at the Exchange. In truth, I'm quite worried about him."

She nodded dismally. "Is it the drink again?"

"Whenever has it been anything else?" the man replied with an exasperated gesture. "All Mr. Desmond seems to want to do is sit by the fire and ramble on about your mother."

"And what of my aunt, Mrs. Love Desmond? Have you seen her?"

Fitzhugh's bushy brows shot up. "Mrs. Desmond is not still with you?"

"No. She left our home in Charleston about six weeks ago, and I had hoped she might have returned to London by now."

Fitzhugh shook his head regretfully. "I'm sorry, miss. We haven't received so much as a letter from Mr. Desmond's sister-in-law."

Natalie sighed. "Thank you, Fitzhugh. I would like to introduce my friend to my father now." She nodded to Ryder and proceeded toward the study.

Fitzhugh called after her, "Oh, miss, you might want to—"

Natalie turned around. "Yes?"

The butler shook his head. "Never mind, miss."

Natalie and Ryder continued down the hallway, both frowning bemusedly. Glancing over his shoulder at the anxious butler, Ryder murmured, "Things don't bode too well for your aunt, do they, love?"

"I'm afraid not. I suppose I was foolish to hope she might actually be sitting here waiting for me—her strained relationship with my father notwithstanding. But I would like you to meet Father. Perhaps he may have heard something from her."

The large, darkened room they entered was illuminated only by a fire glowing in the grate. The walls were lined with soaring bookshelves stocked with expensive leather volumes. Above the shelves were hung landscapes by Constable and portraits of Desmond ancestors done by Gainsborough and Van Dyck.

Natalie frowned. Her father was nowhere in sight. His desk was cluttered with papers, but his chair was empty. The mahogany and silk damask settee facing the fireplace appeared vacant as well, although the empty brandy decanter on the nearby tea table seemed an ominous sign.

Natalie was about to suggest they search elsewhere when

the sound of snoring alerted her. With her face growing hot, she led Ryder across the room and around the settee.

Her father lay passed out, facedown, on the Persian medallion rug before the fire.

Twenty-one

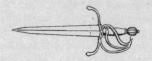

Ryder could only feel intense sympathy for Natalie as he watched her sink to her knees beside her prone father and beg him to awaken. The odor of brandy was heavy in the air.

"Father, are you all right? It is I, Natalie."

When there was no response from the insensible figure, Ryder intervened. "Here, love, let's turn him over."

Ryder gently grasped the man by his shoulders and rolled him over on the rug. He glimpsed a handsome, aristocratic face now eroded by signs of dissipation—a fine tracery of red spider veins across the nose and cheeks, a gaunt color, heavy purple circles beneath the eyes. Desmond's coat hung agape; his fine shirt linen and silk cravat were crumpled and stained with liquor.

Charles Desmond stirred and gazed up at the two newcomers through bloodshot brown eyes. "Natalie!" he gasped. "By Jove, is it you, girl?"

"Yes, Father."

Before she could comment on her father's shocking state, he heaved himself to a sitting position and embraced his daughter. "Ah, Natalie, my dear! How good to see you again! I truly feared I never would!"

Although her father's emotional greeting touched Natalie's emotions, she remained embarrassed that Ryder had seen him thus. "What in God's name are you doing on the floor?" she demanded in a tense whisper.

"Well, I'm not entirely certain," came his befuddled reply. Charles struggled to rise, then fell back with a groan and raised a hand to his brow. "Ah, my poor head . . ."

Natalie glanced at Ryder in perplexity.

He took Charles's arm. "Here, sir, let us get you to a chair."

"Who are you?" Charles demanded of Ryder.

Natalie answered, "This is a friend of mine, Ryder Remington, Marquess of Newbury."

"Pleased to meet you," Charles muttered, flashing Ryder a weak smile.

Fighting back an urge to recoil from Desmond's brandied breath, Ryder remarked tactfully, "May I venture to say, sir, that in your present state it might be imprudent to tarry too long by the fire?"

"Ah, yes." Flushing with obvious embarrassment, Charles allowed Ryder to heave him to his feet.

Ryder led the staggering man to a George I tapestry armchair beyond the fireplace. "Can I get you something, sir?"

Charles drew trembling fingers through his graying brown hair. "I'd give my soul for a double brandy right now. Natalie, be a love and fetch it for me."

She ground her jaw. "I shall not contribute to the madness that got you in your present deplorable state."

Ryder flashed her a look of entreaty. "My dear, he needs it. But a small one, if you please."

With a resentful glance toward both men, Natalie went to the Sheraton sideboard and poured her father a small quantity of brandy. She crossed the room and reluctantly handed him the crystal snifter.

Charles Desmond downed the brandy neatly, drew a convulsive breath, then looked contritely at his daughter. "I am sorry, my dear. This is no fitting homecoming for you. I do trust you are well?"

Natalie flashed her father a wan smile. "Aye, I am."

"Won't you both have a seat?"

After Natalie and Ryder seated themselves on the settee, Charles set down his snifter and said, "If I may ask, what has brought you back to England, my dear? Not that I am not delighted to see you again, but I had thought you and Love had decided to remain in the Colonies on a more or less permanent basis."

"Actually, I've come home because of Aunt Love," Natalie explained. "Have you seen or spoken with her?"

"Not at all."

"Oh, this is terrible!" Natalie exclaimed, wringing her hands. "I had hoped she would be here."

As Charles stared in confusion from his daughter to Ryder, Ryder explained, "Natalie's aunt disappeared from Charleston some weeks ago. We subsequently learned that she had boarded a merchant ship bound for London."

"Love is here?" Charles asked, scratching his jaw. "How odd that she did not make even a courtesy call. Of course, things haven't been right between us, ever since my brother died."

Leveling a cool stare at her father, Natalie spoke up. "It was wrong of you to blame Aunt Love for Uncle Malcolm's death."

Charles gestured vaguely. "Perhaps my stance might have been somewhat extreme," he admitted with surprising humility.

"Indeed," Natalie concurred.

His cheek twitching with the obvious discomfort he felt, Charles turned his attention to Ryder. "If I may ask, sir, how did you become acquainted with my daughter?"

"I met your daughter in Charleston," Ryder replied smoothly. "Later on, we discovered we had both booked passage on the same ship bound for England. I needed to return here to London to check on my grandmother—and, of course, Natalie wanted to try to find her aunt, and to see you, sir. When we disembarked, I insisted on escorting her home."

"So you've both come to London to visit loved ones," Charles remarked with a sad smile. "How I wish my beloved Desiree cared enough to return from Paris to see about me." He glanced toward the fire, his cheek jerking convulsively.

Ryder noticed that Natalie's fingers were digging into the arm of the settee, and her face was gripped by exquisite emotion. How his heart ached for her—and how much better he could understand her now!

"Father, I am sure Mother must still care about you," she whispered without conviction.

The melancholy man suddenly exploded into anger. "I'll not live with a bloody Bonapartist!" he declared, slamming his fist on the arm of the chair. "Why, the woman endorsed the Berlin Decrees and the Continental System, which would have bankrupted our country! Desiree behaved as if she were cruelly and blissfully unaware that I, her husband, earned my livelihood at the Exchange."

"I realize Mother's attitude was extreme, Father," Natalie put in sympathetically.

Abruptly, Charles's irate facade crumpled, and he heaved a raspy breath. "And yet, my life without her seems a curse . . ."

Ryder continued to feel intense sympathy for Natalie as both of them watched Charles hang his head and shudder with emotion. He wished with all his heart that there were something he could do to improve matters for her, but he knew his hands were tied. Charles Desmond, in his shocking state of dissipation, might well be beyond recall.

"Father, we must let you rest," Natalie said helplessly.

Charles wiped his cheek with his sleeve and muttered, "I'm sorry, daughter. Next thing, I'll be on a bloody crying jag. You are doubtless tired and possibly hungry. Please, you must settle yourself in . . . Fitzhugh will see to your needs."

"Yes, Father." Natalie rose, crossed the room to him, and leaned over, gently kissing his brow. "I'll just see our guest out, then."

Ryder stood. "I enjoyed meeting you, sir, and hope to have the pleasure again soon."

"Likewise," Charles replied with a wan smile.

Ryder followed Natalie out into the corridor. As she turned to him, he would have given his right arm to ease the look of anguish on her face. He reached out to smooth an errant curl on her troubled brow.

"I'm so sorry, darling," he murmured.

"Father is in a worse state than ever—and Aunt Love is nowhere in sight," Natalie said dismally.

"Given what your father said, perhaps it is not surprising that your aunt is not here," Ryder pointed out, hoping to cheer her. "Didn't you tell me this rift between them is quite bitter?"

Natalie nodded. "On the night Uncle Malcolm was killed in the duel, Father accused Aunt Love of being a coldhearted woman who had driven his brother to gambling and woman-izing."

"Oh, good Lord."

"It wasn't true, of course. Aunt Love may be an eccentric but she is also one of the finest, warmest human beings I've ever known. She simply could not cope with my uncle's vices and betrayals, any more than I suppose my mother could handle my father's tendency toward profligacy, or his politics—as reprehensible as it was for her to leave him."

Ryder nodded. "No wonder you're determined never to marry."

"Not that your parents' marriage was a model for wedded bliss, either," she pointed out cynically.

"True," he conceded.

"Sometimes I wonder if there is such a thing as a happy marriage."

Ryder smiled wistfully as honesty compelled his answer. "My grandparents had one—for over twenty wonderful years, until my grandfather died in his sleep in Florence."

Natalie flashed him an apologetic look. "I'm sorry. You need to go see her, don't you?"

"I'd like you to meet her," he said solemnly.

"Of course. We'll do that soon. In the meantime, I shouldn't detain you, or burden you with my own problems."

He scowled. "Natalie, please do not talk as if I am not a part of your life now."

She braved a smile. "You must go."

"Shall I call on you this evening?"

She shook her head. "No, spend some time with your grandmother. I need to get settled in as well."

Ryder became momentarily lost in thought as he considered the unpleasant task that could no longer be avoided, no matter what the personal anguish required.

Drawing a heavy breath, he said, "Tomorrow we shall meet with my father."

She raised an eyebrow in mild surprise. "Why, of course I'd be happy to meet the duke. But why—"

"This will not be a joyous occasion," Ryder cut in tensely. "But as Harry said, my father does own a textile factory and he has some contacts in the industry, so I feel a meeting with him may be a good starting point in our search for your aunt."

She stared at him with compassion. "Ryder, if this is too painful for you, I can't let you—"

He pressed his fingers to her lips and spoke sternly. "What did I tell you, love? We are in this together."

"Ah, yes," came her rueful response. "We are truly partners in crime."

He chuckled. "I shall call for you early on the morrow." He flashed her a tender smile. "Be ready, and wear something pretty."

"I'll be ready," she promised.

Ryder left the Desmond town house feeling bemused at his difficulty in parting with Natalie, if only for one night.

Although it had seemed hard for him, it had seemed much easier for her—quite an irritation. Even though Natalie's arrival in London had so far produced no aunt, only a father floundering in quicksand, she had hardly fallen apart and begged for his comfort. On the contrary, she had bucked up her courage and told him not to call on her that evening; she had taken charge of her own life and her responsibilities. Now he feared that their shared mission to find Love was the only glue that still kept them together—at least from her perspective.

Perhaps, as she had pointed out earlier, it was best that they were no longer cabin mates; indeed, his conscience argued that he should let her go, before she became irrevocably ruined, or even pregnant, at his hands. Yet the rogue in him felt more fascinated, more bewitched, by Natalie than ever. The intimacy they had shared aboard ship had been glorious, but also so tenuous; the fact that she had pulled away each time afterward, marshaling her own forces, had left him feeling frustrated and hungry for more. He felt like a man who had been tempted by several delicious morsels; now he wanted a full feast at her banquet. And he knew it still rankled that the prim lady in Natalie remained determined to quash the passionate wench he had held in his arms. In that respect, his mission to awaken her to the sensuous world was far from completed . . .

When Ryder arrived at his grandmother's Adamesque town house off Grosvenor Square, the butler, Carsley, showed him into the salon. Ryder entered the large, sunny room and spotted his grandmother sitting near the French doors, her spectacles on as she concentrated on her knitting. Tenderness gripped his heart at the sight of her. Nonna was a statuesque, lovely, elderly woman with a noble, lined face and silver hair caught up in a bun. She wore a high-necked gown of gray silk brocade, along with the many beautiful rings, the garnet brooch, and the pearl given to her by his grandfather. She was humming an old Italian melody under her breath as she worked—a poignant tune Ryder remembered from his childhood.

Nonna had not even noticed his entrance; her hearing was not what it had once been, and she was immersed in her work. He glanced around at the well-remembered room. Many of the furnishings and objets d'art had been brought over from Italy: the walnut sideboard inlaid with ivory animals, the Venetian gilt wood chairs and settee, the Cozzi vases and exquisitely carved Doccia figurines. He gazed appreciatively at the plaster fretwork ceiling with its gilt embellishments and roundels of art by Veronese, the walls hung with breathtaking scenes of Venice painted by Canaletto and Bellotto.

Remembering a long-ago game between them, he tiptoed across the room to stand behind her, and placed his hands over her eyes. "Guess who?" he whispered, according to ritual.

"Ryder!" With a look of rapt joy etching her face, Francesca Valenza dropped her knitting and surged unsteadily to her feet.

Moving around her chair, Ryder embraced his frail grandmother and kissed her cheek. The scent of her lavender perfume brought back more poignant memories. "Nonna, I hope I didn't startle you. How wonderful it is to see you again!"

Francesca pressed a hand to her heart and stared at her grandson amid tears of love and delight. "Ryder, nipote mio, I thought I would not live to see this day! You are home at last!" She squeezed his hand convulsively.

He grinned. "I realize my appearance here is unexpected, but there really was no time to send a letter. I left Charleston rather suddenly."

"You are here," she replied feelingly. "That is all that matters, my love."

He stared at her with concern. "You are well?"

She waved him off with a slender, wrinkled hand. "I am an old woman, more stiff with each passing day. But I should not complain. I have buried many a friend half my age."

Ryder leaned over to pick up his grandmother's knitting, and laid the half-finished mauve-colored blanket on the chair. "Another afghan for the poor?"

Francesca nodded solemnly. "There are so many suffering in the wards of St. Thomas's, shaking from fever or consumption. The ladies in the St. Thomas Beneficent Society can scarcely keep up with the demand."

He slanted her an admonishing glance. "Nonna, you spend too much time in the seamy parts of town, ministering to the desperately ill. Who knows what malady you might contract—or what ruffians could accost you? Look what happened to Mother, for heaven's sake."

Francesca patted her grandson's arm. "Beloved, do not work yourself up into a state over an old woman such as I. At my advanced age, I have the luxury of not worrying about such threats."

Intensely, he reiterated, "But, Nonna, after your own daughter was—"

She clutched his hand again and shook her head. "One day soon, we will talk about your mother. For now, let us sit down and catch up on our lives."

"Of course." Ryder led his grandmother to the settee, and the two sat down together.

"What brings you back to London, my boy?" Francesca asked.

He beamed with pleasure as he raised and kissed her hand. "I wanted to see you, of course."

"Not the true reason," she replied with a wise smile. As he would have protested, she wagged a finger at him. "Now, Ryder, I know you are devoted to your dear Nonna, but something tells me this journey concerns a woman—a very special lady, I think."

Ryder grinned sheepishly. "You still have the second sight, don't you?"

Her fine hazel eyes darkened with sadness. "Sometimes the visions are more a curse than a blessing." Forcibly, she brightened. "But do tell me of your lady. Did you meet her in Charleston?"

Ryder could only shake his head at his grandmother's uncanny insights. Briefly, he related the circumstances of his and Natalie's meeting and their journey to London—leaving

out, of course, the scandalous circumstances of their initial
acquaintance and the fact that they had become lovers during
the voyage.

But Nonna was not fooled. Narrowing her perceptive gaze
on her grandson, she scolded, "You have made this fine
young gentlewoman your mistress, no?"

Ryder actually felt color shoot up his face. "Nonna! Please,
you mustn't—"

"Oh, I will not tell a soul, you may be sure. But am I correct? Is she your paramour?"

He grinned again. "Well, not quite."

Francesca slanted him a scolding glance. "Meaning you
have only ruined her?"

He chuckled. "Why do women always equate one of life's
greatest pleasures with being 'ruined'?" When Francesca
didn't comment and continued to eye him soberly, he muttered, "You know me too well."

"*Sì*, and you are a bad boy. But I love you anyway."

"And that's what I love about you," he said with utter sincerity. "You accept me the way I am."

"I know your heart is in the right place—albeit the rest of
you could sometimes use a sound thrashing."

He laughed and nodded in agreement.

"Are you going to offer to marry this young woman?"

"Natalie *is* very special, I'll grant you that," he said with
a sigh. "But even if I should offer for her, I doubt she'd have
me."

Francesca's features tightened in indignation. "She
wouldn't have a duke's son? What ails the girl?"

"A very tragic family history," Ryder replied without humor, then told his grandmother of Natalie's background with
her father, uncle, and cousin.

"Bless her heart," Francesca murmured afterward. "But
surely she can't equate you with the others?"

"Natalie is wary of marrying at all—as I am. You should
have seen the disgraceful state her father was in when I escorted her home. I can't say I blame her for being suspicious
of all men."

"*Englishmen,*" Nonna amended with disgust. "It is no
wonder they lean toward dissipation, with the king of England such a wastrel, overspending himself while his poor fa-

ther went mad at Windsor. Now he has John Nash carving up Piccadilly in order to create a monument to his own vanity. Think of the good all that wealth could have done if consigned to the poor!"

Ryder fought a grin; George IV, formerly the Prince Regent, was hardly Nonna's hero.

With a passionate gesture, she continued. "And then there was the debacle last year, when his Majesty had the gall to postpone his coronation while attempting to divorce Princess Caroline. Thank goodness the bill of pains and penalties was withdrawn from the House of Lords. Caroline's behavior on the Continent might have been less than prudent, but the king of England is a cad—with a new mistress to console him, no less."

Ryder chuckled. "It never ceases to amaze me, Nonna, how you deplore every Englishman—with the exception of your own grandson, who was once among the favored at Carlton House."

Francesca drew herself up with dignity. "You, my boy, are half Italian—"

"And most proud of it," he cut in vehemently.

"You have all your mother's goodness and not an ounce of your father's cruelty." She clutched his hand. "Are you home to stay?"

He shook his head sadly. "I think not, Nonna."

"But where will you go next?"

He shrugged. "Perhaps on to sinful Paris, now that the monarchy is safely restored." A sudden image flashed in his mind of taking Natalie there, of spoiling her with pastries and champagne and expensive presents. Lord, she really *was* in his blood!

"I suspect you will be staying in London far longer than you think," Francesca was saying. "Furthermore, I predict that soon you will grow up and ask for the hand of your lady. After all, one day you'll inherit your father's title and all his duties. You'll need a duchess, my boy."

Ryder frowned at the sobering possibilities. To his grandmother, he said scoldingly, "You just want to see me settled—and producing great-grandchildren."

"True. But my motives are not entirely selfish." She touched his arm. "Just because your parents had a loveless marriage, *nipote mio,* doesn't mean you and your young lady can't find great happiness together, as I did with your grand-father, God rest his soul." She crossed herself.

Ryder solemnly followed suit. "As a matter of fact, I was mentioning you and Grandfather to Natalie today."

Francesca beamed. "What did I tell you? We think alike, my boy. And when will I get to meet your lady?"

"I will bring Natalie to dinner some night soon. How will that be?"

"Molto buono."

"In the meantime, however, we must try to find Natalie's missing aunt."

Francesca regarded Ryder with keen sympathy. "You will have to see your father, then?"

"How did you know?"

She shrugged a thin shoulder. "The textile factory in Step-ney. William Remington might be able to provide you with some useful information."

Ryder's handsome features tightened. "Have you seen my father recently?"

"I have not seen William since Carlotta's funeral, nor have I desired to," came her bitter reply. She touched Ryder's hand. "It was wrong and cruel of him to blame you for your mother's death."

"I hardly feel guiltless in the matter," he said bleakly. Be-fore she could comment, he rushed on. "But I will have to see Father if we hope to locate Natalie's aunt." He squeezed his grandmother's hand. "Do you get any feeling for where the woman might be?"

Francesca shut her eyes and concentrated. After a moment, she whispered, "This is so very odd."

"What?" he prodded.

Francesca's words came forth hoarse and ominous. "I see wickedness, evil. Words of darkness and iniquity. 'Famine, fire, pestilence, plague.' " She opened her eyes and stared at Ryder with alarm. "What does all of this mean?"

He felt equally unsettled. "I have no idea. But, good Lord, Nonna, this doesn't bode well for Natalie's aunt at all. Could she be in peril?"

Francesca frowned fiercely. "Of that I am not certain. But I do get a definite feeling of doom and foreboding. I think you had best find this woman as quickly as possible."

Twenty-two

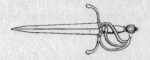

EARLY THE NEXT MORNING, RYDER STOOD BEFORE HIS MOTH-
er's grave in the churchyard of St. Margaret's, Parliament's
church that languished beneath the medieval splendor of the
nearby Abbey. On this mild April morning, he appeared the
proper gentleman in a black tailcoat and silk top hat. He held
in his hands the bouquet of yellow roses he had just purchased from a street vendor.

How his mother had loved yellow roses.

Removing his hat, Ryder leaned over and placed the flowers in the empty brass urn in front of Carlotta's headstone. He
crossed himself, and mouthed a silent prayer for his mother's
soul.

He had not seen her tombstone before, and the sight of it
weighted his emotions anew with the finality of his loss.
When she had died, he had remained in London for the funeral, but then he had sailed for America before the grave-
stone had been readied . . .

Now he had been gone long enough for lichen to begin
creeping up the marker.

Nonetheless, the stone definitely bore his father's mark.
Plain marble, with no embellishments, no sentimental platitudes. There was only Carlotta's name, along with "Wife of
William, Duke of Mansfield," and the chiseled dates which
gave testimony to Carlotta's too-brief, forty-four years.

If only he could have done something to prevent her senseless passing! Yet at the time, he had been too consumed with
his own debauchery to watch over his mother as carefully as
a devoted son should have.

187

"I'm sorry, Mama," he whispered with a catch in his voice.

Shortly before Ryder had left London, he had been a young libertine who gambled with Brummell, courted scandal with Byron, and on several occasions attended the races at Brighton at the personal invitation of the Prince Regent. But all that had changed with his mother's death. Although he had continued to live a licentious life abroad, he had a strong feeling he might only have been running from himself during the past four years.

He recalled Nonna's reminding him of the tug of his heritage—the dukedom, the responsibilities he would one day inherit. Was he prepared for those obligations?

He frowned. Nonna had urged him to grow up and marry Natalie. A scant month ago, he would have scoffed at that prospect entirely. Give up his rakehell ways? Settle down with just one woman? Never! But since he had met Natalie, he had been challenged, intrigued, fascinated, both intellectually and emotionally. Something within him had changed. There was no doubt in his mind that he cared for her, that he had become caught up in her life. Only he didn't really know quite how to express that caring as yet without sounding like a cad—

Which doubtless he was, after seducing her on board the ship, and for lusting after her even now. He had missed her terribly last night, couldn't wait to be with her again—still, to his credit, he realized it wasn't just her kisses he had missed, but all the delights and mysteries of being with her.

Somehow, he sensed his mother would approve that he was at least willing to reexamine the direction of his life. Emotion choked his heart as he stared at her headstone one last time and wiped a tear from his eye. "I miss you, *mamma mia*," he whispered. "And I love you—forever."

Ryder left Westminster in his grandmother's coach, heading toward Devonshire Terrace to fetch Natalie. As the carriage rattled down Park Lane, on the northern fringes of Hyde Park, he thought of the second daunting task before him that day. His spirit rebelled at the prospect of seeing his father again, but if Nonna was right and Natalie's aunt truly was in peril, he really had no choice but to follow every possible lead in trying to rescue the woman.

When he called for Natalie at her father's town house, he found that she looked most fashionable in her gold satin day dress, lacy shawl, and feathered bonnet. Yet her expression appeared equally troubled as he assisted her into the coach. They sat facing each other as the conveyance clattered off.

"How goes it with your father, love?" he asked.

She shook her head. "He kept Fitzhugh up half the night, retching and wallowing in self-pity over my mother's desertion."

Ryder was puzzled. "I'm really sorry. But hasn't your mother been gone for eight years? I would have thought your father's pain would have eased by now."

"Unfortunately, Father keeps getting worse instead of better. He is much more morose now than when I left him. He has truly become obsessed with his own misery."

"And there is nothing we can do to help?"

"I really don't know," she replied with a frown.

"Would your mother come back from Paris if you asked her?"

Bitterness flared in Natalie's golden-brown eyes. "That is out of the question."

"Meaning you aren't willing to ask?" Ryder's tone was gentle.

Distractedly, Natalie glanced out the window. "Not yet, at any rate." Sighing, she turned toward him with a conciliatory gesture. "How is your grandmother?"

"Doing quite splendidly, thank you." Flashing her a tight smile, Ryder warned himself not to alarm her by mentioning Nonna's vision regarding Love Desmond. Instead, hoping to lift Natalie's spirits, he nudged her lacy hem with the tip of his boot, catching an enticing glimpse of white silk stocking. Studying her high-necked gown with its satin-covered buttons, and her virginal shawl, he teased, "You look quite a vision of propriety today."

She dimpled. "You asked me to wear something pretty. And besides, it is not every day that I am privileged to meet a duke."

"I would have thought that every available duke in the *ton* would have vied for you when you came out."

"I never came out," she returned crisply.

"Not even a court appearance?"

"Nor any soirees at Carlton House."

He chuckled. "Ah, yes—you do not hold with such frivolity, do you, my very proper Miss Desmond?"

She smiled, obviously enjoying his baiting despite herself. "Oh, by the time I turned fifteen, Aunt Love began to fret over my debut and to pay court to the various grand dames to ensure that I would receive all the proper invitations and vouchers when I came of age. However, when we subsequently learned that Rodney had been repeatedly arrested for public intoxication in Charleston, and Aunt Love decided to sail for America, I felt I must accompany her. Since then, there has been no time in my life for society and its tiresome rituals of courtship."

Although Ryder smiled at her comments, they caused an inner stir. Once Natalie's life was back in order, would she then relent of her bluestocking ways and seek a husband? The very idea had him grinding his jaw—and also chiding himself. He wasn't ready to offer for her, yet here he was, fully prepared to commit mayhem at the very thought of some other dandy trying to pluck her off Pall Mall.

His musings scattered as the coachman pulled the conveyance to a halt before William Remington's imposing home off Hanover Square. Ryder hopped out and assisted Natalie from the carriage. The two strolled between the wrought-iron gates, passing through stark grounds and up the steps of the three-storied Palladian town house with plain, symmetrical lines and an austere tan brick facade totally bereft of embellishments.

Ryder's knock was answered by a clearly flabbergasted butler, a robust, balding man dressed in impeccable black. "Your lordship! You are home!"

Ryder grinned as he ushered Natalie inside. "Withers, it is good to see you again."

"And you, your lordship. You are well, I trust?"

"Quite. Is my father in?"

The butler nodded. "His Grace is upstairs in the chapel."

"The chapel?" Ryder repeated cynically.

"Three years ago, his Grace had the chapel installed on the second floor, according to a design by William Inwood."

"How very convenient for him," Ryder drawled.

"If you and the lady will kindly wait in the drawing room, I shall apprise his Grace of your arrival."

Withers took Ryder's hat and Natalie's shawl, then showed the couple to the salon. They sat down together on a cane-backed beech settee. To Ryder, the room appeared much as he remembered it—paneled in walnut, dark and cold as a tomb. The furniture was mostly of austere Hepplewhite styling, although Ryder spotted a few newer pieces fashioned along religious lines—a black lacquer cabinet inlaid with marble plaques of the Apostles, a pair of mahogany library chairs with tapestry covers depicting the Crucifixion and the Resurrection. The tables and walls were decorated with religious works of art, including sculptures by Donatello and oils by Titian.

Soon the door swung open and William Remington stepped inside. Ryder shot to his feet, while Natalie quickly followed suit. Ryder found that his father, like the room, had not changed. Still the same tall, angular, ramrod-straight figure, dressed in black; the same piercing gray eyes that so closely matched the gunmetal hair. Still the same look of contempt etching the harsh features.

Yet as William Remington paused for a moment to regard his son, Ryder thought he spotted some flicker of unnamed emotion in the depths of the duke's silver eyes. Soon the spark faded, replaced by the familiar stony facade.

"So it appears the prodigal has returned," William Remington said wryly.

Ryder dipped into a mocking bow. "Your Grace." He turned to Natalie. "May I present Miss Natalie Desmond?"

As the duke flicked is cool, appraising stare to Natalie, she curtsied deeply. "Your Grace."

He expelled an exasperated sigh. "Have a seat, both of you."

Out of deference, Natalie and Ryder waited until the duke had folded his tall frame into one of the tapestry library chairs before they resumed their seats on the settee.

William Remington raised a thin gray brow at his son. "To what do I owe the honor?"

"I have returned to London to check on my grandmother."

"And is Countess Valenza well?" came the older man's disinterested response.

"Quite. I am also in London because of a desire to assist Miss Desmond, whom I met while in Charleston. We subsequently sailed for England on the same passenger ship."

After another cool, assessing glance at Natalie, the duke swung his attention back to his son. "Go on."

"Miss Desmond has an aunt, Love Desmond, with whom she operated a textile factory in Charleston. But their enterprise became threatened by British cloth smugglers. A few weeks back, Miss Desmond's aunt disappeared. We have reason to believe she may have come to London in search of these smugglers."

"Cloth smugglers!" Remington laughed dryly. "How very odd a pursuit for you."

Stiffly, Ryder said, "Since you own a textile factory in Stepney, we wondered if you might be able to provide some insight into Miss Desmond's situation."

The duke shrugged. "I am no longer actively involved in the running of the Stepney facility. However, if you wish, you may contact my business partners, Oswald Spectre and John Lynch—although I have serious doubts that either will have any knowledge of smuggling activities."

"We didn't mean to imply otherwise," Ryder responded evenly. "But the fact remains, Miss Desmond and I must begin our investigation somewhere. We are just about at our wit's end in our search for her aunt. Perhaps Lynch or Spectre can provide some clue that could point us in the right direction. After all, the safety of Miss Desmond's aunt could well hang in the balance."

With an expression of some suspicion, Remington turned to Natalie. "Just who are you, anyway, young woman?"

At once, Ryder grew irate. To his father, he said, "Your Grace, I will not have Miss Desmond addressed in this manner."

A cynical smile played on the duke's thin lips. "You mean I have no right to know the background of a woman my son and heir is obviously . . . involved with?"

As Ryder appeared ready to spring to his feet, Natalie reached out to grip his arm. "It's all right," she muttered to him under her breath. Proudly, she regarded his father. "What do you wish to know, your Grace?"

"You are English?"

"Yes."

"But you met my son in Charleston?"

"Yes."

"Who are your people?"

"I hail from London. My father is Charles Desmond."

"Ah, yes. The younger son of the Earl of Worcester. Good stock—although you haven't quite the pedigree I would want for my son's future marchioness."

His face livid, Ryder shot to his feet. With fists clenched at his sides, he spoke in a low, fierce tone. "You, sir, have no bloody say about whom I may or may not associate myself with or choose as my wife. You gave up any right to offer advice about my affairs on the night my mother died, when we had our cozy little conversation afterward. Furthermore, Miss Desmond is worth ten of you, your title, and your wealth."

The duke only laughed. "Those are not the words of a young man hoping one day to inherit."

"Then disown me, *Father,*" Ryder replied in a deadly calm voice. "By all means, summon your solicitors at once. I'm stunned that you haven't tried to tackle the legal niceties before now."

William Remington stood, his features tight with anger and contempt. "I see you have not changed one iota, Ryder—still the hothead and a wastrel."

Ryder's eyes were bright with scorn. "I see that you have not changed either, your Grace. But I'll reserve the epithets—after all, there is a lady present."

With a muscle twitching in his gaunt cheek, the duke took out an ornately carved gold pocket watch and flipped it open. "This matter is growing tiresome. I have no further time to deal with you, as I am expecting my new prayer companion, Harriet Foxworth, at any moment."

"Don't let us keep you," Ryder urged.

Snapping shut his watch, Remington turned and exited the room, ending their interview.

The coach had barely driven away from Hanover Square when Natalie burst into tears. At once, Ryder became frantically concerned over her plight.

"Darling, I knew I shouldn't have brought you along today," he said, passing her his handkerchief. "The horrible things he said to you. Why, the instant that sanctimonious blowhard insulted you, we should have left—"

"Me?" she cut in incredulously, staring at him. "Do you think I am crying over me?"

"Then what?"

"I'm crying for *you.*"

"Oh, Natalie." Unable to contain himself, Ryder reached out and caught her by the arms. Despite some resistance on her part, he quickly pulled her onto his lap. "Oh, my darling," he whispered, tenderly kissing her brow and stroking her back. "Why would you cry over me?"

She was aghast. "Ryder, release me at once! Someone may see us!"

Muttering a curse, he tugged down both shades in the coach. Then he leaned over and kissed her lips, slowly and thoroughly. "Now tell me why you are crying."

Drawing a convulsive breath, she tilted her anguished face toward his. "Because of you—your father. Do you know the two of you never even once touched each other? Why, you never shook hands, or inquired after each other's health. You even called him 'your Grace.' The one time you called him 'Father,' it was with the utmost contempt. It made me feel so bad for you."

"Oh, Natalie, love." He pressed his lips to her damp cheek. "Please do not cry for me."

"I can't help it," she sobbed.

His arms tightened around her. "Oh, what I would give to have you alone right now," he said feelingly. "I need you."

Touched by his words, yet still saddened, she stared up at him. "You hate this, don't you?"

He was taken aback. "Hate what?"

She appeared on the verge of new sobs. "You never should have come with me to London. You've lost your carefree life and have gone through hell, all because of me. Now you have to dress in stiff, formal clothes, and to deal with your father."

He drew a heavy breath. "Ever since my mother's death, there has been so much bitterness between us . . ."

"Oh, this goes much deeper than mere acrimony. I swear, your father must be made of ice. How could he speak about going off to pray with Harriet Whoever-She-Is when obviously he has no feeling, Christian or otherwise, in his heart—

certainly not for his own son. And the way he was dressed—all in black. Did you see his shirt studs? They were fashioned of black onyx, with small gold gothic crosses. The very sight sent a shiver down my spine."

Ryder nodded soberly. "I suspect my father took my mother's death much harder than he may ever admit. Mayhap he hides his pain behind his religious fanaticism."

"Well, it's not fair that he blame you for everything!" she declared.

He braved a smile and kissed the back of her gloved hand. "Don't worry about it, love. With luck, we won't have to see him again."

"But he is your father!" she cried. Abruptly, she went pale. "And you mustn't bring me around with you again. I cannot let him disown you."

Ryder shot Natalie a glance of heated suspicion. "Natalie, I wouldn't dream of allowing my father's opinion to have the least effect on our relationship."

"And what relationship is that, Lord Newbury?" she asked with some bitterness.

"You know damn well what relationship that is," he said with a deepening frown. "Don't act as if nothing has happened between us, Natalie."

Her jaw tight, she glanced away. "But you could be disinherited."

"As I just informed my father, I am surprised he hasn't taken such steps before now. Besides, do you think I care one whit for his title or his fortune?"

"You doubtless will later on."

Anger flared in his eyes, and he shook a finger at her. "Natalie, I refuse to continue this absurd discussion with you. If you would stop seeing me simply because I 'might' become disowned, then I must presume you truly are a selfish, mercenary creature and that it was indeed my title and fortune you were after all along."

She gasped in outrage. "You—you know that is not true! You are the one who pursued *me*—and made a thorough pest of yourself, I might add! I don't even want to marry—and certainly not *you!* How can you twist things around so?"

"I am taking lessons from you," he snapped with a murderous scowl.

"Well, I am not mercenary in the least," she continued primly. "Indeed, I am being selfless in the extreme. I only want what is best for you."

At this contention, a devilish grin abruptly split Ryder's forbidding countenance. He lowered his face until his lips gently brushed Natalie's, and his bright blue eyes burned down into hers. "Do you? Then open your mouth wide, darling, and kiss me long and hard."

"Oh, you rogue!"

But as his lips moved hungrily over hers and his hands seized her wrists, Natalie ultimately complied.

William Remington entered the darkened, gloomy chapel on the second story of his house. Beneath the somber, carved gothic arches, he spotted his new prayer companion, Harriet Foxworth. Harriet sat on a walnut pew before the granite altar with its ponderous pillars and candles illuminating a large oil painting of the Last Supper.

William's heart warmed at the sight of his dear friend. She was an amiable and welcomed presence, especially following the unexpected and tense meeting with his son.

William sighed. Things had gone badly with Ryder, and he felt at least partially responsible. But the boy was such a libertine—his lack of purpose and industry outraged William's strict sensibilities. Indeed, he suspected that this young woman Ryder was supposedly "helping" was already well acquainted with his son's debauchery.

Laying aside these troubling realities, he continued down the soft red carpeting toward Harriet. She was dressed in widow's black, with a veil draped over her hat. She was staring reverently at the altar; in her lap were her Bible and prayer book.

He smiled. He had recently met Harriet at St. Margaret's, when the two had sat together during mass. Afterward, strolling around Westminster, they had chatted and he had learned her story. A widow who had lost her baronet husband only a year earlier, Harriet had come to London from Bath in order to live with her daughter and son-in-law on St. James's Street.

The two had become instant friends. While Harriet could be termed a novice at ecclesiastical matters, she had a pious attitude, a teachable mind, and a passion for learning that had drawn William to her from the outset. The fact that she might not be quite his social equal had, for once, not mattered. It was rare indeed for William to meet anyone so devout; the two had prayed together practically every day since.

Reaching her side, he murmured, "Good morning, my dear."

She set down her books, rose, and drew back her veil, revealing a lovely countenance with pleasing, finely drawn features, fair rose coloring, and very few wrinkles for a woman of middle years.

"Why, good morning, William," she said in her lilting voice. "I hope I did not arrive early?"

"No, my dear. As it happens, I must apologize for being late. I had quite a surprise this morning—"

"Indeed?"

William frowned. "My son has returned from America."

"You don't say!"

"And he brought with him a most unsuitable young woman, I might add."

"Oh, dear. But I would truly love to meet your son—"

"Ryder and I are not on good terms. He appeared here only because he wanted . . ."

"Yes?"

William's thin lips tightened into an impatient line. "Enough of this. We must attend to our prayers."

"Oh, of course," Harriet said solemnly.

He regarded her sternly. "Did you read the passages from Isaiah and Revelations as I instructed you?"

"I did." She made a nervous gesture. "But frankly, William, it all seemed a bit grim."

"Grim?" he repeated, his expression thunderous.

"Well, yes. You know, dragons prepared to devour unborn children, sea monsters ready to cudgel saints, and all that. As for these prophecies of fire and brimstone—"

"Man is evil and will be doomed for his sin," intoned William.

"Oh, dear," she muttered. "But did not John Wesley believe that man is basically good and can be redeemed by faith?"

"John Wesley?" William's face darkened in outrage. "How dare you speak the name of such a heretic in this holy place!"

"I am sorry, William." Flashing him an entreating look, she reached out to pat his hand. "All of this is rather new to me, you see."

His countenance softened, and his eyes gleamed with an appreciative light. "Ah, but you are an eager pupil."

She smiled. "I am indeed."

He coughed. "That is something else we must repent for."

She blinked rapidly. "But, William, you only kissed me yesterday."

"According to the Gospel of St. Matthew, 'Whosoever looketh on a woman to lust after her has committed adultery with her already in his heart.' "

She laughed. "I am a widow, William—which makes adultery rather an impossibility, I should think."

William actually smiled. "Of course. We must simply avoid the lure of evil."

"So we must," she agreed. "Still, all of this sackcloth and ashes for a mere kiss?"

Slanting her an admonishing glance, William firmly took her arm. "Come, now, we must say our confessions and attend to our prayers. Afterward, my dear, we shall have a very long talk on proper Anglican theology, and on the infamy of heretics such as the Wesleys."

A flicker of mischief danced in Harriet's eyes. "Following our—er—session, we may need to repent even more, don't you agree?"

"Doubtless," William Remington concurred as he led Harriet toward the altar.

Twenty-three

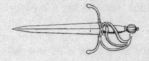

HALF AN HOUR LATER, RYDER AND NATALIE FOUND THEM-
selves amid the squalor of Stepney. The coach clattered down
dark, winding streets fouled by damp, sooty air, rotting garbage, bilge, and sewage. Ryder studied in dismay the various
dreary structures they passed—rattletrap tenements, noisy
taverns, factories of every kind, workhouses, poorhouses, fever houses.

Those unfortunate souls consigned to spend their lives in
the East End of London shared a sad and desperate existence.
Ryder had already spotted several pockmarked prostitutes
plying their trade in the streets, a couple of shifty-eyed river
thieves attempting to sell their ill-gotten gains at the back
door of a shop, and a huckster trying to entice two passing
sailors through the doors of a gambling den. Saddest of all
were the children—flower girls tugging at the coats of passing businessmen, ragged newsboys hawking ballad sheets,
stark-eyed toddlers being towed along by gaunt-faced moth-
ers with deep hopelessness in their eyes.

By now, Natalie had again settled into the seat opposite
Ryder—though he was pleased to note her cheeks were still
tinged with a guilty blush.

"I'd forgotten how much misery there is in the East End,"
she murmured, watching a bent old woman with a broom
chase down a street urchin while shrieking, "Thief! Thief!"

"Aye—I do wish we could somehow solve all of man-
kind's problems," Ryder replied grimly. "I also find it unfortunate that my father has placed his factory in this part of
town. The area crawls with pickpockets, thieves, and charla-

tans. Although I suppose access to warehouses and docks is critical for any such enterprise, I don't like exposing you to danger."

"Ryder, I am not some hothouse flower who will wilt at the first sight of a rat scampering past," came Natalie's stout reply. "Do you think your father's business partners will be able to help us?"

He laughed. "I wouldn't hold out too much hope there, love. Both men are as eccentric as my father."

"In what ways?"

"Oswald Spectre is a notorious skinflint who spends his days counting his gold sovereigns, and John Lynch is a miscreant who stalks the London streets at night, wearing a black cloak and indulging in iniquities too depraved to mention."

"How very disconcerting," Natalie murmured.

The coachman halted the conveyance before the soot-blackened brown walls of a factory. Ryder helped Natalie out and assisted her across the wretched, slime-encrusted alleyway. He pulled her back as a huge rat scurried across their path, missing her slipper by inches. She clutched her chest and stared at the vile creature burrowing its way into an odious pile of garbage and slops.

Ryder raised an eyebrow at her. "What did you say about wilting at the sight of a rat?"

She raised an eyebrow right back at him. "I was merely startled—I did not wilt."

He chuckled. "We can still go back, love. It is not too late. I can interview Lynch and Spectre on my own."

"Don't be ridiculous. I wouldn't dream of not meeting these men."

They entered the establishment through a scarred door and proceeded down a dark, narrow passageway. Already Ryder could hear the high-pitched whine of the looms and the rumble of drive shafts. Turning a corner, they almost collided with a tall, forbidding woman dressed entirely in black. Dark-haired and appearing to be in her mid-thirties, she was large and raw-boned, and had a huge nose, a large wart on her left cheek, and the shadow of a mustache framing her gray, bulbous lips. Her brown eyes radiated an unnerving intensity.

Ryder removed his hat. "Mrs. Lynch," he greeted her.

"Surely you remember me. I am Ryder Remington, William Remington's son."

"Ah, yes, your lordship." The woman's voice was harsh and cold as she dipped into a curtsy.

Ryder turned to Natalie. "My dear, this is Essie Lynch, wife of one of my father's partners, John Lynch." To Essie, he added, "May I present a friend of mine, Miss Natalie Desmond."

"Miss Desmond," Essie said stiffly.

"How do you do?" Natalie said.

With a curt nod, the woman turned and stalked off.

Watching Essie march around the corner, Natalie shook her head. "A very odd woman."

Ryder laughed. "You haven't seen odd yet."

They emerged onto the noisy, cluttered floor of the weaving room, and at once Natalie noticed the differences between the Stepney factory and the facility she and Aunt Love operated in Charleston. The expanse here was dark and grimy, compared with the light and airy weaving shed back in America. A foul haze of human sweat, machinery oil, and lint hung in the air. The workers—mostly women and children manning the clamorous, clanking power looms—were obviously of dire circumstances. Many were emaciated, dressed in little more than rags. Natalie's heart ached as she spotted one pitifully frail, vacant-eyed child threading the warp of an idled loom. The lad could not have been more than six.

"Oh, Ryder." Natalie half shouted to be heard over the din. "They are working children here, and no doubt paying all their workers starvation wages."

"I shall see about that," he replied tightly. "We desperately need to pass laws to prevent the exploitation of children—of *all* factory workers."

"Meaning that one day you may take your rightful place in the House of Lords?" she challenged.

He smiled wryly. "Stranger things have happened, love."

He guided her to a staircase that led to the mezzanine above the looming floor, and from there down a narrow corridor and through an open doorway into a dim, unkempt office. A portly man with sagging cheeks and stubby fingers sat behind a desk cluttered with papers. Intently polishing an impressive ring on the sleeve of his black velvet coat, he did not at first note their entrance.

"Mr. Spectre," Ryder said.

The man—balding, blunt-nosed, with an oily face and dark, beady eyes—glanced up, squinted at them curiously, then stood. Despite his girth, his voice came forth surprisingly shrill and almost effeminate. "Why, Lord Newbury. What a surprise to see you back in England."

Ryder turned to Natalie. "Miss Desmond, I would like you to meet one of my father's business partners, Oswald Spectre."

"How do you do?" Natalie extended a hand, which Spectre shook. She fought a grimace as his rank breath, which smelled of coffee and sausage, wafted over her, and the dampness of his flesh seeped through her glove.

"Both of you, do have a seat," Spectre said with a benign smile, gesturing toward two plain walnut chairs in front of his desk. After they had complied, he asked, "What may I do for you?"

Ryder leaned forward. "Actually, Miss Desmond and I are in London on the trail of cloth smugglers."

"Smugglers?" Spectre emitted a high-pitched cackle. "How queer. May I ask how you became involved in this peculiar pursuit?"

Briefly, Ryder explained about the Charleston factory, Natalie's missing aunt, and the clues that had brought them to England.

Staring from Ryder to Natalie, Spectre rapped a pencil on the desk and scowled. "You think I may be of assistance in this matter?"

Natalie responded, "Mr. Spectre, we have reason to believe the smuggling ring is based here in London, whence the fabric is illegally conveyed into Charleston. Have you heard anything that might be useful to us—rumors, whatever?"

With a shrug, Spectre tossed aside his pencil. "Sorry, Miss Desmond, but I'm afraid I have nothing to offer you."

"You have heard nothing at all about cloth smuggling here?" Ryder pursued skeptically.

Spectre stroked his flabby jaw with pudgy fingers. "Well, you might try the Customs House on the Thames, although it's doubtful the agents will make you privy to any investigations they are conducting. I would hazard to guess cloth smugglers do not worry overly about clearing their shipments through customs here, or paying any applicable export duties."

"A good point," Ryder acknowledged.

Spectre was busy spitting on his ring and buffing it. "Is there anything else I can help you with, Lord Newbury?"

"As a matter of fact, there is." Ryder tossed a determined smile at Natalie, then turned back to their host. "How long have you been employing children in the factory?"

Spectre laughed. "Ever since we commenced business seven years ago."

Ominously, Ryder said, "I doubt my father will approve of your exploiting the young in this manner."

A flicker of mingled caution and annoyance sparked in Spectre's small brown eyes. "Lord Newbury, your father has not been directly involved in the affairs of this enterprise for some years, nor have I ever found the duke to be particularly squeamish or tenderhearted on the subject of child labor."

Ryder's voice was rising. "One day I shall be taking over my father's duties, and your disregard of my wishes in this matter will not be overlooked."

Now Spectre appeared genuinely distressed. His thin eyelashes twitched with each rapid wink, and his tone rose to a whine. "Have you considered that if we release the younger workers, they will only succumb to a worse fate on the streets?"

"Please spare me the milk of your human kindness," Ryder replied. "And let me assure you that I will personally see to it that every child is found a suitable place in a school sponsored by a church or charity."

"A most noble undertaking, your lordship," Spectre sneered.

"You are quite clear about my wishes, then?"

"Quite."

"And I want you to see to it that the other workers are paid more appropriate wages," Ryder went on. "Why, most of them appear starved, and are wearing rags."

"There you must speak with John," Spectre muttered irritably. "He handles the financial end of things."

"Is he in?"

"Probably," came the man's diffident rely. "Although I haven't spoken with him today."

Ryder and Natalie said terse good-byes and left the office, continuing down the narrow passageway to another cubicle, this one just as meticulously neat as Spectre's had been slovenly. Leading Natalie through the doorway, Ryder spotted Lynch. A thin man with coal-black hair and cruel, hawkish features, he sat at the desk making entires in a ledger. Behind him, hanging from pegs on the wall, were a black cloak and a sinister-looking, low-brimmed hat.

Upon glimpsing his visitors, Lynch scowled, snapped shut his ledger, and stood.

Lynch's gray eyes focused on them, piercing and emotionless as ice. In contrast to Spectre, his voice hissed forth in a low, grating whisper. "Ah ... Lord Newbury. It has been some time since I have had the pleasure." His gaze flickered to Natalie and settled there.

"Mr. Lynch," Ryder said briskly, "the lady and I have a matter to discuss with you."

Lynch made a mocking bow. "By all means, come in and take a seat."

There followed largely a repeat performance of their interview with Spectre, except that Ryder found John Lynch's attitude far less helpful and even more guarded and hostile. Throughout the discussion, the man stared rudely at Natalie, his cold eyes probing her, much as a bird of prey might fix upon a small, helpless creature. At one point, when Ryder spotted Lynch licking his thin lips while ogling her, he almost lurched out of his chair to smash in the scoundrel's face. Only Natalie's fingers gripping his arm restrained him.

Once they had exhausted, without success, their inquiries about the smuggling, Ryder said, "By the way, Mr. Spectre told us that you are in charge of the payroll."

Lynch's frosty gray stare narrowed. "That is true."

"I informed Mr. Spectre that I expect all the children here to be released—and that the other workers are to be paid fair wages. I presume that, even now, you pay each worker less than five shillings a week?"

Lynch snorted. "Five shillings is, of itself, exorbitant wages." With obvious contempt he added, "Why don't you let me see to the running of things here, Lord Newbury?" He settled his insulting gaze on Natalie. "Surely you have other, more pleasurable pursuits to occupy you."

In an instant, Ryder was out of his chair, his fingers cruelly twisting Lynch's black silk cravat as he half yanked the other man out of his seat.

"Look at her again, you bloody bastard," he grated, "and 'twill be the last thing you ever see."

In the face of the threat from the giant, enraged Ryder, Lynch was almost frighteningly calm. He regarded the furious man with a chilling smile and rasped, "Really, Lord Newbury, I meant no offense."

Muttering a blasphemy, Ryder shoved Lynch away. "Perhaps I should suggest that my father conduct a thorough investigation of conditions here at the factory—as well as an audit of your books."

That gibe met its mark. The man's mouth tightened to an angry slash, and his eyes grew as sharp and hard as nails. "Are you on such amenable terms with the duke?"

"That is none of your damned affair," Ryder snapped. "Well—shall I speak with my father regarding the conditions I have observed?"

"That will not be necessary," came the cold reply.

"Meaning that the next time I visit the factory, I will not observe children being exploited—or half-starved workers in rags?"

Lynch was silent.

Ryder banged his fist on the desk. "Answer me, you miscreant."

"It shall be as you wish," was Lynch's scornful response.

As they left, Natalie was shuddering. "What an abominable man! He spoke exactly like a snake—if snakes could talk."

"Aye," Ryder concurred angrily. "I'm surprised I stopped short of wringing his wretched neck for the way he kept leering at you."

"Why didn't you?" she teased.

He laughed and wrapped an arm around her waist. "Not a pleasant sight for you, my darling."

"Then I may have saved his neck."

"Not that he deserved it."

She turned sober as they started down the steps. "I only wish the interviews had provided us with more information, but unfortunately, we're really no better off than when we started."

"True." Almost to himself, Ryder muttered, "I wouldn't be surprised if one or both of my father's business partners are hiding something. Spectre is an oily leech, and as for Lynch, I shudder to think of what evil may lurk in that depraved heart."

"What would they be hiding?" Natalie asked.

He shrugged and guided her around the perimeter of the weaving room. "Oh, I don't know—rumors they've heard, mayhap. If they knew anything at all about cloth smuggling, I'm sure they wouldn't tell us."

At the exit passageway, Natalie turned to take one last look at the forlorn child she had spotted earlier. "Do you suppose Lynch and Spectre will really release the child workers?"

"Do you think they will increase wages in this oppressive shop?" he replied humorlessly. Glancing around the room, he set his jaw in a firm line, then tugged her into the corridor. "Don't worry, love. I'll see to it that the Stepney factory stops enslaving children. Perhaps something can be done to help the families. And surely with the proper endowment, I can persuade a church or a private school to educate those unfortunate urchins. I need to find a place for Simon, anyway."

She stared at him with awe. "You really are serious about helping the children?"

He led her out the factory door. "Does it shock you that I can actually think of others, that I can harbor selfless motives?"

"No, it does not shock me at all." As he opened the carriage door for her, she added sadly, "I simply doubt you can ever be truly happy, weighted down with such responsibilities."

After she had climbed in, he took his seat across from her, shut the door, and spoke with biting cynicism. "Ah, yes—not as long as we have *you* to take on all the burdens of the world, leaving me free to be a rake and a wastrel. Right, love?"

She reached out to touch his sleeve. "Ryder, I really do appreciate you—and your efforts."

He clutched her hand, but continued to scowl.

Both were quiet for a moment as the carriage pulled away.
"So it seems we have reached another dead end," she murmured.

"Quite possibly."

Her brow was knitted in concentration. "What shall we do
now to try to track the smugglers? The entire East End of
London is a maze of factories and warehouses. Shall we go
from factory to factory? Dock to dock?"

The look on Ryder's face expressed his anger and steely
determination. "Oh, no, you don't! You, my dear, are not
doing any investigation here."

Her mouth dropped open. "But why not? I investigated in
Charleston!"

"That was different. London is not lazy, provincial
Charleston; it is a maze of madness, vice, and danger, with
footpads and brawlers lurking around every corner. It is un-
thinkable that you should subject yourself to such perils. Thus
I must insist that you allow me to handle all further investigation."

"Now wait just a minute! I'll not let you stop me—"

His voice grated out, fierce and ominous. "Oh, but I shall,
Natalie. I'll have you across my knee before I allow you to
roam the London streets at night."

She flung a hand wide in exasperation. "Why are you all
of a sudden becoming so stern and unyielding?"

"I'm quite unyielding where your safety is concerned."

"Well, I want to go with you."

"No."

"Ryder, I insist—"

"Damn it, Natalie, my mother was killed on the London
streets at night!" he exploded. "I wasn't there when she
needed me, but I shall make certain *you* do not succumb to
a similar fate."

All at once Natalie's anger melted as she understood his
feelings and realized he must care for her in his way. She
knew this was not a prudent moment to press her point. "Ryder, I'm sorry."

He sighed, reaching out to touch her gloved hand and
speaking earnestly. "Tell you what—I'll make a pact with
you. We'll investigate together during the day, if you will allow me to do all the investigation at night."

"Ryder, that does not strike me as a fair deal," she admonished.

"It is the only bargain I'm offering."

"Of course, since you get the best end of it."

In his typically outrageous manner, Ryder changed moods and winked at her devilishly. "Always, love."

"Oh, you rogue!"

When she began pummeling him with her fists, he only laughed, grabbed her wrists, pulled her across the coach, and kissed her into compliance.

That night, Harry Hampton was walking through a foggy, fetid, murky alleyway in the East End when suddenly he was grabbed and pulled into a shadowy doorway. A massive forearm was clamped around his neck in a death lock. At first he fought, flailing out wildly to escape his attacker, and then he froze as he felt the cold barrel of a pistol at his temple.

"Just take my purse and be done with it!" he cried. "It's in my breast pocket—"

"Calm yourself, Hampton," drawled a familiar voice, and he was released.

Harry whirled to face the man who had waylaid him. "Newbury! By god, are you trying to kill me?"

"Sorry," Ryder muttered with a rueful grin. "I guess I'm a bit jumpy after I was accosted earlier by a ruffian myself—not to mention having received several lewd invitations from ladies of ill repute and engaging in a territorial dispute with a very nasty tomcat."

In the darkness, Harry rolled his eyes. "What in God's name is all this balderdash? You send a message that I should meet you in this dangerous part of town at midnight. Then, when I arrive, you all but throttle me!"

"Again, Harry, I apologize. For all I knew, you were a another footpad—or a smuggler."

"A smuggler? How very singular." Harry peered up and down the odious street, his gaze pausing on a scarred doorway illuminated by the yellow glow of a gaslight. "By Jove, that looks like your father's factory over there."

"It *is* my father's factory."

"Then what in God's name are we doing here?"

"Haven't you figured that out yet?" Ryder questioned impatiently. "We are looking for smugglers."

"Smugglers? At your father's factory?" Harry's voice was rising.

"Pray announce it to all of Stepney!" Ryder snapped in a harsh undertone. "Mayhap you can summon a few more pickpockets while you're at it."

"Sorry." Now Harry also spoke in an intense whisper. "Why are you looking for smugglers outside your father's factory?"

Ryder drew a heavy breath. "Hampton, if you ever reveal what I am about to tell you—"

"Please, no further demonstrations of your lethal skills are necessary, Newbury."

Ryder chuckled. "You are aware, of course, of Natalie's situation?"

"Aye. The cloth smuggling back in Charleston—the missing aunt and all the rest."

"Well, I am convinced that the smuggling ring is centered at my father's plant."

"You don't say? But why?"

"In Charleston, Natalie showed me a sample of the smuggled cotton fabric. It clearly bore the distinctive warp of Remington cloth."

"Great Scot! This is terrible."

"Indeed."

"Does Natalie know?"

"Not yet. Luckily, she wasn't afforded too close a view of the finished product when we visited my father's factory today, and she'd half blind without her spectacles, at any rate." Suddenly, a proud grin split his features. "Although she can see me."

"Can she?" came Harry's fascinated response.

At once Ryder remembered himself. Clearing his throat, he continued soberly. "Now that we are in London, where Remington cloth is sold as well as manufactured, it is possible that Natalie may grasp the connection to the Charleston factory before long."

"I see," Harry muttered. "Not a good prospect as far as the honor of the Duke of Mansfield is concerned, is it?"

"Nay. That is one reason I am not yet informing her of my

suspicions. I suppose there's a spot of family loyalty left in my heart after all. The other reason is that, if Natalie knew of my suspicions, the foolish girl would be here tonight in the thick of it."

"And after you lost your own mother on London Bridge," Harry murmured with an unaccustomed touch of compassion.

"Aye," Ryder replied with a catch in his voice.

"What do you propose to do, then?"

"I propose uncovering the ring myself."

"And that is why we are standing here in the pitch blackness, risking life and limb?"

"If you were a smuggler, would you carry out your activities in broad daylight?" Ryder countered irritably.

"Actually, I don't know." Harry peered into the night. "The bloody place is darker than King Henry's tomb."

"It is the only starting point we have, although perhaps we should drop in at some of the punch houses near the docks and see what we can pick up from the locals. Surely some member of the ring must own a ship."

"I suppose so. Who at the factory do you think is the ringleader?"

"One of my father's partners—either Lynch or Spectre. Perhaps both."

"And you aren't willing to go to your father directly with your suspicions?"

"We aren't on such terms. Besides which, I'll be in a much stronger position to confront him if I can first nab the culprits."

Harry sighed. "Newbury . . . you don't suppose the duke is actually involved?"

Ryder shook his head. "I doubt it. He is too busy praying—and condemning the rest of the world for moral turpitude."

"You have my sympathies, old boy." Harry grimaced as he shook a large cockroach off his instep. "I suppose we might as well settle in for a long night."

"Yes, it rather looks that way," agreed Ryder. "And if this avenue doesn't prove fruitful, we'll begin reconnoitering taverns in the vicinity in a night or so."

Twenty-four

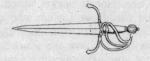

Over the next few days, Natalie saw little of Ryder. He called on her occasionally during the day, but he seemed to have forgotten their bargain that, if she would allow him to do the investigating at night, the two of them would investigate together during the day. Every time she mentioned wanting to go back to the East End and perhaps visit other factories or punch houses in that squalid part of town, he insisted that such activities were far too dangerous for her.

Despite all his high-minded rhetoric about wanting to protect her, she feared he had already grown frustrated with pursuing her and was seeking excitement—and his ease—out in seamy London. Although she remained stirred by memories of their lovemaking on the ship, and of Ryder's stolen kisses since then, she was convinced she should not succumb to him again, putting herself at even greater emotional risk, when she knew that sooner or later they must part. Ryder, on the other hand, seemed to demonstrate through his nightly absences that all he had wanted all along was a tawdry affair.

Natalie spent time with her father, but seemed unable to lift Charles Desmond from his morass of drinking and self-pity. She continued to fret over Aunt Love, and called on many of the widow's friends, hoping to learn news of her aunt's circumstances. Yet her efforts proved fruitless.

One day she received a small hint that she and Ryder were on the right track. She had gone to her old family couturiere on Bond Street to order a new frock—and the dressmaker showed her a bolt of the same cloth that had been her undoing in Charleston! But when Natalie questioned the elderly woman about where the fabric had come from, the couturiere could only apologize, saying she had had it for some time and couldn't remember from which cloth dealer she had purchased it.

Natalie left the shop and was entering the jeweler's next door, to drop off her father's pocket watch for repair, when she all but collided with Essie Lynch, who was attempting to exit the same establishment. On spotting Natalie, Essie stepped back, scowling, to allow the younger woman to enter. Natalie noted that the harsh-featured woman was again dressed entirely in black; she held a small package in one hand, a bouquet of flowers in the other.

"Mrs. Lynch," Natalie said, moving through the portal. "I hope I didn't startle you."

Essie's cold gaze settled on Natalie. "Yes. Well, I was just running my errands."

Natalie nodded toward the bouquet of red roses. "Your flowers are quite lovely."

Essie hesitated for a moment, then said, "Our only child is buried at St. John's-at-Hampstead. I visit her grave each Tuesday."

Instinctively, Natalie reached out to touch Essie's arm. She could feel the woman flinch, but Essie did not pull away. "I am so sorry. I cannot imagine any greater heartache than losing a child."

For a moment, Essie's emotionless facade seemed to waver as she stared at Natalie. Then she nodded curtly and marched out the door.

As a puzzled Natalie proceeded to the counter, the elderly, bespectacled jeweler was shaking his head. "Good day, miss. Tell me, are you a friend of Mrs. Lynch's?"

"Well, I am acquainted with her."

"She's an odd one, she is," the man confided.

"What do you mean?"

"For many years now, Essie has come in regularly to see what I have in. She must have the largest collection of mourning jewelry in the realm."

"Mourning jewelry?" Natalie repeated in astonishment.

"Aye. Today she bought a ring with a royal seal fashioned upon the death of George I. Why she has this fascination with the macabre, I don't know. Each Tuesday, it's by Covent Garden for her flowers; then she pops by here to purchase another expensive gewgaw. Not that I'm complaining—the woman is one of my best customers."

"I suppose she would be," Natalie muttered, feeling bemused as she removed her father's pocket watch from her reticule.

That evening, Ryder called to take Natalie to dinner with him and his grandmother. As they were being driven to Francesca Valenza's home, she told him about seeing the bolt of cloth at the couturiere today. "Don't you agree this is significant?"

He only shrugged, his expression preoccupied. "It could be."

"I am planning to visit other shops in Mayfair to see if I can spot the same cloth again," Natalie said. "Sooner or later I should be able to find someone who can identify where the fabric has come from."

"Why don't you let me handle things?" he responded irritably.

Her own frustrations burst forth. "Because you are shutting me out of your activities."

He flashed her a forbidding look. "For you own protection."

"That is not fair, nor is it completely honest. Lately, you don't tell me how you spend your days—much less your nights."

"Do you think I am betraying you?" he asked tightly.

"Betraying what?" she mocked with an incredulous laugh. "There is nothing for you to betray, Lord Newbury. We have no commitment, do we, you and I?"

Her words rankled Ryder, especially since he found them all too true. "That is not quite how I see things, Natalie," he replied. "And furthermore, you can't browbeat me into risking your safety."

"But I have no idea what you're doing!" she cried, gesturing passionately. "You have become so secretive and distant. I almost prefer the rogue I knew back in Charleston. At least then, you were honest regarding what you were about."

They both well knew what she referred to there. He was silent, scowling, as the coachman drew the carriage to a halt before Francesca Valenza's home. But a moment later, as Ryder escorted her through the dusky, dappled yard toward the front door, he caught her arm and pulled her close beneath the canopy of a huge crape myrtle.

The spring breeze wafted the scent of nectar and the sound of rustling leaves over them as Ryder regarded Natalie hungrily, his gaze lingering on her elegant coiffure and emerald-green silk dress. "You look so beautiful tonight, darling," he murmured with husky longing.

"You look rather dashing yourself," she was compelled to admit breathlessly.

Ryder leaned over and kissed Natalie with a fervor that secretly thrilled her, especially as he nestled her so close to his hard, warm body.

"What brought this on?" she inquired with a telltale quiver.

"Do you still think I am seeking my ease elsewhere?" he asked intensely.

She laughed and caught another shaky breath.

"Well, Natalie?"

"That was not the kiss of a man whose needs are well sated," she admitted.

"Indeed." He nuzzled her cheek with his lips. "I wish we could find a way to be alone, darling. I have missed you terribly over the past days."

Though the urgency of his words did move her, Natalie was determined not to allow her passions to overrule her head again. "Ryder, you know what my feelings are about that. I am fond of you, but—"

"Oh, are you?"

"*But* it is really for the best that we not—"

"To hell with what's best," he interrupted, kissing her again. "I still want you too damned much."

Although rattled and dizzy, Natalie pressed her palms against his chest and met his impassioned gaze soberly. "I'm sorry, Ryder, but I'm afraid not even a charming rogue like you can have everything he wants—and you might find the price too dear."

"Are you saying you want a husband instead of a lover?" he asked in puzzlement.

"I'm saying I want neither," came her tumultuous response. "I'm speaking of the emotional—and other—risks to us both. You know this feeling between us is impossible. And besides, you are already spending your nights elsewhere—"

"To find your aunt," he cut in emphatically.

"If that is true, then why won't you share with me what you're doing?" she burst out in exasperation.

"If I do, will you let me take you off somewhere?" he teased, nuzzling her cheek with his lips.

"Oh, you are incorrigible!"

"Aye." He kissed her again.

"Ryder, please," she murmured breathlessly, pushing him away. "Your grandmother."

Chuckling, he led her toward the door, while she fervently hoped the night air would quickly cool her hot cheeks.

In the glittering salon of the grand home, Francesca Valenza, looking regal in a frock of gold silk brocade, rose from the settee to greet Natalie with open arms. "Natalie, my dear!" she cried, hugging the girl and kissing her cheek. "I feel I know you already. You are a vision, just as Ryder told me. I am certain you are the one for him."

Touched by the effusive greeting, Natalie replied, "And he has told me much about you, Countess Valenza. I am most pleased to meet you."

"Please, you must call me Francesca," the old woman insisted.

"It will be my pleasure," Natalie replied.

"Good evening, Nonna," Ryder added, leaning over to kiss his grandmother's cheek.

"My beautiful grandson," Francesca murmured, embracing him, then winking. "You have done well for yourself, no?"

As everyone laughed, Francesca added briskly, "Now come, both of you, and we shall sup in the dining room, while Natalie and I become better acquainted." Lowering her voice, she confided, "My old chef, Pietro, will have apoplexy if we are late for the first course."

"Is that your latest vision, Nonna?" Ryder teased. "Your Florentine cook expiring in the kitchen over cold, abandoned soup?"

"That is a certainty if we do not proceed with haste," came her rueful reply.

Francesca led them into the oak-paneled dining room, to an Empire table lit with gleaming Boulton candelabra and set with the finest Irish linen, Baccarat crystal, and Florentine china. Ryder seated his grandmother at the head of the table, and Natalie opposite him along the table's flank.

After Francesca returned thanks, two liveried footmen served up the sumptuous feast prepared by Francesca's Italian cook—seafood soup, followed by braised pigeon, roasted potatoes with sage and rosemary, and eggplant flavored with herbs. A different wine accompanied each delectable course, and soon Natalie was feeling mellow and content as she and Ryder chatted with Francesca. Ryder's grandmother managed to learn much about Natalie's background without seeming to pry, and Natalie felt drawn to the witty, gracious woman.

Her own warm feelings toward Francesca were obviously returned. Soon the countess turned to Ryder, tapped his arm, and asked feelingly, "So, my grandson, when are you going to marry this jewel?"

He grinned sheepishly. "Actually, Natalie and I were touching on that possibility in your front garden." He winked at her. "What exactly did you have to say on the subject, darling? Something about the price being too dear?"

Francesca turned to Natalie, whose face was flaming. "What did this rascal do?" As Natalie's blush deepened, Francesca lifted a slim, beringed hand. "Never mind. Now I am being a meddlesome old woman."

"No, not at all, Countess," Natalie put in diplomatically, while shooting Ryder a quick, fuming glance. "Your grandson has been very helpful toward me over the past weeks. But actually, right now I am rather preoccupied with my obligations—such as a lost aunt."

"Ryder told me." Francesca scowled and laid a slim finger alongside her jaw. "The aunt will be found soon, I think."

"Really?" Natalie asked with wide-eyed fascination.

Francesca appeared perplexed. "Ryder did not tell you about my vision?"

Natalie glared at him again. "No."

Ryder offered her a conciliatory smile. "Darling, Nonna had a feeling your aunt could be in danger. I didn't want to alarm you."

"Oh, yes," Natalie said angrily, "you like to reserve all the danger for yourself." She turned intently to Francesca. "Do you get any other feeling about my aunt?"

Staring at Natalie in compassion, Francesca shook her head and patted the girl's hand. "I am sorry, my dear. But do not fret. I'm sure your aunt will appear in due course. Let us speak more about you and my grandson." Her eyes sparkling with merriment, she inclined her head toward Ryder, then asked Natalie conspiratorially, "Perhaps if he will promise to grow up, you will marry him?"

Natalie could only laugh.

"He is a fine boy," Francesca added, "and I know he will come around in time."

If I don't strangle him first, Natalie said to herself, smiling at Francesca.

The rest of the meal passed pleasantly, but over dessert, Francesca turned reflective. Setting down her fork, she gazed at Ryder and said soberly, "My dear grandson, there is something I've been meaning to tell you for years now." She nodded fondly toward Natalie. "And I would like your young lady to hear this as well, since you are obviously so special to each other."

Although Natalie blushed, Ryder stared straight at her. "Aye, so we are."

After a momentary hesitation, Francesca confided, "On the night your mother died, I had a vision."

Ryder tensed, setting down his brandy and sitting up straight in his chair. "Yes, Nonna?"

A terrible sadness etched Francesca's features. "It pains me to tell you this, but I fear your mother's death was not an accident." Closing her eyes in intense concentration, she went on. "I saw hands—cruel hands—shoving my daughter off London Bridge into the freezing Thames."

Ryder and Natalie exchanged alarmed glances; then he said, "But perhaps you mean the thieves—"

"No, no, the robbery was only a ruse," Francesca cut in, shaking her head. She opened her eyes and stared starkly at Ryder. "The true motive was Carlotta's murder."

There was a moment of stunned silence as Francesca's dire words reverberated through the room. "But—but that is terrible, Nonna," Ryder said at last, his expression deeply troubled. "If it could be true, why didn't you tell me at the time?"

Francesca's expression was fraught with anguish and regret. "Oh, my grandson, I could not. Not while you were so torn apart by grief. How could I add to your burdens then?"

"But why have you chosen to tell me now?"

Francesca sighed heavily. "Because lately, the visions keep returning. And all my instincts tell me that the danger has not passed."

Both Natalie and Ryder were lost in thought as they were driven away from Francesca's home. He in particular felt rent with torment over the possibilities Francesca had raised. Good heavens, to think that his mother might have been murdered!

And what had Nonna meant when she said the danger had not ended? Could he and Natalie face additional perils here besides the smugglers? Was there a murderer still lurking about who might do them harm? A disturbing mosaic was forming in Ryder's mind, and he did not at all like the way it was shaping up.

Natalie's thoughts were obviously equally unsettled. She regarded him with keen empathy and sighed. "Oh, Ryder, if what your grandmother said tonight is true . . . Have her visions been accurate before?"

His nod was solemn. "I remember an incident that occurred when I was a child. One of Nonna's scullery maids was found dead—stabbed—in the root cellar. On the night it happened, Nonna had a vision of the girl being knifed by her lover. She related the details to the Bow Street Runners, and the information led them not only to the murder weapon, hidden in a squalid alleyway in the Isle of Dogs, but also to the responsible party—who then confessed and was later hanged at Tyburn."

"Good heavens! How uncanny."

Ryder's brow was creased in a deep scowl. "So if Nonna thinks my mother was murdered, then she most likely was."

"But who . . . ?" Carefully, Natalie added, "You can't suspect your father."

"Nor can I eliminate him," Ryder returned grimly.

"Oh, Ryder. I'm so sorry." Natalie reached out to touch his hand.

He was silent, but squeezed her fingers. He wished desper-

ately that they could be alone, but too many problems stood
in the way tonight.

After a moment, she admonished him. "You know, you really should have told me about your grandmother's vision
concerning Aunt Love."

"Natalie, it would only have worried you, and you know it.
Besides, from what Nonna said tonight, the danger could now
well be over for your aunt."

She laughed mirthlessly. "I think your grandmother was
only trying to humor me there."

"We'll find her, love. For now, I must get you home"—he
raked his gaze over her slowly and sighed—"even though I
wish this evening didn't have to end."

Natalie glanced away, feeling unnerved yet treacherously
aroused by his words.

His voice came low and seductive. "Do you feel it, too,
love?"

Did she indeed! "Ryder, please stop torturing me about it!"
she said helplessly.

"Now I'm torturing you?"

Her gaze beseeched him. "You know there's no future in it.
And I could even become pregnant—"

"Are you?" he demanded with sudden intensity.

She glanced away again, embarrassed as she recalled how
that particular anxiety had been relieved right before they arrived in London. "No."

"And you think I wouldn't be willing to accept the responsibility of that risk?" he asked darkly. "My, you really do
think I'm a cad, don't you?"

She clenched her fists in her lap. "I think—as you well
know—that we will never suit. And why risk subjecting an
innocent child to our own miseries?"

"Like your parents did to you?"

She was silent.

He reached out to pat her hand, but spoke ironically.
"Don't worry, my dear. You are safe tonight. There's somewhere else I must be."

"And where is that?" she inquired, suddenly angered.

A mask closed over his features. "If I told you, you would
only fret needlessly, and you might even end up jeopardizing
your own safety."

"I am sick and tired of your shutting me out!" she flared.
"I am supposed to be part of this investigation, too!"

"And I am not going to risk a hair on your lovely head."

"No, you are only going to go seek your ease with some
slut, now that I have thwarted you," she retorted in a fit of
temper.

In the darkness his voice was charged with passion.
"Natalie, if I didn't have to be somewhere else, I would demonstrate to you —*now*—just how wrong that statement is."

She struggled to overcome her own wayward longings.
"Ryder, please . . . I know it has been a difficult evening for
us both. Just take me home."

He did, but when he left her, he felt as frustrated as he
perversely hoped she was.

Half an hour later, Ryder was striding along a filthy, familiar alleyway in Stepney. Squinting through the foggy darkness, he navigated past rubbish and slops, foraging cats and
dogs. He could hear the raucous sounds of a brawl spilling
out from a nearby tavern.

It had killed him to drop Natalie off just now. In truth, he
had ached to somehow whisk her away for a lovers' tryst. He
especially needed her, following the staggering revelations at
Nonna's house. Even the mentioned possibility of his getting
her pregnant had not stayed him.

Good Lord, what was happening to him? If he didn't keep
his emotions in better check, he might well end up married to
Natalie, in a union she was convinced would spell doom for
them both. Yet he couldn't stop thinking about her, wanting
her . . .

He smiled. She was trying so valiantly to resist him, to
play the proper lady again. To an extent, he couldn't blame
her; just as she had pointed out, there was no actual commitment between them. Of course, he no longer felt quite so un-
committed, and he was by no means ready to give her up.

What if she decided to let *him* go when they found her
aunt, or even sooner? Ryder glowered at the very thought. He
was not accustomed to being on the losing end of a love affair. Usually he had to pry himself away, amid histrionics and
tears. Yet it set him reeling to think of how Natalie might
simply toss her head and walk out of his life. And the fact

that he was shutting her out of his present nocturnal activities—even if for the noblest of reasons—was doubtless not improving their relationship at all. She thought he was out having a rollicking roll in some bawdy house, when he was actually mixing it up with footpads, rats, and cockroaches.

At least he and Harry seemed a bit closer to a potential breakthrough on the smuggling. Over the past few nights, they had noticed lights blinking on the second level of the factory—ghostly pools of illumination that wended their way from room to room. Something underhanded was definitely going on in there.

Stealthily approaching the facility, Ryder touched the pistol at his waist. He was determined to get at the truth of these shenanigans—and soon.

Within eyeshot of the establishment, Ryder froze at the sounds of low voices and horses snorting. He peered through the fog at three men loading crates onto a dray just outside the factory doors! He ducked into the doorway from which he and Harry normally did their surveillance. Encountering a solid object, he glanced down to see the dark outline of Harry . . . slumped against the stoop and snoring.

"Hampton!" Leaning over, he roughly shook his friend and spoke in an urgent whisper. "For heaven's sake, man, wake up. I think the smugglers are loading their booty even now."

"What's that?" Harry asked groggily, rubbing his head.

Ryder hauled Harry to his feet. "What has happened to you? Have you been into the drink?"

Harry grunted and shook his head. "Someone banged me over the head with an iron spanner, by the feel of it."

"God's teeth," Ryder gritted. "Take out your pistol. We must nab these felons—*now.*"

Both men pulled out pistols and stole into the alleyway. Meanwhile, one of the laborers was shutting the gate on the wagon jammed with crates. Ryder realized that the conveyance was surely about to move away.

So, apparently, did Harry. "Halt!" he called out. "I'll have a word with you men."

While Ryder fought an urge to throttle his impetuous friend, the driver of the dray turned and fired a shot, narrowly missing Harry and prompting both men to fling themselves facedown into the fetid street.

"Brilliant strategy, Hampton," Ryder complained as he spat out some odious substance that had splashed in his face. "Why didn't I think of such a clever remark? Damn you and your infernal impatience!"

"Sorry, old man," muttered Harry.

Ryder groaned as he heard the neighing of the horses and the dray clattering away. Then, blessed luck, he heard a frantic voice shouting, "Hey, there, lads! Wait for Mawkins!"

Ryder lurched to his feet. One of the laborers had been left behind!

Ryder tore off after the short, stout man, grabbed him by the lapel, and pressed his pistol to his jaw. "Not so fast, my friend."

"Easy, gov'nor," the portly little man said shrilly. "I ain't the one that fired at ye."

Ryder cocked his weapon. "Perhaps not, Mawkins. But you are the one who is going to talk—and plenty—and fast."

Twenty-five

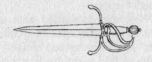

THREE HOURS LATER, RYDER WAS GROWING VERY FRUSTRATED, as well as slightly tipsy. He, Harry, and Mawkins sat in the corner of a seedy tavern not far from the Stepney factory. Although he had tried to remain sober and keep his mind on the issues at hand, he had lost count of the number of rounds of grog the other two had shared while he and Harry had "interrogated" their quarry. Now Harry was passed out, snoring, his cheek resting on the filthy, cluttered table, whereas Mawkins—a short, barrel-chested man with a craggy, whiskered face—seemed to possessed a hollow leg.

Since capturing the laborer, Ryder had learned that Mawkins was undoubtedly the most talkative man he had ever met in his life—yet the man wanted to talk about everything except the smuggling. Ryder had learned about Mawkins's three children, a wife, and widowed mother-in-law, whom he supported. Ryder had become privy to his views on everything from the king's debauchery to the plight of the working class.

"Take all these new machines," Mawkins was now expounding to Ryder. "The steam engines, printing presses and plows, and all the rest. Now, I ask you, gov'nor, have they helped the working man at all? Why, he's been driven from the land to sweat and toil in the factories, and be slaughtered at Peterloo."

"Yes indeed," Ryder replied, "and my sympathies are entirely with the working man. Now would you please—"

Ignoring Ryder, Mawkins continued. "He's been forsaken to spend his days in wretched tenements, with vermin the size of mastiffs. Why, last week, gov'nor, I almost clubbed me own son in the darkness, thinking the poor mite was a gutter rat."

"How unfortunate. But I still must know who hired you to load the wagon tonight—"

Mawkins waved his tankard. "I already told you, gov'nor. Some bloke named George—"

"George *who?*" Ryder demanded with thinning patience. "There must be a million Georges in London alone."

"Aye, could be," Mawkins agreed amiably, taking a gulp of rum. He scowled and laid a stubby finger alongside his jaw. "You know, me aunt Lucy was married to a George. George Mills. Or was it Wills?"

Ryder pounded a fist. "For the love of heaven—"

"Beat me poor aunt senseless, Uncle George did, and drank up the grocer's money. Incarcerated for his debts, he was. 'E died of gaol fever at Newgate—"

"Please, man, can't you tell me anything more?" Ryder beseeched. "There is a gold sovereign in it for you."

Mawkins beamed, revealing gaped, decaying teeth. "Ah, but you are a generous man, gov'nor. Why didn't you say so in the first place?"

"Just speak up."

"All I heard from George is, we was supposed to meet a bloke named Lawson at the docks."

"Why didn't you tell me this in the first place?" Ryder burst out in exasperation.

Mawkins shrugged. "You didn't ask, gov'nor."

During the next few nights, Ryder and Harry took turns watching the factory and making the rounds of grog shops near the harbor. They stayed in touch with Mawkins, and bribed him into their service both to seek information and to relieve their surveillance outside the Stepney facility.

Whenever possible, Ryder and Harry mingled with seedy seamen and prostitutes, trying to gain information about the man called Lawson. Although at first they tried their best to blend in with their squalid surroundings, they made little progress, since the sailors, whores, and tavern keepers they encountered tended to turn taciturn when questioned.

Ryder edged closer to success on a rather chill evening when he got involved in a game of hazard with two sailors in a punch house near the Thames. While he threw the dice, Ryder kept noticing a prostitute—a blond creature with heavily rouged lips and cheeks—eyeing him covetously from across the room. When he grinned at the buxom creature, she slinked over and settled herself on his lap, amid howls of appreciative laughter from the two other men.

"Well, hello, angel," the whore whispered, batting her eyelashes and all but purring as she looked Ryder over. "If you ain't a big, handsome fellow."

One of the sailors confided to Ryder behind his hand, "Watch out, mate, or Polly will wear ye to a stub in no time."

"Aye, she is a hot piece, that one," jeered the second seaman.

Still ogling Ryder, Polly spoke up. "Oh, I don't think we need ter fret over this cannon running short of its balls any time soon."

Amid new roars of bawdy mirth from the men, Ryder grinned back at the wench while inwardly grinding his teeth. He did not at all relish having the pockmarked whore on his lap, or smelling her cloying perfume, which did little to mask her more offensive body odor. But he was aware that he needed to project a certain cavalier image if he was to win the trust of these people.

Gathering up the dice, he said casually, "By the way, I've been looking for an old friend, a bloke by the name of Lawson. Any of you ever heard of him?"

The two sailors exchanged blank glances and shrugged, but Polly at once piped up as she playfully mussed Ryder's hair. "Oh, I know Lawson, dearie."

"Do you?" Ryder asked. "How can I get in touch with him?"

She grinned, looked him over again, and licked her painted lips. "Come outside with Polly, angel, and maybe I'll tell you."

While the sailors chuckled, Ryder told Polly, "You go ahead, love, and I shall join you shortly."

She smirked, got up, and strutted out of the tavern.

Ryder raised an eyebrow to the other men. "Do you think she knows anything?"

Grinning, one of them replied, "She knows she wants to ride your prick, mate!"

Irritated, Ryder said, "Aye—but does the wench know any-thing about Lawson?"

"There's only one way to find out, friend," taunted the other, and both men laughed ribaldly.

Ryder hadn't been aware that Natalie was sitting across from him in the tavern, watching him. Dressed in a plain black frock and a wide-brimmed black hat, her features obscured by its veil, she had been scrutinizing his activities for some time—and seething with anger and jealousy.

Over the past days, she had become increasingly maddened by Ryder's continuing absences. She knew that, in part, her concern had to do with her still-absent aunt. But she also had to admit that she had been feeling eaten up with anxiety that Ryder might indeed be out consorting with doxies in squalid London.

Tonight, she had decided to take matters into her own hands—only to have her worst fears confirmed. For there the lecher was—just as she had suspected—grinning away, with some slut bouncing on his lap. And the Jezebel was actually mussing his hair—something she herself had once done back in Charleston—making Natalie burn to charge over and claw out the trollop's eyes.

All in all, the scandalous display made Natalie all but crazed with jealousy. She mused ruefully that now she could understand how agitated Ryder must have felt in Charleston when he had been impelled to watch her tease other men at the tavern.

Beside Natalie sat her father's coachman, Timothy, whom she had convinced, under duress, to accompany her. Timothy had been Natalie's friend since childhood, and she trusted him. The manservant also liked and respected Aunt Love, and when Natalie had related the story of Love's disappearance and explained how she needed to investigate, he had agreed, albeit reluctantly, to escort her out tonight for the widow's sake. Still, it could not be more apparent that Timothy highly disapproved of Natalie's choice of surroundings as he sat next to her with a huge scowl creasing his thick-featured face. He had not even bothered to remove his cloak, hat, or gloves, and his quirt was clutched menacingly in one hand.

"I tell you, miss, this is no place for a lady to be," he whispered tensely, for at least the dozenth time. "And I fail to understand why we are shadowing Lord Newbury. Why, the man is so obviously a seasoned rakehell—gambling and flirting with prostitutes."

Natalie ground her jaw as she observed Ryder gathering the dice, with the preening whore still on his lap. "I realize as much. But I'm also aware that Lord Newbury is on the trail of the very smugglers who may know my aunt's whereabouts."

Timothy threw up his hands. "None of this makes any sense to me, I tell you. And I surely belong in Bedlam for allowing you to convince me to bring you to this den of iniquity."

Even as he spoke, a drunken character tottered past their table, leering at Natalie. "How 'bout a jig, girlie?"

Timothy stood. Massively built and well over six feet tall, the coachman radiated a menacing height and girth. "How about a swim in the Thames, mate?" he snapped.

At once, the wild-eyed drunk staggered off. Timothy nodded in grim satisfaction and resumed his seat.

Distracted by the incident, Natalie glanced across the smoky tavern, only to watch the prostitute slither off Ryder's lap and leave. Her relief was short-lived, however, as a moment later, she watched Ryder don his cloak, hat, and gloves, and follow the creature out of the tavern.

"Excuse me for a moment, Timothy," Natalie said sharply, getting to her feet.

But he was also up like a shot, grabbing her arm. "Oh, no, you don't, miss. Not without me."

"Very well."

In the foggy street outside the tavern, Ryder was peering around the deserted area for the prostitute, who now seemed to have vanished into thin air. He spotted a shadowy figure in the distance and was striding toward it when a shot rang out, and he felt the bullet whiz by close to his ear!

Ryder didn't even have time to utter a curse. For the second time in just a week, he flung himself onto the repugnant, slimy street. Minus his hat, he looked up and glimpsed the person who had assaulted him, a fleeing silhouette outlined in the wavering glow of a street lamp. The figure was cloaked in black and wore a familiar, low-brimmed black hat.

"Stop, you bloody bastard!" he yelled.

Ryder sprang up and tore after his assailant. He raced along alleyways, sidestepping garbage, dodging drunkards, and avoiding scurrying night creatures. Relentlessly he pursued his quarry through a maze of twists and turns in the smelly, shabby slums of Stepney.

Then, as he rounded a corner at full speed, he was stopped dead in his tracks by an explosion of pain as he was struck a mighty blow to his midsection with a club or a nightstick—

Reeling with agony, the breath knocked from his lungs, Ryder crashed to the street. Catching his breath with a tortured gasp, he barely managed to glance up; again he spotted the familiar cloak and hat, and watched his shadowy assailant flee. Then he heard footsteps approach from behind him, and wondered if the villain had somehow circled around to finish him off.

"Well, I hope you are proud of yourself," said a familiar voice filled with disgust.

"Natalie." Grunting, Ryder somehow managed to roll over and sit up. Torment racked him anew. His ribs felt as if they had been crushed beneath the wheels of a carriage. He glowered up in bemusement to see Natalie hovering over him, dressed all in black and wearing a veil. A scowling coachman stood beside her. "What in hell are you doing here?" he uttered weakly.

"What are *you* doing in the street?" she retorted. "Did you have too much to drink, or is this how you prepare to entertain your lady friends?"

"Damn it, do I look like I'm entertaining someone?" came his exasperated response.

"Timothy, help Lord Newbury up," Natalie continued briskly. "Obviously, the poor wretch knows no better than to put himself at the mercy of prostitutes and ruffians."

Timothy leaned over, grabbed Ryder beneath his arms, and hauled him, groaning, to his feet. "Let us get you home, your lordship."

"By all means," Ryder barely managed to force out.

Somehow, he endured the painful trek to Natalie's carriage. Glancing at her walking beside him, with her fists clenched and her jaw tight, he knew she was furious.

Well, he was angrier still that she had exposed herself to such peril!

Timothy assisted them both into the gleaming black coach and climbed onto the driver's bench. A moment later, the conveyance clattered off. The tension was thick enough to cut as Ryder and Natalie sat in opposite seats, glaring at each other in the darkness.

"All right, Natalie, we may as well have it out," he said heatedly. "And then I'm going to wear out your posterior for your reckless conduct tonight."

"*I* behaved recklessly?" she cried, flinging back her veil. "How dare you even say such a thing following your own reprehensible behavior?"

Grimacing, he tore off his slime-encrusted gloves. "What reprehensible behavior?"

"Drinking, gambling, flirting with prostitutes—and *enjoying* yourself!—while Aunt Love's very life hangs in the balance."

"Ah, yes," he snapped, stifling a new moan of misery. "I was having a grand time dodging bullets and getting my ribs pummeled."

"Don't give me that balderdash! I saw no bullets and no attackers. You were probably just passed out from drink in that filthy alleyway—"

"I was no such thing!"

"And furthermore, I watched you follow that *hussy* outside—"

"She had offered me information—"

"Information about what?" Natalie demanded.

"The smuggling."

"You are lying."

"Fine. In that case, I feel no obligation to tell you anything I know."

All at once, Natalie became riveted to his every word. "What did that creature tell you?"

"Nothing," he retorted in disgust. "She disappeared before I could question her. Then you obviously arrived too late to watch the bullet sail past my ear, or to see me chasing the cloaked figure that fired at me."

"I saw no cloaked figure!"

"Thank God," he uttered feelingly. "One of us nearly getting killed tonight was bad enough."

Natalie paused, a needle of doubt prickling her. "Someone actually tried to shoot you?"

"Yes, and he then proceeded to pummel my ribs with a club."

Natalie was feeling even more uncertain. "You really got hurt?"

Ryder rolled his eyes. "What in hell have I been telling you? After I was shot at, I chased the villain through the alleys, and then, when I rounded a curb, he brought me down with a nightstick."

She stared at him skeptically. "Open your shirt."

At once, maddeningly, he grinned. "Why, my lady—"

"Don't get impudent with me!" she snapped. "This examination will be strictly clinical."

"Ah, yes—strictly." Pulling a wry face, he shrugged off his cloak, then popped open several buttons.

"Oh, my God." Natalie winced aloud, her expression crestfallen as she viewed the massive purple bruise that was already rising across Ryder's beautiful chest. "You did get battered!"

"Aye!" he agreed bitterly. "And I could use a little comfort from you, woman, rather than all these unjust accusations."

She smiled at him crookedly. "If I come over there and soothe you, will you promise not to thrash me?"

"Natalie, right now, wrestling you down and giving you your just deserts would cause me unspeakable agony. But if you attempt such a stunt again, no promises."

She slid into the seat beside him. "So you weren't flirting with that prostitute?"

That infuriating grin lit up his face again. "Jealous minx, aren't you?"

"Answer my question or I shall throttle you."

He whistled. "The question?"

She spoke through gritted teeth. "Did you lust after that Cyprian?"

"Be serious, Natalie. She smelled."

"But—why did you follow her outside?"

"I already told you. She offered information on the smuggling."

"Do you suppose she is involved with the ring?"

Though Ryder had his own distinct suspicions, he was not about to share these with Natalie. "I really have no idea."

She shot him a narrowed glance. "You must tell me everything you have learned."

"No," came his obdurate response. "You'll only get yourself into deep trouble."

Her patience snapped. "Then it is acceptable for you to behave recklessly, but not for me?"

He put his arm around her and grunted from the pain. His grin was forced. "You have it exactly right, love."

"I really do think you enjoy such foolhardy pursuits," she flared bitterly. "I'm not sure you even care whether or not we find Aunt Love. You simply cannot be happy unless you are out confronting danger, flirting with doxies, and clashing with disreputable elements."

He gripped her chin and forced her mutinous face up to his. "Natalie, so far this night has brought me not a whit of pleasure. But all that is about to change. Will you kindly shut up and give me the comfort you promised?"

Fighting a smile, she leaned over and gave his bruise a quick, desultory peck—which only left him hauling her closer and kissing her thoroughly. She moaned with pleasure as he explored her mouth boldly with his tongue. It suddenly seemed forever since they had shared such sweet intimacy. She heard him grunt with more than pain as he stroked her breast. She tired to stay his hand, but he only clutched her fingers tightly to his heart.

He spoke hoarsely. "Tell me, Natalie, when you thought I wanted another woman tonight, did it excite you, make you jealous?"

"I—"

"Tell the truth, Natalie."

"Yes," she admitted shamelessly.

"Shall I let you in on a secret?"

"What?"

He chuckled as he stared down at her expectant face. "I'm not sure I should tell you. It will give you a lot of power, you know."

Now she grinned. "That I would like. Tell me."

He shocked and titillated her all the more when he drew

her fingers boldly lower, to his teeming erection. "Only you can do this to me."

Natalie groaned. She knew she was behaving quite recklessly, that she should pull away at once. She half feared he was lying to her. Yet, feeling the rigid proof of his passion in her fingers, she could only think of how long it had been since they had loved, how badly she wanted him—a yearning that only burned brighter when he again seized her lips in a smoldering kiss. Wantonly, she stroked him, felt him grow even harder at her touch, and imagined that delicious shaft deep inside her. Her mouth would have gone dry except for the hot, wet stroking of his tongue.

Growing extremely agitated, Ryder reached out to pull down the shades in the conveyance. "How long before we are home? At least half an hour, don't you think?"

"Ryder, you can't mean . . ."

He heaved a convulsive breath and caressed her lower belly. "It's been too long, darling."

Natalie was losing ground fast, desperately trying to hold on to some fragment of reason. "Ryder, please, I'm not pregnant—yet."

He chuckled, a low, sensual sound. "You should never say that to a man, darling. It's an irresistible challenge."

"Ryder—"

Despite her protests, as he trailed his scorching lips down her neck, unbuttoned her bodice, and murmured endearments, Natalie felt herself being swept away by the potent emotions welling inside her. She felt out of control, starved for him. Her jealousy had started it all, no doubt, and the atmosphere of danger and excitement that had enveloped them tonight had only further heightened her desires.

Ah, how easily she succumbed to the madness this rogue inspired! And would it be such a sin to give in to those sweet feelings one last time—especially when she quite possibly loved him?

Oh, she surely did! She leaned over and began gently kissing his bruises.

"Ah, love, that is heaven," he murmured thickly.

She ran her tongue over his turgid nipples, slowly tantalizing him. He tangled a hand in her hair and hauled her lips back up to his. Their mouths met and fused, igniting fierce longings in them both. She clung to him as heat racked her with an intensity that made her light-headed.

"It's as if we haven't loved for ages, darling," he whispered into her ear. "I'm bursting for you."

"I know," she murmured achingly. "I can't seem to help myself, either."

Now his voice came rough with emotion as he slipped his hand inside her dress and caressed her bare breast. "Do you think I have no conscience, Natalie? Do you think I don't know 'twould be best to let you go? Well, I know it, love, but I still crave you too much to do it."

His words and touch were so electrifying, Natalie was beyond insanity. She shuddered and ran her lips over his face.

He caught her under the arms, struggled to raise her, then moaned in misery. "Sit in my lap, love. I can't lift you."

Embarrassed, she stammered. "Can you—do the rest?"

A wicked chuckle escaped him. "Aye, with some assistance from you, my lady—and until neither of us can move."

Reeling with desire, she eagerly straddled him. Within seconds, Ryder had finished unbuttoning her bodice and began pulling her skirts up, her drawers down. As she quivered against him, he took the tip of her breast into his mouth and nibbled gently, while stroking between her thighs with his fingers. He teased her with light flicks of his fingers, and then, as she moved against him, he grew more bold. She was panting, almost sobbing with the delight of it. He pressed his face deeply into her bare breasts and burrowed two fingers inside her—

She bucked wildly. He held her tighter. She whimpered with pleasure and dug her fingers into his shoulders. An exquisite moment later, his fingers left her, and she made a small, bereft sound that ended in a squeal of pleasure as she absorbed the full length of him.

"Oh, heavens," she gasped, feeling him so splendid, big, and unyielding inside her, and wondering if she would ever be able to breathe again.

"Move your hips, darling," he rasped. "Don't be shy."

Looking up to meet his burning gaze, she began to move against him, at first with almost maidenly restraint, and then with a woman's raw need. Ryder groaned, locked his forearms at the small of her back, and kissed her fiercely. The coupling might not have been punishment for her, but for Ryder, it was hell. His ribs were a blaze of misery, and not being able to plunder her delicious body as thoroughly as he pleased was equal torture. Yet, rocking with her this way, slowly, deeply, thoroughly, brought a sense of intensely frustrating, feverish delight. His heart roared in his ears, his breath came in excruciating gasps, and every ounce of his being became centered on seeking the exquisite pleasure of release.

Then she began to gasp frantically, to roll and grind her hips—

At last he decided she needed to share equally in the torment. But it was a distinct sob of pleasure he heard bursting from her as he pinned her in his lap and, with a rampage of rapacious thrusts, spent himself with agonizing ecstasy inside her . . .

Natalie shuddered and clung to Ryder, after experiencing a climax that had jolted her as well. Oh, God, what had she done? Given herself once more to a man whom she knew was wrong for her!

But right now, being close to Ryder like this, being cherished against his hammering heart, Natalie simply felt too good to care.

At the sound of a fist banging on his desk, John Lynch glanced up to see a grim-faced Ryder Remington looming over him.

"Why, Lord Newbury. What can I do for you?" he inquired with an air of boredom.

"I think you did quite enough last night," came Ryder's vehement response.

"What do you mean?"

"You know damn well what I mean, you bloody miscreant." Ryder strode over to the wall, pulled a black cloak and hat off their pegs, brought the items over, and tossed them before Lynch. "Someone wearing these garments fired a shot at me last night, battered me with a club, and damn near killed me."

Lynch raised a thin brow and regarded his caller emotionlessly. "It was not I, Lord Newbury."

"Are these items yours?" Ryder asked furiously.

"Of course." Lynch laughed cynically. "But do you actually think I am the only gentleman in London who owns such a hat and cloak?"

Ryder grabbed him by his collar. "I know damn well it was you who accosted me. Got too close to you smuggling game, didn't I?"

Lynch's expression was coolly remote. "And I tell you, Lord Newbury, I still have no idea what you are talking about. Furthermore, my wife will confirm that I was home with her last night."

Feeling extremely frustrated, Ryder shoved the man away and straightened. "Try a trick like that again and I'll kill you."

Lynch fought a deprecatory smile. "It appears to me that you received the worst end of things, Lord Newbury. Perhaps you should take care for your own safety.

Ryder's expression grew murderous. "Is that a threat, Mr. Lynch?"

"Not at all. Merely a friendly observation."

Ryder shook a fist at him. "I shall be prepared next time, you bloody bastard. And I shall catch you at your own game."

"I'm sure I have no idea what you mean." Lynch stood up. "Is there anything else?"

"Yes. I see that you are still employing children here. I have now arranged for all of them to attend a school sponsored by the West End Beneficent Society. Have you increased the wages for the other workers as I requested?"

At last, anger sparked in Lynch's steely eyes. "I will make no such changes without first hearing from your father."

"You shall hear from the duke—and you may very well find yourself in need of a new post," Ryder retorted.

He turned and exited the office. He was rounding a corner when he bumped up against Essie Lynch. With a grunt of pain, he stepped back.

He tipped his hat and spoke in strained tones. "Mrs. Lynch."

Holding a wicker basket, Essie eyed him curiously. "I was just bringing John his meal."

"Can you tell me where your husband was last night?"

Essie's expression grew guarded. "Why, he was at home with me, of course."

"How cozy." Grimacing and pressing a hand to his sore torso, Ryder moved on.

"Oh, Lord Newbury?" Essie called.

He turned to her. "Yes?"

"You move so stiffly," she muttered, looking him over. "I do hope you haven't hurt yourself somehow."

Ryder stared at Essie intently for a moment, but could discern no untoward meaning behind her words. "Thank you for your kindly concern," he snapped.

He turned and left her, his features knitted in a fierce scowl.

Twenty-six

RYDER SPENT THE NEXT FEW DAYS TRACKING DOWN LEADS ON the smuggler named Lawson. Along with Harry and Mawkins, he enlisted three old London friends—James Hutton, Samuel Brandon, and Hugh Channing—in his cause. The men spent their nights either watching the Stepney factory or frequenting the taverns in the harbor district in order to ferret out additional clues on the smuggling ring.

At times Ryder regretted his direct confrontation with John Lynch about the smuggling. His appearance at Lynch's office had certainly afforded him no answers. At the same time, it was doubtful he had really tipped his hand to Lynch; obviously the scoundrel was aware that Ryder was investigating the Stepney plant, or he never would have attacked him outside the tavern. Thankfully, ever since Ryder had interrogated Lynch, no further assaults on his person had occurred, which made him even more convinced that Lynch was involved.

When Ryder was with Natalie, he sensed a new level of longing and sweetness between them, but he also sensed an underlying tension and doubt. He realized that she, like he, must be constantly remembering their torrid encounter in the carriage and wondering what it meant. He found himself in the impossible position of still not being able to express his feelings to her, while remaining equally determined not to let her go. For this reason, he could well understand her frustration with him.

Given his ongoing nightly absences, Natalie continued to accuse him of withholding information from her, though he steadfastly argued that his reticence was only for her own good. He frequently warned her that she must not again subject herself to danger, but she steadfastly avowed that she would do whatever was necessary to find Aunt Love and expose the smuggling ring. Thus, Ryder worried constantly about what outrageous thing she might do next.

He made another breakthrough on a cool night later in April. He was sitting in a grog shop not far from the Thames when Sam Brandon came in, leading a tawdry prostitute with flaming hair, rouged cheeks, and a lewd amount of bosom spilling from her low-cut gown. Sam was grinning from ear to ear, and the buxom whore also boasted a smug smile on her red mouth.

"Ryder," Sam greeted him, "Pearl here has some information on Lawson."

"Do you, now, love?" Ryder asked, smiling at the creature as she and Sam took their seats.

The whore looked Ryder over with an expression of avid lust. "Aye, darlin', but first a bit of the grog might help wet me whistle," she said in a heavy Cockney accent.

"Whatever you say." Ryder motioned to a barmaid to bring a pitcher.

"Aye, that is much better," the whore said a few moments later, after taking a healthy draught.

"What do you know about Lawson?" Ryder asked her.

The woman glanced at Sam, then winked at Ryder. "I hear there's a half sovereign in it for me, lovey."

Ryder took a gold coin from his purse and laid it on the table. As the whore reached out to snatch it, he covered the coin with his palm. "Not so fast. The information first, if you please."

She looked him over greedily. "As handsome as you are, lovey, perhaps we can make us another arrangement."

"Unfortunately, I am already taken," Ryder replied. "But my gold isn't—so far."

The whore laughed raucously and took another gulp of grog. "You wouldn't be meaning to harm old Lawson, now would you, lovey? Him and me is friends, in a manner of speaking, if you know what I mean."

Ryder grinned. "I only have business with the man."

Seemingly satisfied, the whore confided, "Well, lovey, all

I know is, old Lawson is sailing for the Colonies tomorrow night."

"Where is his ship docked?" Ryder demanded.

The woman frowned for a moment, then snapped her fingers. "At the West India Docks, as I recall."

Grinning at Sam, Ryder lifted his fingers, and the whore snatched up the coin.

The next evening, Ryder and his cronies gathered at a filthy, cluttered dock in an area in the East End of London ignominiously known as the Isle of Dogs. The five men were crouched behind a pile of crates, and Ryder mused that even a dog should not venture forth in this odious part of town. The wharves were strewn with refuse, broken crates, and barrels. The air stank of garbage, mold, and fetid water. A nearby garbage bin reeked of its contents of rotten fish. Already Ryder and his cohorts had been compelled to chase off at least a dozen fat rats and a couple of mongrel cats that had rudely sought to share their hiding place.

The area was one of sooty Georgian warehouses and sagging piers jammed with various vessels. Two drunken sailors were staggering along the docks through the curling fog, singing a chantey at the top of their lungs, while just beyond them, a crew of scruffy roustabouts was loading crates onto a frigate.

But Ryder's interest was focused on the sloop that was moored at the pier just beyond their hiding place, the vessel that a dock worker had informed him was Lawson's ship. Yellowed light winked at them from the gray decks of the craft. Sounds of revelry, including high-pitched feminine laughter, kept drifting out from midships. While Ryder could see little through the fog, he was certain the crew must be having a farewell party as they waited for the tide to roll out.

"What are we going to do—sit here and watch the ship all night long?" Harry asked impatiently.

"Surely they have loaded all their cargo, or they wouldn't be celebrating now," said Hugh.

"The old salt I questioned said high tide will be at midnight," Ryder replied. He pulled out his pocket watch. "That gives us two more hours."

"But why are we waiting?" demanded an exasperated James.

"From the sounds of the voices, I've estimated the crew at twelve or more," Ryder said, "which means we are clearly outnumbered. Let them have a few more rounds of rum before we try to apprehend them. We shall need every advantage we can get."

The men grumbled, obviously growing impatient with their lack of activity and the cramped hiding place.

"Damn it to hell!" Harry cried in a disgusted voice.

"What now?" Ryder asked.

"I've just had to skewer another rat. This one was bigger than my aunt Matilda. Well, I've had quite enough, Newbury. I'm going to sneak on board and investigate these smugglers. The rest of you, cover me."

"Harry, no!" Ryder insisted.

But his plea came too late. Hampton was already charging up the ramp with his saber drawn. Meanwhile, a bearded sailor, who was obviously doing sentry duty on the sloop, started toward him with his musket raised.

"I say! What goes on there?" Harry called imperiously.

Ryder groaned. Why did Hampton always have to be such a damned hothead? A moment later, he watched Harry's hat sail off with the force of a musket shot.

Hearing the sentry call out a frantic alert to the others on board, Ryder urgently motioned to his cronies. "Come on, lads! Time to save Hampton from his own stupidity!"

The four men stormed the gangplank, their swords drawn. Within seconds, a dozen angry smugglers, accompanied by a throng of shrieking prostitutes, swarmed down upon them, the men swinging swords and roaring curses.

Locking sabers with a barrel-chested seaman who was bellowing blasphemies, Ryder felt as if they had all landed in the jaws of hell.

"I tell you, Miss Natalie, I don't like this. Not at all."

"Hush, now, Timothy. Do you want to find Aunt Love or not?"

A block away, Natalie was heading toward the pier with Timothy. Under protest, he had taken her out again to follow Ryder. She was now convinced that he knew a lot that he wasn't telling her, and she was determined to ferret out the truth.

They wended their way through a group of warehouses and emerged into the chaos of the West India Docks. The scene unfolding before them astounded her. On the cluttered docks, beneath the murky outline of a moored sloop, stretched a drunken brawl. Ryder and his cronies were battling a group of burly sailors and half-clothed prostitutes. Ryder himself towered above the others with a shrieking woman dangling from his back and beating his head with her fists, even as he attempted to swing his sword at a menacing sailor. From the way everyone was staggering around, and the horrid, slurred curses rising from the group, it was clear they all were drunk.

Oh, she should have known better! And to think she had allowed the cad to seduce her again last week, that she had believed his glib lies!

Irately, she turned to Timothy. "Oh, for heaven's sake. Lord Newbury is involved in a truly scandalous fracas this time. Go see if you can summon the River Police."

Timothy appeared horrified. "But, Miss Natalie, I cannot leave you—"

"Oh, I'll be all right. Now hurry!"

The coachman hesitated for another moment, and then, muttering a protest, he tore off down the docks. Natalie continued to watch the scene with repugnance. Ryder had managed to pitch the harlot off his back, but after he swung his sword at another sailor, the wench followed and bashed him over the head with a board. He reeled crazily for a moment, then careened back into the action. He knocked the sailor cold with the side of his sword, picked up the shrieking, flailing hussy, and heaved her into the Thames. One of the sailors jumped into the river to save the wench, and when both began to scream out frantically that they could not swim, a disgusted-looking Ryder threw up his hands and dived in after them.

"Totally disgraceful," Natalie said.

Suddenly the area teemed with men wielding nightsticks. But the River Police appeared as confused as everyone else. The guardsmen didn't seem to know whom they were supposed to corral—Ryder and his cronies, the prostitutes, or the sailors. Natalie could barely take in all the action. A watchman pounded his stick on a fist-swinging sailor, a prostitute beat on the back of the watchman, while nearby, Ryder dived into the river to rescue another floundering strumpet. Natalie watched Ryder shove the woman up onto the docks and try to climb out himself, only to have the wayward chit kick him back in.

"Shameless," Natalie muttered.

Timothy rushed back to Natalie's side and took in the scene with a look of horror. "Shall I go retrieve Lord Newbury from the Thames?" he asked her.

"Oh, let the fool fend for himself."

Ryder crawled out of the water, at which point the whore smacked him over the head with a dead mackerel. A watchman chased off the whore with his nightstick. A brawling man and woman then crashed on top of Ryder, knocking him to his knees even as he struggled to get up.

Enough! Natalie decided vehemently. With a muttered curse, she started briskly forward. Timothy quickly followed.

As they drew closer, Natalie noticed that the size of the fray had diminished considerably. She looked up to see the sloop slipping away into the night, while Ryder cursed and shook his fist at the departing vessel, and several sailors jeered back at him from its decks. By the time Natalie and Timothy arrived at the edge of the docks, only Ryder, a few of his cronies, and a couple of the prostitutes remained, with the River Police surrounding the group.

Ryder, dripping wet and battered, did not at first seem to notice Natalie standing nearby as he argued with the captain of the police. "But, Officer, my friends and I were only trying to detain the smugglers—"

"Then you should have notified us first, your lordship, or come by the Customs House," came the captain's stern response. "We don't tolerate no vigilantes here. No, sir. I don't care if you are the son of a duke—"

"Very well." Now Ryder glanced in Natalie's direction. "Natalie, what are you doing here?" he cried in astonishment.

"Spoiling your fun, obviously," she retorted.

"*You* summoned the police?"

"Aye—and with the greatest relish."

"Your lordship, will you be leveling charges against these women?" another of the watchmen asked Ryder.

Appearing thoroughly distracted, Ryder looked at the sopping-wet doxies being detained by the other watchmen. He grimaced. "Nay. Just get the maddening hussies out of here."

"Aye, your lordship."

"I assume the rest of us may take our leave?" he asked the captain while leveling a glare at Natalie. "There is a lady here whom I must see safely home."

The captain nodded. "Very well, your lordship. Just don't let it happen again."

The policemen released the whores, who hastily scampered away into the night. Moving closer to Natalie, Ryder glanced at his friends, who stood around dazedly, groaning and shaking their heads. "James, Sam, Hugh. Are all of you all right?"

"Yes, Ryder," said Sam, rubbing his bruised jaw.

"I've one hell of an ache from feeling some wench's knee in my groin," Hugh growled in pained tones, "but I suppose I shall survive."

"Someone smashed me over the head with a belaying pin," muttered an obviously dazed James, "and I am still seeing double."

"Well, enjoy it while you can," quipped Ryder. He looked around in perplexity. "My God! Where is Hampton?"

"Well, I don't know," replied Sam.

"The last time I saw him, he was being chased by a whore with a cargo hook," Hugh offered.

"Bloody hell!" Ryder swore. "We've lost Harry!"

There followed much confusion as everyone, including the River Police, Natalie, and Timothy, was enlisted to search the docks for Harry. The inspection was thorough but futile as all of them scoured the area, kicking aside debris, peering behind crates, and scanning the edges of the Thames for any sign of a body. Ryder even dived in and swam around in a fruitless attempt to find his friend.

Finally, after Ryder had crawled out of the river and the watchmen had given up and left, he strode up to Natalie and the others and said distractedly, "Good heavens, either Hampton's done in for and bobbing around somewhere in the Thames, or I'm afraid the smugglers have absconded with him."

Natalie laughed cynically. "You mean to tell me Harry may

be out there on the open seas with all those prostitutes? I'm sure he thinks he has died and gone to heaven."

"Well, for all we know, he may indeed have died and gone to heaven!" Ryder returned, distraught. "You could at least show a little more concern—"

"Forgive me if I am not feeling overly sympathetic toward you and your dissolute, brawling cronies," she snapped, although she, too, peered out worriedly at the Thames, privately aghast at the thought that Harry might have come to harm.

"Shall we go now, Miss Natalie?" put in an impatient Timothy.

Ryder spoke decisively to the coachman. "You may go on. I shall be escorting Miss Desmond home."

While Natalie rolled her eyes, Timothy glowered at Ryder. "Begging your pardon, your lordship, but I would just as soon see Miss Natalie off with Tom Jones himself."

Ryder's expression was murderous as he swung his gaze back to her. "Are you coming with me or not?"

Although his arrogance maddened her, she quickly decided they might as well have their argument now. She nodded to the coachman. "It's all right, Timothy. I trust Lord Newbury to get me home safely."

"Then you, miss, are as demented as he is."

"Please, Timothy. Go home."

Shaking his head with fierce disapproval, the coachman trudged off.

Bidding his cronies good night, Ryder escorted Natalie to a hansom cab that awaited them nearby. He handed her inside, then spoke with the driver.

As soon as they had pulled away from the docks, he took the offensive. Although she could not fully make out his features as they sat together in the darkness, his tone of voice was charged.

"Natalie, just what do you think you were doing tonight? You ruined everything when you showed up and summoned the River Police. My friends and I were about to meet with success in our investigation—"

"Hah!" she cried. "What possible connection could the debacle I just witnessed have to do with smuggling?"

"Weren't you listening when I spoke with the police?

There were smugglers on that sloop, having a farewell party with a bunch of doxies. We had it on good authority that the scoundrels were about to slip into the main pool of the Thames, their vessel loaded with smuggled cloth. Now they have gotten away—"

"And I think you are lying," she interrupted furiously.

"You *what?*"

"I think you have invented all of this nonsense about smuggling. I think you love spending your nights roaming, brawling, and wenching, and that you fabricated this tale to save yourself from embarrassment when I showed up tonight."

"Natalie, damn it, they *were* smugglers."

"Then how did you find out about them? Why do you always dodge all my questions?"

"For your own damn good."

Stubbornly, she set her arms over her chest. "Well, I do not believe you anymore."

He heaved an exasperated sigh. "Very well, then, I'll tell you. The smuggler's name is Lawson, and we learned about him from a whore in the harbor district. There—are you satisfied?"

"Just what did you have to do to persuade this whore to cooperate?" she sneered.

"I gave her a half sovereign."

Natalie's voice surged with anger. "What else did you give her?"

"I should have given her the sound thrashing I'm about to give you!" he blazed. "Surely, by now you must understand why I cannot involve you in my investigation—"

" 'Investigation.' Now, that is a ludicrous term."

"Deride all you will, but thanks to you, our first real lead has evaporated. Lawson is probably halfway out to sea, no doubt laughing himself silly over our failure, and God only knows what has happened to Harry."

She bit her lip as doubt assailed her. "I didn't like watching that whore ride around on your back," she admitted.

Abruptly, a wicked smile sculpted his lips. "You can ride it anytime you like, m'lady. Or anything else of mine you've a notion to mount." He leaned over and kissed her, pulling her fingers toward his trousers.

She jerked back and grimaced. "Eek! You reek of the Thames."

"We'll be stopping shortly and I'll get cleaned up," he muttered.

"We will be stopping? But where?"

A devilish chuckle escaped him. "Let me surprise you."

Biting back a cynical rejoinder, she removed her gloves and reached up to examine his battered jaw. She yanked her fingers away as he winced. "You really are a mess, you know."

"You don't say? Actually, I doubt there is an inch of me that hasn't been battered."

"I'm sorry," she whispered. "And we really aren't any closer to finding Aunt Love than when we began, are we?"

He was silent, but clutched her hand as the cab drew up to a modest-looking Georgian town house not far from Haymarket.

Watching Ryder hop out of the conveyance, Natalie was bemused. "What are we doing here?"

He took her hand and helped her out. "Ah, but that is the surprise." He reached out, tugging down her veil to cover her face.

"Is it such a surprise that I must hide my face?"

He laughed. "I should certainly advise that you do so."

"But why—"

"Patience, love."

Ryder knocked on the door, and momentarily, a pretty, middle-aged woman in a rose-colored satin gown opened it. "Why, Lord Newbury! We haven't seen the likes of you since you came here ages ago with Lord Brummell."

"Good evening, Favor," Ryder answered, leaning over to peck the woman's cheek. "May my friend and I come in?"

The woman glanced rudely at Natalie, then smiled at Ryder. "Why, of course. Most of our gents don't feel obliged to bring along their own entertainment, you know. But do get inside before you catch your death in the night air."

Ryder towed a scowling Natalie through the portal.

The plump Favor wrinkled her nose as she looked him over in the wan light. "Blessed Saint Bridget, what happened to you tonight, lovey? You look and smell as if you've been dunked in the Thames."

"I have." Ryder handed the woman a gold coin. "I am in need of a room—and a bath."

"Why, certainly, lovey." Favor rustled closer and preened at him. "Is there anything else we can do to please you?"

He coughed awkwardly. "No, thank you. The room, please?"

She sighed in obvious disappointment and pointed toward the stairs. "Upstairs, first door on the right. I'll send the girls up with hot water."

"You are sure the room is vacant?" he asked meaningfully.

She giggled. "Aye, you big rascal."

"Thank you, Favor."

Ryder tugged Natalie down the hallway. Hearing the sounds of giggles, she glanced into a poorly lit, opulent drawing room and saw, to her horror, several scantily attired creatures sitting on the laps of fashionably dressed dandies. Her eyes grew even larger as Ryder urged her up the stairs past garish, crimson-flocked wallpaper and scandalous art depicting half-naked women with blissfully ribald expressions on their painted faces.

He led her inside a room with a large bed covered with a red velvet counterpane—and a huge, gilt-edged mirror hanging directly above it.

"This is a brothel!" she cried.

He threw back his head and laughed. "Did you expect us to stop off at the Abbey for a bath at this time of night?"

"But why must you—"

"Nonna frequently stays up late. I can't go home in my current disgraceful state and risk giving her apoplexy." He stepped closer and pulled her against him. "Besides, I don't at all mind being alone with you."

She shoved him away. "In a *brothel?*"

Further discussion was postponed by a rap on the door. Ryder opened it, and three grinning, younger prostitutes, all of whom resembled the voluptuous Favor, strutted in bearing buckets of steaming water.

"Hello, Ryder, lovey," preened the first, eyeing him greedily.

"Hello, Felicity," he murmured.

"Why haven't you come round to see us, dearie?" pouted the second, who batted her eyelashes at him.

Ryder winked at a glowering Natalie and answered the woman. "I've become a smitten man, Modesty."

"So we see, handsome," said a third woman as she tossed a hostile glance toward Natalie.

"Sorry, Comfort," he replied, "but I must say you ladies don't appear to be suffering for my absence."

"Ah, darlin', you are wrong," Felicity protested, licking her lips as she ogled him. "We have all of us been pining away for you—haven't we, girls?"

The whores erupted into a chorus of laments.

Natalie endured the humiliation as the strumpets flirted with Ryder throughout several more trips with hot water, until the tub was at last filled. From the lustful glances the wenches cast at Ryder—and the resentful looks they tossed her way—it was clear that all of these harlots had previously shared his bed.

After the women left, Natalie charged on him furiously. "You have actually consorted with those—those loathsome creatures?"

"Long ago, love," he assured her as he unbuttoned his shirt.

"Where did they get their ridiculous names?"

He chuckled. "A family tradition, I presume. Favor opened the brothel. Modesty, Felicity, and Comfort are her nieces, who later joined her."

Natalie's expression was one of sheer repugnance. "Oh, the very thought! Corrupting one's own nieces! And to think that you have—"

"Not anymore," he cut in vehemently, shrugging off his shirt and eyeing the steaming tub covetously. "Now, why don't you come over and scrub my back?" He grinned. "If you're a really good girl, maybe I won't spank you after all."

"Why don't you go to the devil!"

He chuckled and stripped off the remainder of his clothing. As much as she wanted to kill him, Natalie could not take her eyes off his glorious body as he stepped into the bath. He was all flawless tanned muscle and smooth flesh. She even felt a stab of sympathy, watching him settle his stiff body into the tub and seeing him wince from the pain the movement brought.

A moment later, another knock sounded. Natalie stormed

to the door, cracked it open, and glowered at Felicity, who stood smirking in the hallway.

"What is it now?" Natalie demanded.

"Auntie Favor says if you'll give us his lordship's clothes, she will rouse the maid to scrub them and hang them by the kitchen fire to dry."

"Splendid." Natalie grabbed Ryder's foul-smelling garments and all but hurled them at Felicity.

She slammed the door shut to the sound of Ryder's insufferable laughter. "Still angry at me, are you, love?" he called.

She whirled around and tore off her hat and veil. "What do you think? I can't believe you have had the gall to bring me to this sleazy bordello—not to mention flaunting your former doxies in my face."

He winked at her solemnly. "But you're forgetting our secret, aren't you?"

She harrumphed. "You are so obviously a man who *loves* to share his secrets."

"Especially with you," he teased her. Then, as she continued to glare, he added silkily, *"Only* with you."

Fighting the scandalous tug on her senses, Natalie snapped back, "That I shall believe when I see it."

"Is my lady begging for a demonstration, then?"

"Is my lord begging for a bruising?"

Undaunted, he held up the soap. "Why don't you come shampoo my hair?" He sniffed a raven strand and grimaced. "It does reek of something far worse than fish, I fear."

She glowered at him, then relented. "As a matter of fact, I would love to get soap in your eyes right now."

Natalie crossed over to kneel beside Ryder, and moved the soap through his raven strands until she had worked up a lather. He lounged back with his eyes closed and an expression of sublime pleasure sculpting his noble face. Her mouth went dry as she ran her gaze over him. His chest gleamed in the mellow light, his legs were beautifully shaped and covered with coarse black hair, and his manhood appeared beautiful and thick beneath the water. Fighting back a desire to curl her fingers about the delectable shaft, she reminded herself that she was justly infuriated with this rogue—especially for bringing her here.

Then, observing the nasty bruises rising along his jaw and

shoulders, she felt her anger being tempered by tenderness and desire. At least he had tried to champion her cause tonight, and she did feel intensely relieved that he hadn't really been consorting with those doxies. She realized she was coming to think of him as *hers*. Oh, mercy! She might as well try to own the moon, or the stars, or the wild horses she had once seen running on the English moors.

Still, he was hers tonight, wasn't he? That traitorous thought excited her terribly. She set down the soap and ran her fingers through the thick, silky mass of his hair.

He moaned. "Ah, love, that feels wonderful."

At the husky longing in his voice, she caught a sharp breath and continued her slow massage of his scalp. Lust was gnawing at her insides, and she had to admit that their scandalous surroundings only intensified the forbidden thrill.

She continued to bathe him, albeit with trembling hands, her fingers lingering on his smooth skin, his splendid muscles, while her fascinated gaze kept straying over his body—and, all too frequently, toward the decadent crimson bed.

At last her curiosity got the better of her. "What do you suppose that mirror is for?" she asked.

He howled with laughter. "Natalie, love, have you so little imagination?"

Miffed, she picked up a pitcher of water one of the women had left and summarily dumped the ablution over his head. She smirked at him as he coughed, sputtered, cursed, and wiped suds from his eyes.

"Now tell me what that mirror is for," she reiterated.

All at once he stood, water sluicing off his magnificent nakedness. The menacing intent in his eyes was both thrilling and frightening as he drawled, "On second thought, I think I shall show you."

Natalie shrieked protests as Ryder sloshed out of the tub and grabbed her, bearing her squirming body to the bed. Laughing, he wrestled her down beneath him and kissed her rapaciously. The scandalous situation, along with his wet, glorious nakedness, was electrifying to her senses.

"You brought me here to seduce me again, didn't you?" she managed to gasp.

Totally unrepentant, he thrust his tongue inside her ear. "Why, Miss Desmond, at last you have noticed."

"You rogue!"

"Aye, and mayhap 'twill take a thorough bedding to set you in your place and put a halt to your mischief, wench."

"You are one to talk of mischief!"

Even as she spoke, his mouth seized hers roughly, and a sound of strangled pleasure escaped her. Her inhibitions soon went spinning off as Ryder pulled down her gown and chemise and sucked her breasts, nipping her soft flesh as he impatiently tugged her garments off her body. She reeled with bliss and tangled her fingers in his wet hair.

A moment later, he rolled her beneath him. His eyes were blazing down into hers, his features fierce with desire. With the hard tip of his manhood pressed against her, he hesitated, his expression passionate, yet equally tender.

Natalie felt as if she would lose her mind if he did not take her—now.

He stroked her cheek and smiled. "Last week I shared one of my secrets with you, Natalie. Tonight I want to unveil one of yours."

"What?" she whispered.

He leaned over to nibble to her earlobe, and she shivered. "Give yourself to me," he urged huskily. "You always hold something back. You don't have to be afraid to let go completely with me, darling."

His words were exciting her to a fever pitch, making breathing difficult. Still, she managed to protest, "I—don't know what you mean."

"Oh, yes, you do." He drew back and pinned her with his fervent gaze.

Indeed, gazing up at him, she *did* know, and her heart pounded in delirious anticipation at the very thought. Still, it smarted that he was expecting so much but was willing to give so little in return.

"So I am to sacrifice my soul, my lord, just to give you one more night of passion?" she asked with uncertainty and some hurt.

All at once his expression grew very serious. "I'm afraid another night won't get it done, love . . ." He paused to kiss her gently, and slipped a finger inside her until she gasped. "I think it's going to take a year of nights . . . mayhap a lifetime of nights."

Natalie squirmed, only to arch herself into a spasm of delight. "I—if I do it," she whispered convulsively, digging her fingers into his shoulders, "will you show me what the mirror is for?"

"Minx!" The resolute light in his eyes promised he would show her a great deal more.

Ryder aroused Natalie with unhurried kisses, mating his mouth with hers, thrusting slowly and deeply with his tongue as his hands caressed her breasts. She was panting by the time he began trailing his lips down the arch of her soft throat. She watched him in the mirror, her gaze now shamelessly riveted as she whispered encouragements. His hot tongue roved in circles over her breasts, then streaked steadily lower. His lips, tongue, and hot breath trailed over her quivering belly.

"Now watch this, darling," he whispered.

How he knew she was watching them, she did not know. But when he leaned over to kiss the soft chestnut curls at the joining of her thighs, she bucked wildly and tried to wiggle free. His response was a husky chuckle as he held her down firmly, parted her thighs, and brushed his lips and tongue over her most intimate recesses. She writhed crazily and whimpered with pleasure—and then she dared to look up at the mirror again and thought she would die of the rapture. With a groan, she ceased her struggles and let him have his way.

Hearing the sound of her surrender excited Ryder to a fever pitch. He wanted to make her completely vulnerable to him, completely his. He hooked her knees over his shoulders and took his time, teasing her endlessly with feathery strokes of his tongue, roving his hands boldly over her silken thighs and delightful bottom, feasting on her, until she moved against him and soft sobs shook her. He held her fast and sucked deeply as she cried out her climax.

Letting her knees slide down his arms, he stared up at her face. Her cheeks were burning hot, her mouth open, her eyes dazed, her expression one of shattered ecstasy. She had given herself to him in a most special way—and in that moment he realized he loved her.

Before he could fully contemplate this wonderous, staggering revelation, he felt her soft fingers curl around his distended shaft. The pleasure was agonizing.

"Please," she whispered, "I want you inside me—now."

"Darling, you don't have to beg me. My God, I can never get enough of you!"

Ryder pulled her legs up tightly around his waist. Natalie felt a combined thrill of fear and lust as she realized the power he would soon unleash on her. Glancing upward again, she caught an image of his bronzed, muscled backside just as he thrust into her. He filled her until she was taut and throbbing, bursting with pleasure, and she met each devouring stroke hungrily. Watching what he was doing to her excited her more unbearably by the moment. She sobbed her delight and grew fascinated with the rhythmic motions of his buttocks as he possessed her with such vigor. She breathed in ragged gulps and clawed at the sheets.

He smiled as he observed her wantonly watching them. "Do you understand fully now, darling?" he murmured between hard thrusts.

"Ah, yes . . . I think I see," she panted, arching against him and prompting a forceful response.

"Are you certain?"

"Y-yes."

A wicked laugh escaped him. "I think, my love, that we must still take this wonderful lesson one step further."

Natalie was confused, but only for a moment. She was amazed by the dispatch with which Ryder withdrew from her and rolled her over onto her knees. Hot ecstasy flooded her senses anew as he eased into her womanhood from behind in this new and provocative position.

"Now I can't see us in the mirror," she muttered between gasps of passion.

"Oh, but I can," he replied devilishly.

Indeed, he could. Ryder glanced up to see their bodies aligned so sensually and moving in perfect harmony. He caught Natalie against him and slowly, thoroughly, savored her. He kept a forearm clamped at her waist as his free hand kneaded her breasts. The heat, the friction, of her were heaven. Love welled in his heart at her moans of rapture and surrender. When she moved against him, wantonly urging him on, his desires broke free, hot and untamed. He drove into her tightness with deep, riveting strokes, until she cried out her climax and he shuddered with release . . .

Long afterward, Ryder gently withdrew from Natalie and lay on his side, watching her sleep. She appeared utterly peaceful, done in by his passion, and the sight of her thus filled him with pride.

He knew he must soon rouse her and fetch her home, but for now, he couldn't take his eyes off her. He gazed at her beautiful body, her disheveled chestnut hair. He spent a long moment coiling a silken strand around his finger, and sniffed its heady fragrance. He trailed a finger down her creamy back, the curve of her hip, and groaned as he remembered the sweetness of her surrender.

How could he *ever* let her go, when just the thought of escorting her home tonight was torture?

His eyes stung with unexpected tears. She had given herself to him, all right—but his heart had been lost in the taking.

Twenty-seven

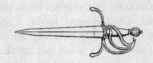

TWO AND A HALF WEEKS LATER, NATALIE SAT IN HER BEDROOM at the dressing table, touching up her coiffure as she waited for Ryder to come by and fetch her to attend a soirée in Regent's Park.

She smiled. He had been rather sweet ever since the night they had made such beautiful love at the bordello—indeed, she blushed every time she remembered that night of torrid, extraordinary passion. Lately, Ryder seemed like a mischievous child with a big secret. Of course, she knew all about one of his big secrets—and doubtless, by now he knew most of hers.

Several times a week, he called during the day, taking her out to tea or for a drive through the park. He teased her with titillating remarks, gave her lustful looks that made her stomach do somersaults, and showered her with gifts—roses, gloves, bonbons, a new hat.

Natalie was very much afraid she was in love with the rake, and feeling very vulnerable to the inevitable heartache her love would be dealt. As different as she and Ryder were, they were sooner or later bound to part, and it saddened her to think that this tender period between them could not last.

As if a portent of things to come, Ryder continued to disappear each night, and he told her virtually nothing about what he was doing. She remained doubtful of his motives—fearing he was enjoying seamy London and all its tawdry temptations, and suspecting that he was still withholding information from her. To her deepening dismay, they seemed no closer to locating the smugglers *or* Aunt Love. Unfortunately,

255

she had been able to do little else to try to find her aunt, since her father appeared to slip further into the abyss of profligacy and depression with every day that passed. His debacles were approaching bizarre and frightening proportions. In the middle of one recent night, Fitzhugh had found Charles drunk in the middle of the square, feeding the birds and singing a loud, melancholy ballad. On the next night, Charles had slipped and fallen on the stairs, badly twisting an ankle. Natalie had tried to pry her father away from his drink and interest him in more wholesome activities, such as a drive in the country or even an evening at the Royal Opera House, but she simply could not lift him out of the slough of despond.

Natalie also felt uneasy on another level. Tonight would represent her first foray among the London *ton* in more than six years. Ryder, as the son of a duke, would no doubt be readily accepted back into society; as far as she knew, he had caused no scandal before leaving for his years of exile, and the *ton* tended to be far more forgiving of the male of the species, in any event. Ryder's grandmother, who would accompany them tonight, had obviously long ago secured her place in the polite world.

But Natalie had doubts about how she herself would be received, after spending years living with her aunt in the still-disreputable "Colonies." At twenty-two, she would also be considered a spinster and a definite oddity.

Hearing a rap at her door, Natalie called out, "Come in," and her elderly maid, Cara, a tall, gray-haired woman with a kindly, lined face, slipped inside.

She smiled at Natalie. "Lord Newbury is downstairs waiting for you, miss—and a fine, handsome lad he is."

Natalie chuckled at Cara's calling Ryder a "lad." "I still have doubts about our stepping out tonight, especially with Father in such a state," Natalie fretted as she straightened an earring. Then, catching Cara's woebegone expression, she touched the curls so skillfully arranged on the top of her head. "Although, as usual, you did a splendid job on my coiffure."

Cara beamed. "You need to go out and enjoy yourself, miss. Don't worry about your father—Fitzhugh and I shall see to him. As for your aunt, she will surely show up in due course. Begging your pardon, miss, but Mrs. Desmond has always been a flighty one."

Natalie couldn't restrain a smile. "Well, I certainly won't find her tonight." *Although I may keep Ryder out of trouble for once,* she added to herself.

"Now, hurry, miss. Your gentleman is growing impatient, I would reckon."

Nodding, Natalie rose and headed for the door in a rustle of silk skirts and satin petticoats. Cara handed her a knitted, jeweled reticule and wrapped a light cashmere shawl around her shoulders.

"Oh, miss, you look so beautiful," the maid whispered, wiping away a tear.

Natalie touched the woman's arm. "Thank you, Cara. Is my father in his study?"

Cara shook her head sadly. "If you're aiming to pop in there with your young man, you may as well forget it, miss. Fitzhugh found him passed out on his way back from the Jericho, and had to summon the gardener to bring him inside and carry him upstairs."

"Oh, dear," Natalie muttered, distraught. "I must look in on him as I head downstairs."

"Very good, miss, but step lively. His lordship is waiting."

Natalie left the room and proceeded down the hallway. She rapped on her father's door and, receiving no response, stepped inside—"

Charles Desmond lay sound asleep in the magnificent rosewood tester bed, snoring loudly and appearing pale as death.

"Oh, Father," Natalie whispered to herself with great sorrow. "What are we doing to do about you?"

She crossed the room and gently shook his arm a few times. He blinked, then, a moment later, tried to focus his bleary gaze on her. "Hello, m'dear," he slurred.

She forced a kindly smile. "Are you all right? Cara told me Fitzhugh found you passed out in the garden."

"I shall live," he muttered with a weak wave of his hand. "Unfortunately."

Natalie's hackles rose at her father's continual self-deprecation. "Well, if you don't stay away from the brandy, I have my doubts."

"Does it matter?" he said morosely.

"It matters to me!"

"I know, m'dear," he replied, his expression all at once contrite. "You deserve far better than your rummy old man."

Natalie sighed. "Father, I must leave now. Lord Newbury is escorting me to a soiree. Will you please try to stay sober tonight?"

Ignoring her question, he gazed at her with a father's pride. "Ah, my dear, how lovely you look in that gown. You know, you are the very image of your mother at the same age."

"Am I?" Natalie asked with a catch in her voice.

"Aye." A poignant light gleamed in Charles's brown eyes. "Seeing you thus reminds me of happier times with Desiree—our courting days, when I escorted her to the Carlton House levees, to the theater and Vauxhall; and the early years of our marriage, when we took such glorious excursions to Brighton and Bath."

"I remember some of those times, Father," Natalie whispered.

"Now they are gone forever."

"Don't say that!" she admonished him. "Please, can you not at least try to keep your spirits up for my sake?"

He nodded. "I shall try, my dear."

But his voice held resignation, and Natalie felt all the more worried and depressed as she kissed him good-bye and left the room.

In the hallway, she encountered the butler approaching her father's room with a supper tray. "Fitzhugh, please try to keep Father away from the brandy tonight," she implored.

The old family retainer could only shake his head. "You must know how hard I have tried, Miss Natalie. We pour out the brandy; then he threatens the footmen with dismissal unless they go right out and fetch him more."

"I know, Fitzhugh."

"The surgeon came by to check on him the other day, while you were out running errands on Oxford Street," Fitzhugh continued anxiously. "He mentioned to me that there is little left to do but to commit Mr. Desmond to St. Pancras for—er—observation."

Natalie was outraged. "I won't see my father consigned to a hospital's mad ward—at least not yet."

"Very well, miss," Fitzhugh answered sheepishly. "I was only passing along the surgeon's comments."

She touched his arm. "I know, Fitzhugh. And your devotion to my father is unquestioned."

He smiled. "Do have a good evening with Lord Newbury."

"Thank you, Fitzhugh."

Natalie's spirits lifted a bit as she started down the staircase and spotted Ryder waiting for her in the foyer. He might be all rogue, but her heart tripped with excitement when she saw him. Lord, but he did look dashing in his formal black velvet cutaway and matching satin waistcoat, pleated white linen shirt, and buff-colored pantaloons. His scandalous black hair was drawn back in a queue, and he held a silk top hat in one white-gloved hand. His appreciative stare was riveted on her, which increased her own sense of breathless anticipation.

Ryder was equally entranced with the vision sweeping down the stairs toward him. Natalie wore a gown of rich burgundy silk, with extravagant beret sleeves, a low décolletage, high Empire-style waist and straight-lined skirt that flared to a fine sweep at her lovely, silk-stockinged ankles. Her rich brown hair had been pulled away from her face and piled in intricate curls atop her head, setting off in exquisite relief the delicate contours of her countenance. She wore a pearl tiara, along with a matching necklace and earbobs.

During the past weeks, his feelings for her had only intensified, he mused tenderly. God help him, he did love her so. He knew what all this meant now, though it still scared him a little.

"Good evening, darling," he murmured, taking her hand and kissed her glove. "You look good enough to gobble up on the spot."

She blushed. "Please, Ryder, we are going out in polite company tonight." Glancing around, she frowned. "Where is your grandmother?"

"Waiting for us in the carriage."

She sighed. "It is just as well. I had hoped to take you both in to say hello to my father, but he is upstairs in bed again, after collapsing in the garden."

Ryder flashed her a look of intense sympathy. "I'm sorry, sweetheart."

"I still say we shouldn't be going out," she continued worriedly. "This is a fine time for us to be socializing, when God only knows where Aunt Love may be."

"I know, but we really cannot miss the festivities," he soothed. "It is Lord and Lady Litchfield's twenty-fifth wedding anniversary, and their son Sam Brandon has been my good friend ever since we were both at Eton."

"Oh, dear. I hadn't realized it was their anniversary. I didn't even get a gift."

"Don't worry, my love, I went by Bond Street and purchased an appropriate gewgaw." He offered his arm. "Shall we go? Nonna is waiting."

Natalie placed her fingers on his sleeve. "Of course." As they headed out the front door, she asked, "Any news of Harry?"

He shook his head. "Unfortunately, no. I've been stopping by the River Police Office every day, but no luck at all so far." He sighed heavily. "Thank God Hampton's parents are touring the Continent at the moment. I should wager Sir Jasper and Lady Millicent will both have a stroke if they learn their son and heir is missing. We can only hope Hampton will surface before they return from Naples."

Natalie nodded sympathetically.

A handsome black coach with a pair of matched gray horses awaited them at the end of the walk. Watching a liveried footman hop down to open the door with its gleaming gold coat of arms, Natalie mused that they would attend the affair tonight in high style.

Ryder handed her inside the conveyance, and she slipped into a seat next to Francesca.

"Natalie, my dear, how good to see you again!" Francesca greeted her, warmly kissing her cheek. "And you look simply divine—I swear I have never seen a lovelier frock."

"You look wonderful yourself, Countess," Natalie replied, admiring Francesca in her gown of pale gray silk.

"And I have the pleasure of escorting the two loveliest ladies in town to the ball tonight," Ryder added as he sat down across from them and shut the door.

Francesca winked at her grandson. "Isn't he the gallant one?" she asked Natalie.

"Oh, yes," Natalie replied.

The carriage lurched into motion. "Ryder tells me that your

dear aunt is still missing," Francesca remarked sympathetically.

"Unfortunately, yes."

Francesca frowned. "It is most strange, but I get the feeling
that you may learn something of importance tonight."

"You do?" Natalie queried.

"Why tonight, Nonna?"

"I really can't say. It's just an intuition."

Vehemently, Natalie said, "Any information at all would
certainly be welcomed, but at this point it is difficult for me
to hold out too much hope."

"I know, dear," Francesca said, patting the girl's hand. "Although I do trust you are not letting this unfortunate situation
prevent you from marrying my grandson as soon as possible.
You are the one for him, you know."

Ryder and Natalie exchanged shy smiles.

"My fondest hope is that I may live to see you and my
grandson celebrate your wedding anniversary, as Lord and
Lady Litchfield are doing tonight," Francesca went on. "Although I understand that rascal Teddy Brandon is still consorting with the fast young actress who is doing *King Lear*
over at the Drury Lane."

"You don't say," murmured Ryder.

Francesca turned to Natalie. "If the boy ever disgraces you
in such a manner, you have my permission to shoot him—as
long as you avoid anything vital."

"Oh, I will—on both counts," Natalie replied mischievously, and Ryder threw back his head and laughed.

The three continued to visit, Francesca sharing other tidbits
of gossip as they headed into Regent's Park. Natalie gazed
out at John Nash's classical masterpiece, even now half finished, of magnificent estates spaced around the boundary of
verdant parkland and trees. The coachman halted the conveyance before a soaring, four-story white Greek villa with classical carvings on the pediment, urns and statuary gracing the
balustrades, and soaring Corinthian columns with carved cap-
itals. The mansion was beautifully lit, and at the doorway a
butler was admitting an elegantly attired couple.

Ryder escorted the two ladies out of the carriage, up the
wide steps, and into a home of palatial proportions. Natalie
was accustomed to luxury, yet it was hard not to gape at a

marble-floored entry hall that was easily the size of a small chapel, and was lavishly appointed with Greek statuary, magnificent roundels of classical art, and a high, soaring white dome decorated with swirling scrolls and flowers sculpted in pale yellow plaster fretwork with gilt embellishments.

The butler led them toward the ballroom, from which the sounds of music and happy voices drifted out. At the archway to the huge, circular saloon, Natalie gazed inside and tried to take in everything at once—the women in their glittering ball gowns, swirling in the arms of men in swallow-tailed coats; the string quartet on the dais sawing out an elegant baroque minuet; the stunning gold-paneled walls and the mellow parquet of the floor; the magnificent Italian frescoes on the ceiling. The air was thick with the perfume of flowers, and the sounds of laughter and bright conversation mingled with the swell of the music.

The butler announced, "Countess Valenzza, Lord Newbury, and Miss Desmond," and, amid gazes of frank appraisal from the guests, the three entered and headed for the reception line. They were greeted pleasantly by Lord and Lady Litchfield; Ryder offered congratulations and presented their gift. As Teddy Brandon, Lord Litchfield, kissed the hand Natalie offered, she studied the pompous, potbellied gentleman with his balding pate and monocle, and found it hard to believe he was such a lecher.

Natalie's fears about being snubbed rapidly faded as Francesca led them around and introduced them to her granddame friends. Natalie could not doubt the countess's high standing when she was greeted politely by the haughty social matriarch Lady Castlereigh, and warmly by the king's friend Lady Anne Barnard. They chatted briefly with the charming Sir Walter Scott, who, in his rich Scottish brogue, was enthralling a small group of attendees with the story of his adventures in uncovering the lost crown, sword, and scepter of Scotland. They met the royal painter, Sir Lawrence Thomas, and the poet laureate, Mr. Southey.

Soon Francesca drifted off to sit with some friends, while Ryder and Natalie joined his cronies Sam, Hugh, and James, who were in attendance tonight with their wives or fiancées. Although Natalie felt much more comfortable around Ryder's contemporaries, she was dismayed when the entire group began to gossip about the king.

"I hear the coronation may finally be set for July," said Hugh.

"Aye, but will Caroline be crowned queen?" James wondered.

"Not if the king has anything to say about it," remarked Sam. "Granted, the divorce proceedings in the House of Lord were a debacle that never brought his Majesty the desired pound of flesh. Nonetheless, he seems determined that Caroline will never sit beside him on the throne."

"Can you blame him?" asked an indignant Hugh. "The Princess of Wales is little more than a doxy—and a pig."

"Well, she cannot possibly be more of a profligate than the former prince himself," protested Hugh's wife, the vivacious Lady Bess.

"Aye," said Miss Sarah Truesdale, James's fiancée. "I've lost track of all his mistresses."

"These days it is Lady Conyngham—with all her diamonds and ultra-Catholicism," James informed her.

"And with the spurned Ladies Hertford and Jersey forever weeping in the wings," added a laughing Sam.

"Do you suppose the king will be sober for the coronation?" Ryder asked wryly.

"Possibly—as long as he and Lady Conyngham aren't up too late, *praying* the night before," quipped Hugh, and everyone laughed.

As the group began chattering about a well-known married lady who had recently disgraced herself by showing up at her lover's club on St. James's Street, Natalie tried to hold on to her patience. She found the gossip both tedious and appalling. Ryder evidently sensed her state of mind, for soon he asked her to dance. Together, they went out to the middle of the room and joined the other couples in an elegant quadrille.

Before they had completed their first few steps, Natalie paused as she spotted a familiar, black-clothed figure across the room. "Ryder, isn't that your father?" she asked.

He turned to stare at the tall gentleman with broad shoulders and gunmetal-gray hair. "So it is. I wonder what possessed him to attend."

"We must go over and say hello to him."

He scowled. "After the way he treated you when we called?"

She touched his arm. "Ryder, we must honor protocol. This is an important occasion after all. Surely you can't wish to embarrass him."

"Very well."

Grimly, Ryder escorted Natalie off the dance floor and across the room. They encountered William Remington as he left the buffet table with two filled cups of punch.

"Your Grace," Ryder said, bowing before his father.

"Why, Ryder, Miss Desmond," the duke returned, appearing pleasantly surprised.

Natalie curtsied. "Your Grace."

"Natalie and I were just wondering what brought you here tonight," Ryder remarked coolly.

The duke laughed dryly. "Not my usual sort of haunt, is it? Actually, I am here with my prayer companion. Harriet has been arguing for weeks now that I should get out more."

"Good for Harriet," Natalie put in, and was surprised and pleased when Ryder's father actually smiled at her. She mused that when he relaxed, he appeared almost as handsome and masterful as his son.

"Come along—I'll have you meet her," he said imperiously.

Ryder and Natalie dutifully followed him toward a tall, brown-haired lady who stood with her back to them, conversing with several other matrons. Observing the woman, Natalie felt uneasy; something about her was very familiar.

"Well, there you are, Harriet, my dear," the duke greeted her. As she turned, he handed her a cup of punch and said, "I would like you to meet my son, Ryder, and his friend, Miss Desmond."

Before the duke could finish his introductions, everyone turned to Natalie, who had gasped loudly.

"My dear, are you all right?" Ryder asked with concern, reaching out to grab her arm.

Natalie was staring wide-eyed at the woman. "Why, you are not Harriet Foxworth!" she exclaimed. "You are—"

And before she could utter another syllable, the woman who called herself Harriet Foxworth lurched toward her, and Natalie was drenched from bodice to waist with wine punch.

Twenty-eight

DURING THE NEXT FEW MOMENTS, NATALIE SEETHED WITH frustration as the alleged Harriet Foxworth first entreated their hostess for help, then towed Natalie off to Lady Litchfield's boudoir upstairs. Natalie sat at the dressing table, glowering at the woman who hovered over her while trying to remove the stain from her dress.

Natalie noted resentfully that "Harriet" appeared no worse for wear due to her ordeal; her brown hair had acquired no more gray strands, and her features were as classically etched and pleasing as ever. She possessed the same tall, graceful figure. Yet her actions and attitude demonstrated that, at heart, this woman was as flighty, capricious, and eccentric as ever.

"Oh, dear," she lamented, dabbing at Natalie's frock with a wet cloth. "I have made a dreadful mess of your gown."

Natalie's exasperation exploded into anger. "Will you kindly stop fretting over my gown and tell me what in God's name you are doing here, *Aunt Love?*"

The woman gasped. "Well, I might ask the same question of you, Natalie. And there is no need to resort to profanity."

"No need!" Natalie's hand sliced through the air. "I've been driving myself insane for two months, terrified that you were lying dead in some seamy alleyway, and all this time you've been amusing yourself by *praying*—with a duke!"

"Well, you needn't announce it to the entire realm, for heaven's sake," Love scolded. "I had a perfectly legitimate excuse for doing what I did."

"What possible excuse could you have for frightening me out of my wits?"

Love was busy straightening an earbob. "When I arrived in London, I posted you a letter, Natalie," she said with strained patience. "In it I explained everything. I had assumed you would continue to run the factory in Charleston, like a dutiful niece—"

"How could I run the factory when, for all I knew, you had been taken off by a press gang or something? After I finally unearthed a clue that you had sailed for London, I came here in search of you—"

"Which is evidently why you never received my letter," Love pointed out irritably.

Natalie drew a seething breath. "Obviously we are getting nowhere with this discussion. Now, let's start from the beginning. Why did you leave Charleston in the first place, without consulting me, and what are you doing in England—posing as Harriet Foxworth, no less?"

Love glanced into the mirror and smoothed her coiffure. "Why, the explanation is quite simple. I was impelled to go undercover, dear, just like I told you in the note I left behind. As things turned out, I had to leave Charleston in a great hurry."

"Why?"

"Because I learned the name of a ship that had smuggled English cloth into Charleston, and I stole on board just prior to its return voyage to England."

Natalie was stunned. "You actually became a stowaway?"

Love grimaced, and began playing with her pearl choker. "Indeed, and it is not a life I should recommend. I swear I shall never again cross the Atlantic in the dank, smelly hold of a ship. Why, there were the most nefarious creatures skulking about—cockroaches, beetles, rats—"

"I cannot believe I am hearing this," Natalie muttered, shaking her head.

"But I did manage to befriend a young sailor. Properly bribed, he provided me with adequate food and water."

Natalie remained flabbergasted, and was even wondering if her aunt belonged in Bedlam. "So you came here to London. Then what?"

"I followed the smugglers from the docks, of course. And they led me straightaway to a cloth factory in Stepney."

The hairs on the back of Natalie's head began to stand up. "You can't mean—"

Love's eyes gleamed with triumph. "But I do."

Natalie groaned. "Oh, heavens."

"Haven't you as yet discovered the lay of the land, my dear?" Love went on excitedly. "Our competition has been smuggled Remington cloth."

"Oh, my God!" Natalie gasped, as all the horrifying implications reverberated through her mind. "So that is why you've become the Duke of Mansfield's prayer companion?"

"Certainly. And isn't it fascinating that you came here tonight with his son? And such a handsome young fellow he is, I must say."

Natalie laughed bitterly. "You do not know the half of it."

"What do you mean?"

Natalie's eyes gleamed with bitterness. "I met Ryder Remington in Charleston when *I* went undercover to try to find you—and the smugglers."

Love's slim hand fluttered to her cheek. "Oh, my. You don't suppose the boy is involved, do you?"

"It is possible," Natalie related grimly. "You see, I showed him a sample of the smuggled cloth back in America. He had to have known that it came from his father's factory—"

"Especially with its distinctive warp," Love put in.

"But he never admitted his father's involvement to me."

"Oh, my."

"What a fool I've been!" Natalie wailed.

"You mean you had no idea where the cloth came from?"

Natalie shook her head. "I did locate one sample here on Bond Street, but could not track down the source. And to think that I walked through the Stepney factory with Ryder and never made the connection. Of course, I didn't see the cloth at close range."

"And you are near blind without your spectacles," Love reminded her.

"True."

Love's lips were twitching. "So the two of you actually inspected William's factory together?"

Natalie nodded. "The duke suggested we question his partners, John Lynch and Oswald Spectre. Neither was of any help, of course."

"Not surprising," commented Love. "I suspect one of those scoundrels may be behind this mischief."

"And not William Remington himself?"

Love waved a hand. "With all his wealth, why would he need to smuggle anything? Besides, the man is far too busy praying all the time."

Natalie was tempted to shout at her aunt. "Well, if you do not think he is responsible, then why do you keep carrying on this ruse?"

Love smiled. "I've been able to gather information about the Stepney plant from William—and besides, I've become rather fond of him."

"You must be jesting!" Natalie declared. "You have become enamored of some religious zealot? And do you actually mean to tell me none of your friends have recognized you since you engineered this masquerade?"

"Oh, fiddle-faddle," said Love. "You know I've never before run in these high circles. Besides, tonight is the first occasion on which I've convinced William to venture forth in society. Granted, I was given some curious glances by Ladies Cowper and Castlereigh when William first introduced me. No doubt they both wondered who Harriet Foxworth might be, but I was received politely enough. After all, who would contradict or criticize a duke?"

"Whatever you say, Aunt Love," Natalie muttered in mystification.

"Natalie, please don't think badly of me for enjoying myself."

"Enjoying yourself," her niece repeated ruefully.

"Don't you think it is high time?" Scowling, Love began to dab at Natalie's gown again. "Why, when Malcolm was alive, he managed to keep us in perpetual disgrace with all the duels, the women, and the gambling. And don't you remember how, when you turned fifteen, I was already tearing my hair out over your future debut, wondering how I would ever secure your invitation to court and all the proper vouchers for the season?"

"I realize our family history has weighed us down," Natalie murmured.

"Indeed, things were in such an appalling state six years ago that Rodney's collapse in America was truly a godsend for us both."

"A peculiar way to look at it."

"But to get back to your original question. Over the past few weeks, a couple of friends have recognized me while I was out running errands, but I managed to swear them to secrecy."

Natalie's outrage surged again. "You might have at least notified Father that you were here."

"After the way he blamed me for Malcolm's death?" Love countered.

Natalie sighed. "I see your point. But what of William Remington? Sooner or later he is bound to find out about your ruse, and that you deceived him to gain information."

"Yes, I suspect that when he learns the truth, the man will be annoyed, to say the least. But I did manage to get him out in public tonight. Isn't that marvelous? Especially after he has been torturing himself for years over his wife's death."

Now Natalie had to smile. "Oh, Aunt Love, you are impossible! What am I going to do with you?"

"Well, are you going to hate me for the rest of my life, or give me a hug and say hello properly?" she demanded.

Laughing, Natalie rose and gave her aunt a warm hug. "I am most happy you are safe and sound, even if you have decimated my life—and my gown."

"Yes, we must see what we can do about that." Love wet the cloth and resumed her blotting efforts.

A few moments later, the two women returned to the ballroom amid curious glances. When they rejoined Ryder and his father, Natalie was surprised when the duke asked her to dance. Although Ryder frowned in obvious disapproval, he voiced no protest concerning his father's overture. Natalie had little choice but to take the hand the duke offered and stroll with him to the dance floor, even though, following Aunt Love's revelations, she was actually dying to get Ryder alone—to browbeat and likely strangle him.

The duke whirled Natalie around to a Schubert waltz, holding her at the proper distance.

"I see that Harriet has managed to bring some order to

your gown," he murmured, looking her over with his shrewd, appraising gaze.

"Yes, your Grace."

"Do you two know each other?"

A feeling of alarm streaked down Natalie's spine, followed by a flood of awareness. So that was why he had asked her to dance! Ryder's father was curious as to her connection to his "prayer companion."

She flashed him a quick smile. "Actually, your Grace, Miss Foxworth and I became rather well acquainted while she repaired my gown."

He actually chuckled. "Harriet is a fine woman—and she seems to like you, young lady."

"I shall hope my wardrobe will endure her goodwill," Natalie quipped, and again the duke laughed.

"You are a spirited creature," he murmured. "I like that."

She met his gaze evenly. "But not for your son?"

He sighed, his amused expression giving way to a regretful frown. "Actually, I may have responded precipitously when I met you, young lady. I suppose I was rather taken aback the day you appeared with my son—and no doubt I felt exasperated with him as well. Things have not been good between us for some years."

"So I understand."

"But since I've met Harriet . . ." He smiled with an unaccustomed wistfulness. "Suffice it to say I have arrived at a point in life where I would like to see Ryder happily settled, and accepting the responsibilities of his station."

"And perhaps you would like to mend your relationship with him?" Natalie suggested.

"You are a very perceptive young woman."

"Your condemnation has not been easy for Ryder to bear," Natalie felt impelled to add.

For a moment, the duke appeared taken aback. Then, with a surprising touch of humility, he asked, "Have you any suggestions, Miss Desmond?"

Natalie shook her head. "I am afraid the two of you will have to resolve this on your own."

Across the room, Ryder, standing next to Sam, was irate as he watched his father waltz with Natalie. It galled him to see the man he so hated touching the woman he loved.

"I can't believe Father had the nerve to ask Natalie to dance," he muttered angrily to Sam. "I'm going to go over there and break up their little tryst."

Sam's mouth fell open. "Have you taken leave of your senses, Newbury? Your father is dancing with the woman you love—all but a written endorsement of her as your future bride. Now you want to go botch things up?"

His bride, Ryder thought with sudden, fierce possessiveness. Aye, that was exactly how he wanted Natalie—as his bride. Enough of this nonsense about not getting to have her when he wanted her, which was turning out to be every tormented moment of his life.

To Sam, he burst out furiously, "But they are waltzing, for heaven's sake!"

"That does not mean you must have a conniption over it," Sam argued. "Do you yearn to be disinherited?"

"I couldn't give a damn!"

"But what of Natalie? Won't she care?"

Realizing he was trapped by the constraints of propriety, Ryder stared at his father holding Natalie, observed the two of them sharing a laugh, and ground his jaw. Natalie had caught the appreciative stares of other gentlemen in the room, too, he noted darkly, which only exacerbated his irritation.

When the dance ended, he crossed the room and took Natalie's arm. To his father, he said curtly, "Your Grace, if you will excuse us, I do believe Natalie could use some air."

William Remington was barely able to murmur in the affirmative before his son towed Natalie off.

Outside on the veranda, Ryder hotly confronted her. "Did you enjoy your waltz with my father?"

"Ryder, he is a duke and he asked me! What choice did I have?"

"You could have told him to go to hell."

"Oh, yes, that would have gone over just splendidly."

"I don't like watching him anywhere near you!"

Studying his angry countenance, Natalie felt a mixture of sympathy and exasperation. In a low, intense voice, she said, "Aye, I suppose your attitude is not at all surprising, considering what I have just learned."

His gaze narrowed on her, and his voice snapped. "What did my father tell you?"

She laughed ruefully. "*He* told me nothing. But he might have. And that is why you are so indignant, isn't it?"

Ryder began to pace the small terrace. "Natalie, I simply did not want that blackhearted cad touching you. Otherwise, I have no idea what you are talking about."

"Don't you? Why did you not tell me from the beginning that our competition has been smuggled Remington cloth?"

"What?" Ryder swung about to face her, his expression stunned. "How did you learn this—if not from my father?"

"So you admit 'tis true!" she cried.

He seized her arm with steely intent. "Natalie, tell me how you found out."

Her eyes blazing at him, she retorted, "Your father's new prayer companion—Harriet Foxworth—has turned out to be none other than my aunt Love!"

Astounded, he released her. "You must be joking."

"Not at all. Aunt Love followed the smugglers to England—and to your father's Stepney plant."

Ryder drew his fingers through his hair. "Oh, Lord. I knew you would find out sooner or later."

"Then why didn't you tell me the truth from the very night we met?" she demanded.

With equal fervor, he replied, "Natalie, I swear, the first time I knew we were dealing with Remington cloth was when you showed me the sample at your factory."

She laughed bitterly. "Why is it I do not believe you? And even assuming you are finally telling the truth, why couldn't you have told me when you saw the sample?"

"Because when I realized that my father's factory was involved, I knew I had to come to England and investigate. I wanted to find out who at the Stepney facility was responsible for the smuggling. But unfortunately, my efforts, like yours, have largely been fruitless."

"Not fruitless," she sneered. "You have been having a grand time roaming the streets of London at night, haven't you?"

He clenched his jaw. "Natalie, I swear to you, I have *not* been enjoying myself."

"But you still haven't explained to me why you didn't tell me the truth from the outset!"

He met her gaze earnestly. "There was your safety to consider, and my father's honor. Besides which, you would have become suspicious, Natalie. Aren't you very suspicious now?"

Unmoved by his arguments, she asked, "Are you involved in the smuggling, Ryder?"

A short, sharp breath escaped him, as if he had just been punched in the stomach. "You can't be serious!"

"Maybe I am!" she shot back, close to tears. "And maybe you are still hiding something, or protecting someone. The hell of it is, I don't know what to believe anymore! But I should have known I could never trust you. Now I have no choice but to go to the British customs authorities and report the smuggling."

He laughed. "Best of luck, my love, in trying to enforce your most unpopular American tariff."

"Then what do you propose we do?"

He sighed with resignation. "I am already planning to speak with my father tomorrow. I will inform him of the smuggling and insist he put a stop to it. I didn't want it to come to this, but I realize now that only my father will be able to conduct the type of thorough internal investigation at the factory that should uncover the true culprits."

She eyed him suspiciously. "Will you give me your word that you are not involved and that you will follow through on this?"

"You have it on both counts."

"Good."

As she started to go past him, he grabbed her arm. "What about us, Natalie?"

She could not believe what she was hearing! "You can ask that after the way you have deceived me?"

He laughed ironically. "Very good, Natalie. I knew you would find a convenient excuse to break things off."

"This is not just some flimsy excuse! It is a major breach of trust!"

"Is it?" His eyes blazed with emotion. "But then, you never did think we would suit, did you? And now that you have found your aunt and your mystery is solved, you have no further need of me, do you?"

"Don't you dare try to blame me for your own misconduct

and lies!" she flared. "I never should have expected you to be more than a cad—and an adventurer!"

Before he could respond, she swept past him and returned to the ballroom.

Ryder stood in stunned silence, his fists clenched at his sides. He could not believe this was happening! Just as he was realizing how much he loved Natalie, how much he wanted her in his life, he was losing her!

Twenty-nine

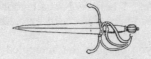

THE NEXT MORNING, RYDER CALLED ON HIS FATHER. HIS FEEL-ings were in turmoil following last night's scene with Natalie, and he fully realized that his relationship with her now hung by a thread—a thread he was determined to cling to. Perhaps he could begin to redeem himself by putting a stop to the smuggling. He also realized he could no longer avoid his responsibilities—not just his future with Natalie, but the entire issue of who he was, his heritage and identity.

Withers showed him to the duke's study, which was lined with hundreds of leather-bound theology books. He spotted his father sitting at his desk, writing in a journal. The duke glanced up distractedly as his son entered.

"Why, Ryder, this is a surprise," he said, getting to his feet.

Ryder affected the slightest bow. "This is not a social call, your Grace."

"Then I won't ring for tea," William replied wearily. "Please, have a seat."

The two men took seats flanking each other—Ryder on the cane-backed settee, William in an armchair—and regarded each other warily.

"What I have to discuss concerns Miss Desmond," Ryder began.

William raised an eyebrow. "Don't tell me you are asking my permission to marry her?"

Ryder's voice crackled with anger. "As I have told you before, my intentions toward Miss Desmond are none of your affair. If I were planning to marry her, yours is the last counsel I would seek."

"Pray continue," the duke said coldly.

"I am here to discuss a matter of some gravity. You are aware of the difficulties Miss Desmond and her aunt have encountered with their textile factory in Charleston?"

William sighed and flicked a bit of dust from his black wool sleeve. "Yes, I believe I recall your mentioning how their enterprise had been threatened by cloth smugglers. How does this concern me?"

"It concerns you because the smuggled cloth in question has been conveyed out of your very own Stepney factory."

At last Ryder had his father's full attention. The duke's head snapped up, and his features darkened with fury. "Surely you must jest."

"Not at all, your Grace."

"What proof do you have that the Stepney factory is involved?" William demanded.

"Miss Desmond showed me a sample of the smuggled cloth back in America. It clearly had the distinctive Remington warp."

William laughed cynically. "I tell you, this is absurd. I would have known if the Stepney facility were involved in smuggling."

"You would have known?" Ryder mocked. "As far as I have been able to discern, you have totally divorced yourself from the running of the factory. And as for those two degenerates you call business partners, I've never seen a more suspicious pair of scamps."

A fierce frown gripped the duke's features. "What other proof do you have that this smuggling has occurred—other than your dubious peek at the ostensibly smuggled cloth?"

"I have been watching the Stepney factory after hours, and there have definitely been suspicious goings-on there late at night—strange lights appearing on the upper story, drays pulling away in the darkness. Indeed, for some time now, I've suspected that John Lynch is the ring leader—"

"And what brought you to this brilliant conclusion?"

"Because one night while I was out investigating, the bastard took a shot at me and pummeled me with his nightstick."

The duke regarded Ryder with unaccustomed apprehension. "Are you all right, son?"

"Spare me your kindly concern," Ryder sneered. "The point is, Lynch tried to kill me."

"Did you question John about the incident?"

"Aye, and not surprisingly, he denied everything. My friends and I eventually tracked the smugglers to the port, to a shipper named Lawson. We tried to detain him at the docks, but without success."

The duke was silent.

"Well, your Grace, what are you going to do about this?" Ryder pursued tensely.

William scowled. "Whether the charges you have made are entirely true or not, there is clearly sufficient evidence to prompt a thorough audit and internal investigation at the factory. If such illegal activity is going on there, I assure you the responsible party will be discharged and his crimes brought to the attention of the authorities."

"Good."

"I have one more question," added the duke.

"Yes?"

"Why have you waited so long to tell me this?"

"I was hoping to be able to apprehend the culprits myself," Ryder admitted. "And believe it or not, your Grace, I was concerned about your honor. As a matter of fact, Miss Desmond herself did not know of the possible involvement of the Stepney factory until last night at Lord and Lady Litchfield's reception, when we finally found her aunt."

The duke raised an eyebrow. "Miss Desmond found her aunt at the soiree?"

"Indeed." Ryder smiled wryly. "As a matter of fact, you were a witness to the touching reunion."

William went pale. "You can't mean—"

"I think you will have to question Harriet Foxworth regarding the rest of it," Ryder said.

"Oh, I will," William rejoined vehemently.

Ryder stood, nodding to his father. "Then I will wish you good day, your Grace."

The duke rose. "A moment, Ryder." He forced a thin smile. "How is your grandmother? It was good to see Francesca last night, although she and I exchanged only a few words. She did look well, however."

"She is doing quite splendidly," Ryder replied. He hesitated for a moment, then added, "And by the way, she doesn't think Mother's death was an accident."

The duke frowned deeply. "She doesn't?"

Bitterly, Ryder related, "Perhaps now you can accuse me of being not just irresponsible, but also a murderer."

A flicker of pain crossed his father's features. "Ryder, perhaps I—"

But the duke's entreaty was lost in the slamming of the door as his son left.

Moments later, William strode into the chapel to find Harriet Foxworth waiting for him in her pew.

"Good morning, *Harriet,*" he said mockingly.

Appearing flustered, she popped up with her Bible and prayer book in hand. "Good day, William. I must say you seem rather—er—preoccupied this morning."

"Do I?" He smiled tightly.

She forced a cheerful expression. "Are you prepared to discuss the passages from Revelations?"

"Ah, Revelations. Perhaps I have experienced a few *revelations* myself."

Her face drained of color. "What do you mean?"

He raised an eyebrow at her. "Could it be that I have learned a certain person I trusted has betrayed and deceived me?"

"Oh, heavens!" she cried, setting down her books, her hand fluttering to her heart. "So you have already found me out?"

"Shall we say I have just had a most illuminating discussion with my son concerning various smuggling activities—and two rather unorthodox women who ran a Charleston textile factory together."

Her mouth fell open on a gasp. "Then you know—"

"That you are actually Love Desmond, the aunt of my son's—er—friend?" the duke finished furiously.

She wrung her hands and regarded him entreatingly. "William, I meant to tell you in time—"

"Did you?" His scowl was formidable. "But before that, you had to lie to me, betray me, and exploit me in order to accomplish your own nefarious ends, didn't you—*Love?*"

Her expression was crestfallen. "No! No! You don't understand at all."

"Then pray tell me the truth, from the beginning."

She nodded miserably. "As you already know, I did run the textile factory in Charleston with Natalie."

"Go on."

"Once the smugglers began to ruin our enterprise, I went undercover to find them. I stole aboard their ship and ended up here in London. I followed them to your Stepney factory, and that is why I subsequently initiated contact with you—"

"To gain information about the smuggling?" he demanded in a rising voice.

"Yes," she admitted wretchedly.

"And at church, no less," he went on in an outraged tone. "You claimed you were the widow of some obscure baronet, and were there praying for his soul. You chose a holy vehicle for your unholy deeds."

She hung her head. "Yes, I suppose I did, William. My actions were entirely reprehensible. But you must understand that soon after I began this ruse, I realized you could not possibly be involved in the smuggling."

His features softened a flicker. "Then why did you continue to see me?"

She stared up at him with worshipful eyes. "Because . . . well, frankly, by then I had become quite fond of you."

He almost smiled then, but soon a look of angry suspicion returned. "Why should I believe you now?"

She stepped forward and touched his arm. "Because I swear to you, by all I hold sacred, that I am telling the truth this time. I might have begun our association under a ruse, but I remained your friend for sincere and honest reasons. Will you forgive me, William?"

He glared at her for another long moment; then his forbidding countenance wavered. "Well, I am not certain. You have been a very bad girl."

"Ah, yes, I have been. I am utterly contrite."

He edged closer, a hint of devilment now shining in his eyes. "Shall I punish you, then?"

"Punish me?" She smirked at him. "You mean, like you did last week when we were both so wicked?"

He chuckled as he pulled her into his arms. "Love . . . You know, I rather like the sound of that."

"Isn't that indeed what our sessions are all about?" she

asked with a mixture of mischief and piety. "Prayer . . . hope . . . love . . . and punishment, of course."

"Hmmm," he murmured, pressing his lips against her throat. "I may have to make punishing you a lifelong endeavor."

That afternoon, Ryder called on Natalie. He found her sitting in the rose garden behind her father's home. A book lay open in her lap, and she was staring wistfully at the flowers. The day had turned heady and warm, and the scent of nectar was thick in the air. In the distance, the gardener was pruning the formal spice garden, adding a riot of smells, from sage to mint to lemon verbena, to the already perfumed atmosphere. Birds sang in the chestnut trees and fought noisy battles in the effervescent fountain.

He noted that Natalie appeared a luscious splash of color in the vibrant setting. She wore a pink muslin day dress, and her shiny chestnut hair was arranged in curls on top of her head. He marveled that she could be so close, and yet, emotionally, she seemed a thousand miles away from him. Was she still angry about the information he had withheld? Perhaps he could now make amends.

Ryder approached the stone bench on which Natalie sat, leaned over, and kissed her cheek. "Good afternoon, darling."

"Ryder." Glancing at him, she no longer appeared irate, only sad and resigned, and somehow this unsettled him even more. She gestured to the place beside her. "Please, sit down."

He complied, again taking in the setting with an appreciative eye. "It's really quite lovely here."

"Aye. Father keeps the house so dark and oppressive that sometimes I have to escape."

"How is he doing?"

She groaned. "Don't ask. I have insisted that we have Aunt Love by for dinner soon, although I rather dread the reunion between her and my father."

He squeezed her hand. "At least you know Love is safe and sound now."

"Yes. That is a blessing."

His expression turned to one of cynical amusement. "Although now I'm afraid your aunt will have a bit of explaining to do to my father."

She glanced at him sharply. "You have already spoken with the duke?"

"Yes. This morning. I told him everything." He reached out to run his index finger over her lush mouth, then grinned wickedly. "Well, almost everything."

"And what was the result of the interview?"

"As we suspected, my father is not involved in the smuggling himself. Nevertheless, he has promised to do a thorough internal investigation at the Stepney factory in order to expose the culprits."

"Good." She sighed. "I suppose that is it, then."

"Not quite. There is still the matter of you and me, my love." He took her hand, stared into her eyes, and spoke earnestly. "I want you to marry me, Natalie."

"What?" Setting aside her book, she lurched unsteadily to her feet. "What prompted this sudden declaration?"

He stood and touched her arm. "Do you really think it is so precipitous, considering what we have shared?" He smiled. "I know I should have spoken with your father first, but I just can't seem to contain myself."

"You never can," she muttered, still feeling staggered by his proposal.

"You know I can provide for you well," he continued seriously. "In time, I will inherit my father's title and all his wealth."

"Oh, will you?" she responded tremulously. "Knowing so well your rakehell nature, I am certain you are straining at the bit, just anticipating all the obligations of your future station."

"For you, Natalie, I'll take those duties on."

She regarded him with clearly mixed emotions. "You still haven't told me why you want to marry me."

"Because I find I cannot let you go, darling. No other woman moves me as you do. I must have you all the time."

That remark rankled. Although it had been highly titillating to Natalie, back in the carriage, to first hear of Ryder's "secret," having his lust for her be the sole basis of a marriage proposal was not flattering!

Hotly, she retorted, "That is so typical of you! What makes

you think I even give a damn what woman you hoist your flag for?"

The infuriating rogue only chuckled. "It seems to me the last time we were alone, m'lady, you were quite eager at the hoisting."

She almost slapped him. Fighting tears, she snapped, "Well, I do not care!"

He lifted her chin with his fingertips, his expression now utterly solemn. "Do you care if I love you?"

She cared. Indeed, the revelation caused her to sink back down on the bench, where he at once joined her. With her fingers clenched in her lap, she stole a glance at him from the corner of her eye, and again caught his sober, expectant expression. Mercy! That she aroused him was one thing—marginally a compliment, certainly no commitment. But love . . . With love there were possibilities, albeit frightening ones.

"When did you reach this conclusion?" she asked hoarsely.

"In the bordello—right after you gave yourself to me," came his unabashed answer.

Her face burned crimson. "Ah, yes—so you would have."

He squeezed her hand. "Well, Natalie? Will you marry me?"

While at first a clear rush of emotion moistened her eyes and softened her features, she soon shook her head in regret. "I—I appreciate the sincerity of your proposal, Lord Newbury, but you know I cannot."

"Why?"

A spark of resentment flared in her eyes. "After all that has happened, you can ask that? How can I trust you?"

"Didn't I explain the reasons for my reticence?" he argued, squeezing her hand again. "And haven't I now set matters right?"

"Perhaps you have," she admitted. "But the fact remains that you withheld important information from me—and you might do so again. You also deserted me night after night, to spend your time in the seamy London underworld."

"Natalie, that was a necessity."

Her gaze flicked sharply to his. "A necessity that evidently amused you greatly."

He groaned. "Darling, can't we put this behind us and move on?"

She glanced away. "I don't think so, Ryder."

"You're not willing to forgive me anything, are you?" he demanded.

"It is not just a matter of forgiveness."

"Isn't it?"

Her anguished eyes met his. "We're too different, Ryder. I refuse to be the one who places your unfettered spirit in shackles."

He lurched to his feet. "But this makes no sense! Why would I offer for you if I view marriage in such restrictive terms?"

She shook her head fatalistically. "I am not sure. Perhaps our sense of duty and honor."

"Not love or need?"

She rose and spoke intently. "Ryder, can you honestly tell me you've been happy since we've been here in London?"

"Not completely. But that is not really a fair question, either. Since we have been here, we have faced one problem after another—"

"And that is just my point. You need to go back to the world where you belong. You will never be truly content anywhere else. You must live where you can be free, where you can spend your nights at whatever libidinous pursuit catches your fancy."

"Natalie, I want to spend my nights with you!"

"Because you're caught up in your passion for me," she protested. "Because you see me as another passing fancy, an amusement. Even if we did marry, sooner or later you would tire of me, and we would be headed straight for disaster."

"You really cannot trust or believe me, can you?" he asked with pained resignation.

She hung her head. "No, I cannot."

"That is your final word on the subject?"

"Yes."

He gripped her chin, forcing her face up to meet his forbidding visage. "Tell me something—do you think you are too good for me?"

"No, never!" she denied vehemently. "Our love affair has—has meant everything to me. You have opened my eyes to a world I never knew before, and for this I shall always be grateful."

Ryder noted with new hope the tears welling in her eyes
the sudden trembling of her lower lip. "You love me, don'
you?" he demanded.

The unexpected, jolting question left Natalie flounderin;
even more. "I—I think that is beside the point—"

"Oh, is it? Forgive me, my dear, but I think that is *pre
cisely* the point."

"That is because you always allow your emotions to rule
your life," she burst out, "and I simply cannot live that way
You have known from the outset that I am a spinster and a
bluestocking—and most set in my ways. The truth is, I am nc
more suited to marriage than you are."

"Should I console myself with the knowledge that no one
else will have you?" he rejoined bitterly.

She fought tears. "Yes."

He dropped his hand and spoke with acrimony. "It's scan
comfort, love. And you know I could force your hand. Afte1
what we have shared, I would definitely characterize your behavior as a breach of promise."

"You would risk that sort of scandal?" she cried, aghast
"Think of the disgrace to your own family—"

"I don't give a damn about gossip or infamy, as long a:
you marry me."

"Now you are being impossible!" she declared, his arrogance thoroughly exasperating her. "You just can't accept de
feat, or being less than the conqueror of *all* women, can you
Ryder?"

"Be serious."

"I am serious! I find it telling that you do not propose tc
me until you are sure you are losing me. Then, all at once
you are professing your undying love and devotion. It mus'
be quite a blow to your vanity—the one who got away, anc
all that."

He spoke with increasing frustration. "Natalie, that ha:
nothing whatsoever to do with my motives. I have simply
come to my senses, and realize we belong together. I know
you love me, and one way or another, I am going to have
you. You will marry me or you will rue the consequences."

She shook her head in pained disbelief. "Oh! So now I am
supposed to fall at your feet, simply because *you've* decidec
you do want me after all? Well, you can forget your plans tc

discredit me. As it turns out, a scandal will have little effect on my life, since shortly, I plan to return to Charleston with Aunt Love and continue running the factory." She raised her chin and regarded him with trembling bravado. "So you see, you have no hold on me."

Hurt seared Ryder. How could she say such things to him after all they had shared? Had she no feelings? Was she made of ice?

Abruptly, he hauled her close, his blue eyes burning down into hers, the angry intensity of his expression battering her proud facade. "That's not how it felt the last time we made love, when I was so deeply inside you, and you were so hungry for me you clawed at the sheets."

His words were indeed tearing Natalie apart. "Ryder, please don't make this more difficult than it already is." Brokenly, she finished, "Please don't make me cry."

But he was unmoved, his expression remorseless, his words fierce. "If it takes bringing you to tears to make you my wife, then prepare to cry, my love."

She did, barely holding in the sobs until after he had turned and walked away from her, his perfect body outlined in bright sunshine.

Thirty

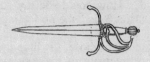

Two nights later, Ryder sat in a punch house with Sam and Mawkins. He was unshaven and bleary-eyed, his rumpled black hair hanging over his shoulders and his shirt half unbuttoned.

The scene was teeming with revelry. Scruffy customers drank, played cards, threw darts, laughed and argued at the top of their lungs. Across from Ryder's table, a quartet of drunken sailors was gathered around the piano, belting out a ribald ballad, as an equally tipsy prostitute plunked out a tinny accompaniment.

Not that Ryder and his companions were in any condition to take note of the carousing. The three men had drunk grog and played quadrille and hazard until the cards and dice swam before their eyes. Now they merely swilled their rum and continued their philosophical discussion regarding Natalie, and women in general.

"Who can understand this female?" Ryder darkly implored the others. "I was her champion—I took on her cause like a knight in shining armor. I risked life and limb for her benefit. I helped her find her aunt, and I solved the mystery of the smuggling. Now that she has no further use of me, she has discarded me like so much offal."

"That's a woman for you, gov'nor," Mawkins put in, leveling his bloodshot stare on Ryder. "They do it to you every time—use a man up and spit him out."

"I offered to marry her, to go respectable," Ryder continued. "Did she even listen?"

"They never do, gov'nor."

"Why would she think that I prefer spending my nights here?" he demanded, gesturing at their seamy surroundings and taking another gulp of rum.

"Who can conjure what goes on in the mind of a female, gov'nor?" Mawkins replied. "Take me cousin Rose. She up and married a haberdasher. Spent all his money, she did, till the landlord threw the both of them out on the street. Then she run off with a traveling portrait painter, Rose did. Now her poor husband has cooked his brains with rum, and is blubbering away at Bedlam."

"Disgraceful. How much does a man have to sacrifice, I ask you?"

"They want it all, gov'nor."

"And don't forget about Harry," a barely conscious Sam interjected.

"Aye, Harry!" Ryder expostulated, pounding a fist on the scarred table. "Thanks to her, Hampton is lost, and God only knows if we'll ever find him. But does she care, I ask you?"

"None of them care, gov'nor," answered Mawkins. "All them females is the same. None of them is ever content until they have spent a man's money, cut off the jewels, and de-masted him."

Ryder shuddered at the horrifying mixed metaphors. "Don't forget the damage they do to a man's heart."

"Aye, a man's heart is fair game for any wench. She'll rip it out, stew it good, and serve it up with the Sunday cabbage."

Even as Mawkins tossed out this new appalling image, a hefty whore strutted past the table and fixed her conniving gaze on Ryder. "Why, hello, lovey," she crooned in a sultry voice, reaching out to ruffle his hair. "Pining away for female solace, are ye?"

Ryder's eyes smoldered with violence as he yanked himself away from the woman's touch. "Be gone, you evil Cyprian. My jewels will be safe tonight."

"More's the pity, lovey," said the whore.

While Ryder was drowning his sorrows, Natalie sat dining with her father and Aunt Love. After much coercion on the part of Natalie, Love had finally been persuaded to join her niece and brother-in-law for an evening.

The dining room of the Desmond home was lit by ornate gold candelabras and a fire blazing in the grate; the table was set with snowy linen, gold-edged Derby china, and Sheffield silver. The footmen served a lavish repast of roast pheasant, steamed salmon, asparagus, potatoes in cream sauce, and sweetbreads.

While the food was clearly first-rate, Natalie found that she had little appetite. Although she had known that declining Ryder's marriage proposal was the only right choice for her, the parting with him had nonetheless been emotionally wrenching and devastating. To make matters worse, she had been experiencing digestive queasiness ever since Lord and Lady Litchfield's soiree. The fact that her malaise had been coupled with the lateness of her monthly time suggested a possibility so wondrous, yet so daunting, that she became frantic every time she dared to think about it.

The strained atmosphere between Charles and Love only exacerbated her feelings of tension and indisposition. After giving his sister-in-law a cool, cursive greeting, Charles Desmond had said little, swilling his wine and slurring the few words he uttered. Natalie and Love exchanged superficial conversation regarding the king's anticipated coronation this summer and the continuing furor over whether or not Queen Caroline would ever actually be crowned. Charles glanced up once with interest when Natalie and Love discussed the recent news of Napoleon Bonaparte's death on St. Helena, and how the former emperor's demise might finally restore a much-needed stability to French monarchial rule.

Finally, as they all shared the dessert of wine and toffee pudding, Natalie knew it was time to address the impasse between her aunt and her father. She glanced from one to the other and said, "Father, Aunt Love, I have brought the two of you together tonight for a purpose."

"Obviously," Charles slurred, sipping his wine.

"Father, don't you think you've had enough wine?" she asked gently.

Lifting his goblet, he quoted dramatically, " 'Give wine unto those that be of heavy hearts.' "

Natalie glanced at Love, who offered a sympathetic smile. Then she cleared her throat, deciding she might as well strike the issue head-on. "Father," she said, "haven't you been angry at Aunt Love for long enough?"

Charles scowled. "After what she did to Malcolm?"

"Father, Uncle Malcolm—"

"Was a reprobate who disgraced his wife and child through brazenly drinking, gambling, and chasing women," Love finished indignantly.

Charles turned on Love, shaking a finger at her. "Ah, yes, blame Malcolm!" he declared with a sweeping gesture. "Never mind that you drove him to behave as he did!"

"So you are still blaming *me* for your brother's failure?" Love shot back in angry disbelief. She tossed down her napkin. "I do wonder why I ever came here tonight."

"By all means, do not let us keep you," Charles sneered.

But Natalie grabbed her aunt's sleeve as Love would have risen. "Please, Aunt Love, we need to get this resolved—especially since you and I are now free to return to Charleston."

"Natalie, I have no intention of returning to Charleston."

"What?" Natalie cried. Then, noting that her father was nodding off to sleep, she said sharply, "Father, can't you and Aunt Love—"

Charles's head snapped up, and his bleary eyes popped open. "Oh, go back to Charleston, both of you!" he said in disgust. "Prey on my nephew Rodney again. That's all any of you women are good for—controlling a man's life and driving him to ruination."

"I'd wager you would kill to have Desiree back, running your life for a change," Love put in with sudden spite.

The barb had more than its desired effect. Charles's ferocious expression crumbled; he buried his hands in his face and groaned.

At once appearing crestfallen and contrite, Love rose and went to him, laying her hand on his shoulder. She spoke with surprising humility. "I'm sorry, Charles. Deeply so. I am far too impulsive for my own good. What I said was cruel . . ."

"You are right!" His voice was half a sob. "It's our fault," the Desmond men. We spell disaster for every woman we love. That's why Desiree left me. I—I never deserved her!"

"Charles, please!" Love entreated. "Don't torture yourself so. If it helps, I . . . I did love Malcolm deeply."

Charles clutched Love's hand. "I know," came his muffled reply. "And I don't blame you. Truly I don't. I blame myself."

"You mustn't," Love urged. "Mayhap you indeed cannot help the way you are. It was an unfortunate accident of heredity, perhaps. Who knows what makes a person as he is?"

Charles's words were tortured. "I know I am doomed, just like my brother. I know I shall never again know sweet Desiree's love . . ."

Shaking her head, Love left Charles to his sorrow and towed Natalie out into the hallway. "I'm sorry that things did not turn out better, dear. You know how it is with your father—and he does, unfortunately, seem to bring out the worst in me."

"I know, but at least the two of you are speaking now," Natalie replied. She regarded Love quizzically. "What is this about your not returning to Charleston with me?"

Undaunted, Love was smoothing her coiffure. "I think we had best not get into that now, dear. Besides, I must make this an early evening—William is taking me to hear Rossini at Covent Garden."

"He is?"

Love beamed with happiness. "He has forgiven my little deception."

"Oh. You mean your pretending to be Harriet Foxworth?"

"Aye. And now that this smuggling business is out in the open, there is no more need for chicanery."

Natalie's brow tightened with suspicion. "Just what exactly is going on between you and the Duke of Mansfield?"

"Can't talk now, dear," Love replied briskly, leaning over to peck Natalie's cheek. "But we must have tea soon. For now, why don't you go sit with your father? I've never seen Charles in such a morose state. Frankly, I am quite worried about him."

"So am I," Natalie concurred.

"He really is lost without Desiree, even after all these years," Love murmured fatalistically. "Let's just hope your mother's absence won't be the death of him." True to her flighty character, Love abruptly brightened. "Well, I must step lively. Chin up, dear."

As Natalie turned back toward the dining room, she felt anything but cheerful.

In the days that followed, Natalie prepared for her voyage back to America. She fretted over her father, who had improved not at all. She also worried about herself, for her monthly time had still not come, and she was beginning to experience even more nausea at odd moments. She was becoming increasingly suspicious that she was pregnant, a possibility that spurred both awe and panic. Guilt nagged at her that she had not discussed the prospect with Ryder.

Yet how could she tell him what she feared when he was bound to insist on marriage—a marriage that would ultimately doom them both? In this respect, the likelihood of pregnancy only increased her determination to return to America, rather than trap herself in a match in which she, Ryder, and the child would all ultimately suffer.

Ryder came by to see her a couple of times, but she kept the visits brief, claiming concern for her father. Again he proposed marriage; again she turned him down, even as it broke her heart to do so, and guilt repeatedly assailed her over the possibility that she could be taking his unborn child with her back to America.

Two days before she was scheduled to depart London, Natalie visited her aunt at the cozy little hotel in Mayfair where she was staying. In the sitting room of the matron's suite, the two women shared tea, scones, fresh strawberries, and cheese.

After the courtesies had been exhausted, Natalie got straight to the point. "Aunt Love, what did you mean the other night when you told me you aren't planning to return to America with me?"

"I meant exactly what I said."

"But why?"

Love smiled radiantly. "Because I have decided I want to marry William Remington."

Natalie shot to her feet. "What? You must be jesting!"

"Sit down, dear. And no, I am not jesting at all."

Stunned at the news, Natalie sank back into her seat. "But—but the Duke of Mansfield has to be the coldest man I've ever met. Plus, he is a religious fanatic."

"I realize William's religious fanaticism can be tedious," came Love's offhanded reply as she nibbled on a scone. "However, he's rich as Midas, and I love him, so who cares?"

"Aunt Love!"

"One can certainly forgive a few eccentricities in a duke, don't you think?" Love forged on brightly. With a slight blush, she added, "Actually, some of William's eccentricities I rather like."

For a moment, Natalie was too mystified to speak. "But how can you contemplate living with a man who has no feelings?"

Love reached out to pat her niece's hand. "Now, dear, you are judging William far too harshly. Granted, he tends to act aloof, but I have discovered that there is a world of hurt buried beneath that cold veneer. Not to mention passion."

"Passion?" Natalie's eyes were enormous.

Love laughed. "It is too much to believe that I might succumb to such carnal delights at my advanced age?"

Natalie rolled her eyes. "Nothing you do surprises me anymore. So you are determined to remain here?"

"Quite."

Biting her lip, Natalie asked, "But what about the factory in Charleston—and Rodney?"

Love shrugged. "Oversee it yourself if you've a mind to. Otherwise, I say it is high time we left Rodney to succeed or fail on his own." She frowned. "Perhaps your father uttered a grain of truth the other night. Mayhap we Desmond women do interfere too much—and our machinations haven't done much good for the Desmond men, as far as I can tell."

Natalie sighed, pressing a hand to her suddenly roiling stomach, while was rebelling against the cream cheese she had just eaten—and, no doubt, against the sobering prospects of her own future. "Suit yourself, then. I am returning to America."

"And what of your young man—William's son? Ryder seems such a fine, handsome gentleman. And just think, you could become a marchioness, and one day a duchess."

"You'll become a duchess sooner," Natalie pointed out resentfully.

"Oh, yes, and won't it be fun?" Love clapped her hands. "Why not keep it all in the family?"

Natalie fell tensely silent. Her aunt's words renewed her feelings of guilt over leaving Ryder, and to make matters worse, her stomach was now threatening a full revolt.

"Aunt Love," she said finally, in a strained tone, "Ryder is a fine person in many ways, but—"

"You are not still angry at him for not telling you William's factory was involved in the smuggling?"

"No, it goes much deeper than that," Natalie confided with pained resignation. "He's a rogue at heart, and I fear he will never make any woman truly happy. Our marrying would eventually make him feel smothered, would crush his unfettered soul, and we would both be miserable because of it. Despite what he says, I'm convinced he would never truly settle down."

Love appeared unconvinced. "But hasn't he been very committed to you, dear—coming with you to England, helping you solve the mystery?" She paused, looking perplexed. "He hasn't offered for your hand?"

Her niece sighed heavily. "He has. But I've turned him down."

"Oh, Natalie!"

"Aunt Love, you for one should understand, after all you endured as Uncle Malcolm's wife!"

"Ryder Remington is not Malcolm Desmond, my dear," Love replied soberly. "I've met the boy only briefly, but I sense he has a great deal of his father in him—"

"And those are the very qualities that will bring him to grief if he marries me!" Natalie declared. "He is not meant for a life of titles and responsibility and social constraint. He will never be happy unless he is free."

"Then why has he offered for you? I sense that there is a deep bond there."

Her aunt's last words assailed Natalie with new guilt. Turmoil and doubt churned within her, even as waves of nausea continued to sweep her. She got unsteadily to her feet and moved to the window, staring out at the cobbled street, watching a fruit vendor clatter past with his cart.

"I must go home," she muttered.

She heard her aunt rustle to her feet. "Natalie, what is wrong with you? Why, you've turned as white as a sheet, child."

"I . . . The scone did not agree with me. I feel—"

"Nauseated?" her aunt provided.

Red-faced, Natalie turned around. "Certainly not! It's just a touch of indigestion."

Smiling wisely, Love came forward and touched Natalie's arm. "You are pregnant, aren't you?"

"Of course I am not!" Natalie denied hotly, then staggered as a new spasm of distress gripped her.

"Come over here and lie down before you fall down," Love scolded. She led Natalie to the silk brocade settee, then went to wet a cloth and wiped the girl's face and forehead. "You are carrying Ryder Remington's child?"

"Aunt Love, that is preposterous!"

"The two of you crossed the Atlantic together, didn't you?" Love asked wisely.

"That does not mean we were lovers! Just what do you think I am, anyway?"

"A woman in love—and scared to death she has chosen the wrong man."

"I am not some courtesan who goes around having love affairs!"

"I never said you were, darling. But, as you're also aware, I have met your young man, and I know his father—er—*very* well."

Natalie's mouth fell open. "You actually mean that you and William Remington—"

Love winked. "As I said, William is a man of intense passion."

"I can't believe I am hearing this!"

"And now you are experiencing morning sickness—"

"Yes! At four o'clock in the afternoon."

Love wagged a finger and flashed her niece a mischievous smile. "My dear, you cannot fool me. You see, I knew your mother, and she, too, experienced nausea at odd moments when she was carrying you."

Natalie was quiet, clenching her fists.

Love touched her niece's coiled hand and spoke fervently. "My dear, you cannot go back to America. You must tell Ryder that you are carrying his child."

Teary-eyed and distraught, Natalie turned to her aunt. "But then he will insist I marry him."

"That is the idea, darling," Love said gently.

"I can't tell him," she whispered miserably, shaking her head and blinking at tears. "I just can't. It will be all of my worse fears coming true."

"But what will you do back in America—a woman alone, pregnant, unmarried?"

"I—I don't know! I'll find a husband—or invent one."

Love shook her head. "You must tell him. 'Tis the only fair and decent way."

A horrible suspicion dawning, Natalie glared at Love. "If you tell Ryder, I'll never forgive you."

"Me?" Love flashed Natalie a look of wide-eyed innocence as she squeezed her niece's hand. "Would I ever act so impetuously? You must know you can trust me, darling."

Thirty-one

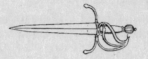

"**Y**OU ARE GOING TO TAKE *MY HEIR* WITH YOU BACK TO AMERica?"

The next morning, Natalie was sitting at breakfast with her father when Ryder burst into the dining room unannounced and asked his abrupt, demoralizing question. She could have died on the spot, especially because of her father's presence—although, thank goodness, all the servants were out of the room.

When Ryder made his angry demand, Natalie could only stare at him. He appeared every bit the forbidding, enraged stranger—dressed in formal black, his features set as resolutely as stone—and for once, she felt genuinely frightened of him. She had no idea how to respond.

Ryder, in turn, was gazing at Natalie with both rage and hurt. He could not believe she had done this to him—that she now carried his child and yet had no plans to inform him. Did she have no regard whatsoever for his feelings? Did she trust him so little? Thank God her aunt had intervened and told him the truth, before it was too late and she was lost to him.

As the tension stretched to an unbearable tautness, the two continued to regard each other warily. Then Charles Desmond, for once almost sober, filled the gap. Getting unsteadily to his feet, he glowered at Ryder. "Lord Newbury, what is the meaning of this intrusion, and how dare you infer anything so—so scandalous about my daughter!"

Ryder turned to Natalie's father with an attitude of icy courtesy. "Mr. Desmond, I apologize for my outburst, and for intruding on you in this fashion. However, it is critical that I

speak with your daughter alone, at once. It is regrettable that
I must reverse the normal order of things—ordinarily, my solicitors would have contacted you first, with a formal written
proposal." He paused to glare at Natalie. "However, your
daughter's deceit has made it necessary for me to act in a far
more peremptory fashion. But I do assure you that my repre-
sentative will call on you first thing on the morrow."

Obviously extremely discomfited, Charles coughed. "Well,
yes. Then I suppose I should leave the two of you to—er—
discuss the matter."

Natalie looked beseechingly at her father. "Please do not
leave me alone with him."

"Natalie!"

Ryder's charged voice compelled her to look at him, and
she struggled not to wince at his expression of formidable
fury. "Yes?" she whispered.

"Do you really want to lay out all the details in your father's presence?" he asked with menacing mildness.

Miserably, she shook her head.

Ryder turned to Charles. "Sir, if you will excuse us?"

Nodding, Charles left the room.

Ryder fixed his wrathful gaze on Natalie. He shoved a
chair aside and started toward her. Panicked, she fled. He
caught her by the window, pulling her into his arms.

He held her firmly, but not roughly. Nonetheless, she
flailed at him and struggled to get away.

Frantically, she cried, "Don't you dare! If you hurt me,
hurt my child—"

"*Our* child!" Ryder caught her face in his hands and spoke
passionately. "*Our child,* Natalie. Just who has been hurt
here? Who has been deceived? You are the one who was going to take away my baby—and with him the woman I love."

The woman I love. The words lashed at Natalie's heart. She
stared up at him, her expression exquisite with conflicted
emotion. "Ryder, I did what I felt was right—for us both."

"Nonsense. You hurt me, Natalie."

The pain in his eyes wounded her all the more. "Oh, you
weren't even supposed to know," she cried abjectly. "I am so
furious with Aunt Love!"

"She is not the one to blame here. Thank God she had the
decency—and the sense—to tell me."

"I won't marry you, Ryder!" she burst out.

His hands dropped, and his smile was frightening. "My dear, you have no choice. A formal proposal of betrothal will be presented to your father tomorrow, and it will be accepted."

"Of course! Following the scene you just created!"

"For which you have only yourself to blame. Furthermore, if you continue to resist, I swear I shall go to my father and, if need be, bring to bear all his power. I am sure that even he will not allow you to steal my child—and his grandchild."

She stared at him, now a dark, relentless stranger, so full of implacable intent. For once, he seemed very much a duke's heir, and the demoralizing glimpse of his future identity was devastating to her. "Oh, no, I cannot do this! I'm turning you into your father!"

His words came in an emphatic whisper. "Defy me again, Natalie, and you'll see worse."

She turned away to hide her stinging eyes. "You know you are making a dreadful mistake. You know that we shall never suit—"

"Then we'll suffer together, my love, for I shall never let you go."

After uttering the fierce words, Ryder moved up behind her, clamping his forearms gently at her midsection, drawing her close, and pressing his lips to her cheek. An anguished cry escaped her as his unexpected tenderness ravaged her emotions.

Her fingers clenched on his forearms. "Ryder, won't you please—"

"No more arguing, darling," he cut in firmly. "The decision has been made."

She realized he was right; there truly was no escape now. Her fingers uncoiled in a gesture of resignation. He snuggled her closer against him. She wished desperately that he would simply leave before she fell apart, but clearly he was granting her no emotional reprieves today.

His hand moved low on her belly, to where their tiny child lay. Poignant feeling brought a knot to her throat.

"When did you know?" he asked.

She shivered. "About a week ago."

"And you did not tell me?"

"I didn't want to trap you."

"And now you are the one who feels trapped?"

"I—I don't know."

"Do you want my child?" he asked intently.

She almost wept then. "Oh, yes."

He expelled a relieved breath, moved aside her hair, and kissed the nape of her neck. "Then it is all going to be all right. Trust me, darling."

She wiped tears away with her sleeve. "Didn't you tell me that earlier, right before you carried me off and bedded me for the first time?"

He smiled. "You were quite willingly bedded, my lady— and in time, you will become a willing bride, too."

"You are that sure of yourself, are you?"

"Aye—sure we will make this work, for ourselves and for our child." He nibbled on her ear. "You know it will have to be a rushed affair, with no time for a full reading of the banns. But perhaps we can get a message to your mother in Paris."

"No," she disagreed weakly.

"Did she hurt you so badly, darling?"

Her voice broke. "You hurt me, too."

"More than you have wounded me?"

She was silent, shuddering with the unshed sorrow that she still somehow kept at bay.

"Will it be so terrible being married to me?" he asked gently. He turned her slightly in his arms, tilted her face upward, and captured her trembling lips, smothering her raw cry.

It was the most bittersweet moment Natalie had ever known. Ryder's kiss was one of utter possession, but also of incredible sweetness.

Afterward, she sniffed at tears and turned her face away. "You know, you have gotten your way now. You have made me cry."

He sighed. "I never truly wanted to make you cry, only to make you mine." His hand moved low to stroke her belly again. Pride and love gleamed in his eyes. "And you said I had no hold on you."

She began to quiver all the more.

"What is it, darling?"

Miserably, she confessed, "The future Duke of Mansfield was conceived either in a carriage or, more likely, in a brothel!"

He chuckled and tucked her head beneath his chin. "I think it was at the brothel. I think I knew as I watched us coupling in the mirror."

"I didn't get to watch," she pointed out, sniffing. "Not then. I was on my knees at the time."

"So was I," he teased her tenderly. "And I'm on my knees to have you now."

She hiccuped. "You know what the worst part is?"

"What's that?"

Her fingers dug into his wrists. "I'm really sorry I hurt you, Ryder."

At last, she turned in his arms and sobbed.

Later that day, Ryder called on his father. He still felt a lingering hurt over Natalie's former reticence, yet hope and joy surged within him anew. They would marry now; he would make things work. With Natalie by his side, anything would be possible.

William Remington rose as his son entered the study. "Ryder, what may I do for you?"

Ryder's tone was coldly formal. "I have come to inform you that I am marrying Natalie Desmond. Out of respect to my mother's memory, I am giving you this one chance to grant your approval. But I must also warn you that one word said to slight Miss Desmond will result in your never seeing either of us again."

William looked most taken aback by Ryder's diatribe. "Son, I—you have my blessing. But you must tell me, is this young woman carrying your child?"

"That is none of your damned affair!" Ryder glared at his father and turned to leave.

William followed him. "Ryder—please. Natalie's aunt told me."

Ryder stared at him speechlessly.

"Love explained that Natalie was being obdurate in the matter. She thought you might need—well, some help with the legalities. If so, I shall be happy to place my solicitors at

your disposal, and if you are in need of a special license, I am
in good stead with the archbishop."

Ryder regarded his father with bitter skepticism. "Why this
change of heart, your Grace?"

William Remington was silent for a long moment, then
spoke carefully. "First, I do regret my initial condemnation of
Miss Desmond. I have become well acquainted with her aunt,
and realize now that she is a young lady of good stock. Indeed, it is quite likely that Love and I may marry."

Ryder was pleasantly surprised. "You don't say?"

"My other concern is the child. You cannot, of course, allow an issue of yours to be born illegitimate, nor can you allow Miss Desmond to choose another husband."

"Is that all?" Ryder asked in a tense whisper.

The duke shook his head and continued with obvious
strain. "Moreover, I feel that perhaps I did not do my best by
you, son, and I should like to have another chance—with you,
I hope, and certainly with my grandchild."

Ryder gazed at his father with clearly mixed emotions. "I
cannot make any promises, your Grace, but, given your obvious sincerity, I will accept your help."

"Thank you, Ryder."

"And you, Father."

It was the first time in many years that Ryder had called
William Remington "Father" without rancor, and when he
shook his father's hand before leaving, it was the first time
the two men had touched since before Carlotta had died.

Thirty-two

Less than a week later, Ryder and Natalie stood before the altar of St. Margaret's, Westminster, as the vicar intoned the nuptial ceremony from *The Book of Common Prayer.* Behind them in the lovely Christopher Wren church sat the wedding party. The gathering had deliberately been kept small but respectable, with members of both their families, selected friends, and even a couple of cabinet ministers who were acquaintances of Ryder's father in attendance.

Natalie glanced at Ryder as he repeated a vow. He appeared splendid, if quite stern, in his dress coat of black velvet, ruffled shirt, tan pantaloons, black shoes with brass buckles, and white gloves. His long black hair, tied back at the nape, hinted at his hidden recklessness, although his visage was utterly solemn and properly patrician as he pledged his troth.

He was trying so hard to be respectable, she thought tenderly. But could he be happy in the long run under the constraints of marriage and giving up his roguish ways? She feared that he was deluding himself regarding his love her, that he was caught somewhere between his passion for her—which, admittedly, was strong—and his desire to do the honorable thing. She fervently hoped their union would work out, even as she still secretly feared they could be embarking on a disaster course that would eventually leave him feeling trapped, leave her feeling powerless to change things, and bring misery to them both.

Ryder, too, was studying Natalie as she said her vows. She looked utterly divine in her wedding dress of French lace

over white satin. She wore a small wreath of white tea roses
in her hair, and her coiffure was crowned by a gauzy veil that
trailed away from her face and down around her creamy
shoulders. Admiring the low neckline and high Empire waist
of her gown, he mused that the current style would suit her
well as her belly grew larger with child . . .

His child. Over the past week, he had thought much of the
baby they would have, wondering if it would be a boy or a
girl, imagining holding the child in his arms for the first time,
picturing Natalie with his baby suckling at her breast. She
had wounded him when she had planned to take his child—
and herself—away from him. Even now, a slight frown puck-
ering her beautiful mouth, and the fine worry lines beneath
her eyes, gave evidence to the fact that she was marrying him
under duress. Why couldn't she believe he would change for
her, that he would become a good husband and father?

As they had rushed ahead with the wedding plans during
the past week, they had remained distant. He intended to see
to it that the rift would end tonight. And he would start by
wooing his bride, seducing her, and then loving her all night
long—thoroughly but gently, too, so as not to harm her or the
baby. Excitement and a deep hunger stormed his senses as he
anticipated holding his bride in his arms, being alone with her
again, at last.

A feeling of powerful possessiveness and pride washed
over him. What a fool he had been ever to think something
less than marriage to Natalie would do. Loving her as he did,
he could never settle for having less than all of her. Now,
never again would they be compelled to sneak off to express
their love in secret. Tonight, he would bring them together as
man and wife. Afterward, he hoped they would finally be on
the road to mutual trust and understanding.

Soon, Ryder experienced the joy of placing his ring on
Natalie's finger, and soon afterward, the vicar pronounced
them husband and wife. Ryder turned to his bride, and his
heart soared when she smiled at him tremulously. He leaned
over and gently brushed her sweet lips, smiling as he heard
appreciative murmurs rise from the congregation.

As he and Natalie went back toward the sanctuary, his father and Love Desmond were the first to come forward, Wil-

liam looking austere and dignified in formal black, Love wearing an elegant gown of lavender silk.

"Congratulations, son," William Remington said with a kindly smile.

"Thank you, Father." As Ryder shook William's hand, he felt oddly tempted to embrace him, for the first time in so many years. Watching the duke move on to kiss Natalie's cheek, he turned and hugged Love.

Natalie was also pleased by the warm wishes offered by Ryder's father. As William kissed her cheek, it sank in upon her that she was part of the Remington family now, Ryder's wife until death parted them. She again hoped things could work between her and Ryder, especially for the sake of their child. Next to her, her bridegroom looked supremely happy and proud as he chatted with Love, yet she still had doubts that he could remain content throughout their marriage.

Love now swept up and embraced Natalie. "Congratulations, darling. You've never looked more beautiful." Pulling back, she wiped away a tear and added tentatively, "You're not still angry at me for spilling the beans, are you?"

Natalie flashed her aunt a forbearing smile. "If I stewed in resentment every time you did something outrageous, I'd be angry at you all the time."

Love patted the girl's hand. "It is for the best, darling. You'll see."

Natalie found it difficult to doubt Love's words as Francesca came forward with tears welling in her eyes and warmly hugged the bride. "Oh, my darling Natalie, I cannot tell you how happy I am to see this day," she said in an emotional voice. "You and my grandson make the most splendid couple."

"Thank you, Countess," Natalie returned graciously.

"This marriage is meant to be. It will be long and fruitful, you will see."

"Is that another vision?" Natalie asked.

Francesca squeezed her hand. "It is an absolute certainty."

After a moment, when Francesca began to speak with Ryder, Natalie's enhanced mood sank as she saw her father advance toward her. Even though Charles Desmond was sober and dressed in proper formal attire, his coloring appeared particularly bad this morning, his eyes were bloodshot and jaundiced, and he was all but swaying on his feet.

He continued to wobble as he hugged Natalie. She could feel the bad shaking of his body and smell the telltale odor of liquor.

"My dear, I am so happy for you."

She eyed him with grave concern. "Are you all right, Father?"

He waved a white-gloved hand. "Of course. Don't fret."

Yet Natalie's brow was deeply puckered as she watched him stagger on to shake Ryder's hand.

After the register had been signed, and the legalities disposed of, the guests traveled to the Desmond home for the wedding breakfast. The twenty guests crowded inside the dining room, where the servants had squeezed in two extra tables, arranging all three in a U shape to afford a feeling of intimacy. After all were seated, the liveried footmen served the meal of eggs, ham, fruit, scones, wedding cake, and champagne.

A moment later, Natalie's father stood to offer the first toast. "My friends," he began unsteadily, "let us drink to my lovely daughter, Natalie, and her new husband, Lord Newbury." Staring poignantly at her, Charles paused to sniffle, his voice cracking slightly. "May they know the lifelong happiness that never blessed Natalie's mother and me."

The guests exchanged bemused glances at the unusual salute, but dutifully raised their champagne glasses. Charles quickly drained his own glass and motioned to a footman to pour him another round.

During the repast, the guests gossiped gaily. There was mention of the current clash in Parliament between Tory and Whig, of the ongoing battles over reform of the common laws and of Parliament itself. But mainly the talk was centered, as it had been at Lord and Lady Litchfield's recent soiree, on the upcoming coronation.

"Do you suppose the king will actually see himself crowned this July?" inquired the vivacious Lady Litchfield. "Or will the carpenters again be pulling down the tacked-on galleries at the Abbey, as they were required to do last summer?"

"I hear the invitations will be in the post any day now," put in Francesca. "So it seems the king is serious this time."

"If he is in earnest," remarked the pompous, monocled Teddy Brandon, "then he had best have the carpenters construct a cage to restrain Queen Caroline during the ceremony."

At Teddy's audacious words, there was a collective cry of dismay from the ladies, and soon the entire gathering became embroiled in a spirited debate pitting the ostensible virtues of the disgraced, corpulent queen against the alleged attributes of her equally dissolute, gluttonous husband.

"With Princess Charlotte dead," declared the elderly, outspoken Lord Chalmsley, "one would think the king might reconsider his intractable stand on the separation from Caroline. He has lost his heir, and in the event of his death, to whom will the monarchy fall? The infant Victoria?"

"Perhaps it is difficult to become a prolific sire," remarked Teddy Brandon, "when one is perpetually suffering the throes of gout, pleurisy, and obesity."

Brandon's indelicate comment prompted suitably scandalized utterings from the ladies, while one of the men was heard to mutter sardonically that King George's preference for grandmotherly types would no doubt not increase his chances for ever attaining another issue. At this juncture, Ryder's father stepped in, firmly steering the conversation away from the king and toward some recent theological writings of the Archbishop of Canterbury. Quickly bored with the discourse, the guests turned their attention back to the food and champagne. Natalie wondered if her new father-in-law's effort had been made for her sake, to save her embarrassment at the indiscreet subject matter, especially considering the possible parallels to her own life.

About ten minutes later, Ryder nudged her and whispered in her ear, "Darling, I'm afraid your father is about to pass out."

"Oh, no!" she whispered back, glancing over to see Charles with his head lolling toward his plate.

Fortunately, Love had already motioned to the footmen, who dashed forward and saved Charles from doing a nosedive into his poached eggs. The servants helped Charles up, and all attempts at dignity soon gave way to absurdity as the embarrassed men were compelled to half drag their insensible employer from the room, amid snickers and snide glances from the guests.

A few moments later, Fitzhugh, appearing agitated, entered and hovered in the archway. Love rose discreetly and went over to speak with him. Natalie excused herself and joined the other two, who were already conversing intently.

"What is it?" she asked Love in a tense whisper. "Is Father quite ill?"

Love flashed her niece a reassuring smile. "It's nothing, dear. Fitzhugh simply cannot awaken your father."

"Oh, no! I must go to him!"

"Don't be ridiculous! You cannot leave your own wedding breakfast. I shall go to Charles, and if need be, I shall summon the surgeon. Now go back to your place at once, Natalie. I assure you, my dear, that to leave the celebration now will only bring your father even more disgrace than he has already heaped upon himself."

Nodding dismally, Natalie swept back to her place.

"What's wrong, darling?" Ryder asked as he sprang up to seat her.

"Father is quite unwell."

"Do you need to leave?"

She shook her head. "Aunt Love is seeing to him."

"And we shall as well, once everyone goes home," he said firmly.

Beneath the table, he took her hand and squeezed it. She smiled at him. At times he could be very dear.

After the guests had offered the newlyweds their fond wishes and left, Ryder and Natalie went upstairs, just as the physician was emerging from Charles's room.

"How is my father, Dr. Sturgess?" she asked.

The thin, bearded man shook his head. "Not good. His color is abominable."

"I've noticed he has gotten quite jaundiced of late," Ryder remarked.

"Indeed. The drink is going to be the death of him." Sturgess regarded Natalie grimly. "But I fear it is not just the liquor that is killing him, but a broken heart. He simply refuses to let go of his self-destructive obsession with your mother. At this rate, my dear, he will not last out the year."

Natalie nodded morosely, thanking the physician as he left

Afterward, Ryder stood watching the exquisite struggle on his bride's face. So much pride. So much fear. So much love It dismayed him that her family problems had brought her such pain.

"Darling, what can I do to help?" he asked gently.

She was silent, biting her lip.

"Natalie?" he prodded.

At last, she turned to him earnestly and touched his arm "We must go to Paris and fetch home my mother."

Ryder reached out to caress her cheek. "Of course, darling When have I denied you anything?" Leaning over, he added tenderly, "Except, of course, permission to leave me. We'll board a steamer to Calais first thing on the morrow—and we shall bring your mother home."

"Oh, Ryder, thank you."

She smiled at him then, quite radiantly, and thrust herself into his arms. Ryder held his bride close and felt heaven within his grasp.

Thirty-three

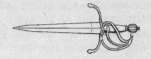

A FTER SPENDING MUCH OF THE DAY WITH NATALIE'S FATHER and informing Francesca, William, and Love of their plans to leave for Paris, Ryder and Natalie went to the hotel in Piccadilly where he had reserved rooms for their wedding night. Their suite was lavish, with its Louis XIV furnishings, flocked wallpaper, Oriental rugs, and velvet draperies. Natalie and Ryder sat at a small table near the front window, eating lobster and sipping champagne by candlelight. She wore a lacy pale blue gown and negligee, he a burgundy-colored dressing gown.

Ryder had been staring at Natalie for some moments, as he found her to be far more of a temptation than the delectable food and drink. Her chestnut hair cascaded over her shoulders, and he could not wait to run his fingers through that rick silk. A flush of expectation colored her lovely cheeks, and her eyes held a glow of combined uncertainty and longing. He intended to see to it that the uncertainty soon fled her visage, and that the longing was kindled into unbridled passion. He could not wait to take her in his arms and begin their marriage in earnest.

Natalie found her husband's smoldering, intense expression both thrilling and unnerving. Thinking of the night to come, and of the lifelong commitment the consummation of their marriage would represent, she felt her stomach lurch slightly. Muttering an excuse, she rose and went to stand not far from the window. A soft breeze caressed her face as she stared at the magnificent lines of St. James's Church, etched in gold by the setting sun.

She felt Ryder move up behind her and wrap his arms around her waist. "Not hungry, darling?" he murmured, nibbling at her throat.

Fighting a shiver at his nearness, she turned in his arms. "Not terribly."

He frowned with concern as he stared at her—so close, so tormentingly beautiful, yet still so far away. She was his wife now, but he retained doubts that she was truly his, that she would trust him with the rest of her life.

"You know you have a baby to eat for now," he admonished.

"I know. But I cannot help it if my appetite is not the same of late."

He cuddled her close and kissed her brow. "We must see what luscious delights we can tempt you with in Paris."

She smiled tremulously, but her eyes were troubled. "I doubt I shall be overly concerned about food there."

"You are worried about your father?"

She nodded. "If nothing changes, he could die, Ryder. And soon."

"Do not fret," he soothed. "We'll find your mother and fetch her back here."

She smiled. "You are always taking on my problems—first Aunt Love, and now my father."

Ryder touched the tip of her nose. "Darling, it is my pleasure to champion your causes. As for our journey to Paris, what lovelier spot could we choose for a wedding trip? And we may be able to accomplish some good while we're there."

"If Mother will even agree to come back to London with us," Natalie replied with bitter skepticism.

He lifted her chin and stared down into her eyes. "You are still very angry at her, aren't you?"

She nodded solemnly. "Can you blame me? She turned her back on Father and me, as if neither of us existed."

"I know. It just pains me to see you upset."

Abruptly, she moved out of his embrace. "It does not pain you enough to keep you from forcing me into this marriage," she muttered pointedly.

Hurt seared him at her words. "Have I made you so miserable by wedding you?"

She twisted her fingers together. "No, not miserable ex-

actly, but you know I still have doubts about our marriage being viable in the long run."

"Did we have another choice, Natalie?"

She flashed him a poignant smile. "No, I suppose not,
though I fear you will be the one who ends up feeling confined."

He closed the distance between them and embraced her
once more. "Why don't you let me worry about that?"

"It seems you want to take on all my worries, don't you?"

He took her face in her hands. "Natalie, look at me."

Defiantly, she lifted her gaze.

He stared into her tawny-brown eyes and spoke vehemently. "I know you are concerned about your father and apprehensive about dealing with your mother. I know you are
still angry at me for forcing your hand. But we're married
now, and we shall make the best of things. If you're planning
to use these problems to throw up barriers between us tonight, I'm telling you now that it won't work."

Her expression suddenly guilty, she again broke away and
moved off. Again he followed her, wrapping her in his embrace and holding her tightly to him. A moan escaped her as
she felt the urgency of his desire rising against her backside.

"Do you know how long I've waited to be alone with
you?" he murmured intensely.

She shuddered. "Yes."

"Are you afraid I'll hurt you? Hurt the baby?"

"No." The word came out choked.

"Then why the tears?" He cupped her breasts with his
hands and pressed his mouth to her soft throat.

Natalie sighed as the scent and heat of him made her tingle
with desire. "Because when we're so intimate, I—I feel close
to you, a part of you. And that frightens me."

"Because you're afraid you'll have to give me up eventually?"

"Yes."

"Not a chance!" He stroked her belly tenderly. "Remember
once when I told you we might be more alike than you
think?"

"Yes."

"Perhaps you are afraid of giving in to the part of yourself that is like me—the reckless, passionate streak—the very soul of the scandalous wench I met back at the Charleston tavern."

She turned to regard him with mingled curiosity and resentment. "If by that you mean, am I afraid of losing control of my own life, then yes, I certainly am."

Though his eyes sparkled with amusement, his tone was earnest. "Darling, you don't have to be afraid with me. You can be a shameless wench or a straitlaced bluestocking—whatever makes you happy. For I am convinced we can find a way to live together that will satisfy our conflicting sensibilities."

"Do you really believe that, Ryder?" she asked with forlorn hope.

He clutched her close. "I have to, darling, because the alternative is unbearable. Although it may take effort, I know we can be happy together."

She stared up at him tremulously. "Oh, I hope you are right."

He smiled back tenderly. "Will you make me a promise?"

"What?"

"A promise that at least you'll try?"

"Of course I'll try," she said feelingly.

He sighed with relief and began kissing her neck. "And will you let yourself enjoy it?"

She laughed breathlessly. "With you, how can I not?"

"Not just our moments in bed, darling, though God knows they are heaven. I want your promise that you'll let yourself go a bit with me—not let all those worries weigh down our wedding trip."

"I suppose that's the least a bridegroom should demand," she conceded with a smile. "You have my promise, then."

His passionate gaze impaled her as he lowered his face toward hers. "Tonight we will make our beginning. There will be no barriers—only you and me, and our love."

She did not answer, but her gasp of desire as he captured her lips was answer enough. He crushed her closer and she felt the hardness of his passion pressing against her. Her hands caressed his spine.

"Don't worry, darling, I shall be gentle with you," he whispered. "But do not doubt for a moment that you are mine—my wife, my love. Tonight and always."

Ryder took his wife's hand and led her to the bed. Next to
it, he undressed her, removing her gown and wrapper. She
still appeared uncertain, trembling, and her emotional suscep-
tibility excited him all the more. He would prove himself
worthy of her trust, of the total intimacy his heart would demand. He cast his hot gaze over her ripe, beautiful body, and
joy filled his being that she was his. He drew his finger
through her hair, kissed a silken chestnut strand, and inhaled
the luscious, perfumed scent of her.

"My God, you are so lovely."

He touched one of her swollen breasts, and at the sound of
her sharp pant, leaned over to take the dark nipple in his
mouth.

She emitted a cry that was half pleasure, half pain, and he
quickly pulled back, gazing at her face.

"My breasts are very sensitive," she murmured.

"A state for which I'm doubtless responsible?" he asked
with pride.

She smiled. Then arousal seared him anew as she reached
out and undid the sash on his dressing gown, drawing her
gaze greedily over him—and then her fingers.

Ryder lifted her onto the bed, doffed his dressing gown,
then joined her there, kissing her ardently. Their tongues
played and plunged. After a long moment, he moved his lips
down her throat, kissing her neck, then running his tongue
over her breasts and nipples. She responded with fierce abandon, lifting his face to her nipple, encouraging him until he
sucked deeply. Now her pants of pleasure, and the way her
body writhed against his, told him there was no discomfort,
only bliss as he stroked and sucked and kneaded the delightful, firm globes.

He moved lower, searching the contour of her belly with
his lips, seeking signs of a change. She was still very flat, and
she trembled beneath him.

"I can't wait until you are large with my child," he whispered, caressing her belly with the palm of his hand, "and I
can feel him moving, watch your body change with each day
that passes."

"And what if he is a she?"

He chuckled, running his tongue around her navel. "A
dozen or so girls first might suit nicely. I wouldn't want you

to claim you had done your duty by me once you had produced an heir."

"I would never try to claim that," she said breathlessly.

He stared up at her fervently. "And I would never allow
you to."

With those impassioned words, he eased his lips even
lower. When he parted her thighs, she tensed, more with
emotional reticence than with true shyness. Gently he held
her thighs apart and whispered, "We're married, darling. Now
be my wife."

She shuddered and relaxed with an aching sigh. He planted
hot kisses that left her squirming with pleasure and digging
her fingers into his hair. When he explored her with his fingers, she gave a demented cry and tossed her head. He
glanced upward, studying her expression of complete vulnerability and shattered restraint. He slid his fingers inside her
and watched her reaction as she bit her lip and clutched the
sheet. She was so gorgeous, with her nipples so tight with
passion, her rich chestnut hair spread wide on the pillow. And
she belonged to him . . .

By now, his blood was roaring in his ears and his manhood
felt ready to burst. Still, he lingered between her thighs,
wanting to heighten the torment for them both. He leaned
over and possessed her with his lips and tongue until she sur-
rendered completely and succumbed to her pleasure with a
feverish cry.

He stared up at her incredibly expressive face—the hot
cheeks, the deeply dilated eyes, the wet, parted lips. "Do you
love me, Natalie?" he asked hoarsely.

Her eyes were bright with tears. "Yes."

"Then say it."

"I love you, Ryder."

The sound of those sweet, dearly coveted words on her lips
almost brought him to tears. When he surged upward to take
her, she surprised him by pushing him over, easing him back
until he sat up against the headboard. The mindless look in
her eyes as she straddled him compelled him to pull her to
him tightly, ravishing her breast in his mouth as he roamed
his hands freely over her back, her soft bottom.

"Let me . . ." She breathed hard. "Let me kiss you."

He released her, only to groan as she roved her lips over

him, beginning at his strong neck, moving down his muscled chest. She took his hardness firmly in her fingers—

Raw lust raged through him. He was panting, barely able to contain the urge to grab her and take her before he spent himself in her fingers—

Then she leaned over and took him in her mouth. Wet, velvety heat engulfed him. He closed his eyes and clenched his teeth. A feral groan rumbled through his throat and he tangled a hand in her hair. Her tongue was performing a wild, wicked dance on his agonized manhood. He could not endure it.

"Natalie, you do not know what you are doing," he rasped. "My God, woman, you are going to kill me—if I don't kill you first."

In answer, she chuckled, straightening to kiss him, and thrust her tongue deeply into his mouth. By now Ryder was beyond madness—

His touch was insistent, almost rough, as he caught her, lifted her, pressed her down on her back, and then positioned himself between her spread thighs. He reached down and stroked her raw pulse with his rough thumb, caressing her until she cried out. He could feel the blood roar in his ears as he entered her so slowly, barely thrusting himself into her—

God, she was so hot, so tight. He was careening through a fiery haze of dementia—

So was she, writhing beneath him, whispering, "Take me, Ryder. Oh, please."

"Tell me you're mine," he whispered back. "All mine."

She was sobbing. "I am. I'm yours, darling."

Ryder could not bear the sweetness of it. He pushed an inch deeper, felt her clenching around him. He shuddered violently, and then she lurched upward to take him, and cried out with a ragged joy that twisted his heart—

He fought for restraint in a fulminating haze of passion. He expressed his hunger with a wild kiss as he possessed her with gentle, thorough strokes. He drew back and stared into her eyes, watched the wildness of desire consume her as she worried her lower lip with her teeth. He clutched her hands and interlaced her fingers with his. An exquisite arch of her hips broke his control and he lowered himself onto her, mating her mouth with his, pumping into her until they climaxed together with a shared, wanton cry.

Thirty-four

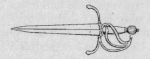

Just over a week later, Natalie and Ryder stood at the window of a different hotel, this time in romantic Paris, where their third-story room overlooked the enchanting Place de la Concorde. Following their long journey from London, the couple was tired; after sharing an early supper in their room, both were dressed for bed. Ryder stood behind Natalie, his hands at her waist, his chin resting on her head as they shared the sunset together. It was a moment of great joy for him as, with his bride in his arms, he looked at Paris through the eyes of a happy newlywed.

The splendid Mansart building overlooked the tranquil square. On this find June evening, elegantly dressed strollers circled the octagon with its lush plantings and impressive statues dotted with pigeons. A perfume of mingled flowers and greenery rose from the garden moats ringing the plaza. To the west stretched the majestic, chestnut-lined Champs Élysées, culminating in the half-finished Arc de Triomphe; to the east rose the gates of the Tuileries Gardens. To the south, citizens promenaded along the Quai des Tuileries or across the Pont de la Concorde with its soaring memorials to French heroes. Beyond the glittering Seine with its clog of vessels loomed the impressive Greek facade of the Chambre des Députés on the Left Bank.

Ryder wondered how Natalie felt, seeing Paris for the first time. This was hardly his first visit to France. As a child, he had toured the Continent with his parents, in the days before the Napoleonic conflict had heated up. As a young man, he had fought with Wellington's cavalry at Waterloo, and had been among the forces that had occupied Paris in the summer of 1815, as the French *tricolore* bit the dust and the white flag of the Bourbons was again hoisted over the metropolis. Now, with Bonaparte dead, the monarchy seemed firmly restored, after nearly three decades of war, turbulence, and death. Looking out at the peaceful square, Ryder found it hard to believe that Louis XVI, Marie Antoinette, and at least a thousand other luckless French souls had been guillotined in the Place de la Concorde during the bloody days of the Revolution. And he had to wonder what so many years of turmoil had really accomplished for France. Despite the revolutionary fervor that had swept the country for so long—the endless battles between king and revolutionary, Jacobin and moderate, royalist and Bonapartist—there were still millions of French peasants struggling for their bread and shoes.

Yet not even these unpleasant realities could quell Ryder's feelings of tenderness as he observed the captivating landscape with his wife. He thought of the baby she carried, and hoped the events of the past week had not tired her overly. The day after the wedding, they had taken one of the new steamships from Dover to Calais, and had then embarked on their long journey overland to Paris by mail coach. The inns they had stayed in each night had not been of the best quality, but the lovemaking they had shared had been superb. Ryder felt so much closer to his bride after the days of intimacy, but he well knew there were parts of her troubled heart that she still withheld from him. Now that they had arrived in the carefree city of Paris, he hoped their entire time would not be taken up by family troubles, and that he would also have time to pamper and spoil her, take her to the best shops and restaurants, the opera, the theater and museums . . .

Natalie, too, was filled with tender, poignant feelings as she viewed the lovely scene. The first week of her wedding trip with Ryder had been idyllic, despite the rigors of travel. Her husband had proved himself to be a charming, ever-attentive companion, and a superb lover. Tingles of excitement streaked over her as she recalled the glorious lovemaking they had shared. She recalled one night in particular, when it hadn't mattered that the inn where they stayed was tawdry, the tick they slept on lumpy. Ryder had spent hours arousing her, until she was insane, frantic. Then he had loved her so slowly and thoroughly, falling asleep while still inside her. Twice before dawn, he had awakened her to possess her again. It had been glorious, and by now she was completely addicted to the intimacy they shared—and more deeply in love than ever. She was beginning to suspect she was a true wanton at heart—a thoroughly fascinating, yet equally daunting, prospect. Still, she had enjoyed this delightful period, and could only pray it would last for them both.

Now they were in Paris, and the wonders and vibrancy of the city only added to the feelings of magic between them. But as Natalie thought of their other purpose here, a small frown knitted her brow.

Ryder noted that tiny scowl. He smoothed her hair and leaned toward her. "You look troubled, my love. Does the view not please you?"

Glancing up at him, she smiled. "Oh, it's splendid—I had no idea Paris is so beautiful. My mother always wanted the family to tour here, but by the time I was old enough, Father insisted that it was too dangerous for us to come. I've read of the city, and remember my mother describing it to me, but nothing really prepared me for this."

"Then why the frown? You are thinking about tomorrow?"

"Yes. And meeting my mother."

"It should be quite a surprise for her as well—assuming we can even find her. Too bad there was no time to send a letter ahead."

Natalie was quiet, her expression abstracted.

"What was it like the last time your family was together?" Ryder asked.

"Turbulent." She frowned grimly. "I was fourteen at the time."

"Was your father's drinking problem as pronounced then?"

"No. I recall he had a predilection for gambling and drink, but at least he was halfway responsible back then, going almost daily to the Exchange."

"Do you remember just how your parents parted? You say it was over political reasons?"

She nodded. "I recall Mother and Father having a particularly violent argument, around the time Wellington was charging through Spain and Napoleon was busy defeating Prussia. I'm not sure of the details of their quarrel, although

I could certainly hear the shouts coming from the drawing room. The next morning my mother left London, never to return."

He kissed the top of her head, inhaling the dusky, enticing scent of her hair. "Poor love. Didn't she even say good-bye to you?"

Natalie stared ahead. "In fairness to her, she tried. She knocked on my door to tell me she was leaving, but I refused to let her in."

"And she had made no attempt to stay in touch with you over the years?"

"She sent letters for a time. I tossed them, unopened, into the fire."

He clutched her closer. "Are you still so embittered, darling?"

She turned in his arms and raised an eyebrow at him. "And you are not toward your own father?"

"That was different," Ryder pointed out gently. "He blamed me for my mother's death."

"And my mother deserted me, a child of fourteen."

He nodded. "You are right. I'm sorry, love."

She shrugged. "Perhaps it is time I told her off, anyway. Still, I have my doubts she will ever return to my father."

"Not even now that Bonaparte is dead?"

She turned to stare out at the Seine, with its cavalcade of barges and ships. "Napoleon's demise might have an impact, though my guess would be, not much of one. If anything, my mother is likely more furious at the British than ever for putting her champion out of power. She always was very opinionated, very self-centered, and vain."

"We'll change her mind, love," he vowed. He nodded toward their lavish Louis XVI bed with its silk brocade hangings, and the iced champagne on the night table. "But for now, I know you must be exhausted. May I convince you to come to my bed?"

She warmed his heart with her smile. "You never need to convince me there," she whispered, stretching on tiptoe to kiss him.

It was early the following afternoon before Ryder and Natalie set out to call on her mother. They had awakened late, made love, and then Ryder had insisted on pampering his wife with a long brunch in bed.

Now they walked from their hotel, strolling along the arcaded Rue de Rivoli, with its verdant glimpses of the terraces and statues of the Tuileries Gardens. They appeared quite the proper married couple, Natalie wearing a high-necked day dress of fine blue muslin and a straw hat with silk flowers, Ryder wearing a single-breasted black tailcoat, a silk top hat, and buff-colored pantaloons. The day was mild, birds were singing in the nearby chestnut trees, and a handsome cabriolet was clattering down the boulevard at a fine clip.

At the corner, they turned north along the Rue de Castiglione, wending their way past shops and eateries, and soon entered the Place Vendôme, the stately former parade ground now surrounded by Louis XIV apartment buildings. Ryder glanced at the central bronze column, absent of the statue of Napoleon that had once loomed at its top.

"You are sure this is where your mother lives?" he asked, gazing around at the awe-inspiring stone archways and soaring colonnades.

"Not positive—but her return address did list a building in the Place Vendôme."

Ryder shook a finger at his wife. "Aha! So you did at least peek at the envelopes before you tossed them into the fire."

She made no direct comment as they moved past the Colonne Vendôme. Staring in perplexity at the bare metal pillar, she asked, "Shouldn't there be a statue at the top of that column?"

"Indeed there was—of Bonaparte himself," answered Ryder. "Following the battle of Austerlitz in 1805, Napoleon had the thousand or so cannon he had captured melted down, and the column and his image fashioned from the molten bronze. His statue was pulled down during the Restoration of 1814."

Natalie shook her head. "Pulled down? They are so bellicose, these French. But now I am certain my mother lives here. She would have chosen a residence within viewing distance of her hero—even if his likeness has since been removed."

They found their way to the appointed number and moved through the arched entrance of a magnificent Mansart building. Inside the foyer, they ran across an elderly gentleman, of whom Natalie, in her stilted French, made an inquiry regarding her mother's apartment. Both Ryder and Natalie laughed when the gentleman replied in near-flawless English, "Ah, yes! Madame Desmond! Third floor. First suite on the left."

They climbed the three flights, and all too soon emerged before tall, daunting double doors with handsome panels and hammered gold knobs.

Catching his wife's apprehensive expression, Ryder quickly kissed her troubled brow. "Chin up, love. It can't be that bad."

His knock was answered by a tall, slender butler, who regarded the newcomers quizzically. "Madame, monsieur. *Qu'y a-t-il pour votre service?"*

"Tell Madame Desmond that her daughter and son-in-law are here," said Ryder.

"Pardon, monsieur?" asked the bemused butler.

A moment later, Natalie's heart thudded as she heard her mother call out, "Jacques, *qui est-ce?"*

The three watched a tall, middle-aged woman sweep toward them, wearing a low-cut, blue satin empire gown. Ryder at once saw that Desiree Desmond was an older version of his beautiful wife, complete with the heart-shaped face and tawny eyes. She carried herself with elegance and hauteur, and wore her silver-streaked chestnut-brown hair in curls piled high on her head.

As Desiree spotted the couple at the portal, her face drained of color and her hand flew to her breast. Her gaze became riveted on Natalie.

"Natalie, my darling!" she cried. *"Mon Dieu,* is it truly you?"

Desiree rushed forward, and the next moment Natalie found herself swept, if unwillingly, into her mother's embrace. An unexpected rush of emotion choked her in that moment of reunion, especially as she inhaled the remembered flowery scent of Desiree's perfume. And even through her anger she felt the comforting sameness, the bonding, of being in her mother's arms again. She was also disarmed by the warmth of Desiree's greeting, and thus unprepared for the feeling of connection and belonging that threatened to crush her own defenses.

Desiree kissed her daughter's cheek, then pulled back, wiping a tear. "Oh, my dear, I cannot believe you are truly here! How I have dreamed of this moment, when we could be together again. And you have blossomed into such a ravishing young woman!"

"Thank you, Mother," Natalie returned stiffly, keeping her voice calm and level with an effort. "You are looking well yourself."

Desiree's gaze flicked to Ryder. "And who is this enchanting gentleman you have brought with you?"

"Madame Desmond, may I present my husband, Ryder Remington, Lord Newbury."

"Your husband?" Desiree's astonished gaze went from her daughter to Ryder, then back to Natalie. "But, my dear, I did not even know you had married."

"There is much you haven't known over the past eight years," Natalie rejoined bitterly.

For a moment, Desiree appeared at a loss. She quickly recovered her composure, turning to Ryder and laughing nervously. "My, what a handsome fellow you are, Lord Newbury."

"Thank you, madame," Ryder replied, taking and kissing the hand she offered. "It is truly a pleasure to meet you."

"Come in, then, both of you," Desiree rushed on. To the butler, she added, "Jacques, *café au lait, s'il vous plaît.*"

"*Oui,* madame."

Desiree led the couple into a huge, high-ceilinged, gold-paneled salon with a central seating area of crimson velvet settees and gilt-edged Louis XV chairs. Though Natalie was accustomed to elegance, it was nonetheless all she could do not to gape at the overwhelming opulence of this room. Her amazed gaze flicked from the stunning ceiling, with its masterpieces of swirling plaster fretwork and cascading crystal chandeliers; to the gilt-edged Italian frescoes that lined three of the walls; to the magnificent portrait of a younger Desiree, signed by the renowned Parisian artist Vigée-Lebrun, that hung above the fireplace between the front windows. Natalie felt a new lump of emotion in her throat as she noted the striking resemblance between herself and the portrait, and remembered that very painting hanging in her parents' London home—before her mother had left.

Desiree gestured for them to sit down. Ryder pulled Natalie over to a red velvet *canapé,* while Desiree ensconced herself in a matching chair flanking it.

"What brings you to Paris, my loves?" she asked brightly. "Dare I hope you have come to see me?"

When Natalie regarded her mother with cool distrust, Ryder quickly answered, "We are here on our wedding trip, madame."

Desiree's gaze shifted to her daughter. "How long have you been married, darling?"

"A week, Mother."

Desiree slanted her a reproachful look. "And you did not even invite me to attend the ceremony?"

Natalie avoided her mother's eye. "Actually, I did not think you would be interested, or that you would attend if invited."

Desiree's expression was crestfallen. After a moment, she sighed. "I cannot blame you, my sweet girl. I tried to explain things to you in my letters—"

Natalie's bright gaze locked defiantly with her mother's. "I did not care to read them."

Desiree uttered a low gasp. The tension was alleviated as the butler stepped in with the coffee service. Desiree handed both Ryder and Natalie their *café au lait* in Sèvres china cups, along with luscious pastries topped with cream and strawberries.

As the three shared the repast, Desiree braved a new smile at her daughter. "Well, dear, the important thing is that you are here now, and we can properly catch up on our lives. You must tell me all about what you have been doing these past years."

Natalie dutifully launched into an account of her activities over the past eight years, telling her mother that she had moved with Aunt Love to America to run the factory, then had later returned to England, on the trail of smugglers and her missing aunt.

While Natalie paused to sip her coffee, Desiree winked at her. "So you went on the grand adventure, did you, my darling?"

"Not totally grand," Natalie replied stiffly. "I was terrified for Aunt Love's safety."

"But of course you were." Desiree regarded Ryder with frank admiration. "And where does your dashing husband fit into your tale?"

Natalie deferred to Ryder, who delivered a laundered version of his background and the circumstances under which he and Natalie had met. He also completed her story, telling Desiree of how they had sailed to England together, uncovered the smugglers, and found Aunt Love before they married.

Desiree was clapping her hands. "Oh, I have never heard such a divine or romantic tale! I am so happy the two of you have shared such a gay escapade." She glanced at her daughter. "You were such a sober child when I left."

"A reality not improved by your departure," Natalie pointed out acrimoniously.

Another awkward silence ensued, but soon Desiree, forever ebullient, flashed both her guests her cavalier smile. "Oh, we will have such fun together! I must show you the town, introduce you to my friends. As a matter of fact, I'm due at a reception at Monsieur Talleyrand-Périgord's tonight. You must both come with me. Where are you staying?"

"Our hotel is in the Place de la Concorde," Ryder replied.

"Why, Talleyrand's *hôtel particulier* is practically next door! Furthermore, you must stay here with me! I've plenty of room." Then, watching Natalie and Ryder exchange dubious glances, she laughed. "Oh, what am I saying? You are newlyweds, but of course! You will want to be alone! And what more romantic spot could you choose than Paris?"

"We appreciate your understanding, madame," Ryder told Desiree. "And we will want to be alone—but also to visit with you while we are here."

Desiree glanced compassionately at her daughter. "A pity so many years had to pass before we could be together." She sighed, then asked tentatively, "Are you still angry at me for leaving, darling?"

Natalie's eyes blazed at her mother. Instead of answering the fervent question, she took the offensive. "Aren't you even going to ask why I have come here today?"

Desiree scowled in perplexity. "Did you not say you came to Paris on your wedding trip? Naturally, you would want to see me."

"We came to Paris specifically to see you, Mother." Catching Desiree's suddenly eager expression, Natalie held up a hand. "But don't get your hopes up about our having a heart-warming little reunion. I long ago gave up on having you as a parent."

While Desiree gasped her dismay, Ryder took his wife's hand. "Darling, show some care," he cautioned.

But Desiree dismissed Ryder's admonition with a wave of her hand and regarded Natalie soberly. *"Ma chère,* I understand your anger. But you must know that leaving you caused me untold anguish."

"Did it really, Mother?"

Desiree's gaze beseeched her daughter. "Why did you come to see me, then, if not for your own needs?"

"I came about Father."

Desiree tensed and remained silent.

"Aren't you even going to ask about him?" Natalie burst out.

For once, Desiree's undaunted facade wavered. She glanced away and blinked rapidly. "Do you really think he was ever out of my thoughts?"

"Oh, yes," came her daughter's ironic reply.

Ryder again laid his hand over his wife's. "Natalie—"

"No, let her speak her feelings," Desiree urged, turning to Ryder, even as emotion twisted her own visage. "It is the French way, and in truth, I cannot blame her."

"Well, Mother?" Natalie prodded.

In a low voice, Desiree asked, "How is Charles?"

"Dying," Natalie said.

"Oh, *mon Dieu!*" cried a wild-eyed Desiree.

"He's drunk himself halfway into the grave." Natalie's eyes blazed with bitterness and triumph. "And the doctor says he won't last out the year. He also said that it is not just the drink that is killing him, but a broken heart."

A pallid, obviously shaken Desiree rose unsteadily and made her way to the window. "I—I had no idea Charles had taken my departure so hard."

"How could you? You didn't know—or care."

"That is not true."

"It is! Tell me, will you even consider coming back now, if just to save Father's life?"

Ryder watched Desiree grip the windowsill with such force that her knuckles turned white. "I cannot, Natalie."

Natalie sprang to her feet. "Then that is my proof. You do not care."

Desiree whirled. Her eyes were bright, and she spoke in a trembling voice. "And you do not understand. It is not simply a matter of caring. There is a matter of heritage. Your father could have chosen to live with me here—"

"To gamble on horses and taro? To lose himself in the debauchery of the Palais Royal?" Natalie reinforced her outcries with angry gestures. "The man is barely staying alive in London as it is, but to bring him here to sinful Paris? And you actually would have subjected him to the dangers of immigrating while England was at war with France? Why, that bully Napoleon likely would have imprisoned my father in the dungeons of the Conciergerie."

While Ryder groaned at his wife's lack of restraint, Natalie relished her own small victory as she watched her barb score. Anger flared in Desiree's eyes at the indictment of her beloved Bonaparte. "Oh, I can see there is no reasoning with you," she returned with equal passion. "You are just like Charles—opinionated and stubborn to the end!"

"And you are not? Although we must clearly add selfishness and supreme vanity to your list of attributes—"

Desiree stepped forward and spoke vehemently. "You do not understand, Natalie. Just because I had to leave does not mean I was disloyal to you. There are certain hurts a woman cannot endure."

"Then, pray, explain yourself. If you can."

Before Desiree could proceed, the butler entered. "Madame," Natalie heard him say in French, "Monsieur Dubois has arrived to take you to luncheon."

Desiree went pale, and Natalie regarded her mother with contempt. "Weren't you just trying to explain how you haven't been disloyal to Father and me? By all means, Mother, go on to your assignation. We would not want you to miss your rendezvous with your lover."

"Natalie, please, you must allow me to explain," Desiree pleaded.

"Ryder and I are leaving now."

She started out of the room and Ryder dutifully followed, flashing Desiree an apologetic glance.

Desiree hurried after them and caught his sleeve. "Make her come back. Please."

He smiled kindly. "Madame, I must ask you to forgive Natalie's lack of restraint. Do not worry, I shall see that she returns. However, as you've just observed, my wife has inherited your spirit—and doubtless your temper."

"Oh, *oui!*" Desiree replied.

Thirty-five

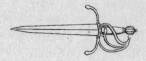

NATALIE WAS MOODY AND TACITURN AS THEY LEFT DESIREE'S building. Sensing an explosion in the offing and seeking to defuse the bomb, Ryder insisted they stroll over to the Boulevard des Italiens for a glass of wine—and she reluctantly agreed.

Ryder actually felt a great deal of sympathy for his wife, understanding her feelings of betrayal and abandonment at the hands of her mother. Yet he also realized that she was allowing her outrage toward Desiree to stand in the way of what she hoped to achieve in Paris—and ultimately, such self-defeating behavior would only bring her grief. Ryder knew that if Natalie was to accomplish her goal here, he must help her see reason.

They selected a small sidewalk cafe on the colorful boulevard, and sat sipping wine and nibbling on cheese as the Parisians strolled by. A passing organ-grinder played a jaunty tune on his instrument while his monkey dashed around begging for coins. Ryder smiled as he observed Natalie handing the chirping little animal a franc. But the mischievous monkey grabbed Natalie's reticule and scurried off, screaming gleefully.

Ryder and Natalie dashed after the monkey. The chagrined organ-grinder tried his best to help, alternately apologizing effusively and bellowing at the animal, which hastened to hide itself, screeching, behind Natalie's skirts. By the time the little drama had played itself out and the reticule was retrieved, Natalie and Ryder were both back at their table, laughing.

He winked at her. "It's good to see a smile on your face again, my love."

At once she felt contrite. "I'm sorry about the scene with Mother. And I promised you I'd try to enjoy our wedding trip."

He smiled lazily. "I think I shall have to exact appropriate revenge—tonight in bed."

She chuckled, blushing at the delicious prospect. But as she lifted her glass, her expression grew pensive again.

"What are thinking, darling?" he asked.

She sighed. "Sometimes I wonder if any marriage is truly happy, if eventually they don't all disintegrate into lies and betrayals."

He reached across the table to grasp her hand. "Ours never will."

She smiled. "I appreciate how hard you are trying, Ryder."

"It is not just an act," he replied solemnly.

Although his tone was persuasive, she remained troubled. "I realize you think that now. But after the blush of passion wears off—" she paused, glanced at him quickly, and scolded, "Now, don't you dare laugh! I'm just saying that something more abiding must take its place."

Ryder was still struggling not to grin. "Darling, first of all, the 'blush of passion,' as you call it, is not going to wear off for us. I keep finding myself more hungry for you, rather than less. On the other hand, if it wears off for you, my lady, I'll make you put up with it, anyway. Better yet, I'll find new ways to make you blush."

"You would!" she accused, laughing.

"I will. As for our having 'something more abiding,' we already have it—our love, our child, and your determination to wreak havoc on my wayward ways."

Yes, if she didn't end up making him miserable for it, she mused. She smiled at him tenderly, dearly hoping he was right.

He squeezed her hand and said carefully, "Natalie, about your mother . . ."

"Yes?" she said tensely.

"You were rather hard on her back there."

She set down her wineglass and sighed.

"You know, she greeted us both with surprising gracious-ness and warmth."

"Out of guilt," Natalie declared.

"It couldn't be love for you, now, could it?" he suggested.

"A loving mother does not desert a fourteen-year-old child!"

"Whether she does so or not, the fact remains that you still love her."

"I do not!"

His fingers lifted her chin. "Really? Then why the tears?"

Indeed, Natalie was trembling, struggling to hold back a flood tide of hot, raw emotion. "Because she hurt me—and hurt my father—so much."

"I know, darling. But you never gave her a chance to ex-plain things, did you?"

She was silent, brooding.

"You burned her letters, and even now, when she tried to tell her side of things, you shut her out with your anger."

Silence again.

"As for your parents' alienation, problems between hus-bands and wives are rarely so one-sided, I think," he added.

Her challenging gaze flashed up to his. "You blame your father entirely for the failure of *your* parents' marriage."

He smiled. "My, but you do not give an inch of quarter, do you, love?"

"Well, it is the truth, is it not?"

"It may have been in the past," he conceded, "but perhaps I have reached a point when I realize life is seldom etched out strictly in black and white. For instance, take your moth-er's friend. What makes you think he is her lover?"

Her gaze beseeched the heavens. "Ryder—this is *Paris!*"

He tweaked her chin and chuckled. "Do you hear yourself, you bad girl? Could it be perhaps you are condemning in your mother what you find in yourself?"

She stared at him and fought a smile.

"Aren't you scared because you discovered today that you are more like your mother than you want to admit? Maybe you have also learned that Desiree Desmond is not nearly the monster you have painted her to be. You've held on to your outrage and hurt for eight long years, and now you're faced with the prospect of letting go of some of your preconceived

otions. And that scares a sober, set-in-her-ways Englishwoman such as you, doesn't it?"

At her husband's incisive wisdom, Natalie lost her battle
with a guilty smile. "Perhaps I am a little like her—and yes,
it is frightening."

"Not to me," he teased huskily.

Demurely she sipped her wine. "You always did want to
bring out the passionate Frenchwoman in me, didn't you?"

"And have I succeeded?"

She laughed. "I'm sure you have, in more ways than you
know."

"Well, Natalie? Will you give your mother a chance?"

She released an exasperated breath. "What do you want me
to do?"

"Go see her a few more times, get reacquainted. Lay aside
the past and your anger for the moment. Then, when you
know her better, mayhap that will be the best time for the two
of you to really talk."

"Why should I?" she flared in sudden mutiny.

He ran a finger over her petulant lips and replied sternly,
"Because your father's life hangs in the balance."

She nodded, much sobered, as suddenly all of her own re-
sentments seemed petty. "You are right. God knows Mother
has her faults, but I was too uncompromising today. We shall
go visit her again tomorrow."

"Good girl." He nodded toward her drink. "Now finish
your wine. Then we shall peruse some of these delightful
shops, and I shall see if I cannot find an appropriate bauble
to further lift m'lady's spirits. After all, I have the rest of the
day to corrupt you, don't I?"

"You devil! My mother is going to love you—if she
doesn't already."

A moment later, their shared laughter echoed down the
Boulevard des Italiens.

Thirty-six

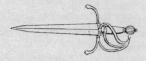

DURING THE NEXT WEEK, NATALIE FOLLOWED HER HUSBAND'S
advice. They spent much time with her mother, and Natalie
struggled to rein in her bitterness and become reacquainted
with the parent who had deserted her long ago.

Holding back her anger became easier than she would have
expected in the captivating city of Paris. The sunny metropolis soon wove its magic spell around her. Being a newlywed
and hopelessly in love only added to her feelings of enchant-
ment. Although she still had doubts that Ryder could remain
content in their marriage permanently, she felt too happy to
devote much time to fears for her and Ryder's future, or to
anger toward Desiree.

Natalie found herself enthralled with this city of Voltaire
and Racine, Lescot and Goujon, Percier and Fontaine. Along
with Desiree and her companion, Monsieur Dubois, Ryder
and Natalie strolled through the Louvre and the gardens of
the Tuileries, fed the pigeons on the steps of the Sacré Coeur,
and supped on the quaint terrace of the Café de la Rotonde.
They attended a performance of Moliere's *L'Ecole des
Femmes* at the Théâtre Français, and a splendid presentation
of Spontini's *La Vestale* at the Académie de Musique. They
strolled the wide boulevards with their colorful vendors, acrobats, bands, choir and funeral processions. They shopped,
Natalie buying a new frock at Petite Jeannette on the Boulevard des Italiens, Ryder purchasing a stylish hat in the
Marais.

Just as the Parisians around them loved observing the visitors from England, Natalie watched her own mother, becom-

ng reacquainted with Desiree's outlook on life and her
opinions. She discovered what a skilled social tactician her
mother was. While privately Desiree still shamelessly ad-
mired Bonaparte and found the Bourbon king Louis XVIII to
be an abysmal bore, she kept her republican views to herself
and was in every way as adroit a politician as the esteemed
Talleyrand, with whom she remained longtime friends, even
though in the end Talleyrand had deserted Bonaparte. Desiree
did not hesitate to take Ryder and Natalie along for a public
reading by the literary lion Chateaubriand at the Académie
Française, although the viscount was another Bonapartist now
turned peer and royalist. And despite Desiree's apparent an-
tipathy toward Great Britain, she eagerly brought the newlyweds to a dinner party hosted by Sir Charles Stuart at the
British Embassy on the Faubourg Saint-Honoré. Indeed,
Desiree hardly wore mourning for the recently deceased emperor, and Natalie was left doubting the true depth of her
mother's allegiance to the former First Consul.

The relationship between mother and daughter remained
polite and cordial, if strained. Natalie knew her resentment
came out in little ways, when she failed to laugh at one of
Desiree's typically outrageous remarks, or gave a terse response to one of her questions.

She also learned about her mother's reckless streak.
Desiree was addicted to the *tierce,* the French style of gambling on the horses, as well as to hazard, taro, whist, and a
host of other games. She gambled, but unlike most of
Natalie's male relatives, she set limits for herself and kept
them. Quite frequently, she won.

Of course, having so much in common, Desiree and Ryder
became instant friends. One sunny afternoon when Monsieur
Dubois was away for his standing chess game at the Café de
la Régence, Desiree and Ryder spent hours sitting at the
Louis XVI card table playing war, the popular French card
game. Natalie sat on the settee, ostensibly reading Scott's
Ivanhoe, as the two took turns dealing, shrieking with laughter as their nimble fingers snatched up the cards. Actually,
Natalie would have liked to join in on the fun, but she was
growing increasingly frustrated with her mother's total lack
of concern for Charles Desmond; indeed, Desiree had not
mentioned Charles once over the past days. Natalie equally

resented the fact that Desiree was almost perpetually in the company of the ever-attentive Monsieur Dubois.

After Desiree lost her fifth hand to a grinning Ryder, she gathered up the cards amid expostulations in French. Turning toward her daughter, she declared, "Oh, this husband of yours is a demon with the cards. I am sure you can never best him—"

"We don't play," Natalie interjected primly.

"Not these sorts of games," Ryder added wickedly.

Desiree roared with laughter and leaned across the table to playfully slap Ryder's sleeve with a sheaf of cards. "Oh, you are a rogue, *mon ami,* and so big and handsome." To Natalie, she said, "How can you keep your hands off this rascal, if only for a day?"

At Desiree's typically shameless query, Natalie demurred, while Ryder again filled the gap with a broad grin. "She doesn't."

Even Natalie had to chuckle at that. Then her attention was again drawn by Desiree.

"Henri! What are you doing back so soon?" the matron cried.

Natalie glanced toward the archway to observe the butler showing in Monsieur Dubois, a wiry little Frenchman with a waxed mustache and a perpetual gleam of laughter in his dark eyes. During the time the four had spent together, Natalie had found Henri to be amiable enough, although she disliked the way he perpetually hovered over her mother. Today he wore a black swallow-tailed coat, a silver moire waistcoat, and gray trousers that showed off a physique remarkably trim for a middle-aged man.

The elegant Frenchman strode to the card table and kissed Desiree's hand. *"Ma chère."* He nodded in turn to Natalie and Ryder. "Madame. Monsieur."

"Oh, stop genuflecting and take a seat," Desiree said in exasperation.

Smiling, Henri complied.

"Your chess game ended early, monsieur?" Ryder inquired.

Henri chuckled. "Alas, my friend Pierre was easy prey today. A disappointment, but the poor fellow is distraught over his failed love affair with Madame Renault."

"A pity," agreed a nonchalant Desiree as she shuffled the cards.

"I thought I might take us all for an early supper at the Café de Paris," Henri added.

"Natalie and I would be delighted to join you," Ryder replied, "but I must insist on buying dinner this time."

"Oh, *non, non,* you are our guests," declared Desiree.

"Ryder is right," Natalie chimed in. "You and Monsieur Dubois have been spending too much on us—dinners, theater tickets, barge rides."

Henri winked at Natalie. "Then, madame, perhaps we can settle this small dispute with a set of whist."

"You French and your mania for games of chance," Natalie remarked drolly.

Undaunted, Henri began gathering up the cards. "The winner pays, no?"

"I think the loser should pay," Ryder argued mischievously.

"But that makes no sense," said Desiree.

The three debated the issue for a few more moments, finally agreeing to Ryder's terms. Natalie was persuaded by her husband to join in the game. By silent conspiracy, Ryder and Natalie then proceeded to lose the set to Henri and Desiree.

"It seems we have bested the newlyweds, eh?" Henri murmured ironically to Desiree.

"You know they lost on purpose," she replied, slanting a chiding glance toward Ryder.

He grinned. "Ah, but your skill at whist is not inconsiderable, madame. You might have defeated us in any event."

"Ah, yes, Desiree is lethal with the cards," agreed the admiring Henri. He took Desiree's hand and again fondly kissed her beringed fingers. "You are a woman of many talents, eh, *ma belle?* We have a free dinner to show for it, no?"

Natalie gritted her teeth as she watched Monsieur Dubois drool over her mother's hand for the second time in just an hour.

Observing his wife's suddenly mutinous expression, Ryder coughed. "Shall we leave for the restaurant, then?"

"I would like to go back to the hotel first," Natalie said with a frown.

"Are you feeling all right, my dear?" Desiree asked with concern.

"Actually, why don't you three go on to dinner?" Natalie replied, setting down her cards. She rubbed her forehead and grimaced. "I seem to be developing a headache."

"Oh, my poor darling," cried Desiree.

"Madame, we would not dream of depriving you of your husband at such a critical time," the gallant Henri put in.

Gazing dubiously at Natalie, Ryder spoke up. "Can we postpone our dinner until tomorrow night? I think Natalie could use some fresh air."

"But of course," Desiree agreed.

Ryder and Natalie said their good-byes and left Desiree's building. They strolled along in silence for a few moments, heading toward the Seine.

"You don't really have a headache, do you, darling?" Ryder asked.

"No," Natalie admitted with a guilty smile. "But you are right that I needed to get out of there."

"Do you want to talk about it?"

She bit her lip. "Can we just walk for a while first?"

"Of course."

Holding hands, the couple strolled along the *quai*, gazing out at the river, the boats, the fluttering trees, the people passing by. The late afternoon was mild, the air heady with the scents of greenery and the muskier smell of the river.

Natalie found the setting dreamy and romantic—especially with Ryder beside her—and she could feel her spirits lifting. Then she spotted a colorful hot-air balloon on a distant *pont*, and her face lit up with excitement.

"Ryder, look! A balloon launching!"

He glanced ahead and smiled eagerly. "Let's go watch it."

Like two excited children, they hurried down the *quai* to the Pont Neuf, the Parisian bridge extraordinaire. Humanity jammed every speck of space, the public winnowing its way past vendors and booths, and amusing itself watching everything from tightrope-walking to juggling demonstrations to fencing matches.

For Ryder and Natalie, the dazzling sights and sense of fun were infectious. Watching him eye the swordsmen with gleeful interest, she caught his arm and firmly steered him toward the launching at the center of the bridge. They stepped up to join the other spectators just as the beautiful blue balloon—as colorful as any Easter egg with its gold fleur-de-lis embellishments—sailed up into the perfect cloudless sky, the two male aeronauts on board waving proudly to the effusive crowd.

Watching the lovely craft glide away over the Seine, Natalie felt a pang of disappointment. She grabbed Ryder's hand and tugged him back toward the *quai.* He laughed as they both rushed along, dodging people and pigeons and craning their necks to watch the balloon.

Soon a boatman on the Seine spotted them and called out, "Madame, monsieur, *s'il vous plaît.*"

They descended the *quai,* and Ryder paid the boatman and helped Natalie into the small vessel. The grinning oarsman rowed them along the path of the balloon, which was still drifting over the river. Ryder sat happily with his wife at the stern, and both watched the jaunty craft overhead, amid the splendor of the passing buildings of the Louvre on one side and the Left Bank on the other. Sunlight sparkled on the Seine and dappled the other vessels floating past. They watched, entranced, until the balloon drifted off and became as small as a bright blue marble.

"Feel better now, darling?" Ryder asked.

Natalie nodded and smiled.

He raised her hand and kissed it. "Want to tell me why you're still so angry with your mother?"

She gazed at him with clearly mixed emotions. "Must I?"

He nodded. "Is it because Monsieur Dubois was fawning over her?"

"Partly."

He drew a deep breath. "Natalie, I've been watching you and Desiree over the past week. She has done everything in her power to effect a reconciliation, and you have certainly been polite enough. But you are still holding her at arm's length."

"I know. But can you blame me?"

"No, not entirely. But how are you ever going to convince her to return with us to London if you remain so aloof?"

"I don't know," she muttered. "It's just that—Mother does make me so angry sometimes!"

"And why is that?" he asked gently.

"Because she takes nothing seriously!" Natalie burst out. "Her entire life is taro and whist and the gambling and shopping—*and* her ever-faithful lapdog, Monsieur Dubois. She doesn't give a thought to my father, or to any other of her obligations, while I—"

"Yes, darling?"

Through clenched teeth, she exclaimed, "I have all these responsibilities that I take so seriously!"

"I know," he commiserated, kissing her cheek. "And I do hope loving me is at the top of your list."

Natalie had to laugh, her head of steam diffused by Ryder's teasing. He appeared so endearingly earnest. "You know, this is not really fair to you," she remarked. "It is our wedding trip and we shouldn't be caught up in my familial struggles."

"Am I complaining?" He grinned and wrapped an arm around her waist. "As long as I can have plenty of time to pamper and spoil you—and am provided my nightly revenge—I don't care."

She smiled and quickly kissed him, stroking his jaw with her fingertips. "You are being too wonderful, you know."

He flashed his white teeth. "That's how I keep you off guard, my lady, so I may entice you to my more wicked purposes."

She chuckled, then asked thoughtfully, "Would you prefer being with someone more like her?"

He appeared astonished. "Her? You mean Desiree?"

She nodded.

"You must be joking, Natalie."

"And why is that?"

"Oh, Natalie." He pulled her closer and shook with mirth. "Darling, I would never want to marry a woman like Desiree—not that she isn't delightful."

"Why not?"

"Because she and I are too much alike—outrageous scamps, the two of us. There wouldn't be any challenge in it."

"And I'm a challenge?"

"God, yes." He groaned.

"Don't be blasphemous," she admonished him primly, ghting a smile.

His blue eyes gleamed with merriment. "See what I mean? can't even complete a sentence without getting a lecture om you—albeit I have known you to be plenty blasphemous ourself, my love. At any rate, you are much more fun."

"My scoldings are fun?" she exclaimed, but from the smirk ill pulling at her mouth, he knew she was wavering.

"Believe it or not, Natalie," he went on, "I want a wife ho does take her wifely obligations most seriously—as long s her principal obligation is *me*."

"Oh, you scamp!"

He leaned over to kiss her. Natalie gave him her lips, then udged him away, embarrassed, as she caught the boatman aring at them.

He drew back to look at her face. "Now, darling, I really o think it's time for you to speak with your mother lone—to get your feelings out in the open."

She sighed. "I suppose you're right."

"How about tomorrow?"

"Tomorrow? Must I?"

He squeezed her hand. "You'll feel so much better when 's done. Besides," he added wickedly, "I'll make you glad ou did it."

Intrigued, she stole a glance at his face. "Oh, will you?"

"Indeed. And speaking of making it worth your while . . ." Ie nuzzled her ear with his lips and said huskily, "You know, ιy love, there is something so romantic and seductive about ιe motion of this boat. Do you feel it, too?"

Flustered, she stammered, "I—I—"

"Remember what we did in the carriage?"

Natalie was aghast. "Ryder, you can't be serious! The boat-ιan!"

Ryder shrugged. "He doesn't speak English."

"He'll see!"

Ryder only chuckled, and Natalie's next protest was smoth-red by his lips. He held her close and whispered wicked tterings in her ear that made her toes curl and her face burn. ιst as she began to fear he truly *was* going to stage a rep-tition of their torrid encounter in the carriage, boatman or no oatman, he pulled back and winked at her solemnly.

"See what I mean, darling? You're so delightful to tease—and so easily beguiled."

"Oh!"

The boatman laughed heartily as Natalie lashed Ryder with her gloves.

Thirty-seven

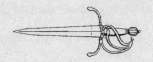

THE FOLLOWING AFTERNOON, RYDER INVITED MONSIEUR Dubois out for drinks at Tortoni's so that Natalie could speak with her mother alone. After the men left, Desiree joined Natalie on one of the settees in the salon. Touching her daughter's arm, she said, "Darling, I do hope you are feeling better today."

Natalie answered forthrightly. "Mother, I did not have a headache yesterday."

Desiree's features twisted in perplexity. "The headache was a ruse? So why did you postpone our dinner?" Then she grinned and snapped her fingers. "I know—you wanted to be alone with your husband."

"No. Not that I do not love being alone with Ryder, but actually, I needed ..." Natalie drew a deep breath and blurted out, "I wanted to get away from you."

"But why?" Desiree appeared crestfallen.

Natalie gestured angrily. "Why? You can ask that? You are having an affair with Monsieur Dubois, aren't you?"

Desiree met her daughter's gaze steadily. "No, Natalie, I am not."

"Well, I do not believe you."

Desiree shook her head sadly. "So your mind is made up, *ma chère?* What can I say? Granted, Henri would be delighted if things should proceed further between us, but long ago he accepted that I still consider myself a married woman and can offer him no more than friendship."

"But why does he play court to you?"

Desiree laughed gaily. "Natalie, he is French! A French-

341

man would never acknowledge defeat—and certainly not in
matters of the heart."

Natalie was silent, playing abstractedly with a bit of lace
on her cuff. "Do you mean to tell me that for all these years,
you haven't taken a lover?"

Desiree's response was cool and firm. "I have not committed adultery."

"But you carry on as if you do not care a whit about Father!"

"Natalie, when I returned to France, I had a broken heart.
Sooner or later I had to either pick up the pieces and go on
with my life or die from the pain."

"And it makes no difference that Father is dying now?"

Desiree's light brown eyes bespoke an eloquent sadness.
"It makes a difference. There will always be a tender spot in
my heart for Charles. But I cannot allow him to destroy me
again."

"Destroy you?" Natalie was flabbergasted. "But you are
the one who left, without giving a thought to our feelings.
And if you do still care for him, why won't you return?"

Desiree touched her daughter's hand. "Oh, Natalie. You
never read any of my letters, did you?"

"No."

Desiree rose and went to the window. The golden light
slanting in outlined her sad, wistful expression as she stared
out at the Place Vendôme.

"Charles and I had terrible political differences, and horrible fights as a result. He considered Napoleon a cruel despot
who would not be content until he brought all of Europe to
its knees, while I found the emperor to be a man of great daring and vision, and I truly felt the destiny of France lay in his
republican regime." She flashed her daughter a wan smile
over her shoulder. "In fairness to Charles, his business at the
Exchange did suffer due to Bonaparte's Continental System,
but neither did Charles ever fully understand the vast political
differences separating our two countries. Soon after the emperor triumphed at the Battle of Dresden, Charles demanded
that I renounce Bonaparte as a ruthless tyrant."

"And you would not?"

"Of course I would not!" Desiree exclaimed passionately.
"Your father had no right to tell me what I should or should

ot believe, or to demand that I abandon France. Then
e . . ." She gestured helplessly.

"What happened, Mother?"

In a voice hoarse with pain, Desiree confessed, "Charles
lenied me his bed unless I would make the denunciation and
enounce my French citizenship."

Natalie was stunned. "And that is why you left?"

Desiree stepped forward and spoke amid vehement ges-
ures. "Natalie, I am French! I could not turn my back on the
:ountry of my birth! Nor could I live with my husband in a
narriage that was a mere shell. Surely now that you are a
narried woman, you must understand that!"

Natalie managed to quell a guilty smile. "But how could
ou leave him if you loved him?"

"I left him *because* I loved him—because I could not bear
he pain any longer." She sighed deeply. "And I still care for
im today."

"I don't believe that."

Desiree swept over to sit by her daughter. "I know you are
itter, darling. I fought with Charles long and hard over
ou—demanded he let me bring you with me to Paris—but
e adamantly refused."

"I—I did not know that," Natalie said, feeling a strong tug
n her emotions. "Still, how could you leave your child? I
imply cannot believe any loving mother could do that, espe-
:ially now that—"

"Now that you are *enceinte,* darling?" Desiree asked
visely.

Natalie glanced away in embarrassment. "How did you
<now?"

Desiree touched her daughter's hand. "Oh, Natalie, a
woman can always see that joy in another."

Natalie's questioning gaze met her mother's. "Was it such
a joy to carry me, Mother?"

With heartfelt sincerity, Desiree replied, "Oh, darling, it
was the greatest pleasure of my life."

Natalie was silent, choked with emotion.

Desiree squeezed Natalie's trembling fingers. "Tell me,
larling, did your pregnancy precipitate the rather rushed wed-
ling?"

Natalie coughed awkwardly. "My, but you are perceptive. As a matter of fact, Ryder all but dragged me to the alter."

Merriment sparkled in Desiree's eyes. "Oh, that devil you are married to! He is not the type to leave a girl a virgin for long, no? As for you, *ma chère,* perhaps you have a little more French blood in you than you thought."

"Perhaps," Natalie admitted with a sheepish smile.

"But you are happy, no?" Desiree added with unaccustomed tentativeness.

Natalie's expression was radiant. "Never happier."

"Oh, *très bien!*" Desire tightly clutched her daughter's hand and pleaded, "Darling, now that you know the joys of wedded love, surely you must understand how I could not endure the alienation between me and your father."

"I'm trying to, Mother."

"As for you—"

"Yes?"

Desiree shook her head, her voice etched with deep regret. "You seemed lost to me even then. So much like Charles."

A hint of wistfulness tugged at Natalie's mouth. "But now you think I may be more like you than you had thought?"

"*Oui.* I can only pray you will give me another chance." Desiree looked at Natalie with her heart in her eyes.

As much as Desiree's contrition moved her, Natalie was still not completely prepared to give up all her anger and hurt. "I—I will try, Mother," she said with sincerity. "I can only promise that much."

"Then I shall cling to that promise with all the hope in my heart," Desiree replied fervently.

Natalie felt moved to flash her mother a look of compassion. "You know, it would help so much if you would go back to Father. Especially if you still love him. And now with Bonaparte dead—"

"I am sorry, Natalie. It is too late."

"Father is going to die, you know."

Desiree's tear-filled gaze met her daughter's, and she nodded sadly. In a barely audible voice, she whispered, "I know."

Several hours later, Natalie was back at the hotel room, sharing a bath with Ryder before they went to dinner with Desiree and Henri. As the steam of the scented water rose round them, Ryder held his wife cradled against him and tenderly stroked her back and kissed her hair. Being in his arms thus, listening to the strong thud of his heart, was heaven to Natalie. She loved him so much, she thought achingly. For bringing her here, for helping her with her mother. Her resentment toward him for forcing her to the altar was long gone. At moments like this, her doubts seemed absurd. He was so good to her, and so irresistibly sexy, kind, and charming. Indeed, loving him was like falling into a pit with no bottom. Exhilarating. Frightening.

She pressed her lips against his wet chest and listened to his moan of pleasure, the quickening of his heartbeat. Did he feel the same thrill? Or did he already feel weighed down by their marriage? Was he making a good show for the sake of their child?

Their time here had been so idyllic, despite her own frustrations of dealing with Desiree. When they returned to their world of uncertainties and responsibilities, would they still be as happy—and Ryder as carefree? He had spoken yesterday of how much he and Desiree were alike. Would his wayward, devil-may-care qualities eventually strain their marriage, just as Desiree's capriciousness had contributed to her breakup with Charles? As for herself and Ryder, was there a true meeting ground between their worlds? Could she continue to love him without changing him?

"How did it go with your mother?" he asked.

She twisted around to stare up at him, looking so sexy with his damp, slick hair and the beads of moisture on his face. "I think we cleared the air a bit. You know, she wanted to bring me to Paris with her, but my father wouldn't allow it."

"Does it help you to know that?"

"Yes. I feel closer to her now."

"I'm glad. Did you ask her to return to London with us?"

"Yes. I think she still loves Father, but she won't agree to go back."

Ryder lifted her chin and stared into her anxious face. "We'll bring her around, love. I'll do my best to help."

"You always do," she whispered with tender gratitude. She paused, a thoughtful frown drifting in. "I know now why my parents parted."

"And why is that?"

"My father cast my mother from his bed."

"Ah—that puts the alienation in some perspective, then."

She nodded solemnly. "I think it would be hard to live without passion."

Obviously amused, he raised an eyebrow. "Why, Lady Newbury, however did you arrive at this fascinating conclusion? You can't exactly claim you've had to live without passion since we've been wed."

Natalie giggled but didn't answer.

Wickedly, he whispered, "Could it be that after I first claimed you on board ship, you found yourself pining away for my amorous attentions?"

Although she blushed, she responded pertly, "You overestimate your charms, Lord Newbury."

"Oh, do I? Is that how it came to be that you were dragged, pregnant, to the altar?"

She flung a handful of water in his face. "Scamp! Only a cad would mention that!"

He was chuckling. "I can certainly rise to that challenge when needed."

She moaned as she felt his body rising to quite a different challenge. "Well, maybe it was a *little* hard to live without your passion," she admitted mischievously.

He chuckled again, caught her hand, and pressed her fingers to his stiff manhood. "Sometimes it's hard to live with it, eh, love?"

She tilted her face saucily toward his. "Are you expecting me to stroke your vanity now, my lord?"

"Don't stroke my vanity. Just stroke me."

She did. He groaned. His blue eyes grew hot, intent. He was very aroused.

Feeling very amorous, Natalie abruptly turned in his arms, splashing water in every direction as she straddled him with her knees. "I think I would like my reward now."

"Your reward?" he repeated, laughing heartily. "But you already claimed that in advance, last night."

She gave him a sultry look and rubbed her most intimate parts against him. "Remember the double portions of ice cream we had at the Café de Paris?"

"Natalie . . . Oh, love." Ryder was caught in a vise of unbearable pleasure as she sank herself onto him. "Take care, love, for the baby."

"I will. Trust me, darling, I'll be gentle with you."

She was, but by the time it was all over, Ryder was blissfully exhausted and most of the water had been splashed out of the tub.

Thirty-eight

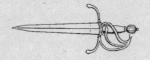

On a sunny afternoon a few days later, Ryder and Natalie were strolling through the gardens of the Palais Royal. Ryder mused that his wife looked truly gorgeous in her new frock of striped, plum-colored taffeta with its Empire waist, short, puffed sleeves, and rounded neckline. She wore a charming hat decorated with silk roses, and carried a lacy parasol.

He also felt a sense of devilish pride that he had convinced her to come with him to this fascinating, decadent haunt of saint and sinner. Natalie was truly letting go and enjoying herself with him, and how he loved her for this.

Now he delighted in her reactions as, wide-eyed, she took in the scene. The promenade swarmed with people and activity. Couples and entire families ate meals or ice cream on the terraces spilling off the colonnade. Old men played dominoes and drank coffee in the shade of leafy chestnut trees; small, fluffy dogs scurried about underfoot, barking shrilly. Portrait painters in stained smocks performed their craft amid the chaos of humanity trooping by. Vendors in ramshackle stands tried to tempt passersby with everything from the finest silks, bonnets, hats, and jewelry to ornate clocks and hand-painted china. A mishmash of smells—strong coffee, hot French bread, tobacco, greenery, perfume, human sweat—laced the air.

Around the quadrangle were grouped cafés, coffee shops, and billiard parlors. Prostitutes openly enticed Royal Guardsmen on the pillared galleries, while cigar-smoking cardsharps lounged in the shadowed archways of gambling dens, forever scanning the crowds for wealthy dandies to pluck dry at faro or billiards.

They paused near a small table where a colorfully dressed huckster was enthralling a small crowd with *le jeu des gobelets*. Natalie watched intently as the man maneuvered three walnut shells with lightning speed. Once the cups came to rest, a young dandy pointed to one of them, and a gasp sounded from the assemblage when the grinning huckster picked up the shell and there was no pea underneath. The gambler snatched a franc from the scowling dandy as a new gentleman came forward to place a bet.

"How does he do that?" Natalie asked Ryder as she watched the shells being propelled about. "I could have sworn the young man made a correct guess."

Ryder chuckled and leaned toward her. "The whole thing is a ruse, darling. Sleight of hand. The pea is actually hidden in his palm, clutched between two of his fingers."

"Oh! That is disgraceful." She stared up at him. "But how do you know such things? Don't tell me you've ever played such a deplorable trick on anyone."

"Me?" His expression was all pious innocence. "Never."

Watching the huckster snatch up yet another coin, Natalie said irately, "Give me a franc."

With a chuckle, Ryder obliged. Natalie stepped forward and held up her coin. She watched the man put the pea under one shell and then move the shells around swiftly. At the end of the game, she pointed to the center cup, and was not at all surprised when there was no pea underneath. But instead of giving up her coin, she quickly overturned the other two shells—so the amazed crowd could see firsthand that everyone had been duped. As cries of outrage rose from the spectators, Natalie grabbed the man's wrist and held up his hand, causing the hidden pea to drop to the table.

Pandemonium broke loose, the irate bystanders charging the huckster with blasphemies spewing forth and fists flying. The besieged man fled, wild-eyed, minus both his table and his shells.

Nodding to herself with grim satisfaction, Natalie handed the coin back to Ryder, who appeared amazed. "Is something wrong?"

He shook his head. "A vindictive little minx, aren't you?"

"Well, he deserved it."

"Remind *me* never to misbehave in your presence."

"Hah! You do it all the time."

"Aye, and I rue the consequences."

Both were laughing as they headed on. Taking Natalie's cue, Ryder lunged into the middle of a juggling demonstration, grabbing three bright balls, much to the amusement of the children gathered there. He attempted to juggle the balls, and ended up thoroughly bungling the effort and even knocking off his hat. The children, as well as Natalie, were howling with mirth by the time Ryder returned the balls to the bemused juggler, retrieved his hat, and swept on with his wife.

As they passed a stand displaying British pottery, Natalie's smile faded to a pensive look. "Ryder, are we going back to London soon?"

Feeling a pang of disappointment, he tugged her to a halt beneath a small tree. "Darling, aren't you happy here? Don't you like Paris? Are you afraid the decadent city will get into your blood and turn you into a hedonist forever?"

She laughed. "Oh, Paris is delightful, and I do wish we could stay forever. But, truth to tell, we don't seem to be making much progress with my mother, and I am becoming increasingly worried about Father."

"The doctor assured us that his life is not in imminent danger," Ryder pointed out. "And I feel it's too soon to completely give up hope on Desiree. She may yet come around and decide to return with us."

"I realize this, but I still don't want to be away from Father too much longer," she muttered. She glanced around, craning her neck. "Do you suppose we could buy him a gift here?"

"Of course." He took her arm and moved forward, his gaze scanning above the sea of heads. "I seem to recall seeing both a tobacconist and haberdasher somewhere near the colonnade—"

All at once Ryder stopped in his tracks, not far from a puppet show. Yet his gaze was riveted not on the theatrical display but on a familiar figure standing among the spectators with a lovely young lady on his arm.

"Harry Hampton! My God, is it you?" Ryder called out.

Both the man and the lady turned, the man grinning in shocked pleasure. Waving, he rushed forward to join them,

with his companion in tow. Ryder was amazed to note that
the gentleman was indeed his old friend Harry Hampton, who
now appeared no worse for wear, especially since he was escorting a ravishing, dark-eyed beauty dressed in an Empire-
style frock of lacy white.

"Ryder!" Harry exclaimed, pumping his friend's hand.

"Hampton! What a shock."

"By Jove, what are you—and Natalie—doing in Paris?"

Ryder wrapped an arm around his wife's waist and grinned
proudly. "We're married, and here on our wedding trip."

"Married?" Harry winked at Natalie.

"And now I must ask the same question of you," Ryder
went on irately. "How on earth did you end up in France?"

Harry's hearty laughter boomed out. "It is a long story, my
friend."

Ryder was about to pursue the matter when the two couples had to spring apart to allow a small troupe of acrobats to
march between them. Ryder cupped his hand around his
mouth and called out, "Meet us at the Café de Foy and we'll
have an ice."

Harry waved in the affirmative, and within moments, the
four were seated on the terrace of the café enjoying strawberry ices.

"So it seems congratulations are in order," Harry began.
"Just when did you two become Lord and Lady Newbury?"

"About two and a half weeks ago," Ryder replied. He
grinned at Harry's charming companion. "And it looks as if
you have been playing the amorous suitor yourself. Will you
kindly introduce us to your lady friend?"

"Oh, yes. Sorry." Flashing a tender smile toward the girl,
he announced, "Lord and Lady Newbury, may I present Ma-
demoiselle Genevieve Foulard."

Extending a gloved hand, Natalie smiled at her and said,
"How do you do?"

The young woman shook Natalie's hand and smiled back
shyly. *"Enchanté,* madame."

Natalie raised an eyebrow at Harry. "She doesn't speak English?"

"Not a word."

"And do you speak French?"

"Not a word."

Ryder and Natalie exchanged meaningful glances. "I'm sure they communicate in the way that matters," he murmured.

"Oh, yes," came her disapproving rejoinder.

Ryder cleared his throat. "Well, Hampton, are you going to tell us how you ended up in France?"

"Oh, that.". Harry laughed. "Do you remember the night at the docks?"

"How could I forget?"

"Well, during the fracas, someone bashed me over the head. I was staggering about afterward, with stars shooting off in my head, and all I could remember was my plan to steal on board the smugglers' ship. So I started up a gangplank—only it must have been the wrong gangplank and the wrong ship, for after I passed out in the hold, I didn't wake up until I was in France!"

"You can't be serious!" Ryder exclaimed.

"I swear I am telling you the God's truth," Harry replied.

"Then why didn't you dispatch us a message?" Ryder demanded indignantly. "We had visions of you being carried out to sea by the smugglers, doubtless to become food for the sharks."

"Sorry, old man," Harry said sheepishly. He took Genevieve's hand and kissed it, causing her to blush prettily. "I suppose I became distracted when I came across Genevieve near the docks of Calais."

"No doubt." Ryder said.

"And you brought her with you to Paris—unchaperoned?" added a scandalized Natalie.

Harry wrapped a protective arm around the girl's shoulders. "She was rather in a spot of trouble."

"So she still is," quipped Natalie.

Ryder and Natalie visited with Harry and his lady for several more minutes. Natalie tried to converse with Genevieve, using her own limited French. Though the discussion was fragmented and confusing, Natalie did manage to learn that Harry's girl was only seventeen, a shoemaker's daughter, and seeing Paris for the first time.

Once everyone had finished the ices, Ryder invited Harry and Genevieve to join them, Desiree, and Henri for dinner that night. The other couple graciously accepted.

"Aren't you glad we have found Harry, love?" Ryder asked as he and Natalie strolled back through the gardens. "I remain astounded by it all."

Natalie harrumphed. "And I am horrified. Harry has obviously been busy seducing a seventeen-year-old. Did you see the way he kept touching her, kissing her cheek, and whispering in her ear?"

Ryder scowled. "Yes, I must speak with him about her."

"She is practically a child!"

"Not quite. Couldn't you see they are deeply in love?"

"Does that give him the right to ruin her?"

He sighed. "Perhaps his intentions are honorable."

"Not as far as I can see!"

Ryder chuckled as he wrapped his arm around Natalie's waist. "Oh, love. Poor Harry may rue the day you found him."

Thirty-nine

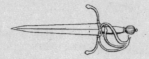

THAT NIGHT, AS PROMISED, THE THREE COUPLES SUPPED TO-
gether, enjoying champagne and roast duck at the elegant
Tour d'Argent on the Left Bank. By now all were enchanted
with the lovely, shy French girl, Genevieve. Desiree spoke
with the young woman in her native tongue for long, intense
moments, then patted her hand and turned to the others.

"This is terrible, my dears," Desiree murmured. "Poor
Genevieve was thrown out of her home by her drunken fa-
ther. She was selling flowers at a market near the docks of
Calais when Harry found her."

"Indeed she was," agreed Harry, with a tender smile at
Genevieve. "But she need never worry about supporting herself ever again."

"And just what are your intentions toward her?" an outraged Desiree demanded of Harry. "You realize, of course,
that she is only seventeen?"

Harry took Genevieve's hand and kissed the back of it.
"She's far older in all the ways that count."

While Desiree rolled her eyes and Natalie gritted her teeth,
Ryder spoke up to his friend. "What *are* you intentions,
Hampton?"

Harry shrugged and said with a cocky grin, "To begin
with, I think I shall take her home to meet my parents."

"*Sacre blue!*" cried Desiree, crossing herself. "To being
with, you must summon a priest."

Harry chuckled, while Natalie said, "Genevieve is welcome to come to London under the protection of my husband
and me."

Desiree added, "She is welcome to stay here with me."

"You may abandon that invitation, madame," Harry responded with unaccustomed sharpness. "Genevieve is coming back to England with me, and that is final."

"Have you asked Genevieve what she wants?" challenged Natalie.

Harry deferred to Desiree. "Madame, if you will?"

Desiree turned and asked the girl several questions in French. After she had answered the queries, Genevieve's eyes widened in fear, she glanced distraughtly at Harry, then grabbed his arm and spoke frantically.

Harry spoke soothingly to the girl until she calmed down. To Desiree, he said with a proud grin, "I think you have your answer, madame."

Desiree threw up her hands.

"Perhaps there is a solution that will please everyone," Ryder murmured. He nodded to Desiree. "Madame, could we speak for a moment on the balcony?"

Though Desiree's expression was bemused, she dutifully rose and accompanied Ryder outside, where the two stood amid the spectacular view of the Quai de la Tournelle and the gothic towers and gargoyles of Notre Dame.

"Desiree, if you are indeed so concerned about the welfare of Genevieve Foulard," Ryder began, "then perhaps you should accompany all of us back to London. With you as the girl's chaperone and to make the needed translations, an air of propriety would be ensured."

She shook a finger at him. "And this is just another ploy, *mon ami,* to convince me to return to Natalie's father."

"We're not suggesting you live with the man again," he argued patiently, "only that you should make a visit. You will be welcome to stay with Natalie and me at our lodgings in London."

Desiree frowned, clearly vacillating.

Ryder touched her arm. "Desiree, the Revolution is over. Bonaparte's empire is gone, he is dead, and the French monarchy has been restored. England and France are at peace."

She raised a delicate brow. "And what is the purpose of this history lesson, *mon ami?*"

"I am trying to point out that the reasons you left London no longer exist."

Desiree conceded the point with a small, morose nod. "I must agree that the climate of France has changed with Napoleon's defeat and passage. Paris has lost much of its former glitter, and even Versailles is abandoned. Now we have reactionaries in the Chambre des Députés, and the public sentiment has been so ultraroyalist ever since the Duc de Berri was assassinated by a Bonapartist last year."

"That is just my point, Desiree," Ryder insisted. "The France you loved no longer exists. Go back to London. There is nothing left for you and Charles Desmond to argue about!"

Desiree raised an eyebrow and made a sound of contempt. "Don't count on that, *mon ami*. Charles and I fought passionately throughout our marriage."

"Ah, but where there is anger and passion, there is also often love," Ryder pointed out wisely. "That has certainly been the case with Natalie and me." He nodded toward the dining room. "Natalie wants to return to London right away. Am I going to have to tell your daughter that she and I have failed, that we must return to England empty-handed?"

Desiree looked back toward the dining room, her eyes filling with tears as she stared at her beloved daughter.

Quietly, he asked, "Do you think Natalie will ever forgive you if Charles dies before the year is out and you have made no attempt to see him?"

Trembling, she turned to him. "Oh, you are ruthless."

He squeezed her hand. "And your daughter needs you, madame. Make the visit so Natalie will know you have at least tried." He grinned ruefully. "And if you can help us save pretty Genevieve from Hampton's corruption, we shall all sleep so much better, shan't we?"

That night at their hotel, Ryder said to Natalie, "Your mother has agreed to return to London with us."

Sitting at the dressing table, Natalie dropped her hairbrush and turned to him with a expression of incredulous joy. "She has? What made her change her mind?"

He walked over to her, picking up the brush and drawing it through her thick, silky hair. "She has agreed to come along as Genevieve's sponsor and chaperone."

"Oh." While Natalie felt relieved for the girl's sake, she

also felt a stab of resentment. "Mother will return to England for the sake of a stranger, but not for her own daughter?"

He leaned over and kissed her cheek. "Of course she's coming back for you, my love, and to see your father. She just needed the proper excuse. Desiree has been wavering for days, long before we ran across Harry and Genevieve. I think tonight I managed to reach her when I reminded her that if she doesn't see your father soon, it may forever be too late."

Natalie rose and thrust herself into her husband's arms. "Oh, Ryder, thank you!"

"You're most welcome, my darling."

She raised her exultant gaze to his. "Now you have fought—and won—another battle for me."

"Don't you know by now that I delight in winning your causes?" he teased.

Suddenly wistful, she asked, "Would you rather be free?"

"Never!" he whispered vehemently, sweeping her up into his arms and carrying her to bed.

Natalie could only hope that Ryder was truly as happy as she felt at the moment. Her mother's decision to return to London also gave her a new infusion of confidence regarding her own marriage and the home she and Ryder would make for their child.

The five began their journey to London two days later, traveling overland by mail coach. Natalie noted that as soon as they arrived at the port of Calais, Genevieve turned as pale and nervous as a little white rabbit, clinging to Harry until they were all safely aboard the small steam and sail packet Ryder had chartered to take them across the Channel and on to London. She seemed a different young woman, relaxed and carefree, once they had pulled away from the docks.

The early summer morning was balmy, the Channel less choppy than usual. Natalie reclined with Genevieve and Desiree on folding Venetian chairs. The three women sipped wine, with Natalie and Desiree continuing the English lessons they had begun for Genevieve on their overland journey. The young woman was quick and bright, and had already acquired a vocabulary of several hundred English words.

Soon Natalie become distracted from the lesson as, across from them on deck, Ryder and Harry began practicing their swordplay. She groaned at the sight. She might have known she would never make it through her wedding trip without having to endure another fencing demonstration. Evidently Harry had brought his sword with him to France, and Ryder had embarked on their wedding trip armed, in case they should be waylaid while traveling overland.

Now, watching the two men dance about with precision, their sabers gleaming and banging, the sun drenching their tall, lithe bodies, Natalie wondered if the two demented cronies would ever change. The deckhands chuckled and shook their heads at the mad antics of the two Englishmen.

In no time at all, Desiree and Genevieve set down their empty wine goblets and dozed. Natalie marveled that they could be so complacent while Ryder and Harry were leaping about wildly and hacking away at each other like maniacs. She mused that her mother and Genevieve were two Frenchwomen who could dismiss the crazed swordplay with a wave of their hands and a *"C'est la vie."* She, on the other hand, was an Englishwoman on the verge of apoplexy.

Perhaps she should try to become more French, she mused. If she and Ryder were to find an enduring love, she would have to learn to let him go more and trust him a little. She had always clung to the safety of being staid and conservative, and had judged others by her own rigid standards. But Ryder had loosened all her inhibitions on their wedding trip, and now such conventions no longer seemed quite so important. She just wanted to see Ryder happy, as happy as they had both been in Paris.

Watching Harry's saber slice within a hairbreadth of her husband's neck, Natalie gasped and averted her gaze. She watched Genevieve open her eyes and stare up at her confusedly.

"Sorry, dear," Natalie muttered.

Genevieve smiled.

"I do hope Harry is planning to marry you," Natalie added.

"Pardon, madame?" whispered Genevieve.

"Never mind." She reached out to pat the girl's hand. "Go back to sleep, darling. Perhaps if we're fortunate, Ryder will skewer Harry to bits, and then we shall all have the pleasure of finding you someone far more suitable."

"Oui, madame."

Obviously not understanding more than a few syllables of Natalie's lecture, Genevieve drifted back to sleep.

When at last the fencing ended and Harry strode off to harass the helmsman, Natalie strolled over to join her husband at the railing. He winked at her, looking totally the rakish devil with the wind whipping his raven hair. His shirt was open almost to his waist, revealing a sexy sheen of sweat on his muscled chest.

She looked him over carefully, feeling relieved when she detected no telltale streaks of blood. "Have you managed to retain all your toes and fingers—and your head?" she asked primly.

He pulled her into his arms, laughing. "Around you, my love, I never keep my head."

"You rogue."

He studied her amused countenance with a curious smile. "What's this, love? You are not throwing your usual fit over the fencing."

She shrugged. "Perhaps I've resigned myself to being married to an overgrown boy."

"Ah, but think of what an entertaining companion I'll make for our children."

"If you and Harry don't turn them all into daredevils."

He chuckled. "Don't worry, love. With any luck, Hampton will be far too busy with a certain young lady to lock swords with me often in the future."

Natalie stretched on tiptoe to catch another glimpse of the lovely, sleeping French girl. "If Harry isn't prepared to marry Genevieve, I want you to call him out."

Ryder whistled. "My, what a bloodthirsty wench you have become—I'd say almost as outrageous as your mother, who, by the way, also has insisted I make Hampton see the light."

"Mother is right," Natalie said piously. "It is the principle of the matter. I'll wager my dowry Harry took Genevieve's virginity—"

"He did," Ryder admitted sheepishly.

"Oh, the scoundrel!"

Ryder's expression turned serious. "Natalie, he is wild about her."

"Then let him do right by her!"

Ryder smiled and nodded toward the girl. "Look, love."

Natalie turned to observe that Genevieve had awakened and was sitting up in her chair, sobbing. Natalie let out a low cry of dismay and was about to rush off to comfort the girl when Ryder caught her hand, shook his head, and pointed toward the stern of the ship. She watched an obviously frantic Harry dash across the deck to Genevieve. He knelt in front of her chair and took the distraught girl in his arms. She clung to him as he rubbed her back and kissed her cheek.

"What is going on?" Natalie demanded. "Genevieve is sobbing! By God, if Harry has made her cry—"

"He hasn't." Ryder turned Natalie toward the railing and put his arms around her.

"Then what has happened to her?"

"Genevieve has nightmares. Her father used to beat her horribly. She was half-starved, exhausted, and terrified when Harry found her near the docks of Calais. She couldn't sleep nights without him there beside her. Harry told me he tried his best to do the noble thing, but . . ." He smiled slowly. "Well, love, you know how tempting it can be when two people share the same sleeping quarters night after night."

Natalie raised an eyebrow while fighting a smile.

He placed a hand over his heart. "I swear, love, I am telling you the God's truth."

"But how does Harry know these things about Genevieve when he doesn't speak French?"

Ryder caught his wife close and pressed his lips to her hair. "I already told you, darling. They communicate in the way that matters. As do we."

Natalie turned to stare at the couple again. Desiree had awakened and was observing the touching vignette with an expression of helpless confusion. "But what of their future? Is Harry—"

"He is going to marry her. He's taking her home to meet his parents and do it up properly. Indeed, he is delighted about your mother's chaperonage for the girl."

"Then why has he been playing the devil-may-care cad around the rest of us?" she asked in exasperation.

"He simply resented the interference—and our questioning motives that turned out to be quite noble all along."

"Oh, Ryder."

Snuggling against her husband's comforting strength,

Natalie again regarded the couple—Harry on his knees, speaking soothingly to the trembling girl in his arms, and Genevieve with her arms tightly coiled about his neck. It was the sweetest sight Natalie had ever seen. And it gave her additional hope that even the most jaded rogue could be reformed by love.

Forty

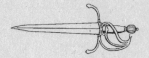

Late that afternoon, Ryder and his bride pulled up to Francesca Valenza's house in a hansom cab. He knew that Desiree would join them later; she had gone with Harry and Genevieve to the Hamptons' house farther west in Mayfair, there to ensure that Genevieve's introduction to Sir Jasper and Lady Millicent would occur with the required air of propriety.

Ryder and Natalie had already stopped off at Charles Desmond's home to check on him and break the news that Desiree was back in London, but Fitzhugh had grimly informed them that Charles was indisposed and would likely be bed-bound for the remainder of the day. Ryder had felt heartsick for Natalie as he had watched his bride rush upstairs to look in on her ailing father. Afterward, heeding the butler's advice, they had decided to call again tomorrow. Ryder knew Natalie was now more worried than ever regarding her father's health, and he hoped they would be able to convince Desiree to accompany them on the visit in the morning.

Ryder escorted Natalie toward Francesca's door, down a path lined by the full blooms of early summer—roses, mums, and marigolds spilling their lush perfume into the air. At his knock, the butler showed them through the house to the rear terrace, where Francesca sat painting with watercolors.

On spotting the couple, she at once set down her brush and rose. "Ryder, Natalie! Thank God you have returned."

Ryder hugged and kissed his grandmother. Francesca turned to welcome Natalie with open arms. After the greetings were completed, the three went over to a stone bench, where Ryder seated his grandmother between himself and Natalie.

"Your trip to Paris, it was good?" Francesca asked.

"The best," replied Ryder. He regarded his grandmother with a thoughtful frown. "Nonna, you look well, but you sounded near frantic when you greeted us. Has something happened?"

She nodded unhappily and clutched his hand. "Grandson, I am afraid it is your father."

Ryder paled. "Go on."

"He has been injured—knifed through the shoulder."

"Oh, good heavens!" Natalie gasped.

"Is his life in danger?" Ryder asked tensely.

Francesca quickly shook her head and patted Ryder's hand. "No, my love, not anymore. The incident happened about a week after you left. At first we feared for his life, but now the surgeon says he has passed the crisis. He is weak, but mending."

"How on earth did this happen?" Ryder demanded.

With a nod toward Natalie, Francesca continued. "The episode occurred in the evening, after Natalie's aunt had dined with the duke."

"Is Aunt Love all right?" Natalie cried. "Don't tell me she was harmed as well?"

Francesca flashed the girl a reassuring smile. "No, she is perfectly fine—although she was a witness to the horrible incident, bless her heart."

"What incident?" Ryder exclaimed.

"Well, according to Mrs. Desmond, the altercation was precipitated by the fact that your father was conducting an audit of the Stepney plant."

Ryder nodded. "I was aware of Father's plans to uncover the smuggling ring, but not that his efforts would put his life in peril."

"It seems William did get too close," lamented Francesca. "I understand both of his business partners—John Lynch and Oswald Spectre—were most resentful and uncooperative regarding the proceedings."

"Go on."

"Evidently John Lynch was the true culprit, for he is the

one who came to your father's home that night and knifed him."

"Oh, my God," Ryder muttered.

"How terrible!" Natalie said.

"How did it happen?" asked Ryder.

Francesca laid a slender finger alongside her cheek. "I don't know a lot of the details, but apparently Lynch sneaked into the house through the back way and attacked William in the drawing room."

"And my aunt saw this?" Natalie asked.

Francesca touched her hand. "Mrs. Desmond may indeed have saved the duke's life, for it was when she entered the room and screamed that Lynch fled."

As Natalie shook her head in horror, Ryder asked, "And how does Oswald Spectre fit into the picture?"

"He likely was not involved, for right after Lynch knifed the duke, it seems he paid a visit to Spectre and hit him over the head with an iron doorstop."

"Did Spectre survive?" queried Ryder.

"Yes, but he has been bed-bound and subject to sinking spells ever since."

"And what of Lynch? Is he still at large?"

Francesca grimaced. "That is the most gruesome part of all. After attacking both your father and Mr. Spectre, John Lynch was found hanged. His death was presumed to be a suicide."

With a cry of horror, Natalie flung a hand to her breast.

"John Lynch hanged himself?" Ryder repeated.

"Evidently so. His wife, Essie, found him."

"This is incredible!" Ryder exclaimed.

"Indeed," said Francesca.

Natalie threw her husband a beseeching glance. "We must go to your father—and to Aunt Love—at once."

Reaching across Francesca, he clutched her hand. "Of course, darling."

"Yes, you two go on," Francesca urged. "But you will come back here this evening, won't you? Your room is ready."

"You are too kind, Nonna," said Ryder. "But I had thought my bride and I might stay at a hotel until I can find us suitable lodgings."

"Don't be absurd," protested Francesca. "I've half a dozen guest rooms that are never used. I realize you newlyweds must be anxious to secure your own residence, but surely you can tolerate a silly old woman for a few days first?"

Ryder and Natalie exchanged smiles; then Natalie said warmly, "It would be our pleasure to stay with you, Countess—if it is not an imposition."

"Certainly not."

"But there is a complication," Natalie added. "We brought my mother with us."

Francesca clapped her hands. "Ah, then you were successful in your mission?"

"Yes. Actually, I was hoping the three of us could stay at my father's house—you know, give my mother and father a nudge in the right direction—but Mother adamantly refused."

"But if she is not with your father, where is she?"

This time Ryder spoke. "She went with Harry and his fiancée to his parents' home."

"You found Harry?" Francesca gasped. "And he has a fiancée?"

Ryder smiled. "It is a long story, Nonna."

"I understand."

"I asked my mother to meet us here later," Natalie remarked. "So if she shows up—"

"If she appears here, then I shall show her to her room, of course."

"Nonna, you are a jewel," Ryder said proudly. He took his wife's hand and helped her to her feet.

"You just go see about your father," Francesca replied. When her grandson leaned over to kiss her, she murmured, "And, Ryder . . ."

"Yes?"

As Natalie stood nearby, smoothing her skirts, Francesca whispered intently, "For days now, I have had the strange feeling that the danger has not ended. Be careful, my love. And for Natalie, too."

Ryder's expression was troubled as he left with his wife.

At the home of the duke, Ryder spoke with the butler. Withers went upstairs to consult with Love Desmond, who was sitting with Ryder's father. A moment later, the manservant reappeared to escort the couple up to the duke's suite of rooms on the third floor.

Ryder and Natalie slipped quietly into the duke's bedroom. Ryder caught a glimpse of his father. Remington lay asleep on the carved Chinese bed, surrounded by regal burgundy brocade hangings. He looked much paler and thinner than Ryder recalled, and Ryder felt besieged by unaccustomed emotion, a mingling of fear and tenderness, as he observed the powerful, cold man he had known all his life lying there pale, bed-bound, and helpless.

Love sat next to William's bed in a straight chair. On spotting the couple just inside the door, she rose and hastened over to join them. Her expression was one of great happiness as she hugged each of them in turn and whispered, "Oh, my loves, I am so glad you have returned!"

Ryder nodded tensely toward his father. "How is he?"

"Fine when he is sleeping, but very cross when he awakens," Love replied. "The Duke of Mansfield does not take well to being bed-bound."

Ryder fought a faint smile.

"Are you all right, Aunt Love?" Natalie asked anxiously. "Ryder's grandmother told us what happened. We were appalled, of course."

"That demon John Lynch!" Love declared. "You heard that he hanged himself, I presume?" As Ryder and Natalie grimaced in unison, she continued. "Good riddance is what I say, after what that villain did to poor William!"

"Nonna told us you were a witness," Ryder said.

A look of anguish and remembered horror clenched Love's features. "Oh, it was a nightmare! I was in the library, fetching a book for William, when I heard him cry out. Of course I came charging right into the drawing room. Imagine my terror when I saw him bleeding on the floor, with the knife protruding from his shoulder and that scoundrel Lynch hovering over him—about to move in for the kill, I imagine. Naturally, I screamed like a banshee, and Lynch fled out the French doors."

"Did you see his face?" Ryder asked.

Love shook her head. "His back was to me, but I did see his black cloak and that low-brimmed, sinister hat which William later told me he often wore. Evidently he was still wearing the cloak when his wife summoned the Bow Street Runners to cut him down from the rafters where he had hanged himself."

Natalie shuddered, and Ryder wrapped his arm around her.

"Are you all right, my dear?" Love asked her niece solicitously. "I neglected even to inquire about your wedding trip."

"Heavens, under the circumstances, that is the last thing we would have expected," Natalie replied feelingly.

"Well, did you have fun, you two?" Love demanded with the old twinkle in her eyes.

"We had a grand time," Ryder answered, "and we even managed to bring home a few surprises."

"Oh?" Love glanced from Ryder to Natalie.

"We fetched back Mother," said Natalie.

Love smiled. "I'm so pleased for you, my dear!"

"We also found Harry—and his new fiancée," Ryder remarked.

"My goodness! What a surprise!"

The three conversed in intent, hushed tones for a few more moments, until a groggy, grumpy voice called out from the bed, "Love, who is here?"

She turned toward the bed. "William, dear, I hope we didn't awaken you."

"Stuff and nonsense. If I rest anymore, I may as well be lying in my grave."

"Ryder and Natalie are here, back from Paris."

"Well, then, bring them over here, where I can see them."

At the bed, Ryder stared down at his father. Again he found that William looked wan and frail, lying there on his back and staring up at his son so expectantly. Remington's eyes no longer gleamed like ice, but instead seemed to glow with a far more human need. Gone was the formidable, invincible duke; in his place lay a fragile, wounded man who had almost died. This realization of his father's mortality and vulnerability touched feelings long buried in Ryder. He gave in to a sudden instinct to touch his father's hand, and felt a tight welling of emotion in his throat when the duke clutched his fingers.

"Your . . ." Ryder paused to clear a suddenly raspy throat. "Father, Natalie and I were horrified to hear of—the appalling attack on your person—and we are so grateful that you are going to be all right."

"Thank you, son," William replied with a catch of emotion in his own voice.

"You are sounding strong, sir," Ryder added.

"So Love keeps telling me." The duke turned to Natalie and, surprisingly, winked at her. "How is the bride?"

Natalie, feeling equally impulsive, leaned over and kissed William's forehead. As she straightened, she felt relieved to note a smile on his face. "I am doing splendidly, your Grace."

"And taking good care of my future grandson?" William asked. When Natalie blushed, he quickly said, "I do not mean to embarrass you, my dear, but after all, we are all family here."

"When William was so gravely wounded," Love put in, "I reminded him numerous times that he couldn't possibly die and miss seeing his first grandchild—and of course he agreed."

Natalie smiled at William. "Your grandchild is also doing just splendidly, your Grace."

The four talked for a few more minutes, Ryder and Natalie trying to keep the discussion cheerful, giving details of their trip to Paris, while avoiding the subject of the duke's ordeal. Then Ryder, noting that his father was beginning to show the strain of the visit, took his wife's hand and they said their good-byes.

Love accompanied them out into the hallway. "I can't tell you how glad I am that both of you are back."

"How long will Father be bed-bound?" Ryder asked.

"The surgeon is already permitting him to get up for a short while each day, but he is quite weak, and his wound still pains him. He was cursing at the poor valet yesterday after the man helped him take only a few steps."

"Perhaps I could come round and help Father get some exercise," Ryder mused aloud. "He's too proud and arrogant to show any such weaknesses around his son."

"Oh, would you, Ryder?" Love asked. "That would indeed be so helpful—and William needs you in other ways as well."

"Such as?"

"Well, he has been in bed for almost two weeks now, and his business affairs are truly in a shambles. His secretary is doing what he can, but with both Lynch and Spectre out of the picture, there is no one to run the Stepney plant. William's other holdings are suffering, too, plus there is a bill he had presented to Parliament—some proposal about repealing the game-poaching laws that really has him fretting—and that is now caught in limbo . . ."

"I will help out wherever I can," Ryder assured her.

"Oh, bless you."

Withers stepped up to join them. To Love, he said, "Madame, Mrs. Lynch has again called to pay her respects to the duke."

"Oh, bother!" With an exasperated sigh, Love explained her reaction to the couple. "Poor Essie drops by most every day now. Evidently she feels guilty for John's treachery. Will you two go have a word with her, help her wring out her hankie or something? Frankly, her calls are becoming tiresome, and I dislike leaving William alone while he is awake."

"Of course we'll speak with her," said Ryder.

Downstairs, Ryder and Natalie entered the drawing room as a black-clothed Essie Lynch rose and swept toward them. Just as Love had warned them, the woman appeared tense and anxious; she was twisting a handkerchief in her fingers, and Natalie was disturbed to note a large, fading bruise along the woman's jaw.

"Lord and Lady Newbury—this is a surprise."

"We have just returned from our wedding trip to Paris," Ryder said.

"How is the duke?" Essie inquired.

"He is mending well."

She continued to worry her handkerchief. "I am relieved to hear that." Lifting her chin, she added with a mixture of pride and uncertainty, "You must both know that I was horrified by John's crimes."

"We realize as much, Mrs. Lynch," Ryder said.

Essie began to dab at her eyes and gesture nervously. "Why, I really had no idea he was involved in smuggling—and was robbing the Duke of Mansfield, no less! I must extend to you both my sincere apologies for his despicable deeds."

"And we extend to you our sympathy for all you've had to endure," Natalie added sincerely. She stared at Essie with concern. "Mrs. Lynch, I do not mean to pry, but I cannot help but notice that bruise on your chin. Did John strike you?"

Now Essie appeared extremely agitated; a blush stained her haggard cheeks as she fingered her jaw and avoided the gazes of both Ryder and Natalie. "When I found John," she muttered at last, "I was so overcome with horror that I fainted and hit my chin on the desk."

"You did?" Natalie gasped. "We are so sorry—"

"Yes. Well, then, I must be going," Essie cut in briskly. "Please give the duke my regards."

"We shall," Ryder said, frowning.

After Essie left, Ryder wrapped an arm around Natalie's waist. "A very odd woman—and nervous as a cat."

Natalie nodded. "I think she lied to us about falling. I think that scoundrel John Lynch must have beaten her."

"Quite possibly he did. And if so, good riddance to him—albeit it is not easy to feel warmly toward Essie, either."

"At least she has expressed concern for your father." Natalie stared at Ryder with her heart in her eyes. "Oh, Ryder, I feel so responsible!"

"You?" he asked, perplexed. "Why should you feel responsible?"

"If I hadn't forced the issue of the smuggling, none of these horrible events would have occurred—especially your father's being attacked. Perhaps Aunt Love and I should have just given up and tolerated the situation back in Charleston."

"Don't be ridiculous," Ryder said, pulling her closer. "We mustn't condone wrongdoing out of fear—and I think my father would wholeheartedly agree with that."

She sighed. "At least the mystery is solved."

He stroked her hair and frowned. "Is it? I sincerely hope so, my love. However, I must confess I find it hard to believe John Lynch hanged himself—that's almost too macabre a twist."

She stared up at him "Then what?"

Already regretting his imprudent words, he kissed her forehead. "Do not worry, my love. I'm sure you are right that the danger has passed."

Yet Ryder's heart remained troubled. What a day of frightful disclosures! Had the menace truly ended? He couldn't get Nonna's warning out of his mind.

* * *

"Good evening, gov'nor. Well, here I am, just like your coachman ordered."

"Mawkins, good to see you again, my friend," Ryder replied with a smile.

Late that night, in the darkness outside his father's Stepney factory, Ryder shook Mawkins's callused hand, then frowned curiously toward the companion the man had brought along.

Mawkins jerked his thumb toward the hulking stranger with a scarred cheek, who was dressed in the dark jacket and cloth cap of a dock worker. "I brought along me uncle Tom. He ain't the one what died at Newgate, o' course."

"I'm relieved to hear it," Ryder rejoined with a dry chuckle. He shook Tom's hand, then turned back to Mawkins. "Very good, then. I've plenty of work for both of you."

Mawkins glanced around in perplexity. "Begging your pardon, gov'nor, but why did you have us meet you at the factory in the dead of night?"

Ryder gestured toward the darkened facade of the textile facility. "Because I want you men to watch the factory each night for any signs of suspicious activity."

"Suspicious activity?" queried a puzzled Tom.

"Not the smugglers again, gov'nor?" said a scowling Mawkins.

"Aye," replied Ryder grimly. "One of the scoundrels just tried to murder my father."

"Blimey!" cried Mawkins.

"And I have it on good authority that the danger may not have passed."

Mawkins scratched his stubbled jaw. "You don't say, gov'nor. What would you have Tom and me do, then?"

"Just keep your ears cocked and your eyes peeled," Ryder ordered. "I especially want you to be on the lookout for a man named Oswald Spectre, and I shall describe him to you in detail. Let me know at once if you see Spectre, or spot any other unusual activity at the factory. If you two men follow orders, there will be sovereigns in it for you both."

Mawkins and Tom exchanged glances of gleeful relish, then listened carefully to the rest of Ryder's instructions.

Forty-one

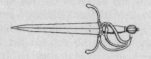

"I TELL YOU, NATALIE, I HAVE NO DESIRE TO SEE THAT INSUF-
ferable man!"

The next morning, Ryder and Natalie were all but dragging
Desiree up the path to Charles Desmond's town house. Since
late yesterday afternoon, when Desiree had joined Ryder and
Natalie at Francesca Valenza's home, the irrepressible
Frenchwoman had made up one excuse after another regard-
ing why she should not call on her estranged husband today.
Ryder and Natalie had gotten Desiree out the door only amid
much coaxing and even a few threats.

Natalie noted that her mother did look divine in her low-
cut, Empire-style, blue silk dress and lace cap. Her coiffure
was impeccable, and her expensive perfume had obviously
been liberally applied. Natalie felt rather bewildered by the
contradictions in her mother's attitude and appearance. While
Desiree claimed to be an unwilling visitor, her lavishly feminine image bespoke otherwise. Perhaps there lurked in
Desiree Desmond's heart more feeling for Charles than the
stubborn matron was willing to admit, Natalie mused with
frail hope.

"Mother, you know Father has been ill," she reasoned.
"Seeing you might be just the remedy he needs."

"Seeing him will be the death of us both," Desiree declared.

Ryder and Natalie exchanged exasperated glances.

Ryder's knock was answered by a beaming Fitzhugh, who
exclaimed, "Madame Desmond! We are so thrilled to see you
have returned!"

372

Desiree harrumphed, *"Bonjour,* Fitzhugh. My daughter and her husband have all but kidnapped me, insisting that I call on your master. Is Charles in?"

"Of course, madame. Please follow me."

The threesome entered the drawing room to observe Charles slumped in his chair by the fireplace, snoring softly. Natalie, who yesterday had caught only a brief glimpse of her father in his darkened bedroom, now studied him closely. To her relief, she noted that his physical state had not worsened appreciably since her wedding day. His coloring remained bad, but his jaundice had not deepened, and at least he was up and properly dressed.

Then she glanced at her mother to gauge Desiree's response to seeing her husband after many years of estrangement. Her features were tight, and she was obviously trying to maintain a stoic facade, although a slight softening of her tawny eyes hinted of more turbulent emotion, and further fueled Natalie's tenuous optimism.

Natalie tiptoed to Charles's side and gently shook his shoulder. "Father . . . Ryder and I have returned from Paris, and we've brought Mother back with us."

Charles Desmond jerked awake and glanced around the room in mystification. His bloodshot gaze settled on Desiree, who stood across from him next to Ryder. He appeared as if he had seen a ghost.

He swayed to his feet and spoke unsteadily. "Desiree! My God, you are back!"

"You always did have a predilection for stating the obvious, Charles," Desiree retorted, if in an equally quavery voice.

"But—but what are you doing here?"

Proudly, she replied, "Your daughter and son-in-law all but dragged me out of Paris so that I could save you from yourself."

"Save me?" he repeated confusedly. "From myself?"

"What Mother means is, we all felt a visit from her might greatly improve your spirits," Natalie put in tactfully.

"At least, those spirits that you don't consume," Desiree added sarcastically.

While Ryder rolled his eyes, Charles reddened in anger at his wife's insult. "How generous of you to come, madame," he sneered. "But then, I suppose you always were a champion of lost causes, weren't you?"

Watching Desiree puff up in fury at Charles's gibe, Natalie tossed Ryder a beseeching, near-frantic glance. He, in turn, grinned, clapped his hands, and said with forced enthusiasm, "Well, isn't it grand that we're all together? Shall we take seats and have Natalie ring for tea?"

The couple grudgingly complied, Charles and Desiree positioning themselves as far apart as possible, like opposing generals sizing each other up. Natalie rang for tea, and Fitzhugh promptly brought in the service. Unfortunately, the hot brew and freshly baked crumpets Natalie doled out did nothing to warm up the chill atmosphere in the room. For some time, Desiree and Charles merely glowered at each other, while Ryder and Natalie made small talk, filling her father in on the details of their wedding trip.

Try as they might, the newlyweds could not hold at bay the building tension between Charles and Desiree. Indeed, while Natalie was rattling on nervously about the new wardrobe she had acquired in Paris, Charles abruptly turned to Desiree and mocked, "You look rather like a fashion plate from La Belle Assemblée yourself, my dear. What—no black crepe for your sainted Bonaparte?"

Tossing down her napkin, Desiree retorted, "How dare you malign the emperor!"

"He is no one's emperor now," Charles shot back. "Unless, of course, you count the worms. 'Emperor of the Worms'— that has a nice ring to it, don't you think?"

"I think you are a callous cad!"

Charles's eyes gleamed in bitter triumph. "And I think you are not so proud, are you, madame, now that Bonaparte has tasted his final defeat and found his proper place six feet under?"

"You never had a whit of respect for the emperor or anything he stood for!" Desiree exclaimed.

"And you never had one ounce of esteem for your own husband—or the country he loves!"

Desiree lurched to her feet. "I do not have to listen to this treason any longer!"

Charles followed suit with a telltale wobble. "And I do not have to take back a faithless wife who deserted me and has no doubt been fornicating with every rakehell on the Continent!"

While Natalie gasped in horror and Ryder grimaced, Desiree was trembling with ire and shaking a fist at Charles. "That is a contemptible lie! And how dare you even presume I am amenable to a reconciliation with you!"

"Perhaps I should petition Parliament for a divorce, just as the king attempted with his own faithless wife last year!"

"As if George himself is a paragon of virtue! I might have known you would respond to my presence in this appalling, ungrateful manner. I shall save you the trouble of seeking a divorce by returning to France."

"Good riddance!"

Desiree was turning on her heel and charging headlong toward the archway when, abruptly, Ryder stepped into her path, shaking his head sternly.

"Sacre blue!" she hissed savagely. "Get out of my way! The man is impossible!"

"Madame," he whispered hoarsely, taking her by the shoulders and turning her, "you will give this a chance!"

For a moment, Charles and Desiree continued to glare at each other.

Natalie stepped between them and spoke plaintively. "Father, Mother, you haven't even seen each other in over eight years. Can't you at least exchange a civil word or two—for my sake?"

"And for the sake of your future grandchild?" Ryder added sternly.

The two stared each other down for another charged moment, and then, surprisingly, Charles was the first to give way. He coughed, then muttered stiffly to Desiree, "You are looking well."

Yet the cease-fire proved lamentably short-lived. "And you are looking wretched," Desiree retorted. "Does your entire diet now consist of brandy?"

"And yours of dandy libertines?" Charles demanded, his voice rising.

"Ah, yes!" Desiree scoffed with an extravagant gesture. "Why, just last week I enjoyed a charming *ménage à trois* with the two British exiles Byron and Brummell—and Lord

Byron has even dedicated his latest romantic epic to me. Such a darling lad! No wonder I so easily tired of your bed!"

While Ryder groaned and Natalie wrung her hands, Charles flung his arms wide. "I give up! Get this harlot out of my sight—I beg you!"

Realizing that further intervention was futile at the moment, Ryder grasped Desiree by the arm. "We shall return, sir," he informed Charles.

"We shall not!" cried Desiree.

"Indeed—do no bother!" Charles seconded.

Without another word, Ryder escorted Desiree and Natalie from the room.

"The man is a beast! An imbecile!" declared Desiree.

In the coach going home, Ryder was trying to reason with his mother-in-law, perched across from him having a fit, while his wife sat next to him in explosive silence.

"Desiree, please don't give up so quickly," Ryder said patiently. "Today was only your first meeting with Charles. I thought it went rather well, under the circumstances."

"You must be delirious," Desiree scoffed.

"We shall go back tomorrow, when you both have had a chance to cool off," Ryder continued calmly.

"In a pig's eye, we shall!" retorted Desiree. "I am returning to France on the next tide."

"That's right, Mother," Natalie joined in angrily. "Just give up, go back to France, and let Father die! I might have known I could expect no sense of loyalty from you!"

"But, darling," Desiree reasoned with a beseeching glance, "the man insulted me horribly. You were there. He called me a whore—"

"You were the one who claimed you had consorted with two men—at the same time, no less—and had one of them writing love poems to you!"

"That was only because your father drove me past sanity with his insults. Natalie, you must know that I would never—"

"Don't bother defending yourself to me, Mother," Natalie cut in hotly. "You cannot expect me to heed the arguments of a woman who deserted her child and her husband."

Desiree turned pleadingly to Ryder. "Please, make her see reason."

Ryder touched his wife's hand. "Sweetheart, it is clear there was fault on both sides—"

"And it is also clear that there will be no hope of a reconciliation unless *someone*"—Natalie paused to stare pointedly at her mother—"makes a sincere effort."

Desiree was about to protest, but Ryder forestalled her when he raised a hand and shook his head firmly.

They returned to Francesca's house, where, just inside the doorway, Natalie rushed off upstairs. Watching with resignation as his wife fled, Ryder pulled his mother-in-law inside the small office which Francesca had put at his disposal so he could handle his father's business affairs.

He leaned against the closed door and spoke with urgency. "Desiree, you are going to have to give this another chance."

She crossed her arms over her bosom. "The man is insufferable!"

"And you were a paragon of conciliation?"

Desiree glowered.

Ryder took a step toward her. "Madame, if Charles dies of the drink, Natalie is going to blame you."

Desiree threw up her hands and began to curse in rapid French and pace the small room.

"Do you want to lose Natalie?" he asked quietly.

She turned to him with a look of helpless anguish. "After it has taken me so long to get her back? Of course not!"

"That is not the way it appears to her now."

"Then what do you want me to do?" she cried.

Staring at her, Ryder thought of how like Natalie she was—strong-willed, defiant to the end. It was ironic, he mused. He had bargained with his wife in Paris to give Desiree a chance, and now he would bargain with his mother-in-law to give Charles a chance.

Calmly, Ryder said, "Desiree, I want to make a pact with you. I want you to call on Charles again, every day for a week—"

"A *week?*" More cursing followed.

"Please, just do as I say. Only for a week. At the end of that time, if the two of you are still not reconciled, then you may return to France with my blessings."

"But why try for another week?" Desiree asked, her voice tortured. "What is the point, *mon ami?*"

Ryder laid a hand on her shoulder. "Because at the end of that time, whether you and Charles are back together or not, I know I can convince Natalie that at least you have made the effort. Can you actually return to France now and let your daughter believe you didn't care enough to try?"

Desiree was silent, scowling and rapping her slippered toe on the Persian carpet.

"So, Desiree? Do we have an agreement?"

"We . . . do." Releasing a heavy breath, she added with unaccustomed tentativeness, "Charles did not look well, did he?"

Ryder shook his head sadly. "If he doesn't change his ways, he will die. Isn't his life worth a week of your time?"

Blinking rapidly, Desiree turned away to stare out the window, her expression eloquent with conflicted emotions. Momentarily, she breathed a heavy sigh and replied, *"Certainement, mon ami."*

"Then perhaps there is more feeling there than you are willing to admit?" Ryder asked gently.

Desiree's countenance remained troubled as she turned to face him. "Feelings have very little to do with whether or not a man and a woman can truly live—and be happy—together."

Leaving the room, Ryder frowned, feeling sobered by the possibility that Desiree's words might have had a ring of truth—not just for her life with Charles, but for his own with Natalie. Just like her mother, Natalie was the one who kept insisting that they were too different—and he was the one who was determined to convince her otherwise.

He hurried up the stairs to the room he shared with his bride, striding inside to the sound of her sobs. Torment twisted his heart as he spotted her sprawled across the bed and shuddering with emotion. He hadn't realized the meeting between her parents had upset her quite so much . . .

On the bed, Natalie was indeed feeling overwrought. Her parents' argument had revived unhappy memories from her youth. The disastrous scene she had witnessed—coupled with the likelihood that Charles and Desiree would never reconcile—not only made her fearful that her father was headed toward certain death, but also made her wonder anew if she and Ryder would succeed together, especially now that they were both in the real world with all its attendant problems and responsibilities.

And they had a baby to think of, too—bless the precious little life. Would she and Ryder eventually end up trapped in a miserable marriage, screaming at each other, ruining their child's life, just as her mother and father had done to her?

Ryder joined his wife on the bed, pulling her into his arms and stroking her back. "Darling, please don't cry."

"She doesn't care!"

He kissed her brow tenderly. "Yes, she does. She has agreed to visit your father every day for a week."

Natalie looked up in awe. "She has?"

Ryder brushed a tear from Natalie's cheek and smiled. "I'm convinced Desiree really does care for your father—and even more than that, she hates the prospect of hurting you."

"B-but she deserted us both so callously eight years ago!"

"Oh, Natalie." Ryder brushed his lips over her cheeks, her swollen eyelids. "If Desiree has agreed to give your father a chance, then I think the least you can do is to give her a chance, too."

Sniffling, Natalie didn't reply.

"Will you give your relationship with your mother another try?" When she still didn't respond, he said, "Think of the joy it brought you to give me a chance."

She considered that for a moment, then harrumphed. "You are certainly much more agreeable than Mother is."

He appeared fascinated. "Oh, am I?"

A smile tugged at her lips. "Very well. I will try."

"No more tears?"

She sighed and reached out to toy with his cravat. "I do seem to be very emotional these days—it must be the baby."

"Poor darling."

Tentatively, she added, "And I guess I'm wondering if we'll end up like Mother and Father, ruining our own child's life."

All at once, Ryder appeared very serious as he brushed a wisp of hair from her brow. "I don't think either of us is that selfish, darling."

She stared up at him tenderly. "You certainly are not—putting up with me, my family, my impossible moods . . ."

He kissed her quickly. "You are pregnant, m'lady. I'm proud to tolerate your moods."

Suddenly turning impish, she wrinkled her nose at him. "I'm very difficult, you know."

"Aye. I know."

She slowly curled her arms around his neck. "And I also expect worlds of sympathy."

He chuckled. "I think I can conjure a way to comfort you, m'lady." He began unbuttoning her frock and kissing the soft skin of her neck.

Feeling soothed already, she caught a blissful breath and smirked at him. "That is just your excuse to take advantage of my favors."

"Take advantage?" he repeated in mock outrage. "If you were not pregnant, Lady Newbury, I would tickle you senseless for mouthing such treason."

Her eyes grew dark and languid. She took his hand and pressed the palm low against her belly. "I can think of far lovelier things for you to do with your fingers."

Ryder groaned. With his free hand he ran his index finger suggestively over her lips. "And I can think of far lovelier things for you to do with your mouth."

"Tell me," she teased impudently.

He playfully swatted her bottom. "You already know, you little minx. Now come closer and show me."

During the next exquisite moments, each of them was blessed with a thorough demonstration.

Forty-two

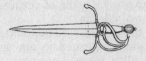

THE NEXT WEEKS KEPT RYDER AND NATALIE SWEPT UP IN A whirl of activities. Ryder became preoccupied with his father's duties, taking over much of the duke's business affairs and also trying to shepherd a bill the duke had sponsored through the House of Lords and on to the Commons.

The talk of the town was, of course, the coming coronation of George IV on July 19. Along with Francesca, Ryder and Natalie received invitations to the coronation and banquet, and to the levee on July 25. Even Desiree became caught up in the celebratory mood, and announced she would likely put off her return to Paris in order to enjoy the festivities with them. Ryder and Natalie viewed Desiree's postponement as a positive sign.

Each morning, as Ryder and Desiree had agreed, the couple took Desiree calling on Charles Desmond. At first, as Ryder and Natalie sat waiting in the corridor while the "visits" were carried on in the drawing room, they cringed and shuddered at the sounds of Desiree's shrieks in French, Charles's shouted replies, and even the clamor of glass breaking. But as the days passed, Natalie and Ryder grew heartened when there were also long moments of silence—and both noticed that Charles Desmond seemed to look better each time they saw him, his jaundice fading and his skin taking on a more natural hue.

This feeling that Charles's health might be returning was reinforced one day when Fitzhugh cheerfully confided, "Mr. Desmond has hardly touched a drop of brandy since Madame arrived from Paris, and he has ordered a new wardrobe for

himself over on Bond Street." Then, when the allotted week
had passed and Desiree continued to make visits to Charles
on her own, Ryder and Natalie happily concluded that true
progress was being made. Charles even began sending gifts
to Desiree. To Natalie's astonishment, she caught her mother
preening over an expensive bottle of perfume, and waving an
elegant, hand-painted silk fan.

Given the fact that Ryder was overburdened with his father's duties, Natalie volunteered to run the Stepney textile
plant. At first, recalling Nonna's warning, Ryder stoutly re-
sisted her offer. But when the watchmen he had hired spotted
no further suspicious activity at the plant, and a stop by
Oswald Spectre's home confirmed that the man was still ailing and thus could offer no threat, Ryder ultimately gave in
to his determined wife. In truth, it was difficult not to acqui-
esce to Natalie, since she was so bored while he was so
busy—and because, indeed, he needed her help so badly.
However, he continued to have Mawkins and Tom monitor
the facility at night and report to him regularly.

Natalie found conditions at the Stepney factory chaotic. She
set up a work station for herself in John Lynch's office. For the
first few days she was there, the duke's solicitors stayed on site,
trying to complete their audit of the confused, disorganized
books. The head solicitor informed Natalie that a goodly sum
of money was missing from the factory accounts and that a
quantity of inventory appeared lost as well. The solicitors suspected that John Lynch had been behind the thefts.

The conditions of the workers appalled Natalie; men and
women remained overworked and underpaid. She spent long
hours hiring additional workers, devising a more equitable
work schedule and pay scale, and seeing to it that the entire
plant was given a much-needed cleaning.

One afternoon she looked up from her desk and was startled to see a familiar, black-clothed figure hovering in the
doorway, staring at her with an odd intensity. She gasped and
flung a hand to her breast.

"Mrs. Lynch, you gave me a start," she said breathlessly.

The woman stepped forward and demanded rudely, "What
are you doing in John's office?"

Natalie rose. "I'm sorry, Mrs. Lynch. It must be a shock
for you to see me here."

"Indeed."

Quickly, Natalie explained. "With both the Duke of Mansfield and Mr. Spectre so ill, I have volunteered to oversee the factory for the time being. You see, I once ran a similar facility in America."

If Essie was shocked by Natalie's announcement of her unorthodox background, she made no direct comment. Instead, she snapped, "You should not be meddling in affairs that are none of your concern."

That remark galled Natalie, and she drew herself up with dignity. "Mrs. Lynch, while I understand your feelings, I must totally disagree. I am now a member of the Remington family, and as such, this factory *is* my concern. I consider my contribution here to be the least I can do while my father-in-law is recovering."

At this second mention of the duke, Essie backed down. "I—perhaps you have a point, Lady Newbury. How is the duke?"

"Still mending well, thank you." Perplexed, Natalie asked, "Mrs. Lynch, why are you here today?"

All at once, Essie avoided Natalie's eye. Awkwardly, she said, "I came to—er—gather John's personal effects from his desk."

Natalie groaned. "I'm sorry. How callous I must seem, standing in your husband's office and questioning your presence. What a difficult and painful occasion this must be for you."

While Essie was silent, a muscle twitching in her haggard cheek gave evidence of her inner turmoil.

"As a matter of fact," Natalie continued tactfully, "I was just about to go downstairs for my afternoon inspection of the factory floor." She gestured toward the desk. "Please feel free to go through the drawers and take anything that belonged to John."

"Thank you," Essie said stiffly.

Starting out of the room, Natalie added, "Is there something I can do to help?"

"No, thank you."

At the doorway, Natalie hesitated, biting her lip. Making a quick decision, she said, "Mrs. Lynch, it pains me to have to tell you this, but the solicitors have found a large sum of money missing from the factory accounts, and it seems that much inventory has also disappeared over the past months."

Essie glared at Natalie. "And you think I know something about this perfidy?" she demanded shrilly.

"No, not at all. I just wondered if perhaps John might have said something to you . . ." When Essie only stiffened in anger, Natalie added, "I see I am mistaken. I'll leave you now, Mrs. Lynch."

Daily, Ryder called on his father. Although the duke remained weak, the surgeon insisted that his patient needed to get up for a few minutes each day to walk. Late in the afternoons, Ryder would help his father stagger up and down the third-floor corridor. He rather liked his father's having to depend on him for physical support. Ryder knew the sessions were painful for the older man—he often appeared white-faced and short of breath. But, just as Ryder had surmised, William Remington was too proud to complain to his son.

However, one afternoon, while the two were taking their constitutional in the hallway, the duke seemed to be experiencing unusual pain from his healing wound. As he and Ryder were coming to the end of the hallway, he gasped, "God's teeth, son, can we not give it a rest?"

"Of course, your Grace." Ryder helped his father to the settee that rested against one wall, and William Remington all but collapsed onto it.

Ryder sat down next to him, watching William flex his arm, grimace, and breathe raggedly. "You should have told me you were in such discomfort. Are you sure your wound is not festering?"

Grimacing, William shook his head. "The surgeon says I am healing splendidly, but that I should expect this sort of pain as I use my arm and shoulder more."

"At least you are faring better than John Lynch's other victim," Ryder related grimly. "I called by Oswald Spectre's home the other day, and he is still bed-bound."

"That monster Lynch!" William shook his head. "I had no idea my business partner was such a villain."

Ryder spoke with genuine concern. "And I deeply regret that my putting a stop to the smuggling exposed you to such peril."

William was quiet for a long moment. At last he met Ryder's eye and said contritely, "I am sorry, too, son."

Ryder laughed. "Why? Because you are a grouchy patient today?"

"No—but because for so long I have blamed you for your mother's death."

Ryder was silent, his features tight with suppressed emotion.

William touched his son's clenched fist. "Ryder, you must understand that after I lost your mother, I was eaten up with guilt. I was the one who was truly responsible for Carlotta, and I failed her badly. I was always too busy with my duties at Parliament, or had some other excuse not to be a truly attentive husband. When she was killed so senselessly, so cruelly, I had to do something to ease the pain, the hellish guilt. So I lashed out at you, my boy—cruelly and unjustly. I buried my own shame by blaming you, and by losing myself in religious fanaticism."

"And what has brought about this change of heart now?" Ryder asked skeptically.

"Knowing—and loving—a wonderful woman," the duke confessed quietly. "I realize now that although I claimed for years to be devout, I was actually a sanctimonious hypocrite. My heart was consumed by hatred and bitterness. Yet my dear Love has changed all that. She has brought hope into my life once again, and has made me believe the redemption of my spirit is possible."

"I'm glad to heart that, Father," Ryder said sincerely. After hesitating for a moment, he added, "But you must know that I felt guilt for Mother's death, too."

"That does not excuse my attitude toward you—or absolve me of my own responsibility," William replied humbly. "Will you forgive me?"

Ryder drew a heavy breath. "Consider it done," he whispered.

A smile of happiness and gratitude lit the duke's face. "Thank you, son. You are very happy with Natalie, aren't you?"

Ryder met his father's gaze evenly. "To tell you the truth, your Grace, if not for Natalie's love, I doubt I could forgive you now—or myself."

William clutched Ryder's hand. "Then your bride has my undying gratitude." Bracing his hand on his son's shoulder, he struggled to get up. "Well, I suppose I had best get back to my room——"

He winced and wobbled on his feet, and Ryder hastened to grab him. For a moment he stared down at the duke's frail, vulnerable face. And then, for the first time in many years, Ryder embraced his father.

As the days passed, Natalie saw less and less of her husband, and this dismayed her greatly. Of course, she was busy with the Stepney factory, but he often spent late nights either in the study taking care of his father's business or at sessions of Parliament. Natalie realized Ryder would make a perfect duke, and that this was the one thing he should never become. His visage was often strained and preoccupied, and she found herself longing to see the old roguish glint in his eyes. She wondered how she had ever convinced herself that she wanted to change him. For she realized increasingly that she did not want to transform him into some sober, stolid gentleman—but rather, to find a way that the rogue and the lady could live happily together. Every time she thought about how much she loved him, every time she fantasized about their unborn child, she vowed that surely they could find a way to attain that dream. The fact that their various family problems seemed gradually to be getting resolved added to a building feeling of optimism regarding their future.

Late one night, when Ryder had still not come to bed, she decided to take matters into her own hands. Putting on her wrapper, she tiptoed down to the kitchen and packed up wine, cheese, bread, and fruit in a picnic basket, while peeking out the back window at Francesca's lovely garden in the moonlight and watching an owl fly past. Taking in the enchanting scene, she thought of how much Ryder had awakened her to the joys of the world surrounding them. Now those joys were denied him, and she was determined to change that.

Taking the filled basket and humming a happy melody, she went to the door of his study and knocked softly.

"Come in," came his preoccupied voice.

With basket in hand, she slipped inside and shut the door. Her husband sat awash in stacks of papers, his hair rumpled, his jaw darkened by stubble, and his shirt hanging open.

Ryder glanced up to see his lovely wife standing at the

door in her gown and wrapper, with a picnic basket in hand. Despite his distracted state of mind, the sight of her warmed his heart. He set down the papers he had been working on and smiled at her quizzically.

"Natalie, what are you doing up so late?"

She grinned and stepped forward, setting the basket on the edge of the desk. "I thought I would surprise you with a midnight picnic."

Ryder had to chuckle. "That sounds like something I would do."

"Not anymore," she rejoined meaningfully.

"I'm sorry, love," he said, stifling a yawn. "I appreciate your thoughtfulness, but I have hours of work left to do. Go back to bed like a good girl."

She shook her head. "No."

Fighting a grin, he got up, moved around the desk, and leaned against it. "So you are going to be difficult again?"

She nodded and stepped closer. "As you well know, pregnant women have that right."

He reached out to toy with a ribbon on her wrapper. "But aren't you going to the factory in the morning?"

"Yes. But I shall not go to bed until you do."

Again he chuckled. "Well, love, that does sound promising."

She glanced toward the hearth. "And the fire looks inviting."

"Ah, yes. It is a rather cool night for late June."

She edged closer, teasing, "I can always help warm you up."

He pulled her close and kissed her. "Now, that prospect sounds irresistible."

She took his hand. "But first, come outside with me for a moment. There's something I want to show you."

He appeared astonished. "At this hour? Natalie, the weather is cool, and you are barefoot."

She laughed. "Come on. Now you're sounding like even more of a 'proper person' than I am."

Quashing further protests, she tugged him out of the house and into the garden, where they stood amid dew and moonlight, the sound of the fountain and the smell of the roses.

"Why did you bring me here?" he asked with a bemused smile.

She drew a deep breath and glanced upward. "The stars."

He followed suit. "Ah, yes. Stars."

"And listen."

"To what? The fountain?"

"Yes. But if you listen very carefully, you can also hear the nightingale calling."

He listened, and heard the sweet, plaintive song. "Yes ... a lovely sound."

"There's a robin's nest in the chestnut tree, too," she went on, pointing toward it.

"Is there?" He craned his neck to see.

"All the little birds are asleep now—"

"As you should be," he put in, trying to look stern.

"But earlier, at sunset, I watched the mother robin flit back and forth, feeding her young. The chirping was so sweet, it made me think of our baby."

With a fervent sigh, he pulled her close. "Oh, Natalie, you're becoming as much of a sensualist as I am."

"Because you have shared your world with me," she admitted happily. "And I didn't even tell you the best part."

His look was one of wonder. "What is that?"

She pointed toward the plantings next to the fountain. "Look—the roses. All the tiny buds are opening. Remember how you once described a rose blooming? Isn't it beau—"

Natalie could say no more. Ryder was kissing her, crushing her close.

"You're trembling," he whispered.

"Aye, my lord. But not with the cold."

He swept her up into his arms and spoke huskily. "Barefoot and pregnant. Just the way I like you."

Ryder carried Natalie back inside his study and tenderly laid her down on the rug near the blazing hearth. He fetched and opened the picnic basket, and they reclined together, sipping wine and nibbling on cheese and fruit. The fire curled about their senses with its crackling glow, drugging heat, and scent of cedar.

Ryder tenderly kissed her cheek. "What made you decide to pry me away from my labors tonight? Not that I'm complaining."

She stretched lazily next to him. "I have decided that your world is too weighed down with problems and responsibilities, my lord."

He all but howled with laughter. "Minx! Now my own words come back to haunt me."

"But they are true," she said solemnly.

"So you really are moving closer to my perspective?"

"Just as you may have moved too close to mine."

"Now I've given you a dose of your own medicine!" he teased.

"Aye." She dimpled. "And 'tis a bitter pill to swallow, m'lord."

"Why, Natalie!" He feigned horror. "Are you actually inferring that you are prepared to spend even more of your time having fun?"

"I never knew what fun was until I met you," she confessed. "Now I suppose I am a convert."

He grinned and plopped a grape into her mouth. "We'll have our time, love. It is just that now our world *is* burdened by problems and responsibilities."

"But in a sense, won't it always be?" she argued. "Won't you one day have to assume your father's duties? I'm afraid that our marriage is strangling your carefree spirit."

He laughed. "But isn't that what you have wanted all along, my love? For me to grow up and assume adult obligations?"

"Actually, I'm not so sure about that anymore."

"You aren't?"

Staring at him with her heart in her eyes, she whispered, "I want back the rogue I fell in love with in Charleston."

For a moment, he stared at her in delight, but then a thoughtful frown creased his brow. "And what of the fact that I'll soon be a father? Can I remain a rogue and still project the proper paternal image?"

"You can enjoy life—and enjoy your children," she countered. "There must be a meeting ground somewhere between our worlds."

A passionate determination gleamed in his eyes. "Ah, yes, and we shall find it, love."

"If we keep communicating with each other," she added poignantly. "I've missed that over the past days."

He clutched her hand. "Aye, so have I. So tell me something, my love—share with me."

A look of delight crossed her features. "I do have a wonderful secret to tell you."

He raised a brow lecherously. "A secret? I can't wait."

She blushed. "But you be first."

He was thoughtfully silent, then murmured, "I reconciled with my father today."

"Oh, Ryder! I'm so happy for you!"

"He asked my forgiveness for blaming me for Mother's death."

"It is about time."

"And in many ways I must thank you, and your aunt," he went on solemnly. "Knowing Love has helped Father to give up his guilt and bitterness."

Her smile was radiant. "You know, Ryder, we do have much to be grateful for—finding Aunt Love, just as she and the duke have found each other. Now you and your father have reconciled, and there may be hope for my parents as well. It makes me feel that maybe there are happy endings—and maybe we can have one, too."

He lifted her hand and kissed it. "Of course we will, darling. Now tell me your secret."

She smiled shyly. "It really is just a small secret."

"Tell me."

Her eyes large with wonder, she pressed his fingers to the tiny mound curving outward in her lower belly. "I think I can feel our baby starting to grow."

Running his hand over the slight swelling, he glanced up at her in awe and joy. "So can I! Has he—or she—moved inside you yet?"

"No, not yet, but I hope to feel her—or him—soon."

He stroked her belly lovingly. "Oh, Natalie, that is not a small secret. It is a small miracle."

Ryder clutched his wife close for a long moment, and when at last he drew back, she saw tears in his eyes.

"Ryder." She felt so deeply touched that her own eyes stung. "You really do want this child, don't you?"

"More than life itself—and as much as I love you," he whispered fervently.

He pressed her down beneath him and tenderly showed her that love—and much more—there by the fire.

Forty-three

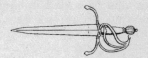

EARLY THE NEXT MORNING, RYDER WAS AWAKENED BY A knocking at the door. He glanced at the rumpled bed beside him and noted that Natalie was already gone.

The sound increased, and he heard Nonna's voice call, "Ryder, you must get up!"

He got out bed, threw on his dressing gown, and stumbled to the door, flinging it open and staring at Nonna's worried face. "What is it?" he asked groggily.

"There are two men waiting for you downstairs. They said they have urgent business with you concerning the Stepney factory."

Distraught, Ryder drew his fingers through his hair. "Oh, Lord, I hope there is no trouble. Natalie must already be bound for there!"

He accompanied his grandmother downstairs to the foyer, where Mawkins and Tom awaited him. Bot men appeared tired, grim, and unshaven, and held their ratty caps in their hands.

Ryder addressed Mawkins tensely. "Yes?"

Mawkins shifted from boot to boot. "Good day, gov'nor. Tom and me been watching the Stepney factory each night, just like you asked us—"

"Yes, yes. Please forgo the preliminaries. What has happened, man?"

"A few hours ago, we seen Mr. Spectre sneak in there, and he also let a couple of dock rats in the back door."

"Dock rats?"

"You know, your lordship—river-pirate types."

"Oh, God." Ryder groaned. "I was not even aware that Oswald Spectre had recovered sufficiently to go to the factory! Are you certain it was him?"

"Aye, gov'nor—that or his twin brother. And the bloke is still there, far as we know."

"Damn! Spectre must have been in on the smuggling all along. And Natalie could be arriving there even now!"

Nonna grabbed his sleeve. "I warned you that the danger had not ended."

Ryder's mind was teeming with horrifying possibilities. "Good heavens—Natalie! I must go to her!"

He tore off to get his clothes.

As Ryder was rushing toward the East End of London in his grandmother's coach, Natalie was arriving at the Stepney factory. She liked to show up half an hour or so before the workers to plan her day and attend to paperwork. Crossing the factory floor, she noted with pride the clean and orderly expanse of machines and raw materials, the bins piled high with mule yarn and roving.

She climbed the steps to the mezzanine and headed toward John Lynch's office. She stepped inside, only to gasp, as she spotted a man's body on the floor, the black-trousered legs protruding from behind the desk!

Her heart pounding in horror, Natalie rushed around the desk to investigate. She stifled a scream as she recognized Oswald Spectre—he was dead, lying in a pool of blood which still oozed from his chest, his eyes open and staring. From the small hole gaping through his saturated shirt linen, he appeared to have been shot. Near him, several boards had been pried loose from the floor, and Natalie saw a small, opened chest of gold sovereigns. A couple of the coins were clutched in Spectre's lifeless fingers!

Natalie was backing away in revulsion when a flicker of motion danced across her peripheral vision. Terrified, she whirled to watch a figure step out from the shadows behind the door. She gaped at the approaching phantom, certain as she viewed the black cloak and low-brimmed hat that she was looking at a ghost! A ghost that held in its gloved hand a deadly pistol!

"John Lynch!" she gasped, flinging a hand to her heart. "Don't tell me you are alive?"

Abruptly, the apparition removed its hat, and Natalie stifled a scream as she found herself staring into the eyes of madness.

Ryder tore out of the carriage and raced across the odious alleyway toward the factory facade. Thank God the door was unlocked! He flung it wide and ran down the darkened corridor toward the weaving floor.

The area was deserted, and he rushed for the steps to the mezzanine. Natalie was up there and in horrible danger—somehow he knew it, and his heart was sickened with fear for her and their child.

Let there be time, he silently implored the heavens. Please, let there be time!

"Oh, my God! It is you!" Natalie cried.

"Yes, it is I," replied the phantom. "Did I fool you, Lady Newbury?"

Horrified, Natalie could only nod.

"And didn't I warn you not to interfere where you were not wanted?"

Natalie managed to find her voice. "Then it was you all along who was responsible for the smuggling!"

"Aye," said Essie Lynch, a glow of mingled pride and derangement in her eyes. "And I was more clever than the lot of you, wasn't I? I duped everyone, didn't I? Even your husband the night I accosted him near the harbor."

"You mean that was you?" Natalie asked. "You masquerading as John Lynch?"

Essie laughed, a demented cackle. "It was I. And imagine the shock I gave Mr. Spectre a few moments ago, when I caught him here and killed him."

"You—killed him?"

Essie nodded with vengeful pleasure. "When Spectre spotted me dressed as John, I thought the poor fellow was going to die of apoplexy and save me the trouble of dispatching his worthless soul to hell. He was certain John's ghost had returned to seek vengeance. In a way, I suppose he was right."

Natalie fought her rising panic. "Oh, merciful heavens! You truly are a murderess!"

"Aye." Essie's hand on the pistol trembled and her voice held the shrill edge of lunacy. "I did not want it to come to this, since I have no quarrel with you. But now that you have discovered me, you, too, must die."

"Oh, no, please, you mustn't," Natalie pleaded, growing desperate as she thought of her unborn child.

Even as Essie's menacing form edged closer, loud footsteps sounded from the nearby stairwell. Essie shrank back into the shadows as a third person charged into the room. Natalie's heart surged with overwhelming relief when she spotted Ryder and viewed the frantic concern and desperate love in his eyes. But this feeling was soon followed by despair as she realized the danger to his own person.

How could she warn him?

Before she could even open her mouth, Essie cried out, "That's far enough, Lord Newbury!"

Ryder whirled. Spotting Essie near the door, he placed his body protectively between his wife and the threatening woman who now advanced pointing a pistol at them both!

"Mrs. Lynch, what is the meaning of this?" he demanded. "Why are you dressed as a man and threatening my wife with a gun?"

"I regret you have come here, Lord Newbury," Essie replied in a piercing voice. "Now I must kill you both."

As Ryder stared at the woman in stunned disbelief, Natalie whispered behind him, "It was Essie who was behind the smuggling all along. She impersonated her husband, and even killed Oswald Spectre."

Ryder glanced at Spectre's corpse on the floor, then quickly shifted his gaze back to Essie. A muscle was twitching in her gaunt cheek, and the hand that held the pistol was trembling badly. The woman was clearly unhinged. He knew that somehow he had to reason with her, humor her, catch her off guard.

"Is what my wife says true, Mrs. Lynch?" he asked. "Were you the mastermind behind the smuggling?"

"Yes!" she cried. "With the cooperation of my weak, stupid husband! He filched the inventory, while I doctored the books and planned all the shipments. But John thought he was too smart for me. The bastard started holding out on me, hiding the proceeds here at the factory."

"So that is why you came here the other day!" Natalie cried.

"Aye. John's greed ultimately became his undoing. He was a miserable coward anyway—and stupid beyond redemption." Staring proudly at Ryder, she added, "He had your mother killed, you know."

"What?" Ryder's query was barely audible.

"Years ago, Carlotta Remington became suspicious of John. Actually, your mother was a meddler—much like your wife—and became concerned about conditions at the factory. She soon discovered John was paying the workers starvation wages and pocketing the rest. John always was a greedy bumbler. When Carlotta caught on to his game, he was the one who hired the brigands to waylay your mother's carriage on London Bridge."

"My God!" Ryder exclaimed.

"More recently, when your father became suspicious of John, he decided to betray both the duke and me. He was going to take his ill-gotten gains and run off with a prostitute. But I was too smart for him."

"You killed him?" Natalie asked.

"The day I confronted him, we had a terrible fight. You saw the bruises on my face, didn't you, Lady Newbury?"

Natalie nodded.

"But I was always the strong one," Essie continued with fierce pride. "I knocked John cold, tied a rope around his neck, then hoisted him over a beam in our drawing room." She smiled cruelly. "He woke up, and it was my pleasure to watch him kick, choke on his own screams, and slowly strangle."

"Oh, merciful heavens!" Natalie gasped.

"Then you were the one who posed as Lynch, knifing my father and bludgeoning Oswald Spectre," said Ryder.

"Yes! None of you would heed my warnings. Spectre was suspicious of our scheme for years. After John died, Oswald was still determined to ferret out John's hiding place. And the scoundrel thought he could move in where John had left off, and take over the illegal smuggling trade. Imagine his surprise when I was here a few moments ago, ready and waiting to wreak my vengeance on him when he found John's secret cache."

Ryder began advancing slowly toward Essie. "You're never going to get away with this, you know."

"Oh, yes, I shall!" She began to back away toward the doorway. "I shall kill you both."

"Not with one shot, you won't," he told her firmly, still moving toward her. Over his shoulder he said vehemently, "Natalie, if she shoots me, run for help at once before she can reload."

Essie's hand trembled on the gun as she stepped into the hallway. "Shut up! Don't tell her to run for help, or I shall kill her first."

"You would kill a mother and an unborn child?" Ryder asked incredulously, moving steadily forward.

Essie's expression grew desperately uncertain. "You're with child?" she cried to Natalie.

"Remember your daughter, Mrs. Lynch," Natalie begged. "Please don't rob my child of its father."

Still backing away, Essie began to waver, her haggard cheeks twitching. "On the night my sweet Mary died, John—may he rot in hell!—refused to summon a surgeon." To Ryder, she added spitefully, "He claimed the duke did not pay him sufficiently to warrant the expense."

"We're very sorry about your daughter, Mrs. Lynch," Ryder said softly. "Please, don't risk harm to another child."

As Essie vacillated in terrible indecision, Ryder advanced again. By now she had backed well into the hallway.

"Stop right now or I'll shoot!" the crazed woman warned.

Natalie watched, stifling a scream, as Ryder made a dive for Essie. "Ryder, no!" she cried, certain that the woman would kill him.

Then she heard Essie's harrowing wail. The woman had unwittingly backed up too close to the steps. In the space of a split second, her arms flailed out wildly and her pistol sailed out of her hand as she lost her balance. Ryder tried to grab her, but too late. Then, as both of them stared in horror, the woman tumbled backward down the stairs and landed with a sickening crash on the factory floor, her neck cocked at an unnatural angle and her eyes wide open in death.

Natalie fell into Ryder's arms. "Oh, Ryder! That horrible

woman!" She stole another glance at the corpse and shuddered violently. "Still, it pains me to see her thus."

"Please don't look, darling." Ryder's arms trembled as he clutched Natalie tightly. "Essie Lynch was a greedy murderess who no doubt just got what she deserved."

Natalie gazed up at him with brimming eyes. "I know. But ultimately, she wouldn't hurt our child."

Ryder's voice shook with emotion as he pressed his hand possessively to her lower belly. "I would have died before I let her do that."

"Oh, Ryder! I love you so much—so much!"

His desperate kiss communicated feelings every bit as deep.

Forty-four

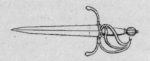

"Oh, my poor darling, you must have been terrified," Desiree said to Natalie for the tenth time that evening.

"I'm all right now, Mother, really," Natalie replied earnestly.

Natalie and Ryder were sharing dinner with Charles and Desiree at Charles Desmond's house. Natalie knew all of them remained sobered by the events that had transpired early that morning.

In the afternoon, as Natalie had looked on helplessly, Ryder had informed Francesca Valenza of the true circumstances of her daughter's death. Both grandmother and grandson had wept during the emotional retelling, yet Natalie had sensed the spirit of healing and peace that ebbed over both in the wake of the tragic disclosures. Afterward, Ryder had called on his father to inform him of what had happened at the factory.

Now, Natalie took heart in the awareness that her parents seemed to be getting along so much better. Her father in particular looked almost like a new man, with his color restored, his eyes almost clear, and the veneer of his former handsomeness shining through. And Desiree appeared especially lovely and bright-eyed tonight.

"At least the danger has ended now, and Natalie is all right," Ryder remarked.

"*Oui,* but the poor darling had such a scare!" Desiree lamented. "I hope the child was not harmed."

Natalie stared at her husband with adoring eyes. "I was not

truly frightened, Mother—not from the moment Ryder appeared."

Ryder gazed at his wife with equal love. "And there was never any question of Natalie or our child being harmed, since the woman had only one shot in her pistol."

Desiree shuddered at the frightful image, then said to her daughter feelingly, "Ah, how very romantic. To have a man who would die for you."

"I would die for you, my love," Charles told his wife, reaching out to squeeze her hand. "Indeed, haven't I been trying my best to kill myself with drink all the years we've been apart?"

Charles and Desiree exchanged a look of joy and communication, while Ryder and Natalie regarded each other with secret pleasure.

After a moment, Charles nodded to Ryder. "Your father was duped by a trio of scoundrels who cheated him shamelessly and murdered your poor mother. But at least none of them will do your family harm ever again."

"Aye, sir," Ryder replied. "And my father is doing so well now that he can handle his own affairs—"

"And marry Aunt Love," Natalie finished proudly.

"How wonderful!" Desiree exclaimed.

"Aunt Love told me today that she and William will marry soon after the king is crowned."

"*Magnifique!*" cried Desiree, clapping her hands. "We'll all have so much fun—the coronation festivities, the weddings—the duke and Love's, Harry and Genevieve's. Why, when I visited the Hamptons the other day, it was evident that Harry's parents simply adore the girl."

"Who wouldn't adore any young lady who can reform Hampton?" put in Ryder drolly.

"Desiree and I have an announcement, too," declared Charles.

"Yes?" Natalie and Ryder asked in unison.

Glancing at his daughter, Charles announced, "My investments in the East India Company have paid off handsomely, and your mother and I have decided to take an extended tour of the Continent."

Natalie was stunned, glancing from a smiling Desiree to her father. "What does this mean, Father?"

With pride and emotion, Charles replied, "It means, saints be praised, that your mother and I are back together."

Natalie turned in delight to Desiree. "Oh, Mother, is it true?"

"Yes, my love," Desiree said, glowing.

"Oh, I'm so happy for you both!" Natalie exclaimed. "But—if I may ask—what brought about this reconciliation?"

Charles spoke up. "Desiree has agreed to remain with me—as long as I agree to give up my brandy."

"Oh, Mother! And are you really content to stay here?" Natalie asked.

Desiree nodded through her tears. "I have missed too much of your life, my darling. I won't be making the same mistake with my grandchildren."

She grasped her daughter's hand and stared at her child with devotion. In that moment, Natalie's radiant smile conveyed to her mother her own love and forgiveness. And after witnessing her parents' touching reconciliation, she felt more confident than ever that she and Ryder could be forever happy, too.

The next few weeks passed in a whirl of activities. Natalie helped Love plan her wedding, and she and Ryder attended many of the soirees and levees leading up to coronation day.

Now that their immediate problems in London were resolved, Natalie fretted over the fate of the factory in Charleston. One day she communicated her concern to Love, and was surprised when her aunt merely laughed and handed her a letter she had just received from Charleston. Natalie read the missive in utter amazement. In it, Cousin Rodney announced that he had sobered up, was marrying Prudence Pitney, and needed no further help with the factory, thank you. Afterward, Natalie laughed almost until she cried, and she silently blessed Prudence Pitney.

On the nineteenth of July, Ryder and Natalie, along with Francesca, Charles, Desiree, Love, and William, attended the coronation. They sat in the upper galleries of Westminster Abbey; Ryder delighted to Natalie's wide-eyed reactions as all of them watched a show of pageantry more colorful than any circus. Like two eager children, they sat on the edges of their seats and clutched each other's hands.

The coronation procession began with the king's herb lady and her maids-in-waiting dancing in, sprinkling the carpeted pathway with herbs. The women were followed by the King of Arms bearing the Crown of Hanover. George himself soon made his appearance—and Ryder noted that the monarch appeared most haggard and was half staggering beneath the weight of dissipation, ill health, and the heavy coronation robes. George was followed by an almost comical entourage of prizefighters dressed as court pages and bearing his royal train.

In the tedious ceremony that followed, Ryder and his bride listened to the pious sermon of the Archbishop of York and saw the king crowned. Afterward, along with three hundred other lucky souls, the small group went to the banquet at Westminster Hall. They sat in the magnificent red-draped chairs and watched the King's Champion enter the building on horseback, wearing a suit of gleaming armor and a feathered helmet, in keeping with the medieval theme. Then the smiling flower girls appeared, flinging rose petals on the path, followed by the king, who was borne in beneath a flowing, opulent canopy. As Natalie and Ryder shared the feast with the others, they learned the shocking news that during the coronation, Queen Caroline had thoroughly perplexed the Life Guards when she had shown up outside the Abbey, pounding her fists on its doors and begging piteously for admittance—an entry that had, of course, been denied.

The festivities ended by early evening. That night, Ryder and Natalie observed the fireworks from St. James's Park. Standing on one of the Chinese bridges that had been erected over the lake in honor of the occasion, they watched spectacular Roman candles shoot dazzling cascades of light into the black sky above them, the firebursts reflected on the dark, gleaming lake.

"A new king—a new beginning," Ryder murmured thoughtfully.

"Aye," Natalie concurred.

"There will be a lot more celebrating for us over the next few weeks, my love," he added. "First your mother and father will renew their vows at Bow Church, then Harry and Genevieve will marry at St. James's, and then my father and your aunt at St. Margaret's."

"I'm looking forward to all of it," Natalie said. "And did I tell you that I received an invitation to court in yesterday's post?"

He chuckled. "That is a rite of passage for every bride of noble station. Now you get to don the absurd traditional feathers and your wedding gown, and join the carnival procession on Piccadilly."

"I would rather stay home," she muttered soberly.

"Nonsense. No one can decline an invitation from the king. I must buy us a shiny new carriage and affix the doors with our family coat of arms for the occasion."

She sighed. "I suppose that means I have arrived in the polite world."

He winked at her. "Aye, you have, Lady Newbury. A bluestocking no more."

"Oh, Ryder," she lamented, "we are becoming so respectable."

He laughed heartily. "You say that word as if it is a pox. Have I corrupted you so much, my love?"

She glanced at him, thinking he looked stunning and rakish in his formal clothes. "It's just that, where do we go from here?"

He pulled her close. "Home to bed?" he suggested hopefully.

She smiled. "You know what I mean. I know we are moving closer to a meeting ground between our worlds, but we cannot spend the rest of our lives running from pillar to post."

"Ah, we must have purpose, be industrious—is that what you are saying?"

"More or less. We should at least think of setting a good example for our children."

"I agree."

"You do?" she asked in surprise.

He tweaked her chin. "So it will be no more roaming about, getting into dangerous escapades, for either of us."

"But what shall we do?"

He frowned. "You can't want to return to America, can you? Frankly, darling, with you pregnant, I won't allow it."

She shook her head. "I don't want to go back now myself. As I mentioned to you recently, Rodney seems to have gotten his life in order, so I'm really not needed in Charleston any-more."

Observing her frown, he whispered fervently, "*I* need you, Natalie. Don't you ever forget it."

She smiled and took his hand. "Our child will need us both."

"Aye. And I have a suggestion, darling."

"Yes?"

"My father has given us an estate in Kent as a wedding present. Why don't we go there, become gentlemen farmers, and see how many babies we can produce in the next decade or so?"

She beamed with happiness. "Ryder! Do you mean it? That sounds like a wonderful idea."

He winked at her. "Particularly making all those babies."

"But what about your father and the dukedom?"

"Natalie, the men in my family live well into their nineties. Let my father and your aunt worry about the dukedom."

She smiled. "It sounds so idyllic. Are you certain you will not miss your travels?"

He shook his head. "When our children are older, we'll take the entire family abroad. In the meantime, I would like Nonna to come live with us, and for the rest of our family to visit often—so our children will grow up to appreciate their many-faceted cultural heritage."

She smirked at him. "You, a farmer! I have never envisioned you settling down in one place, much less giving up your rakehell ways."

He touched the tip of her nose and replied seriously. "But you are forgetting how much I love you, darling. I remember once when you called yourself an anchor and me a piece of driftwood. You were right that I was just drifting with the tide, with no harbor, no constancy in my life. That is what I have found in you. You have brought my life back together again, you have given me joy and meaning, and I shall never give you up, my love."

Feeling much relieved and reassured, Natalie thrust herself into his arms. "Oh, Ryder, I love you, too . . . so much. What you have given me is a way to see the possibilities, to look at life with a fresh perspective. You might have been drifting, but I was landlocked, totally set in my ways. Now I have found my freedom in you. I think that between the two of us, we shall have a wonderful marriage and shall make the best parents ever."

"Amen."

As a spectacular starburst went off over their heads, blazing with its bright promise of a new era, Ryder pulled his wife close for a tender kiss that sealed their love.

Epilogue

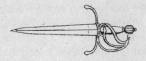

1828

Sunshine swept the halls of the giant Tudor country home. Ryder and Natalie stood in the corridor outside the grand salon. Ryder held their youngest, Franny, christened "Carlotta Francesca" for both her grandmother and her great-grandmother. At twenty-one months old, the baby was a chubby, curly haired-moppet with a sunny disposition, the apple of her daddy's eye.

Ryder and Natalie were eavesdropping, watching and listening intently at the doorway. Inside the sunny salon, Francesca Valenza, in her Windsor rocking chair, was reading a story to their two other, enthralled children, who sat on pillows at their great-grandmother's feet. Both offspring were perfect mixes of their parents, with their mother's thick chestnut hair and their father's bright blue eyes.

Abruptly, the reading stopped as Nonna spotted the two of them hovering in the doorway. She took off her spectacles and glowered. "Come in here, you two! What are you doing skulking about at the door?"

Smiling sheepishly, the couple strolled in with the baby. "We didn't want to interrupt your reading, Nonna," Ryder said tactfully.

All at once, disorder reigned as the two older children took advantage of their parents' interruption.

"Will you take me fishing today, Papa?" six-year-old William piped up from the floor.

"Of course, son. But first you must listen to Nonna."

"May I help you embroider Franny's gown?" four-year-old Love asked her mother.

"Of course, darling," Natalie answered lovingly. "As soon as—"

"Enough of this, you two!" scolded an exasperated Francesca. "You are totally distracting the children from their story! They were as quiet as angels until you two appeared."

"Sorry, Nonna," said Ryder, patting the baby's back as she chortled and tugged on her father's long hair.

"I am getting to be an old woman," Nonna went on forbearingly. "You two can have the children for the rest of the day. Can't I at least enjoy them for a few minutes—uninterrupted—each morning?"

"Of course, Nonna," said Ryder.

"That is only fair," agreed Natalie.

But neither made a move to leave.

Francesca took a moment to make a silent plea to the heavens. "Can't you two find some way to amuse yourselves while I finish the story?"

Ryder considered that for a moment, then grinned. "We'll think of something, Nonna," he said solemnly, leading Natalie away.

"Wait a moment," Nonna called after them.

Both turned expectantly.

"Yes?" Ryder asked.

"Leave the baby," Nonna ordered. "She is old enough to listen with the others."

Ryder regarded the baby with a skeptical frown. Yet Franny, as if she understood her great-grandmother, was already squirming vigorously to get down.

"Are you sure?" Ryder asked Nonna while trying to contain the struggling child.

"Just put her down and see."

Frowning in uncertainty, Ryder set his daughter down. Franny promptly toddled over to take her place beside her siblings. She settled down firmly on her diaper, stuffed her thumb in her mouth, and hurled her parents a defiant look.

"I guess she told us," Ryder quipped with pride. Breathing a dramatic sigh, he offered Natalie his arm. "Let us go, my love. It is obvious we are not wanted here."

They swept out into the corridor while Francesca continued reading the Italian fairy tale, "The Golden Lion."

In the hallway, Natalie slanted a glance toward the happy scene. "Just look at them, Ryder," she whispered. "Three of them, like perfect stairsteps. They are growing up so quickly. Your father and Aunt Love will be so surprised when they come to visit next week.

"As will Desiree and Charles when they arrive the week after. Then, by midsummer, we'll have Harry, Genevieve, and their brood."

"Genevieve is welcome—but Harry!" Natalie protested.

Ryder grinned.

"You two rogues had best behave yourselves," she chided, wagging a finger at him. "No swordplay in front of the children—it sets a very bad example."

He raised an eyebrow mockingly. "Why fence in front of the children when Hampton and I can enthrall all the farmers on the village green?"

"You are impossible!" She smirked at him. "So what will we do until the children are finished with their story?"

Ryder pulled her into his arms. "Well, Nonna told us to amuse ourselves. How about we work on another one?"

"Another child?" Natalie whispered.

"If you are ready, my lady," he teased. "A gentleman should always ask."

"*You* ask?" At his delighted chuckle, she assured him, "I am always ready for you, my lord, and you know it. But if we do have another one, when are we going to take everyone traveling on the Continent, as you have always spoken of doing?"

He laughed. "My love, we are going to live very long lives. There will be plenty of time for travel later on. In the meantime, I'm having far too much fun enjoying the country with you and my children"—he paused to swat her bottom—"and making certain you bear me at least several more."

"Ah, yes—no one could possibly try harder there," she rejoined solemnly. "When you said you wanted to become a farmer, Lord Newbury, I wasn't fully aware of the type of harvest you had in mind."

He clutched her closer and nuzzled her neck. "And speaking of harvests . . ."

Shivering at the touch of his lips, she stretched on tiptoe and stole a last peek toward the salon. "You really want another stairstep?" she asked poignantly.

Ryder stared down at his wife with blue eyes brimming with love and ran his fingertip over her lips. "I want another baby."

She smiled in delight. "Well, if you put it that way . . ." As her husband swept Natalie up in his strong arms and carried her off toward the stairs, she added softly, "So do I."